Camel to Moses

W. D. West

6-3-06

This is a work of fiction. While, as in all fiction, the literary perceptions and insights are based on experience, all names, characters, places, and incidents are either products of the author's imagination or are used fictitiously. No reference to any real person is intended or inferred.

Copyright ©2006 by William West
Cover Design by Dwain Senterfitt

ISBN 0-9777290-0-1

Published and distributed by:
High-Pitched Hum Publishing
321 15th Street North
Jacksonville Beach, FL 32250

Contact info@highpitchedhum.net for more information.

ACKNOWLEDGEMENTS

Thanks to the following for making this book a reality:

My wife and best friend Patty,
Our daughter, Libby,
Her husband and our son-in-law, Dwain
Our daughter, Kelly
And our terrific friend, Kitty.

Camel to Moses

W. D. West

Chapter 1

In 1880, Texas had tamed its enemies the Mexicans, Apaches and Comanche's. But the inhabitants of Southwest Texas, the Big Bend Country, still struggled, as they do today, with other challenges such as a harsh, desolate environment, remoteness, and lack of capital. It is desert country and in the late nineteenth century, only the strongest men and women survived there.

Camel was drunk. He won the drinking contest easily. Winning this poker game might be a little tougher. A slight buzz sharpened his card game; too much whiskey caused mistakes. Camel knew. He'd done it often enough.

He grinned at Hiram's frown as he shuffled the cards. His white toothy grin pissed off Hiram so he grinned a lot. He knew Hiram had hired the two drifters to challenge him to the drinking contest, and had given them seed money to cover the bet. Hiram's plan was so damn simple and deceitful--just like Hiram. Get Camel drunk and then beat him at cards. Camel glanced over at his drinking companions. One was sprawled out in his chair with his head leaning back, snoring and gurgling, arms hanging limp and his legs splayed, while the other man had slipped to the wooden floor and lay sleeping in a fetal position.

The four men at the table made an interesting study in contrasts. Ephraim wore his faded gingham shirt with suspenders holding up his canvas Levi's. He owned a small spread outside of town and was known to be down on his luck.

Judah wore a checkered shirt his wife made from hog-feed sacks. His suspenders were homemade leather straps. He too was a struggling rancher who had recently lost his wife. She bore him eight children, five of them now buried on a hill behind their cabin. Rumor had it the poor woman worked herself to death giving birth and caring for the children.

Hiram was the largest man at the table and the only one wearing a suit. It was black with a white shirt and black string tie. His head and neck were massive. Someone reported seeing him weighed at the mercantile store and the scales topped three hundred pounds. Massive shoulders and upper arms strained against the seams of his coat. Hiram was a carpetbagger from the north who established the town's bank. There were few people in town who didn't owe him. Camel was one of them. Hiram was also the largest landowner in the territory and the most religious man at the table. He loved to quote scripture. He quoted far more than the town's only preacher, Reverend Bilbo McKenzie.

The big man reminded Camel of an overfed hog. His size and fat could be deceiving though. Camel had seen him move and knew he was far quicker with his fists and feet than one would think. There was something else about Hiram that few people other than Camel knew. He carried a Remington short-barreled .36 Colt tucked in back of his belt. Camel learned about it one night after he'd been seen by Hiram courting the school marm. They exchanged angry words on the dimly lit walk and Hiram reached for his gun but Camel drew first. He took Hiram's pistol, examined it and tossed it into the dirt. There was no love lost between them.

Camel sat opposite the big man; their eyes met and held. Camel was dressed in a new store-bought white linen shirt, blue silk neckerchief, and gray serge trousers His Remington .32 caliber pocket revolver was jammed into his broad leather belt for everyone to see. Standing just over six feet, Camel weighed two hundred and forty pounds. At thirty-four years old, his hair was dark brown and his short beard held flecks of gray. Years earlier, he'd been wiry and muscular with broad shoulders and large arms. But, for too many years Camel had elected to live the easy life. His inherited ranch allowed him to sleep much of the day, play cards, drink hard whiskey and court the local widows most of the night. The whiskey, fancy food, and lack of exercise, had turned much of his muscle to fat. He carried a pot belly to advertise his lifestyle. His skin reflected a sickly pallor from lack of sun. He knew he had a problem with alcohol; he couldn't quit it. He also knew the only reason he still had the ranch was thanks to his foreman, Toby Smith.

Ephraim Stoddard sipped his rye whiskey and gazed out the door into the black night. Judah Stutz shuffled his boots, coughed and relit his cheroot. Both were decent men, but Camel knew their luck had run south lately. He would bet his ranch that Hiram had something to do with that. He had a gut feeling they were in this game tonight at Hiram's insistence. Usually both men were home in bed at this time, preparing for a hard day's work on their spreads. But since each man had made large mortgage loans from Hiram's bank, they were in his pocket.

Neither Ephraim or Judah should be here. They look about as comfortable as a whore in church. But Hiram has 'em under his thumb so they got no choice.

"Wait a minute!" said Hiram, as he jumped from his rickety chair. "I damn sure can't concentrate on playing cards with all this noise in here." He reached out with a ham of a fist and yanked one of the drifters by his ankle from the chair where he was sprawled, snoring loudly. The man came to and tried to protest as Hiram drug him across the rough-hewn floor toward the saloon's swinging doors. The drifter's clutching hand tipped over a rusty spittoon. Hiram stopped, lifted the spittoon and poured it's sluggish, brown contents into the man's face. The drifter sputtered and cussed. Hiram slammed the container down and pulled the man out into the purple-black darkness.

He returned and did the same to the other drifter who had not stirred during the commotion. A loud groan was heard as the man's head bounded off the wooden walk. Hiram re-entered the saloon wearing his usual scowl, dusted off his top coat, tugged at the lapels to straighten it, and pulled a long cheroot from his upper coat pocket. All hell broke loose when the first drifter crashed through the doors and jumped on his back. Strings of slimy brown tobacco juice dangled and swung from one ear and his nose. He wrapped his long stringy arms around Hiram's thick neck and chomped down on his ear with yellow, snaggly teeth. Hiram's cheroot shot forward, landing at Camel's heel. He picked it up, examined it, stuck it into his mouth and asked Judah for a light.

Hiram roared and spun like a top. The momentum of the swing broke the drifter's grip and he crashed into the side of the bar. He tried to find his feet, but Hiram was on him. A giant fist slammed into his nose, making blood splatter onto Hiram's white shirt. The blow bounced the man off the bar and he landed in a heap on the floor. Hiram kicked him in the ribs; lifting him from the floor and a pitiful whine escaped his lips. Hiram scooped him up by the collar and seat of his ragged pants, walked to the door and heaved him out. There was a pause before the thud of the body striking the hard, rocky west Texas street was heard.

Snorting like a bull, Hiram scrutinized the damage to his wardrobe. Brushing his shoulders with an almost dainty flip of his beefy fingers, he frowned as he viewed the specks of blood on his white shirt. He pulled a handkerchief from an inside coat pocket and dabbed at the red spots. Giving up, he snorted again in disgust, shrugged his massive shoulders. Looking around for his smoke, his eyes fell on Camel. Camel grinned and blew a smoke ring.

"You got my cheroot?"

Camel held the long, expensive cigar between his teeth, smiled, and said, "I appreciate the smoke, Hiram. It was gentlemanly of you. Of course no one could ever accuse you of being a rude or insensitive man though you did seem a little rough with that last employee of yours."

Hiram ignored the remark. With a grunt, he fell into the chair that squeaked in protest, and pulled another cheroot from his coat pocket. "Looks like ya could find some better riff-raff to have ya drinking bouts with. These kinda people don't help the image of our town." He assumed a look of piety and everyone knew what was coming next, "The good book tells us that he that walketh with wise men shall be wise: but a companion of fools shall be destroyed" He lit his smoke, inhaled, and squinted his dark beady eyes at Camel.

Camel grinned, blew smoke in Hiram's direction, and said mockingly, "I thought they were some of your hands, Hiram. The last few drinks I belted down with the last fella you so gently escorted out, said that you lent him and his partner money to drink and bet with. As for the holy talk about wise men and fools, I guess cards have a pretty good way of separating the two."

"Humph! I don't do business with that type of man as I think the present company can attest to."

Camel stared at him with the same wide smile. His smile muscles were growing weary. His entire system was feeling the thump of the whiskey. In the midst of a false shuffle, which he'd perfected to a high degree of excellence years ago, he lost one. An ace of spades fell onto the table.

All of the men looked at one another. Hiram looked up to the bartender. "Stinky, we need a new deck over here." The thin, pale, bald, cross-eyed bartender nodded and shuffled forward to heed Hiram's command. Talk had it that Stinky was an innocent bystander who took a .32 straightjacket to his lower regions in a barroom gunfight. Some said he lost his member and it ruined him. Others said the bullet castrated him. One story had him shot dead-center in the ass. A more sophisticated version told how the bullet clipped his sphincter muscle and he could not control his bowels. That was why he always smelled so bad. An irritated customer or drunk would sometimes resort to calling him Shitty. Whatever, Stinky did appear to be a sickly type who perched on a stool behind the bar and dozed when business was slow.

Dammit! Thought Camel, *I am drunk. That shoulda never happened. I never drop cards. I can false shuffle, false cut, bottom charge, double-undercut, glide and a half dozen other moves that I've practiced over the years. I better take some deep breaths and clear my head before I screw up like that again.* He handed the deck to Stinky and took the new one. Tearing brown paper from the deck, he felt movement beneath the table.

Ephraim glanced at Hiram and back to Camel. "Uh, Camel, I don't mean nothing by it..." Camel felt the table shake again. Somebody was getting hell kicked out of them, and he knew who it was. Ephraim cleared his throat, talked too fast, "Camel, since you've had a lot to drink, I think maybe one of us should shuffle the cards for the cut."

Camel laid the deck before Ephraim. "That's alright with me, Ephraim." Pushing his chair back from the table, he raised one leg and crossed it over the other. Examining his boot, he said, "Damn if my foot don't hurt. Did somebody kick me under the table?"

Hiram spoke with contempt, "Humph! Why don't we quit dilly dallying around and play poker? Or, are ya too drunk Camel?"

Camel blew smoke toward the booming voice. Damn, he was tired of pulling on this cheroot, blowing smoke, and grinning like a monkey. He wished he could think of something else that would irritate Hiram as much. He couldn't.

As Ephraim awkwardly shuffled with his rough rancher's hands, someone entered the saloon. All of the men turned to see sheriff Dan Libby moving to the bar and asking Stinky for three coffees. Camel was surprised to see him followed by both of his volunteer deputies. The sheriff was a tall, lanky man who always carried a 10 gauge double-barreled shotgun over his shoulder. Sometimes, he wore a .44 Colt in his belt, most often not. The shotgun was his weapon of choice. This night, the barrel of the Colt was stuck in his pant's belt with the handle hanging wide, easily accessible.

The men wore blank expressions. This was unusual. Usually, the sheriff politicked with the regular town folks. Tonight there was no nod, quiet hello or any sign of recognition of anyone.

One deputy was Frank Moseley. He claimed to own the single mercantile store in town while everyone knew he only ran it for Hiram. Frank was a short, bald man who loved to tell lies about his exploits with his Remington Revolver. Most people agreed Frank was a frustrated lawman.

The other deputy was Billy Womack. Billy was a tall, skinny youth and not too bright. Billy's father, Barney, owned the livery stable in town. The young man loved to follow orders and think he was responsible for helping Sheriff Libby clean up the town of Angel Valley. Billy was the only one who wore a gun belt with a holster and a Colt Army .44 caliber. Billy thought slow, but shot fast and accurately.

Camel stared at the three men as they moved to the bar. A bell sounded somewhere in the chasm of his whiskey-soaked brain, but not loud enough.

"Ya gonna draw to see who deals?" Asked Hiram in an angry voice. Camel saw each man holding a card, eyeing him. What the hell? He didn't even see them draw. The lawmen had distracted him. He felt angry with himself. *Come on Camel! Get your horse movin'!* But, something was wrong. *The sheriff never entered the saloon unless there was trouble. He only carried two weapons when a couple of drunk troublemakers staggered into town. Did it have anything to do with Hiram...Hell no! The sheriff, like everyone else in town, gave Hiram a free ride. Most likely if the drifters did report Hiram to the sheriff, he'd lock them up and have them on an outgoing wagon tonight. Cholla or Quiermo, two Mexicans from Adobeville were paid to haul any uninvited folk to the first of the way stations between here and Marathon or Alpine.*

Camel thought it funny that the townspeople, under the leadership of Hiram, had named the town Angel Valley to combat the name of the Devil River. This didn't make much sense to some folks like Camel since the nearest river to them was the Pecos. But, the name stuck and so this led some in town to classify folks as either angels or devils. Camel smiled as he recalled the old busybody, Granny Stutz, pointing her scrawny finger in his face and telling him he was one of the devil's disciples.

This was a Tuesday night, not a Saturday, why would the deputies be on duty? Why would the sheriff be in here, unless...a bell rang a little louder. Could the...

The table rocked and Hiram's booming voice brought Camel back to the task at hand. "Camel, card cheat, womanizer, drunk, laziest man in the territory, are ya gonna draw or just sit there all night?"

Camel felt his face flush. His right hand moved to feel the comfort of his pocket revolver stuck in his belt. "Would ya like to repeat any of that fat boy, shyster banker, carpetbagger, sour hypocrite, greediest man in the territory?"

Hiram's face tightened, his eyes grew smaller, but he forced a smile that showed his widely-spaced teeth. "Now, Camel I'm just trying to get ya to draw so we can get this friendly little game of stud poker underway. Ya know the rest of us have to get up and go to work in the morning." He winked toward Ephraim and Judah.

Camel's anger at Hiram overrode any misgivings he'd felt earlier. *I don't like you. You fat, ugly-faced son-of-a-bitch.* Resting his right hand on the pistol handle, he reached with his left to draw a card. Drawing it quickly to avoid showing it to the others, he saw that he'd drawn a king of hearts.

"Here's mine," said Ephraim, showing a seven of clubs. Judah held up a five of diamonds. Hiram held up a ten of hearts. Camel could not restrain his grin. Looking at Hiram, he said, "I guess I have to be the first to deal Hiram."

Judah pushed the remainder of the deck toward him. Shuffling the cards, Camel's hands riffed the deck and shuffled as he continued to grin at Hiram. Two cards flipped across the table. *Dammit! That cheap rotgut of Stinky's has got me drunk as a skunk.* Hiram pushed the cards back to him too hard.

Dealing seven card stud, Camel played it straight. Hiram came up with three-of-a-kind and took the first pot. The game continued for the next half-hour with Hiram winning the most pots. It was obvious to Camel that Ephraim and Judah were not raising or calling. He bet that Hiram lent them seed money to play with, but they were only filling chairs, the contest was between him and Hiram.

Camel was growing sleepy. Palming a jack of diamonds, he raised the pot and took it with a full house. *To hell with this! Got to get back and get some sleep...may take a room above the bar tonight. Let's take this pot and go to bed.*

In the next game, Judah had two sevens and a two showing, *He's got three of a kind. Ephraim is showing a jack , a seven and a nine, he's sitting on a pair. Hiram has two jacks and a four showing, he's got a full house. How's the fat bastard playing so well tonight?*

Camel was showing two eights and a five. He would need four of a kind to beat Hiram. He was holding another eight, but needed one more. Flipping and playing with the cards, he palmed the last eight and allowed it to drop into his lap.

He hunched forward over the table to cover his dropping of a card to pick up the eight and discard a deuce. "Boys, I see the pot and I gotta raise it. He pushed all his cash forward, over a hundred dollars."

Ephraim folded, dropped his cards and pushed back with a squeaky chair to observe the action as he pulled a small, dark pipe from his shirt pocket and bit down on it.

Judah hesitated. This was the best hand he'd held all night and it showed on his weathered, lean face. Camel felt a slight tremor of the table, Judah's face fell, and he dropped his cards. Like Ephraim, he scooted back in his chair to become an observer.

Hiram wore his usual deadpan poker-face, but Camel knew him. He had a way of holding his shoulders, arms extended, and fists clutching his cards tightly whenever he held a really good hand.

"If you're in a hurry to go to bed, Hiram, you might wanta go ahead and bet sometime tonight," needled Camel. He was flashing his grin again.

Hiram pulled back, and cleared his throat loudly.

"Damn, Hiram, you scared me. You not getting' sick on me are…" Camel froze. He felt something cold and hard pressed against his neck. Turning and looking up, he stared into the hard eyes of the sheriff. The double barrels of the shotgun hurt his neck. The sheriff's voice lost it's usual warmth. "Don't make a move, Camel, or I'll blow your neck off."

The deputy, Frank, slipped Camel's revolver from his waist. Hiram stood, said to the sheriff, "Have him stand, Sheriff and I'll show ya the evidence." They all saw the deuce of clubs fall to the floor as Camel stood. "He palmed an eight and dropped the deuce." Hiram seem to grow even larger and his voice raised, "This crook's cheated everybody in the territory."

"Sheriff, we have a misun…"

"Leave it alone, Camel. Everyone for miles knows ya been cheatin' at cards ever since ya pa died. This is the kinda thing that makes for gunfights and somebody gittin' killed." The sheriff motioned with the barrel for Camel to move toward the door.

"Camel I'm arresting ya for cheating and stealing. I'll hold ya until the judge gets here next week to try ya."

Camel felt his ribs prodded by the steel barrel. He walked slowly toward the door with the sheriff, his deputies, and Hiram following. They turned on the slatted walkway and headed for the tiny stick and wattle jail.

Camel heard Hiram's voice behind him. "Sheriff, I appreciate you and your deputies doing your duty. I want to make a suggestion though." The group stopped as the parley continued. "Ya know, Dan, the judge has not had a case here for months. That makes Angel Valley look real good. If we're serious about attracting more business and folks to our fair city, we need a clean reputation."

The sheriff spoke, "I agree with ya, Hiram. But Camel has broke the law and I got to deal with that."

Hiram's voice grew smooth as Camel had heard it do before when he was making or closing a deal. "You are absolutely right, Sheriff. We can't have this kinda card sharpin' going on. But Camel is a local rancher, or at least he owns a ranch. We all knew his daddy and brother who were upstanding men. For their memory, for our community's sake, I strongly recommend that we handle this matter discreetly."

Camel knew he was drunk, but he must be drunker than he realized. He couldn't believe what Hiram was saying. Knowing him, there had to be a catch somewhere.

"What do you suggest?"

There was a pause. One of the Beaumont boys was yelling down the street somewhere. They were a dirt-poor family. The father died less than a year ago from alcohol poisoning and the mother was referred to as Queenie Beaumont and was known to earn money working in the oldest profession known to man. She often allowed her four boys to be out late at night. It was said the oldest one found customers for her. The sheriff glanced down the street toward more yelling. The family was fighting again. He'd better get down there and check it out.

Hiram's voice was low and soft, "Sheriff, I suggest that your deputies and I walk a ways with Camel and try to talk a little religion into him. You know Reverend McKenzie has preached a lot lately about a man turning from sin and mending his ways. I think that after tonight, Camel might be ready to do that." He grinned, "We need to turn Camel from Absolom to King David."

Camel knew the booze had affected his hearing now. He'd seen Hiram attending the little community church at the end of town, heard him quote plenty of scripture, but had never heard him talk like this before.

There was more yelling. The sheriff looked at Hiram, "I think that's mighty good of you Hiram. I shouldn't do it, but I've always liked Camel, in spite of his sorry ways, and knowing the upstanding stock he comes from, I've always hoped he would turn around."

The sheriff lowered his gun. Moving to face Camel, he said, "You got friends that care about ya here in Angel Valley, Camel.

I'm gonna agree with Hiram this time and let ya go. But, you better think about what these boys are sayin' to you. I won't let ya go again."

The sheriff strode toward the yelling. Hiram spoke to Camel. "Follow Billy!" His voice had lost its mellow tone and sounded harsh and angry.

Camel shook his head, trying to remove the cobwebs. He was drunk, but he was embarrassed too. He had been stupid. Quickness of hand was one of the few areas of his life he still held pride. He had been so drunk and sloppy that he allowed himself to be caught by Hiram. *Now, I know why the sheriff and his deputies were there. Hiram had it all set up.*

Billy walked ahead of him, gripping his pistol butt. They left the walkway and headed toward the train track. Camel stumbled and heard laughter behind him.

Only one light flickered in the darkness; the lantern hung outside the empty train depot. They were nearing the circle of light when Hiram said, "Hold up, Billy."

Camel heard Hiram's big boots crunching in the sand. He heard his name, turned and caught a fist to the forehead. He saw a white flash of light and then he was looking up at the big man standing over him. Everything was spinning. Camel shook his head, trying to stop the movement that was nauseating him.

"Humph! It's time ya got some religion, Camel! Ya need to stop this card sharking, sleeping all day, and staying drunk all the time. 'Wine is a mocker and strong drink is raging! And whosoever is deceived thereby is not wise.'" His voice became tight, "And most importantly, Camel, ya need to stay away from our schoolmarm, Miss Maggie Pickett." He shrugged, grinned and said, "Help him up boys."

The world was still turning, but slower now. As the deputies heaved him up, he sensed the punch coming, slipped a right, twisted his arms free, and hit Hiram flush on the nose. Blood splattered. He heard him cuss. Camel stepped in and upper cut the massive stomach. He was surprised at it's hardness. Hands were clutching Camel's arms again. Stronger this time.

Hiram grunted, laughed a strange laugh, and said, "Hold him, dammit! Camel, the book says, Ye shall not steal, neither deal falsely, neither lie one to another."

The big man stepped forward and flashed a short, powerful right. Camel moved his head just enough for the huge fist to burn his ear. Again Camel jerked his own right free from Billy, though Frank controlled his left. The right was wild; it reflected his drunken condition and grazed the top of Hiram's bull-like shoulder.

"Hold him, Billy, God dammit!" grunted Hiram as his fist smacked solidly onto Camel's chin. Camel tried to move his head to avoid the next punch, but the hammer of a fist landed on his nose. The world was turning faster again, then he felt another right to his chin. Camel felt himself go limp and that's the last thing he knew.

"Hold his head up, Frank!" Hiram grunted. The deputy grasped Camel's hair, pulled the bloody face with blank expression and slack jaw straight so Hiram could hit it again and again.

As the beefy fists pounded Camel's face, chest, and stomach, or whatever was exposed, Billy felt sick and closed his eyes to the mayhem. He could feel blood splatter onto his face. Hiram paused when Billy collapsed onto one knee and vomited.

Frank struggled to hold the limp form erect. "Drop him!" Gasped Hiram. When Camel's unconscious form crunched to the hard ground, Hiram delivered several kicks to his ribs. "Ya know what to do with him," he gasped. Taking his handkerchief from his coat pocket, he wiped blood from his knuckles, face, coat, and shirt, cussed again, kicked the inert form once more, and took a deep breath. Blowing it out, he headed toward town, leaving the still body on the ground and one man standing over it while the other rested on the ground on all fours gagging and heaving.

It was seven minutes after midnight when Billy and Frank heaved Camel's limp body onto the train platform. It was an unusual sight. The platform sat isolated from the town's dwellings; but that's not what made it interesting. Railroad tracks ran fifty yards each side of it and then ended. The train did not come to Angel Valley. The nearest the Southern Pacific Railroad came was to Marathon about sixty miles north. Hiram and some of the other affluent citizens had paid to have the platform and tracks laid. Hiram invited railroad management to visit and observe it.   He thought once the railroad saw how eager the town was for a railroad, it would persuade them to build it. They didn't.   Billy and Frank waited. Frank was pissed. Billy had been little help to him. Frank rolled smokes. Billy sat on the edge of the platform head down, legs dangling and hands in his lap.

After a while, they heard the squeak of a wagon approaching. It was Cholla, a small wiry man who kept to himself. Cholla was a mysterious sort. There was talk that Cholla was a woman. One of the Beaumont boys claimed to see Cholla squatting to pee. If Cholla was a woman, she was the orneriest female that Billy had ever known. She was also the strongest. Billy knew Cholla would transport Camel to a shack halfway to Marathon. Another man paid by Hiram like Cholla would carry Camel the rest of the way and put him on a cattle train to nowhere.

Billy spit, hacked, cleared his throat for the hundredth time and looked at his partner. "He hasn't moved. Do ya think he's dead?"

Frank leaned and peered at him through his smoke, "He's alive. I can hear him breathing...or at least gurgling." Frank stood, nudged the body with his boot, "There ain't much life left in him though. I'd sure hate for Hiram to hit and kick me like that."

Sounds from the wagon indicated it's nearness. Billy said, "I uh...I uh hate it when Hiram does sumthin' like that. I'm sure Sheriff Libby didn't mean for that to happen." Looking down, he shook his head, "It kinda makes me feel bad to be a part of sumthin' like this. How about you?"

Frank grunted as he tossed his smoke onto the track below them. Sometimes, Billy talked too much and got on Frank's nerves. This was one of those times. The boy looked at him with wide, owlish eyes.

Frank detected the tension in the young man's voice. Billy was slow, everyone knew that. The only thing he did remarkably well was shoot his pistol. Frank had never seen anyone shoot a pistol with such accuracy. He was a good boy ordinarily, and would blush if anyone remarked on his shooting skills. He worshipped the sheriff, and feared Hiram. Frank had to give Billy's father credit for the latter. His father was owned by Hiram like everybody else in town and had ordered Billy to always do what Hiram told him to do.

Frank wondered what the young man would do if the sheriff and Hiram's orders ever conflicted.

Frank knew he had no choice in the matter either. Hiram owned him and his mercantile store lock, stock and barrel. He enjoyed assisting the sheriff, but disliked having to provide Hiram a report on the sheriff's activities. Frank figured that Dan Libby would remain sheriff as long as he gave Hiram no trouble. When that day came, Frank figured that he stood a good chance of getting his job.

Cholla said, "You got him hogtied ?" Frank mumbled a cuss and caught the rope thrown from the bed of the wagon. In a couple of minutes Camel's legs were pulled up behind him and his ankles tied to his wrists. All three grunted as they heaved the dead weight into the wagon.

Billy watched the dark night absorb the wagon. He had wondered what happened to the last preacher-man who preached standing on a stump outside Hiram's bank. He said the bank was the devil's store house and the banker was the devil's chief disciple. The next day, everyone wondered where the man had disappeared to. Billy scratched his ear and thought about other men, some of them drunks and undesirables who had...

Billy wondered about a lot of things but knew better than to ask. His pa would probably tell him that it was best for him not to know. Pa always knew the best thing for him.

In the smelly wagon's bottom, Camel's body swayed and shook in rhythm with the bounce of the hard wagon wheels on the rough, rocky road. He showed no sign of life except a quiet gurgle of blood as he shallow-breathed. A dark puddle pooled beneath his face and a stream of the liquid made its way on the vibrating floor to the edge of the back gate where it disappeared.

Back in Angel Valley a sleek, sculptured, brown mare, nickered and nudged the slip knot tethering the reins to the hitching post. Camel had learned in his years of gambling, that when you win all of a man's money, you sometimes need to move on. A slip knot and fast horse were essentials for his trade. The reins dropped to the ground, the horse shook his head in triumph and trotted toward home, the 3C ranch.

CHAPTER 2

When fighting Apaches, white men often saved one bullet for themselves.

Father Pollen was physically and mentally exhausted. His left foot was not clearing the hard earth when he stepped. He knew from experience that this would only grow worse. *I must rest.* Pushing hard as he could with the Mulberry limb he used as a staff, *really a crutch for a cripple rather than an aid for a tired, weary prophet,* he stepped from the shadowy figures that he'd been part of and pretended to be looking up and down the line for some problem that did not exist. This group always amazed him. They moved silently, like ghosts who floated over the earth rather than walk on it. He knew his movement made more noise than all of them put together. His arm trembled clutching the wood as he looked backward and forward as though he knew something no one else did. The dark silhouettes walked single-file and made no sounds. Father Pollen tried unsuccessfully to adjust the limb to ease his aching body. Glancing up, he could see the moon on the horizon. Stars twinkled. It would be another long night.

Walking in the desert at night was a challenge for anyone, but especially for him. The sagebrush and cacti dotted the landscape and while the Indians moved around the thorny, prickly plants with ease, he seemed to possess a unique talent for walking into them and paying the price with bloody hands and torn clothes.

Adjusting his robe, the stooped, knot of a man shook his head in disbelief as he recalled recent weeks. As a sympathizer for the Indians, he had attempted the usual strategies employed by his predecessors of the Presbyterian faith. He had lived on the reservation, tried to teach the children, and even insisted on eating the same rancid meat and beetle-infested floured bread as the Indian. He had practiced the Christian faith to the best of his ability, but it made no difference in the lives of his red brothers and sisters.

In the end, he committed a federal crime by accompanying twenty adults and twelve children who fled their prison known as the Dinehtah. This was supposedly the promised land for the Navajo. For many it was. But for some, like all those with Father Pollen, it was not. They still had to contend with government interference. The Compulsory Indian Education Law passed by congress in 1887, made education mandatory for all Indian children. This was a continuation of President Grant's "peace policy." The policy advocated that the Indian problem would disappear whenever they had been christianized. This began by teaching the children their letters, numbers, and most importantly, the tenets of Christianity. It meant placing them in schools against their will where they were beaten, abused and not allowed to speak their language.

Father Pollen could not continue to be a part of the policy. He supported the Indian's distrust of the government and their need to cling to their culture. He agreed with their cause, but truth be known, had not played a decisive role in the decision to escape. But, the couple of newspapers he'd seen, had made him the leader of this supposedly dangerous renegade, rag tail, motley group of savage killers who had traveled further and faster than the U.S. Army could have imagined. Father Pollen had never placed great emphasis on miracles reported in the Bible, but he had to think it a miracle that so far, this group had managed to escape army search parties, professional trackers, and fearful whites who ran to the authorities if they even heard a rumor that the group was entering their area. *Perhaps that's been part of the miracle--all the rumors have kept the army running and so far, we have somehow eluded our pursuers. But it's only a matter of time before we're caught. We need a real miracle to find a safe haven.*

They had moved on foot with the exception of the one young Navajo father and husband named Spirit Dog who rode a painted gelding. The priest shivered in the night, though it was not cold. *How could a crippled priest from New York who is almost blind and no larger than a twelve year-old get into this position? If --- who am I kidding--- when the army finds us, I will be defrocked by the synod and sentenced to prison. But, I wouldn't go back if given the opportunity. My prayer is that we will somehow find a place where we can settle down, work, build a life and live without fear, disgrace and being robbed of our total culture.* This last thought brought a crooked smile to his homely face. He now identified completely with this group of mostly Navajo and three Apaches.

His thoughts returned to the present when the figures moving before him disappeared. He felt a shock of fear; realized each one had squatted close to the ground. He did the same. His heart was in his throat. Had Spirit Dog spotted the army? For the umpteenth time he asked himself the question, *will the soldiers shoot everyone before giving them a chance to surrender? The soldiers have to be weary and hate us for making them look bad.*

His heart thumped again in his throat when he heard Spirit Dog's voice in his ear. He had not seen him approach; he was just there.

"I smelled dust. Many riders have been here not long ago. We will wait and see if we hear or smell anything else."

The priest moved his head in agreement. Though it was dark, he knew his Indian friend could see it. *Or does he sense it? How do these people move so quietly? How can they ...I know, it's because they've had to learn how to do it in order to survive. Yet, even with all of their skills, they cannot survive the white man's invasion of their lives.* The priest toppled over onto his side. He could not squat very well with his handicap. Lying on the hard earth, he tried to breathe easily and fingered his cross as he breathed a prayer for their safety. A moment later, strong arms lifted him gently to his feet. Again it was the guide's soft voice, "It was a band of mustangs. We will move on now."

Father Pollen breathed deeply to quiet his heart. *Maybe this was for the best. I needed the rest.* Moving up to the rear of the line, he saw one of the figures step deftly behind him. He knew they watched out for him. Walking was difficult for him. He often tripped and fell. Tonight was no exception. He'd already fallen twice and they'd only gone a few miles.

I bet no one had to pick Moses up. He was out front leading, not bringing up the rear and being monitored by others. Oh well!

I'm not Moses or Joshua. I'm just a wild-eyed Indian lover who may well be hurting these people more than I'm helping them. This thought sobered him. One hand worked the staff as the other fingered the cross hanging from his neck. His hand dropped to the leather pouch at his side. He pressed it reassuringly. It held his worn leather-bound Bible.

The double-wick kerosene lamp illuminated Hiram sitting at his massive mahogany desk. His coat draped over the back of his chair. He squinted as he studied the open book before him. His lips moved silently. Leaning his large head back, closing his eyes, he sighed, and rubbed his face vigorously.

Without looking down, he spoke the words aloud from memory, "Fret not thyself because of evil men, neither be thou envious at the wicked." Standing, shrugging his massive shoulders, he massaged his thick neck and said, "Proverbs, chapter twenty-four, verse nineteen."

Lifting the black leather-bound Bible gently, he kissed it's cover and held it aloft. He read his beloved book for a minimum of one hour each day. He memorized a minimum of three verses each day, mostly Old Testament. It's words, he believed, were his guide to life.

Returning the Bible to it's place on the table, he walked toward his bedroom deep in thought. Camel had given him no choice. Hiram felt led by the spirit to rid his town of this corrupt, wicked, hell-bound creature.

In bed, he continued to be miserable. *Did I misinterpret the spirit's voice? Am I suffering from another sin? Am I simply tired, trying too hard to do the Lord's work and Satan is the one behind this struggle? He's the great liar. Is he the one wrestling with me now? Am I having a night like Jacob when he traveled from Beer-Sheba to Haran?* Sleep would not come. His breathing labored. He sobbed. Between sobs, he gasped, "Ye serpents...ye generations of vipers...How can ye escape...the damnation of hell?"

Heaving himself out of bed, he slipped on his pants and headed for his stable behind the house. He was bare-chested and wearing no footwear. Yelping like a kitten as his bare feet touched hard gravel, he entered the stable and talked gently to his riding mare.

She snorted her greeting and took the bridal and bit without complaint.

In less than ten minutes, Hiram reined up before a daub and wattle cabin. His mare was skittish and danced about as several dogs barked and snarled at the intruders. Hiram spoke soothingly to his mount. The door of the cabin cracked open and above the din of the barking dogs, Hiram said, "Cholla, I need you!"

Back at his house, he placed several gold pieces on the table and sat down. With head in hand, he prayed feverishly. He fell silent when he heard footsteps. "I'm here, in the usual place, Cholla." Standing, he pushed the chair back, went to his knees, and placed his elbows in the seat. "Can you see me?"

A sharp voice answered, "Si." The house was dark but Cholla was familiar with the arrangement of it's furniture. He wore a dark robe and held a short leather whip in one hand. Hiram was sobbing again.

"How many, Senor?"

Between sobs, Hiram gasped, "Seven!"

A few minutes later, Cholla gathered the gold pieces, dropped them into a leather pouch hanging from his neck and disappeared into the dark. Hiram's sobs and gasps filled the room, echoed off of the expensive grandfather clock that displayed the moon phases, bounced off of the grand piano and reverberated throughout his mansion.

Captain Yancey Verlander closed his eyes to try to rest them, but only felt his lids burn with the irritation of dust and heat of exhaustion. Raising his small frame in the saddle by standing in his stirrups, he tried to give his hemorrhoids a break, but his ass burned more than his eyes when he resettled in his saddle. *Crazy-ass Indians! Where the hell are you? You sneaky little bastards! When I catch ya, I'm gonna shoot ya lungs out if ya try to run. Shit, I'm gonna shoot ya if ya run or squat. When I get through with...*

His mount stumbled stepping into a dry creek bed. The sensation sent a bolt of fear flashing through his brain. He'd heard of the results of night riding in rough country. He remembered well the story of a young corporal whose horse fell on him while chasing

Apaches in the Badlands of New Mexico. The soldier's back was broken; he never walked again.

How in the hell does this bunch of riff-raff led by a fucking Yankee crippled preacher, keep ahead of us? I only recall seeing the little hunch-backed prick once with his goofy specs and buck-teeth, but damned if I ever would have thought he could pull this shit off. I wonder if the cripple knew what he was doing when he led them south into the Chihuahua Desert country with all it's dry mountains, dead-end canyons, cliffs, arroyos, a million prickly cactus, rattlesnakes, scorpions and damn precious little water, where as much of the country stands up as lays down? Course any idiot ever hearing a tale about this area would know that the country west of the Pecos was fit only for tarantulas, Gila Monsters and wild-eyed crazies.

Blinking and using his peripheral vision, he made out his Navajo scouts sitting their mounts waiting for him. Once again he questioned the skills and loyalty of his scouts. *I'm thinking these guys can't find their horses asses with both hands.*

Knowing the answer before he asked the question, he asked it anyway with more than a hint of irritation in his voice, "Find em'?" There was a long silence, which always pissed him off. The one nearest him, answered in a low guttural voice, "Lost em'. Need to wait til dawn to find trail."

The captain lost it, "Shit!" There were several clinks of spurs against stirrups and creaks of leather reins and cinches behind him in the dark as the company halted. Silence filled the air. Standing in his stirrups seeking relief from his stinging, aching ass, the captain said in a hiss, "This shit has gotta stop! You scouts are being paid good American money and you and your horses are eating from the trough of the government while you bullshit out here and lead us around in circles."

The other Indian spoke in a low, calm voice, "We will go back to Dinehtah at dawn if that is your wish."

The captain aired his lungs with a long tirade of profanity, ending with, "Hell no, you're not going back. We all go back and we go back with these runaway renegades walking ahead of us or we leave 'em as buzzard bait." He continued, "You're on half-rations until you show us your half-assed kin folks."

Dismounting, the captain handed the reins of his horse to a sergeant and pulled on the seats of his pants. Walking a few feet, he paused to unbutton his trousers and piss. He knew he was standing on a good spot to camp because whenever the scouts stopped, they had already picked the location.

The scouts rode their mounts the usual fifty yards from the camp center and dismounted to set up their bedding. If the captain had seen them smiling at one another, his rage would have been even greater.

They were a motley group. Four men and a woman riding single-file along a narrow trail punctuated on each side by Desert Christmas Cactus, Crucifixion Thorn, Soaptree Yucca, Cholla Trees and other varieties of cactus and desert plants that hurt like hell when touched.

The men had tired of cussing each time the plants grabbed their clothing or jabbed them. They were resigned to their situation and too weary to do more than jerk themselves free and continue on silently. They were riding scared too. The Federales almost caught them the day before in that last little dirty wattle and stick clump of huts they had settled in for a couple of day's rest. A rest needed for their horses as much as for them.

The lead rider was a large man. His name, "Big Boy," was an appropriate one. At six-foot six inches and weighing almost two hundred and forty pounds, Big Boy was strong and mean and had made a career of taking advantage of his physical prowess, love of violence, and hatred of almost everyone. His size demanded a large horse, but the Federales coming in on them had forced him to grab a short legged mare. She was a fine horse and most men would have paid well for her, but she was inadequate for Big Boy. His boot-heels swung less than a foot from the ground. He carried a double-barreled shotgun across the horn of his saddle and a thirty-six caliber revolver stuck down his belt.

Second in line was a man known by many aliases, the latest being Kilkenny. He was of medium height and his light-blue eyes had fascinated many women. He was unhappy with his riding partners for several reasons: first, the woman that rode with the group had started out being his companion. But this group of hard-tails had insisted on him sharing her and there was no way he could outshoot all of them. Second, in their hasty escape from the Federales, he had left his Winchester rifle behind. His only weapon was a .44 Colt resting in it's holster, strapped to his leg. Finally, he'd lost his Stetson in the melee and the sun burned his face red.

Third, rode the only woman in the group. Her name was Eunice and the sun, hard riding conditions, no makeup, and rough treatment by the men had taken their toll on her. She was bone-thin and wore her weariness from head to toes. Her dark hair was dirty, greasy, and hung in sweat-soaked strands around her shoulders. She wore a wrinkled, green dress that she'd used a knife to cut off at the knees. Her long, thin legs were sunburned and spotted with insect bites and puncture wounds from the Spanish Bayonets and various cacti that menaced her without letup.

Riding with eyes half-closed was a tall, lanky man known as Jones. He'd had so many aliases, no one knew what his real name was. A dirty, narrow-brimmed Homburg sat at a cocked angle atop his head. His hair was sandy and large reddish freckles dotted his angular face. He half-heartedly pulled his sleeve away from a Spanish Bayonet and allowed the arm to fall at his side. His weapons of choice were a Colt .32 stuffed into his right pants pocket and a Sharps repeater rifle slip-tied onto his leather fender with rawhide thongs.

Next came the mixed-breed named, Sans. His family tree included an Apache grandfather, black runaway slave girl for a grandmother, white father who had been hanged for murder, and a Mexican teenager mother who died giving him birth. He was a small man with deep-set hazel eyes that constantly scanned the area around them and watched their back-trail. He leaned slightly in the saddle. His shirt appeared to have a lump behind the right shoulder. His spine was curved and though all who saw him knew he had a hump on his back, no one had ever seen it. It did not affect his ability to walk, ride, shoot or use a knife. The few who had been in his company long enough and possessed the capacity for introspective thought, had wondered if the hump had affected his disposition. Had it turned him into the cold, calculating killer that he was?

An Evans carbine nestled in it's scabbard was as unique as it's owner. It loaded from the end of the stock and it's magazine tube held thirty-four rounds. Working the lever, the mixed-breed could spread lots of lead around and had killed many a man in a gun fight who thought he had to be out of ammo. A knife with a bone handle housed in a leather case rode his hip. Sans rode drag so as to keep intruders from surprising them, but also to prevent anyone of the group from escaping. His voice was different. He spoke in a raspy whisper. Someone had remarked out of his hearing that he sounded like someone who'd had kerosene poured down his throat and set afire.

All of the men in the group had much in common. They were wanted in Mexico for robbery, murder, horse thievery, and a half-dozen other crimes. They were also wanted in several American states for similar crimes. Each one had worn out his welcome in the states, and rode fast across the Rio Grande to find a new life. But, each one had resorted to his same employment, primarily robbing banks, saloons, and anyplace that had a till. Their luck had run out south of the border and the pursuing Federales were ensuring that they return to the giant of the north that spawned them. Another commonality they shared was their dislike for one another. Although Big Boy and Sans had been together for over a year, their relationship was a business one. Kilkenny despised each one of them. Eunice hated each one of them, but her fear of Sans outweighed her hate. Jones was no different. He rode with this group out of necessity and looked forward to slipping away at the first opportunity. But each one of them knew that there was strength in numbers and their survival depended on them sticking together for now.

Eunice, alone was not a fugitive, at least not from the law. Her pursuers were former husbands and boyfriends. She'd run away from an abusing stepfather at fourteen and been running ever since. She had worked as a prostitute in Abilene, Dodge, Ogallalla, and a host of small towns throughout Texas. Three different men had married her, but she'd abandoned all of them along with a sickly child. She'd accompanied a fast-talking gambler across the border, but hooked up with Kilkenny after he shot her card-cheating boyfriend.

The wagon creaked and groaned and someone spit and said something. Camel had never hurt all over so much in his life. His wrists and ankles burned from the rough rope restraining him. Some parts of his body were numb and he was thankful for that but his chest, shoulders and lower back throbbed with each heart beat. He tried to speak but nothing came out. He tried to roll his head so he could see who had spit but he couldn't manage it. The wagon hit a deep hole, jarred him to the bone and he blacked out.

If he could have observed his surroundings, he would have seen a short, square man with a weeks growth of beard. He wore a patch over one eye that he had lost in a fight in a drunken riot following an argument over a whore in Alpine. He had been in several scrapes with the law in Marathon too and that was the reason he had to slip into town at night because the sheriff had told him he was no longer welcome there.

He waited patiently, whistling softly to himself. The hogtied man would groan every so often, but had never regained consciousness. Even when he had helped Cholla move him and they had dropped him a couple of times, all he ever heard was that groan. He had seen lots of men beat up in his time, but never one this bad. If he hadn't heard the occasional groan, he would have assumed the man was dead and dumped his body in a deep arroyo. He had waited a day to see if he did die and he would not have to make the trip, but the damned bloody mess kept breathing. Whether he lived or not, he bet a goat's tit the man would never be right in the head again. He'd seen it before; a man take a kicking in the head and always be slow in his thinking and speaking. He remembered a big fellow in Abilene who pissed a lot of folks off so one night the whole bar jumped the guy and just about beat him to death. After that the fella walked with a shuffle and lost the use of his right arm. He slobbered a lot and…

His thoughts returned to the present when the train blew its whistle. He watched for the next several minutes as the long black metal snake hissed, clacked, blew, huffed and finally came to a halt. He pulled the brake off and shook the reins for the horse to move out. Up close to the train, he kept his one good eye peeled for the sheriff and was relieved to hear a familiar voice.

"Got me another one from Angel Valley, huh? Sounds more like the devils hell-hole to me."

The two men worked together to lift the dead, slack weight of the unconscious man from the wagon and heave him onto the floor of an empty cattle car. In the dark, they didn't notice the shadow crouched in one corner of the smelly car.

Camel squinted with one eye. It was swollen and would open no further. The other one was closed completely. Both were battered blue. His vision was blurred. Each time the train bumped and shuddered, he felt another pain someplace in his body. Some parts of his body were numb while other parts screamed in burning, nauseating agony.

A voice startled him. Peering through the crusty, slit of a bloodshot eye, he saw a lump of rags, two of them, leaning against the far side of the car. Looking closer, he saw one of them was an older man with a wrinkled, grizzled face staring at him.

"I said I thought ya was dead from the way ya looked when they putcha on last night. You were so still and quiet all night I figured ya had to be dead, hmmmm." He paused, looked through the slatted sides and said, "Ya sure musta made some fella mighty mad back there. They put a bad beatin on ya. Had ya hogtied. I cut ya free, hmmmm."

Camel tried to lift up and look out, but the sharp pain in his head denied it. Rubbing his side, he thought he might have several broken ribs. Each breath brought a flash of fire to his lungs. "Where are we?" He grimaced. Just talking was torture. A high-pitched hum sounding from within his battered head was ever present.

"My guess is between Alpine and Marfa." The wrinkled face grinned, showing no teeth. "In this country ya can't be too sure. I'd say though that these are the Davis Mountains. We been on a little flat country, but it's getting hillier now. One thing's for sure, we somewhere in the Chihuahua Desert cuz it's dry as hell. Taste that hot sand comin up through the floorboards all around us?" He shook his head, "This is some mean country, Mister, hmmmm."

Hiram stood on his back porch humming, washing his face and hands. Pitching the basin of water into the yard, he turned it upside down on the wooden board and hung the gourd onto a peg. He reached for the clean cloth that his maid, Juanita, kept on another peg. He was dressed in black dress pants, white shirt, open at the collar with a black string tie hanging untied around his bull-like neck.

He whistled as he entered the dining room. It was a large room, like most of the rooms in the house. It was a house a man could be proud of. It was a house that needed a woman to give it a special touch. That made him think of the schoolmarm, Maggie Pickett. She had served as the town and territories teacher for a year now, and Hiram had decided she was the woman he would take as his wife. She came from the north, rented a room from the reverend and his wife, and had made it clear from the start that she planned to return to Connecticut. But Hiram saw that she possessed class and beauty, and was the type of woman he was looking for. She spoke with a funny northern accent, but it was proper and correct speech, and that's what he wanted. With that no-good scoundrel, Camel Campbell, out of the way, he planned to court her seriously.

His thoughts carried him from Maggie to the widow, Pearl Manning. It was embarrassing to think that he had considered Pearl a possible match for a while. She owned a two thousand acre spread, but she carried too many liabilities. First, she was known to have cavorted with Camel; second, she had two brats, and third, he was confident she would have financial difficulty at any time, and then he would own her spread anyway. There was a fourth reason; Pearl was a coarse woman while Maggie had class and sophistication. Maggie was the type woman who could help a man run as governor of the state. She would be an asset in a thousand ways. She was pretty and regal too, in a soft, sweet way that made Pearl look like the country-girl farmer and rancher that she was.

Pulling an elaborate chair from the head of the table, he sat and picked up his fork and knife as Juanita sat his breakfast before him. A cup of steaming coffee sweetened with honey beckoned him. She knew he demanded his eggs be cooked over light and his sausage highly seasoned. She had baked a loaf of bread and laid it on the table with a bowl of sweetened figs beside it.

He ignored her as he sipped his coffee and gulped down his eggs. A smile came to his lips as he recalled the night before. It was so sweet. That damn shiftless Camel was out of the picture. The next step was to claim his ranch by picking it up for back taxes. He had contacts in the capitol, and he would use them to help him acquire the land.

Finishing his eggs, Juanita brought in a heaping plate of flapjacks. She was a young Mestizo, single, homely, and very happy to have her job. Her sole mission was to please him. Returning in a moment with a pitcher of cold milk and a canister of syrup, she laid them down as he stared out the window.

The Chisos Mountains rose to the South; the Christmas Mountains to the west, and the Rosillos Mountains stood on the horizon to the north. They appeared purple in the morning light. They would be golden later as the sun rose.

Hiram felt contentment as he poured syrup and thought of his place in the community. He had chosen well. Many thought the country west of the Pecos too wild and rough to amount to anything, but Hiram knew different. The country was craggy and rife with mountains, canyons, buttes, and arroyos and Hiram loved it.

Hiram smacked and grunted as he gobbled the syrup-laden flapjacks. He smiled again as he thought of Maggie. He would find time in his schedule today to visit her at the school. He would stop off at Frank's mercantile, buy a licorice stick for each student, and then go to the school to hand them out and talk to her. It was long overdue that they began a serious courtship.

Toby stood in front of the sheriff's desk twisting the brim of his weathered Stetson with calloused hands. He shifted from one foot to the other. He was no longer a young buck and standing still raised havoc with his arthritis. He was forty-eight years old and in his profession as a ranch foreman, that was a lot of years. His hair was long and white and hung to his shoulders. His beard was white also and reflected a trim a week or so ago. In his prime, he'd been tall, lanky and strong, but now he was hunched and so spare that the hands sometimes joked that he could hide behind a fence post. His sky-blue eyes bored into the sheriff.

Sheriff Libby shrugged his shoulders and stood facing him across the scarred, pine desk. "I don't know, Toby. He could be anywhere. Ya know him better'n I do. Have ya checked out at the widow, Pearl Mannings place?"

Toby said in his raspy, drawl, "No, I haven't, Sheriff. I have checked every gully and bush between the Three C and town. I guess I'm goin' on my gut. I just feel that sumthin's not right." He twisted the hat in his hands. "When I found his horse yesterday, I had a bad feelin' and it's been with me all day."

The sheriff tried humor, "Hell, Toby, he coulda rode a party raft up the Rio Grande to Ojinaga and be layin' up with a big tittied Mexican whore about now. Gotta a tittie in one hand and a bottle of tequila in the other."

Toby's sky-blue eyes stared at him without blinking and carried a sadness that made the sheriff sorry he'd said it.

The sheriff reached for his hat, put it on, and grasped his shotgun. "Tell ya what, Toby, why doncha check out at the widow's place and I'll check with the school marm to see if she's seen him. If she hasn't, I'll ride a few miles out of town each way and see if I can find him."

Toby thanked the sheriff and together they walked out into the sunlight. Toby had to be satisfied with the answer he'd received, but it did nothing to relieve his misgivings. As he pulled into the saddle on his big brown, he spoke aloud to his horse, "Well Babs, guess we gotta keep lookin 'ole girl." He shook the reins and moved into a trot toward the widow's place. His thoughts carried him back to the past.

He'd gone to work for Camel's father, Henry Campbell, over fifteen years ago. Toby began as a bronc-buster. He worked as a ranch hand for over seven years before becoming foreman. Henry had been a strong man and a good man. He lost his wife to consumption when the two boys, Aaron and Matthew, he still called him Matthew like his father did rather than the nickname, Camel, were youngsters. Aaron was the oldest and always a model son. A hard worker, eager to please his father and Toby, he was the spitting image of his father.

Toby's sky-blue eyes scanned the horizon as he recalled Henry changing the name of his ranch from the Rocking C to the 3C. It was named for the owner and his two sons who would carry on after the father had crossed the last river. There was only one C left now, and he was not doing much carrying of anything except marked cards and a whiskey bottle.

Toby raised in the stirrup, adjusted the seat of his Levi's, and frowned as he recalled the day Aaron got kicked in the stomach by a mule. The young man had been treating the mule for screw worm when he took the full blow from the large Missouri mule's hind hoof. Aaron had lived for five days. They were terrible days and nights. Toby could still hear Aaron moaning and sometimes, screaming in pain. Toby remembered thinking that if he had been a steer or horse, they would have shot him to put him out of his misery.

Soon afterwards, Camel told his father he was leaving the ranch to find his own way. Toby could still see Henry standing on the front porch telling Camel that the gate was open anytime he wanted to use it. The lad had left and was not seen by anyone in the territory for over ten years. When he showed up again, his father was on his death bed. Toby always believed Henry had lost a big part of himself when Aaron died and then another big part when Camel left the ranch. Henry was a man of iron will and a lesser man would have given up the fight years before but he hung on for a decade before the iron turned to rust and gave way to the ravages of time.

It still grieved Toby to see in his mind the scene when Camel and his father tried to talk to each other. Neither could do it. Once, Camel left the room, Henry had whispered to Toby that his dying wish was that the foreman would watch out for his only living son. Henry died that night with so much unspoken between he and Camel.

Afterwards, the only thing that interested Camel was a fast horse, faster women, card playing and whiskey, lots of whiskey. Toby tried to talk to him many times, but it was useless. Camel slept most of the day, and stayed out most of the night. Toby finally concluded the best he could do to honor Henry's last request, was to assume responsibility for running the 3C. He lived with the hope that one day Camel would find the right woman, or just grow up and decide to be the man his father and brother had been. He pulled at his shaggy beard; he had lost all faith in Camel's rehabilitation. It pained him to think that the son of Henry, brother of Aaron, and owner of the 3C was a lazy, drunk, cheat and womanizer.

Camel dozed again. The next time he opened his eye, he saw the crumpled figure lying on the floor, snoring. His head throbbed with each heartbeat. The sleeping man's boots swayed with the rhythm of the train. Each sole had a hole in its center. Pawing at his swollen slit of an eye, he gave up. The boot sole fuzzed up and he felt himself drifting off again.

Camel looked again and it was night. He was frustrated with himself. He could not stay awake. The moon cast pale rays through the slatted sides.

He could barely make out the old man who was sitting up staring through the sides. "Where are we?"

The man jerked, grinned, and said, "We about to make a water stop at a little place called Mountain High. I'm gettin off there. Ya might wanta do the same before that mean railroad man comes back here and kicks you off, hmmmm."

Camel tried to raise his head again and thought he might pass out. He attempted to roll over, but it was too painful. "I…can't…do…it."

The old man said, "Ya took a bad lick to the head. I had a friend who got kicked by his horse one time. He was just like you. He lived for…"

Camel felt the train jerk hard again and the old man's rough hands lifting his head. "Ya need sumthin' to drink."

Camel felt life stir somewhere deep within him. *He's gonna give me a drink. Thank God!*

Lukewarm liquid flowed down his parched throat but something was badly wrong. *Whoa! This is water, not whiskey. I need whiskey!*

The train rumbled, squealed, and voices were heard. Camel heard another sound. He listened…it was cattle bawling.

As if reading his mind, the man said, "They getting' ready to fill these cars with cattle. They might use this car or they might not. I ain't bettin' against it. We need to get outta here and I mean now, hmmmm."

Camel could tell they were stopping by the shrill screech of the brakes; iron resisting iron. He pushed up with both his hands, but the effort made the car spin. His head bounced hard onto the rough wooden floor. He gagged. Only a thin gruel slipped from his mouth, all solid food long gone by now.

"Do ya want me to try to help ya up, podnuh, hmmmm?"

Camel gagged again, spit and his face fell back into it. He tried to say something, but could only lie there. There was no way he could get to his feet, even with help.

The voice seemed to be echoing from a canyon, "Damn, I'm sorry I can't help ya podnuh. I gotta go before they catch me. I'm too old to take a lickin' like…"

Camel felt hands poking and tugging at his pockets and that was the last thing he remembered.

When he woke, his face rolled rhythmically with the train's movement. He tried to open his eye, but couldn't. He panicked. He pulled the eyelid open with his finger. It was crusted with vomit. Rolling from his side to his back, made his world spin again. He thought he was going to puke once more. Laying real still, the nausea gradually subsided.

The scent of cattle and hot manure stung his nostrils. From their sounds, he knew they filled the cattle car directly in front of him. It was daylight. The old man was gone.

The train labored to get over a hill, eased it's strain going downhill and then repeated the process. The drafty cattle car rattled and rolled from side to side as it went over hills and down into valleys. The inclines became steeper as it moved westward.

Camel had no idea where he was. How long had he been out? For all he knew, he could be in New Mexico. The tilt of the cars made the cattle bang against the sides, their bawling grew louder, and the stench of manure grew stronger. He fought nausea as his head and entire body pulsed in pain.

Daylight came in waves. The sun's rays were bright at the top of a hill, but it remained dark within the deep gulches, ravines and valleys. Within an hour, full light washed the rough, dry, mountainous terrain.

The clack of the wheels took on a loud, hollow sound when they passed over trestles. There were many of them. Some towered over dry gulches, others crossed low   draws that hardly made an impression in the desert sand.

Fading in and out, he awoke to the squeal of brakes. His pain and queasiness remained. *How long can I lie here? What if they load the car with cattle with me lying on the floor?*

Placing one hand under his head, pushing with the other elbow, he raised himself to a sitting position. He slumped there fighting waves of nausea as the train came to a halt. It jerked forward, almost toppling him.

Men yelling and cattle bawling surrounded him. He sat in the middle of the car, in front of the door. Should he remain there, hoping to be seen, or should he try to make it to the side of the car?

He twisted, placing both palms on the floor, gagged, as a thin gruel slid from his mouth to the floor. He raised to his knees. Loathing sickness swept over him. Each time he pulled a knee forward, he gagged. His head touched the side of the car. He remained in the kneeling position until he heard hands grasping the car door. He raised his bloodied pulp of a face and pulled himself up hand over hand to a standing position. He closed his one eye and held on.

He tried to yell once, but the din of the yells, stomping hooves, and bawling drowned him out. *Please, somebody look in here and see me. Owwww! Dammit that horn took a pound of meat off my back. Owwww! How many beef can they pack in one car? I think I'm gonna pass out. I can't...I'll be trampled.*

Gagging and deep breathing, he held on and feared that he'd be crushed against the siding. Dust from the milling cattle filled the air around the car and in it. Pushing with all his might against the pressing livestock, his head throbbed, his stomach felt like it had been turned inside out like a whole herd of beef had trampled him.

Struggling with all of his might for a corner, he winced and gagged as a horn jabbed his ribs or a steer's hind end pushed against him. The train was moving by the time he felt the other side of the car, telling him that he was in a corner. Fighting to turn to face the steers, he felt himself slipping into a black hole as his body crumpled in the corner amidst the wild-eyed beast and the stinging stench of hot, fresh cow manure.

Something was lashing him in the face. He heard his own voice, "Stop it, dammit!" He peeked through his eye and looked into the ass-end of a giant steer. With distorted vision, it was quite a sight. The tail was swishing him in the face. Holding the tail with one hand, he pushed himself up with the other. His grip on the tail slipped. The steer's tail, like the floor, was covered with manure.

The steer fell back and his rear haunch smashed into the siding just over Camel's head. The press of the steers, the overwhelming smell, the throbbing headache, double vision, all culminated in Camel gagging, choking, spitting but producing only a trickle of yellow bile. Pulling his feet as close to him as possible to avoid the hard, massive hooves, he huddled in the corner, resting his head between his legs and lost consciousness again.

When he came to he was lying on his side, against the back of the car, and it was empty--except for a pair of long legs wearing dingy Levi's and clay-caked boots. Camel looked up into a half-sneering, grizzled face of a man wearing a dusty Stetson. He was holding a bucket. Camel realized he'd been splashed with cold water.

"Time to get your ass off this train, Bum!" The eyes were dark and hard and struck a note of fear and anger deep within Camel. "Get up from there before these number twelve boots start movin' ya. I ain't totin' water and givin' ya no more baths today."

Camel started to speak, but his lips were stuck together from stomach bile. He flicked his tongue to loosen them but the tall figure looming over him interpreted the gesture wrongly. He saw the boot go back and he brought up an arm, but the boot toe found his stomach. *Oh shit, that hurt.*

The next thing he knew, a strong hand gripped his boots at the ankles and pulled him across the rough, wooden floor smeared with cow dung. His one eye showed him the man's face just above his own. Camel saw the man had jumped to the ground, his long arms reached for him, pinched his neck and calf as he pulled him from the car floor. He heard his own voice as he thumped to the hard earth. Gasping for air, he was pulled again by the ankles over hard ground and released.

Camel opened his eye and saw a flat, deadpan expression beneath cold eyes. His vision blurred and doubled. "Bum, ya wait right there for me. I gotta check the rest of the cars, when I get through, I'll bring a bottle back with me."   •

Camel knew the man was lying. It was not just the lie of a man who would fail to do what he promised. There was something sinister in the man's actions, expression, voice, but especially in the eyes.

Camel tried to speak, but he had no air. He listened to the crunch of boot soles on the rocky soil fade away. *I gotta get up! I gotta get outta here!* Turning to his side, he fought nausea, turned on his stomach, waited for the throbbing sickness to pass, and then worked to get on all fours. He made it! Every move required a long pause to allow the drumbeats in his head and stabs of white pain that flashed throughout his system to quite.

He began to crawl. Noise surrounded him: men yelling, cussing, a train whistle blowing, the hiss of steam, cattle bawling, and an occasional crack of a whip. He was weak, but not hungry. His arms and legs trembled. He felt fear as a rider rode close by him yelling at a steer. *Where is the steer? Will I be trampled by a horse or steer?*

Dust choked him. He coughed, gagged and heaved, but kept crawling. His hands and knees burned from the hot, sandy grit. The black point of an agave stuck his shoulder, but he ignored it and crawled for all he was worth.

A voice! A strange, high-pitched, thin voice sounded, "Hey! Mister! I gotta bottle of good whiskey here for ya. Give a holler and I'll bring it to ya." The voice sounded again, "Damn, it's hot out here! Ya must wanta a drink of this good hard stuff to getcha goin'."

Camel felt his pulse racing. The hair on his neck stood on end. Every sense told him this man had something other than whiskey for him. Camel swallowed. *Damn! I'd like a drink right now. But not what this gent's offering.*

Hugging the ground, Camel hoped he was covered with scrub brush. The voice came closer. For all Camel knew, he could be easily visible. He couldn't see well enough to know. The unfamiliar, high voice was very close--so close, Camel could hear the soft crunch of boot soles. *Maybe he's looking at me and will just put a bullet in the back of my head.* He closed his one good eye and held his breath. The voice and feet were silent. It seemed like an hour to Camel, but he knew it was probably a couple of minutes. The voice sounded again, and the footsteps grew fainter until he couldn't hear them at all.

Several minutes later, Camel remained clinging to the hard earth. He heard two voices now. He recognized one belonging to the man who pulled him from the car. The other he knew as the man who had been calling for him. The voices continued. They had obviously split up and were still searching for him. Both voices promised whiskey. Both intended death.

A half-hour later, he heard the high voice cuss and say something else he could not hear. The other's voice spoke, and then he heard them no more. An eternity later, he allowed himself to raise to all fours again and begin crawling.

After a time, he felt certain he was moving in a direction away from the noise and activity. Thinking of the hard face and voices, he did not stop. Someone wanted him dead. Who? *I may be screwed up, but I know who the fatass is. If I make it outta here in one piece, I'm gonna make it back to Angel Valley, call Hiram out and see how well he shoots when a man is looking him in the eye. Shit! I need a drink!* His pain-wracked head and body made him question if he might just die without anymore help from anyone. Recalling the old man's words on the train, he wondered if he would live.

CHAPTER 3

The early west was hard on its women. The sun, sand, wind, loneliness, and desolate landscape drove some to madness. There was a saying that because the country was so barren and bleak, a woman could look out at sunup and know if she would have company that day.

Maggie enjoyed watching Hiram squirm as little Josh read to him from his hornbook. It was obvious that Hiram wanted her to send the children out for recess; he'd asked her in a whisper soon after he arrived, but she refused. Little Josh stuttered and stammered, but continued on.

Maggie hushed the other children when they giggled. She gazed out the open door. She did not like Hiram to interrupt her lessons. She did not like Hiram. He was so pompous and arrogant. The last time he'd visited, he'd stage-whispered to her upon leaving that the Schultz children should be sitting in front of the Stoddard children. She knew what he meant. Hiram was like many of his era who didn't believe in public education, but if it did occur, the wealthier children should be seated in front of the poorer children.

Well, Maggie was of that era but not that philosophy. She sat her student's based upon several factors: size, vision, hearing, behavior, and any other needs they may possess.

She gave David the evil eye for trying to attract the attention of another student. He paled, looked down and then back to Josh. Maggie found Hiram to be offensive in so many ways. First, he smelled like soured dough to her. He was grossly overweight, but it was other things she disliked more, such as his breath. The biggest thing was his haughty attitude. He treated those he was trying to sell with condescending smiles and comments; those below him, he walked on. She thought he was probably the most insincere man she had ever encountered. "And those are his strong points," she whispered to herself as the class broke into applause for Josh's accomplishment. But, she knew she had kept him waiting and aggravated him as long as she dared. His was the most powerful voice in the little town and his vote determined her school's annual budget, including her salary.

She stood wearing a long gingham dress, her light brown hair pulled into a bun atop her head. Maggie was not a beautiful woman, but considered to be attractive. One reason she stood out was due to the limited number of eligible females in the small town. She was tall, willowy, and her smile revealed white, straight teeth. The older boys in class tried to get her to smile because they said it made her beautiful.

She dismissed the students. Desks scraped and feet, many of them bare, echoed on the floor in the little barn-like school house as the children made for the outdoors to play and suck on the licorice candy brought by Hiram.

Watching them go, Maggie thought how her only two suitors were such opposites. Camel was so much fun, but so undependable. More than once, he'd come courting, but she'd smelled liquor on his breath and refused to get into his surrey. Finally, he appeared without the sour mash smell and she went out with him. She flushed as she thought of the couple of times they had parked by the river, under the willows and made love. She knew she was being foolish. As the town's sole teacher of children, she had a reputation to maintain. She had received several warnings from older women about Camel's sordid reputation. She even received a warning from the deputy, Frank Moseley. Something about his words sounded as though they came directly from Hiram.

Hiram was...Hiram. She smiled at him as he approached her desk. "Thank you for the licorice for the children, Hiram. As you know, some of the children's parents cannot afford to buy candy for them. I'm sorry I could not stop the lesson, but we are behind in our studies and have got to complete writing and numbers before the end of the day."

He smiled broadly. "That's alright, Maggie. You're doing exactly what you're supposed to be doing. I just wish I'd had a teacher like you when I was their age."

She smiled, said nothing. He went on, "I never had a teacher as pretty as you, doggone it."

She looked out the door, "Excuse me, Hiram." Walking quickly, she stood at the door and yelled, "David stop teasing him now, or you'll spend a long time in the corner." The yells and laughter outside subsided when she yelled, but resumed as she glanced at the clock atop a battered table resting at the back of the room.

A faint, "Yes ma'am," was heard between laughter and yells. She turned to face Hiram who remained at her desk. She had hoped he would follow her to the door. "I better get out there with them, Hiram, before one hurts the other."

He smiled and said softly, "I came for business too, Maggie." He paused as she moved up the aisle to face him. "You and I need to sit and talk about the council meeting coming at the end of the month. We will be discussing the school's budget for the coming year, and, of course, your salary." He paused again, "I intend to push for every dollar we can get for our children, and especially more money for your salary. You deserve it. These kids are our future. But, I need to get some ideas from you so I can speak with authority."

There was another pause, punctuated by the yells and laughter of kids playing outside. "Can I pick you up at six tomorrow evening? We can have dinner at my place and discuss plans for our school. Hans Stutz and Reverend McKenzie will be there too, of course."

Maggie smiled, saw through his ploy. "I think that's a very good idea, Hiram. I will be ready with projections and a needs list for the coming year."

He smiled broadly, leaned closer. She spun and spoke to him as she picked up William's fat pencil. "I've got to get out there Hiram before Henry and David get into a fight. Thank you, for your interest in the children."

He moved to the hardback chair, picked up his black Homburg and said, "I knew I could count on your professionalism," and walked out. His heavy boots clumped on the hardwood floor. Maggie waited until she heard his horse blow and the clink of stirrups before she moved to the door. She stood on the porch watching the children. She knew that neither Stutz nor the Reverend would hear of the meeting, or else Hiram would make it a short one so he could spend time with her.

Her mind returned again to Camel. Where is he? She knew he was not a suitable suitor. He was too immature and fun-loving. But she sure missed his personality and good humor. She smiled, recalling the way he called her, "Aggie."

Calling the children to line up at the bottom of the steps, she thought for the first time how much Camel and Hiram were alike. Each one knew what they wanted. Each one was totally self-absorbed. Each one was a user of people for their own advantage. As likable as he was, Camel had no redeeming features. He was like a spoiled little boy--fun, fun. At least Hiram made a difference in things. Perhaps she should try to look kinder at Hiram. He could certainly make a difference to these children and to her.

Pearl Manning was bone-tired. She stood from her crouched position in her garden, placed both hands in the small of her back, leaned back seeking relief from the dull ache, and listened for the boys. Their voices told her they were on the front side of the cabin. She blew a lock of brown hair streaked with gray from her eye and looked around her.

Dammit, Earl, you had to bring me all the way out here from Louisiana, get two boys in and outta me as fast as ya could, and then you up and die on me. All I got is a half-dry milk cow, a worn out Missouri mule, a sway-backed mare and a couple dozen steers so wild that they might have run all the way to New Mexico by now. Her eyes brimmed with tears as she thought of Earl, his dying of…what? He just seemed to lose his appetite, began to shrink up, lose more strength every day until he laid down for a week and then died.

The tears were not as much for Earl as for her and the boys. How in the hell can a woman with two kids make it in this wilderness? How could she continue to feed them and care for them? The boys wouldn't be going to school if it weren't for Hiram. He paid for the wagon to pick them up each day and carry them to school. She didn't try to fool herself. She knew he wouldn't be doing it if she did not go to bed with him. Her face burned with anger at herself that within a few months after Earl died, Hiram led her to believe he wanted to court her and make her his wife. She'd been stupid enough to fall for it but soon realized his idea of courting her was to show up in the middle of the day when the kids were at school and romp with her on her feather mattress.

She stooped and picked up the rough-handled hoe. Anger and shame filled her as she thought of how Hiram came at least once a week during the day when the boys were at school to receive his pay. She gripped the handle too hard as she brought it down on some weeds growing near her beans. The impact of the hoe on the hard earth, jolted her shoulder. *That's not smart*, she thought. *How could she grow a garden with a dislocated shoulder?*

At twenty-eight, she remained fairly attractive to men, but she was growing older each day. The hard work and worry was taking it's toll. It all bore down on her face. A couple of years earlier, she had natural curly red hair, pert nose, freckles and an hourglass figure. She was not a beauty, but men found her to be sexy. Now, her hair had lost it's luster and streaks of gray ran through it. Her ample breasts and round bottom seemed to shrink and sag with each passing day.

Anger mixed with frustration as she thought of Camel. She had no idea where he may be. It was obvious that Toby was concerned about him. *Dammit it, Camel! You told me ya loved me and that ya would take care of me and the boys, and I was fool enough to believe ya. I shoulda known all you wanted was some quick lovin'. Because of you, I ran Hiram off, but you only wanted the same thing he did. It sickens me to think of the things I did for Hiram whenever he told me he might be able to arrange for the boys to go to school. I invited him back out...hell, I almost had to beg him.*

Rubbing her lower stomach, she recalled how rough Hiram had been as he rode her like a bronco. He hurt her because of his jealousy over Camel. And Camel...she ached as she thought of him. She loved him. She actually fell in love with the sorry-ass bastard and look what it got her. Thinking she could be the woman to make a man of him and a father for her boys, she'd given herself totally to him. Unlike Hiram whom she gave only her body, she'd given her heart to Camel and he probably never even knew it. Didn't care.

Standing straight, holding the hoe in front of her, she looked up into the blue sky. Tears mixed with sweat and dirt ran down her freckled face; she spoke aloud, "I know! I knew better in my heart. I played the damn fool and look what's it's got me." She pressed her full lips together, and said in a quavering voice through her tears, "Damn you to hell, Camel! I hope they never find ya!"

Sheriff Libby shoveled oats into the bins for his gelding and two mares. Leaning the pitchfork against the side of the barn, he scratched the forehead of the gelding and looked out the barn door to his dog-run house.

Was it really his place? Hiram had set him up here after he'd had him serve eviction papers on the former owner. A skinny, hollow-eyed man whose wife and several children, who like him, carried the weight of defeat in their eyes, body language, and flat voices. The man had cried when his wife read the papers to him. Many on the frontier were not able to make it. This poor, hardworking, half-starved man was one of them. He had borrowed money from Hiram and could not repay it.

Hiram had promised the sheriff he would sell the place to him for next to nothing, but so far, no papers or legal action had occurred. Lighting a pipe, blowing smoke, the sheriff asked himself if he was just serving as a lackey for Hiram and subject to being fired without anything to show for his loyalty and effort. He didn't like the answer to his question.

Turning, walking slowly to the door, he leaned against the jam, puffed on his pipe and once again went over details of the night Camel disappeared. Something was wrong. Bad wrong. He knew Billy had lied to him about that night. Billy was too simple-minded to be deceitful. The lad had kept his eyes averted as he answered the sheriff's questions. He said that Hiram had talked to Camel and then left the three of them in front of the platform. Billy and Frank escorted Camel back to his horse. The last they saw of him was his back as he rode toward the 3C.

Frank had told the same story. The identical story--word for word. The two had agreed on their story and it was all too right to be right. Frank was intelligent and devious, he could lie convincingly. If it weren't for Billy's version mirroring Frank's, and the boy's emotions, the sheriff would have bought it.

He had scoured the territory and found no trace of Camel. What to do next? He had an idea; he would check it out first thing tomorrow morning. Walking toward the cabin, he continued to feel a nagging doubt about the whole thing. He felt the same way about his job and relationship with Hiram.

Sans was the first out of his bedroll each morning. Ordinarily, he'd have kept his mustang close to him during the night. The small, knotty horse he called Bonita served as an excellent sentry, alerting him whenever a stranger neared. But, last night he'd allowed Bonita to roam and crop grass wherever she chose to go. He knew she'd not go far.   This morning, everyone, including him, had rested a little longer. They'd crossed the Rio Grande at dusk and all felt relief at leaving the Federales behind.

Yet, all of the men felt a renewed tension too. They were back in Texas, where each one of them was wanted by the law. Each one knew he was experiencing only a brief respite from being sought by the Texas Rangers and every town marshal in every town large enough to hire someone to wear a badge.

Sans stepped close to a creosote bush and pissed on it. He knew Eunice was awake and watching him, but pretended to sleep. Buttoning his jeans, he scooped up a handful of sand, stood over her, held a fist over her face and allowed a trickle of it to drop onto her cheek and closed eyes.

She covered her face with her hands and scrunched further down under the saddle blanket. He kicked her in the back, and as she groaned with pain, and sat up, elbows wrapped around her face to ward off possible blows, he whispered to her, "Get some wood, Bitch, before I really hurtcha."

Stumbling into a grove of Cottonwoods, she squatted behind one and peed. One hand held her back where the kick had bruised her kidney. She heard rocks bouncing off of the tree and knew it was Sans throwing them at her. She hated him. She hated all of them. Sans did not have his way with her nightly, like Big Boy and Jones, but in a way, he was the worst of all.

Gathering wood, she thought again as she had so many times this last week, how she might escape. She knew this was not the time or place. But at least they were back in Texas. For the first time since being with this group, she fostered hope that she might just survive and live to see this bunch of riff-raff hang.

She heard voices, and recognized them belonging to Sans and Kilkenny. Kilkenny's was louder and closer to her. "I'll get her! Hold ya hosses!"

She had left the cantina in Sonora for him. But, like all of the men she chose, he was weak and allowed them to join with the others. He'd made a couple of half-hearted attempts to defend her but was unable to deal with Big Boy, Sans, and Jones.

At least the only ones using her was Big Boy and Jones. Kilkenny had no stomach for rape. She was sure his looks and personality had always made him a hit with the ladies. Sans didn't use her, but she was convinced he was her biggest threat. She had no doubt that without the others, he would torture and kill her.

Kilkenny appeared and said, "Come on, Eunice, we're waitin!"

Only to him had she dared to allow herself to show anger. "Oh, is that so? Well, Mr. Big Talker, let me hurry up and do whatever these animals order me to do." She stared hard at him as she walked by him carrying an armload of limbs, "I'm sure glad that I got a real man to take care of me."

He looked at his boots, his face no longer turning red. She guessed he was getting use to her sarcasm. He spoke low, "Hang in there, Honey! Things might just get better for us real quick, real soon."

She grunted a "Humpf," but his words did reinforce her glint of hope.

Camel laid on the ground snoring. Something woke him. Lying on his stomach, he heard a frightening sound. He tried to see where the sound came from, but because of his closed eye and slit of another, he had difficulty. Turning his head at an awkward angle, he made out the snake. It was a big one. It's rattlers sounded like buzzing bees. Camel did not move. The rattler was coiled with arched head high and ready to strike. After a minute, he slid backwards away from Camel while holding his coil. Safely away, he straightened and disappeared into the underbrush.

Camel diagnosed his condition. His head ached, but not as badly as before. He could see with one eye, just not very much. Every breath brought a new experience of pain within his rib cage. Whenever he closed his mouth, he felt grit between his teeth. One of Hiram's punches must have realigned his jaw. He hurt all over inside and outside.

Straining and grunting, he raised to all fours, gathered his strength, and then stood up. The horizon began to spin and he sat down hard. After a while, he lurched forward and began shuffling through the brush on his hands and knees. Soft sand cushioned his hands and knees for a few minutes as he crawled as fast as he could. Suddenly the sand was gone and replaced with rocky soil and a million prickly cactus. He made a whining sound as his hand came down on top of a short squat barrel cactus. Licking his wound, he moved ahead only to run head long into a prickly pear that stabbed his head and ear. The next move brought him into contact with a Cholla that tore his shirt and stabbed his shoulder. Mumbling curses, he had never wanted a drink more than right now.

He could no longer hear men or cattle. The only sounds were a hawk screeching overhead and a mockingbird singing a poignant tune. He depended on his hearing; his vision was so limited.

The air smelled clean and pure. The sun was becoming bright and he kept his eye on the ground. He glanced up once and the sun's rays seemed to sear his brain and make his head throb as it had before.

Black-eyed Susan's surrounded him. Their bright gold and orange colors were good for his spirit. Moving through them with his head to the ground, he suddenly felt like the top of his head was on fire. He cussed, sat back on his haunches and touched his head. His fingers felt a strange object; he pulled it out. Placing it close to his eye, he saw it was a cactus point. Looking up he saw that he'd crawled head first into a cactus with it's long, dark green prickly points facing him. He searched his scalp for more cactus points, but found none. His scalp felt like it held a dozen of them.

The terrain was rough and hilly. He crawled over hummocks and into gulleys. His knees and hands stung from scrapes. Camel was aware of several things: he was thirsty, hot, hurting, had no idea where he was, and could not remember beyond a hellish train ride. One thought dominated all others--he needed a drink of hard stuff.

"Wait! I remember fat-ass Hiram whipping up on me as somebody held me. I'll get that lying hypocrite if I live to get out of this. And then I'll get that drink.

Moving his hand forward, he found only air. Tottering on an edge, he squinted down to look into an abyss. The bottom was at least thirty feet down. He'd almost fallen into it. He had to gain his feet somehow.

Lying on his back, he closed his eye and rested. He slept and dreamed. In his dream, a monster with a giant head and mouth filled with razor-sharp teeth, and long tentacle-like arms with sharp claws was chasing him. He tried to run, but it was too fast for him. It's claws clutched his shoulders and held him as the gaping mouth opened to devour him. Waking up cold and in pain, he moaned and groaned, and moved into a fetal position. It was dark and an owl was hooting in the distance. Small feet scurried close to him. He knew the desert was home to many small creatures. It was home to snakes who ate them too. He drifted back into a restless sleep.

He woke up screaming. He was sitting up, swinging his arms to fend off the ugly beast. Breathing deeply, he worked to calm himself. It was only another nightmare. He'd had them constantly since the beating.

At least he was sitting up, this was progress. But, he had to do more. He had to stand and walk. His hands and knees were bloody. Crawling again, he held his head close to the ground to spot dangerous fall-offs and look for a limb to support him.

Stopping intermittently to catch his breath and give his hands and knees a break, he felt for dangers ahead. *What if I grab a rattler?* Sweat stung his one slit of an eye; he swiped at it.

There it was! The skag of a half-rotten cottonwood loomed a few feet above it's prickly cactus neighbors. He crawled toward it, rushing directly into the burning sting of a cactus point. Cussing, he snatched the arrow-shaped point from his scalp. He crawled cautiously now. The devilish daggers surrounded him. His hand touched a round limb. He heard himself grunt in fear that it was a rattler. His hand had instinctively withdrawn. Hearing no rattles, he turned his swollen, face toward the object. A five-foot twisted limb rested between tall cacti.   His heart thumped in excitement. Grasping the limb, he checked it for strength. Grimacing as his bicep felt the pinch of a dagger point, he found satisfaction in the rough texture of the wood. Bark fell from the limb at his touch. This meant the wood was old and possibly rotten.   Lifting it gingerly, he felt its heft. It was the right length and diameter. Satisfied, he used it as a lever to push his weight erect.

Everything's spinning, Dammit! This is terrible. Oh God! I gotta...gotta fight it! I gotta gain my feet or I won't make it. Bracing against it, the limb snapped, sending him crashing into the daggers.

A point pierced his left cheek and the side of another slit his forehead. Lying on his back, he heard a strange sound. *I'm crying.* Wiping his bloody face and squinting with his slit of an eye, he caught sight of a black buzzard sailing above him framed against the blue sky. It's shadow flicked across him. He felt a tremor sweep his frame.

Unless I keep moving and find water, I will be a dead man. A mental image of a blue-faced carnivore picking out his eyes, gave him the incentive to push to a sitting position.

Take deep breaths. Stay Calm. Move slowly and find a limb that will support you. But, if that limb was rotten, aren't all of them? Hold it! Ya can't allow yourself to think like that. Start looking. If only I had a drink to help me think---God, I need a drink bad.

His forehead burned. His cheek throbbed. Hands and knees raw. *How much pain can a man take? How much defeat? How long can I crawl around out here in this heat without water. I want water. I want...I want...whiskey. I want a glass of half water and half whiskey.*

Again his fingers found a point imbedded into his flesh. It took several attempts to remove it. He guessed it was his weakness, trembling, blood-slicked fingers which tingled with numbness. *If only I could be numb all over. Whiskey would...stop it!*

Crawling forward slowly, he touched another limb but it was too small. Another limb---too large. Brushed more daggers but felt no stings. The hairs on his neck raised and heart thumped in his throat as he felt the piercing eyes of the buzzard. Waiting. Patient. Time on his side.

He found it! He clung to the limb for a long time. It was the right size and weight and he hoped it was strong enough to support him. Pushing up with it, he held his breath, but it did not break. Weaving, he thought he was going to pass out. Pushing down on the brown, twisted limb with it's fork on the ground for stability; he breathed deep. The nausea passed enough for him to try walking. It was slow and awkward going, but at least he was up and moving. By shading his swollen, tearing eye, with one palm, he could make out the general terrain and the mountainous horizon. He knew he was far west of the Pecos. The most rugged, dry and dangerous country in all of Texas.

He had heard many stories of men searching for gold or silver who entered this area to never be seen or heard of again. The wild, mostly uninhabited territory was rife with mountain lions, rattlers, and sure death for the man who did not know where the water holes were located. Thirst was his number one priority now that he was on his feet. *I hafta find water. I will find it or die. How about beer?*

Hiram took a swig of beer. Wiping foam from his lips, he told Stinky to bring him another one. He was sitting in a small backroom of the saloon. Hiram never drank in public. The local folks would tolerate a leader inhabiting the saloon to play a friendly game of poker, especially since he assured them he did it only so he could witness to sinners; but the angels of the town frowned on alcohol.

Hiram courted the angels, especially those with money. He was sensitive to his public image. That afternoon he had taken Reverend McKenzie with him in his surrey to visit some of the elderly widows and shut-ins for the church. He burped and finished the beer off as Stinky sat another one in front of him. *I think Stinky's eyes get crossed a little more every day. Damned if I can tell what he's looking at.* Smiling, he recalled the town folks waving to him and the pastor as they rode down the main street.

Reverend McKenzie opened his Bible and stared at the pages without seeing them. He had spent the afternoon visiting church members with Hiram Bishop. They had visited Grandmother Stutz, Mrs. McCormick and Mr. and Mrs. Arlington, all wealthy members.

As pastor of his flock, the Reverend knew most of his congregants were poor. Hiram had no time for them. McKenzie smiled as he recalled the look on Hiram's face when he suggested they visit the Negro family who worked for the Arlington's. Hiram avoided the suggestion by reminding him they had not yet completed the loft which was to be reserved for Negroes, Hispanics and Indians. The Reverend was bothered that work on the loft had been delayed three times. He knew Hiram was working to kill it.

For a small rural church, theirs was unusually ornate, thanks to Hiram. A varnished oak pulpit with gilded woodwork adorning it, a polished communion table topped with embroidered tapestry donated by the Arlington's, cushioned pews for those who could afford to purchase them, all because of Hiram's influence. He regretted he had been caught unaware when Hiram suggested that families be allowed to purchase new pews for their sanctuary. Once the padded pews were in place, in the front, Hiram had the Negro carpenter and custodian of the church make plaques with the families name on them. Hiram himself brought bright red cord to tie the pews off, preventing anyone else from sitting in them. The remainder of pews were hard bottomed slatted things that provided little comfort.

McKenzie frowned. This was unacceptable for a frontier church. Elitism and class status had no place in their church, yet Hiram mocked the pastor's beliefs and established a pecking order based on economics. Standing, he walked to the window of his modest, frame house and looked down the main street. He must take a stand and…

His wife's weak, tremulous voice wafted from the bedroom, "Bilbo, can you come here?" She was sick and growing weaker every day. He thought of Hiram's promise to entice a doctor to set up practice in their town. McKenzie's wife needed a doctor--bad.

"Coming, Dear," he answered. His expression and body language did not match his voice.

Big Boy held the reins to his mount with one hand while he used the other to hold his member and pissed on a wiry Cholla Tree. Kilkenny and Jones did the same. The lone woman, Eunice, stared down at her saddle out of fatigue rather than embarrassment. Sans, the half-breed, sat his saddle and scanned the horizon. No one ever saw him perform any personal act such as the others were doing now.

The three men who'd dismounted adjusted their cinches and bridles. Eunice felt the eyes of the maniac, Sans, bore into her back. She wished for the thousandth time she'd not allowed the handsome Kilkenny to talk her into going with him. She watched him out of the corner of her eye. His fair skin was blistering under the scorching sun without his hat. His complexion had evolved from pink to red and now a bluish hue. She looked away as he turned toward her. She hated him for getting her into this hellhole. In a way, she hated him more than all the others, except for Sans.

Big Boy cussed. Breaking open his double-barreled shotgun, he removed the two shells and walked toward Eunice. Holding it up, he said, "You carry this, Eunice. It'll help ya stay balanced on ya nag."

Her hand jerked away from the hot metal of the barrel and she knew this was the reason he was making her carry it. He pushed the barrel into her bony ribs and it hurt. She took it and quickly moved her hands to the forearm. She knew enough about guns to know a scattergun was not the most effective weapon in the open desert country. And without shells, the gun was useless to her. Just like everything else about this trip.

Big Boy heaved himself into the saddle and the others did the same. As the group moved out, she heard the same refrain she'd been listening to for torturous miles. San's croaky whisper, "Gonna kill the bitch, gonna kill the bitch, gonna cut her guts and leave her squirmin' in a ditch."

CHAPTER 4

Some said that other states were carved or born, Texas grew from hide and horn.

Camel dreamed again. This time he was not running from a monster, he was the monster. He saw the world through green lenses and chased two men. They ran hard, but he was faster. One was older than the other. He was about to catch the older one when the younger one turned to help him. He looked into the faces of his brother and his father.

Sitting up, he gently rubbed his sore face and inventoried his condition. His one slit of an eye opened a little wider this morning. He tried to force the other open with his fingers. It was a relief to find that he could see with it, though everything was fuzzy.

His mouth felt like it was filled with cotton. He had to find water. *A man can go a long time without food, but not without water.* Looking around him, he saw rugged country: hills, spurs, gullies, valleys, and Spanish dagger cactus. Green growth required water. It was around here someplace, but where?

Using the limb as a crutch, he rested his weight on it and eyed the terrain as best he could with his limited vision. Spotting an area about a half-mile away sporting dark green growth, he decided to head for it.

Sagebrush, various cacti, and tumbleweeds were a jumble before him. He had to navigate around each one and it cost him time, energy, and torn skin and clothes each time he took a misstep. Pausing to catch his breath, he eyed the horizon and land around him. The many cacti and sagebrush surrounded him and he thought how each one was his enemy. In this god-forsaken hellhole, survival meant each plant had to fend for itself. Each one had to possess a protective arsenal of sharp thorns and stickers to isolate itself so it could claim any moisture that fell within its immediate area. Each plant was prepared to tear his skin and stab him with its weapons until he bled out the little moisture remaining within his dried and parched skin. He had a fearful thought. *Am I losing my mind from thirst? I'm seeing these cactus as people trying to do me in as though each one was a little Hiram.*

An hour later, he leaned on the limb accepting the realization that the green area was further than he thought. He tried to swallow, but couldn't. His mouth had been dry for so long. His tongue was swollen, filled his mouth. Bending, he almost fell over, but managed to keep his balance. He picked up a small stone and placed it under his tongue. Perhaps it would stimulate some saliva. It didn't. It only irritated his swollen tongue making it harder for him to suck air.

Fear flashed! Would his thick tongue choke him to death? He was in strange, uninhabited country. He could wander for days before locating water. He didn't have days. *How long can a man go without water?*

It was mid-summer and hot. He didn't have a hat to shield his eyes and face from the blazing sun. His clothes were shredded rags. Brown and red streaks covered his torso, reflecting the blend of cow manure and his own blood where his shirt was torn by the unforgiving daggers of the cacti. His thirst was so great that it overrode his many pains.

Hobbling toward a Spanish dagger cactus, he would see if he could pull it apart and find some moisture. Nearing the cactus, he tripped and fell. Sharp pain burned his collar bone and right bicep. On his knees, he ignored the cactus stings and fumbled to pull the daggers from it. He gasped as he tugged at the plant that had become his enemy and refused to give up any of it's moisture. He was too weak. He quit. Tumbling backwards, he lay on his back and cried. It was a tearless cry. His sobs were hacking and dry.

Sitting up, he used his crutch to gain his feet and head for the dark green spot someplace out there. He knew distance could fool a man in this high, clear air, so he resolved not to guess how far he had to go, but to focus on putting one foot in front of the other.

The white, brilliant blaze of sun was arced high in the sky when he stood in the center of the dark green cacti and wild flowers, but saw no sign of water. Falling to the ground, he felt like he had reached the end. His tongue felt fat and bone-dry. His pulse raced. His head felt light and the dizziness that seemed to be abandoning him, had returned. The only positive thing he noted was he could see a little more out of the narrow slit of his left eye.

A scurrying in the brush showed him a horned toad. Glancing about, he saw movement and realized he was looking at a rabbit. If he could somehow manage to catch...the rabbit disappeared into the brush. He sat a long time. The sun's shafts of light pierced his bruised and battered face. Every so often, he caught his own scent. It turned his stomach.

An eternity of falling, gasping, hacking coughs later, he had managed to climb a low spur. Looking down into a low valley, he thought he heard a voice. Shaking his head, he palmed each ear to try and stop the ringing that he'd heard since...since when? Was he hallucinating? His throat felt like it was almost closed and he could hear himself wheeze with every breath.

He made for the voices. A noise in the sagebrush made him pause to catch a glimpse of a roadrunner disappearing into the green and brown foliage. A half-hour later, he realized it was only one voice. It was a man singing. No angel would sound like that raspy voice. The singing was punctuated by spasms of wheezing and coughing. Pushing on, he came to a pile of bones standing at least ten feet tall. He squinted, making out buffalo skulls, antelope limbs, and some large leg bones that puzzled him. He'd heard of men who had collected buffalo bones in the past, but was surprised to see that someone was still doing it. The buffalo had been killed off and disappeared for a decade or more.

The singing stopped, the raspy voice yelled, "Whoeee! I thought Maude stunk when she farted, but she smells like a whore's perfume compared to you!" There was more wheezing, coughing, and spitting.

Camel's eyes followed the voice and found a small, gray-bearded man wearing a battered Homburg and butternut shirt tucked into baggy pants held by rawhide suspenders. The old, wizened man eyed him and said, "Gosh darn it, Mistuh, ya gotta get down to the spring and wash off if ya gonna stay around here. If ya don't clean up, I've gotta get my Spencer rifle and put one of us outta our misery."

Camel tried to talk, but could produce only a hoarse whisper. The old man pointed to a cluster of cottonwoods, "The spring's over there. Use some sand to wash that stink offa ya." Conversation evoked more coughing.

Dropping the crutch, Camel held his hands out and staggered toward the water. The spring was a small pool of water no more that twenty feet in circumference. Camel tottered forward and fell into it. Choking, gasping and spitting, he drank in the cool liquid and thought how water had never tasted so good in all his life. Holding his breath, he held his head under water to wash his aching, burning eyes. One eye remained swollen shut, but his vision improved in the other as he saw particles of sand and other matter that he did not want to think about float atop the water. Sitting up, he sipped the water from his cupped palm.

The little man stood some distance away shaking his head. "Gosh darnit, I'm glad I got my cookin' water afore ya came along. That water ain't gonna be fit to drink for a while." He paused, added, "Cepin by you."

The cool water invigorated Camel. His memory returned with a splash of water in his face. His heart raced, his face flushed as he thought of Hiram. The man had almost beat him to death. He had him put on a train. Camel had no idea where he was. But, the worst thing of all, Hiram had hired someone to kill him. He would not be forgetting any of it.

Unbuttoning his shredded shirt, he grimaced from the pain throughout his body, especially in his rib cage. He peeled off the smelly shirt and dropped it into the water. Rubbing sand onto his sore shoulder and arms and rinsing the cow manure off, Camel made an oath to return to Angel Valley and kill Hiram. The thought, like the spring water made him feel better. He hurt all over, but the biggest hurt was for a drink of something stronger than this spring water.

Sheriff Dan Libby walked slowly to the train depot. As he neared it, he slowed even more and studied the ground. Stopping, he dropped to a squat and examined the dry sand. One hand reached out to a dark spot in the sand. Rubbing the grit between index finger and thumb, he smelled it, stood, dusted his hands together and walked slowly up the wooden stairs to the platform. He walked around on it for a couple of minutes with head down. Again he squatted and rubbed the rough planks. He recognized it--blood.

Ten minutes later, he was sitting in Hiram's bank waiting for him. Customers entered a large room dominated by the bank counter and steel cage that enclosed it; the remaining space held Hiram's large, mahogany desk and chair. The desk faced the door and counter so Hiram had a clear view of anyone entering his business. What no one knew was he had a sawed-off double-barreled ten gauge racked beneath his desk. A door behind the desk led to a small room where Hiram conducted shady business deals.

Sheriff Libby sat with legs crossed, in one of two chairs before the desk, his Stetson resting on the toe of his boot. Hiram stepped from his back room and nodded at the sheriff. Dan was always amazed at how agile and quickly Hiram moved for a man carrying his great bulk. Behind his massive desk, he dropped into his swivel chair which protested with a loud shriek. He eyed his unwelcome visitor for a moment before speaking.

"What brings ya here, Sheriff?"

"Just wanted to check with you again about Camel's disappearance. I'm tryin'…"

Hiram frowned. "Dan, we've been all through that. I told ya everything I know about him. I'm concerned about this, too. Ya know how hard I work to keep our town's reputation as clean as I can. It don't look good for us when a man, a landowner at that, disappears."

Reaching into his desk, he pulled out a couple of cheroots and offered the sheriff one. Both lit up and smoked as Hiram continued, "The truth is, me and Camel always poked fun at each other, but the fact of the matter is, we liked one another." He eyed the sheriff to determine if he was buying his story. The sheriff's poker face told him nothing. Turning to look at the bank door open, Hiram smiled and waved at a customer.

Hiram rested his elbows on the desk top and clasped his beefy hands together. Seeing his bruised and scratched knuckles, he quickly placed his elbows on the arm of his chair, allowing his hands to drop out of sight. "Sheriff, I feel bad about askin' ya the favor of allowin' me to witness as a Christian to Camel, and then he disappears. I don't know if I told ya before, it's no fun makin' a man look bad, but Camel was cryin' drunk the other night. I no sooner told him the Lord loves him and he starts bawlin' like a baby."

"Where did ya last see him?" The sheriff kept his voice low and matter-of-fact.

Hiram frowned, " Like I toldja before, Sheriff. I told Frank and Billy to help him onto that fine Tennessee Walker of his and point it toward home. The last time I saw Camel, he was with them. Ya should ask them. I think you'll find they'll back me up."

Hiram's last words were spaced. He felt anger. The horse! Dammit, why didn't Frank think about Camel's horse! He had to do everything himself or it got botched up.

The sheriff rolled his Stetson around the toe of his boot and stared at it. He had already talked to Frank twice and Billy three times. He knew Hiram was aware of that. Looking into the big man's face, Dan knew he was lying. Dan had come to learn a lot about this man. Whenever he was lying, his voice grew tight and his face reddened. Hiram was on the verge of moving from impatience to hostility.

Appeasing the powerful man, Dan leaned forward and spoke even quieter, "I'm just trying to do a thorough job, Hiram. This is what you hired me to do. *Why even mention the city council, since Hiram controlled it totally.* He worked to maintain his poker face and bland voice. "Like you, I want to keep this town's reputation clean. I don't intend to embarrass you with incompetence."

Hiram's face softened. His body relaxed. "I understand, Dan. You're an asset to this town. You remember that." He paused, assumed his sermonic tone and quoted, "Where there is no vision, the people perish: but he that keepeth the law, happy is he.' That's from Proverbs, chapter twenty-nine, verse eighteen." With that, he stood and Dan knew the meeting was over.

Thanking Hiram, who was now smiling and extending his hand, Dan shook it, felt the pain of the squeeze, noted the condition of

Hiram's knuckles again, walked out and headed toward the livery stable.

Entering the stable, the smell of horses, leather, and burning cedar touched him. His ears rang as steel clanged on steel. Barney Womack, Billy's father, held a hammer in one hand and a rag-covered hand clutched a wagon rim resting on a large black anvil. Barney was a short, muscular man who had little to say. He ignored his visitor, so Dan moved close to a wooden trough setting beside the anvil. At first, he didn't think Barney would stop hammering. Finally, he paused, looked up, and glared at the sheriff.

"Sorry to stop ya from working' Barney. I'm lookin' for Billy."

Barney stared at his work, "Billy ain't well. His ma put him to bed. He has the fever; maybe sumthin' catchin.' I don't know."

Dan thanked him, shared his condolences, but before he could complete his words, Barney was banging the wagon rim. Leaving the stable, Dan knew Barney was lying, just like Hiram. He headed toward Frank's mercantile. He knew he would not get the truth there either.

Changing his mind, he turned into his small office and jail. He flopped into his hard straight chair that wobbled badly. Removing his hat, he tossed it onto the coat rack. He scratched his head.

He talked to these men the day after Camel disappeared and they all said the same thing. Their words and phrases appeared to come from one source, Hiram.

Billy had been so nervous during the questioning that Dan would not have been surprised to see him vomit or start crying. Dan had served as a lawman for many years, and he prided himself on reading people. He knew so far everyone he'd talked to about Camel's disappearance had lied to him. Billy had not been seen by anyone since the last questioning. He guessed that Frank had talked to Hiram regarding Billy's performance, and Hiram had decided Billy needed to get sick for a while. He had to get to Billy again. Billy was the key. He was basically a good young man whose mother had taught him to tell the truth. Leaning his chair back he put his feet on his desk; he figured he would just have to bide his time until he could get Billy alone again.

Camel sat on the bank of the spring staring at it. Water had never looked so good to him before. The little man had disappeared and now Camel heard his approaching steps. Turning his head awkwardly to squint out of one eye, his heart raced. The man was carrying his Spencer rifle.

"I thought I better get my gun. Looks like ya been tryin' to make love to the puma that keeps showin' tracks around here." He continued to cough and spit. "Course, the way ya smell, maybe ya chased him away fer good."

Camel breathed a sigh of relief. "No, I wasn't attacked by a puma. It was a vicious animal though, a man."

"Whoeee! I'm glad to hear that. I only got three bullets left." With that, he sat down on a nearby stump with the rifle butt resting in the sand and the barrel between his legs. "Musta been a bad fella. I hope he ain't lookin' fer ya."

"My name's Claudius Humble Alexander, but they just call me, Bones. What's your name?"

"My name's Mathew Campbell; they call me Camel."

"From the way ya was drinkin' that water, I can see where ya gotcha name."

The old man's words rang a distant bell of regret in the recesses of Camel's mind, but he ignored it.

"I got it because I...I...ya got any whiskey here, Bones?"

Bones shook his head, "I ain't got no whiskey." His faded, gray eyes scanned Camel. "What happened to ya? Was it a fight over a woman?"

"Yeah, ya could say that but it was over some other disagreements too."

Bones squinted his eyes, stared at him up and down and said, "Ya picked up a lotta stingers. Looks like the cactus beat the livin' hell outta of ya, Boy. Lemme get my knife out here and see if I can get some of em.' I got some salt up at the cabin I scraped outta a small salt lake a few miles from here that I'll give ya to wash with to help cure ya sore spots."

For the next hour, Camel winced and grimaced as Bones pulled sharp pricks embedded in his skin from the many desert plants.

"How didja get here? The closest neighbor is over twelve miles from here. In fact, he may," he coughed and spit, "have gone by now, too. The railroad cattle yards are over twenty miles away."

"I came from a little town called Angel Valley. It's in the Chisos Mountain Range. In the Big Bend of the Rio Grande. Ya know where that's at?"

Bones shook his head. "I think I heard of it. But I can't tell ya how far it is from here. I know it has to be a ways though."

Camel felt renewed anger at the response, though he'd already assumed he was far west of his ranch and little town. Staggering, stumbling back to the edge of the spring, he squatted and drank from his cupped hand. It took all of his strength to lift his wet shirt from the water and wring it out. He jumped as Bones yelled, "Whoopee!" Looking around, Camel could see no reason for the yell. Bones's expression was bland. He seemed to see no reason for it either. It was his habit. More coughing, wheezing, and spitting.

Bones went to his cabin and returned a few minutes later with a rusty tin filled with gray-white sand. He handed it to Camel, "This is salt. Wash ya wounds with it so they don't get infected."

After bathing his wounds, Camel shivered. The sun had sunk behind a low mountain. He felt chilled. His hands and lips trembled. "Do ya have any kinda clothes I can wear, Bones?" His head was shaking and he felt weak and nauseated.

Bones scanned him, "I'm a little small for ya, but I'll find something. No women out here so we ain't gotta worry about lookin' purty. What we can do is go to the cabin and you set by the fire and dry ya raggedy clothes." With that, the little man moved off wheezing and coughing.

Camel could not get up. The beating, thirst, and hunger, were taking their toll. He had nothing left. He didn't even have the strength to yell to Bones. In a minute, the little man returned with a look of consternation.

"I can't do it Bones. Could ya lend me a hand?" His entire body trembled and shook. Clutching his wet shirt in one hand, his other arm wrapped around the neck of the old man, together they struggled toward the crude building. One coughed and wheezed while the other hung his head in fatigue.

Hiram grinned.   Sitting in his bronzed tin wash tub, he resembled a fat toad wearing a drenched dark wig. Carmen, Juanita's pretty, younger sister, stood before him nude. She bent slightly as she poured warm water onto his hairy chest and mountainous belly. He reached for a tit but she giggled and stood. Smiling coquettishly, she turned and wiggled her buttocks as she set the bucket down and lifted a long wooden-handled brush from a peg.

Strutting her stuff, she walked past him. He grabbed at a thigh, but she side-stepped him gracefully. Squatting behind him, she scrubbed his back. Laying the brush onto a towel, she walked to the side of the tub, went to her knees, and began washing his torso.

The tip of his member stuck out of the soap suds. She washed around it, down his legs and to his toes. Reaching for the bucket, she walked back to a barrel, dipped the bucket in and returned to him. He stood up in the tub, sloshing water onto the floor. They were participating in a ritual they had performed many times before.

Pulling a wooden chair beside the tub, she stepped onto the seat, holding the bucket.   He hummed as he played with her tits. Standing on tiptoe, ignoring his antics, she poured the water atop his head; reached down for a towel and began to dry him off.   A moment later they were in bed. Hiram wanted to be at his best for the meeting tonight with Maggie. A tumble with Carmen would calm him and enable him to be on his best behavior.

Camel sat before a crackling fire in a small shanty.   It was obviously built with whatever Bones could find: dried cottonwood limbs with creosote bushes stuffed into cracks wherever the limbs bowed; buffalo bones secured with hides of animals, dried rattlesnake skins, several Indian blankets, and to Camel's amazement, there were several faded newspapers stuck to the walls.

At Bones's suggestion, he had undressed, accepted a brightly colored Indian blanket and draped it over his shoulders. Bones spread his tattered clothes on the stone hearth to dry.

Shaking, teeth chattering, Camel continued his assessment of the shack's contents. Not much unless you counted the many colorful Indian-weaved blankets lying about.   The rifle leaned against a corner amidst dried limbs and thin creosote stems protruding from the walls. There was a bunk on one wall and a homemade table with three legs with one end propped atop a stump. Camel sat on a similar stump. It served as Bones's chair. That made up Bones's furniture. A deer hide made a rug beside the bunk. A yellow, greased piece of paper was pegged down against the wall. It's dull glow told Camel that it was a window. In the stone fireplace, a black pot with a heavy wire handle hung from an iron rod sunk into the sides. Whatever was cooking smelled wonderful to Camel.

"I gotta git more wood. Ya set there and I'll git ya sumthin to eat as soon as I git back. Camel heard the sound of coughing fade. Bones was not a well man. Camel noted that with almost every conversation or movement, the old man coughed and struggled for breath.

Dammit to hell! There's gotta be a drink of something around here. Lifting one of the many Indian blankets folded loosely and stacked on the floor, he scanned the contents but found only a pile of raggedy clothes, a rusty lantern and a pick ax. He sat again when he heard Bones cough. A moment later, Bones struggled in with an armload of limbs. Dropping them on the hearth, he stumbled to his bunk and plopped onto it. His wheezing reminded Camel of the train engine.

Bones's face was a hue of blue and he thumped himself in the chest as he struggled for breath. Camel saw a wooden bucket of water on the floor and a gourd hanging from a peg.

"Bones, can I get you a drink of water?" *What about some tonic or cough medicine, dammit. That stuff has some alcohol in it.*

The old man shook his head and waved him away. A minute later, he still sat and wheezed, but his breath came slower and quieter now. "About all I can offer ya is some jack-rabbit stew. Can ya eat some?"

As Camel ate the tasty soup, he noted Bones staring into the blazing fire, holding his bowl without eating. The old man jerked as he tried unsuccessfully to stifle a cough. Camel gulped the delicious gruel, but saw Bones slurp only a couple of spoonfuls.

Camel would find that Bones could tell him little of his past. The old man's physical health was deteriorating and his mental health was doing the same.

Camel sucked the sweet meat from the stewed rabbit leg. Bones had trapped the rabbit and cooked it in an iron kettle over the hot coals in the fireplace. Camel ate most of it and thought again how wonderful it would be if he only had a drink of hard liquor. Observing Bones with his limited vision, the old man intermittently talked to himself, giggled, coughed, spit, shouted or assumed a zombie-like trance.

At the moment, Bones sat on his bunk holding his bowl in one hand and pulling at his gray beard with the other. His eyes appeared to dilate as he stared into the fireplace and the hand touching his beard dropped to his lap. The only sound he made was a whistling each time he exhaled. The old man sat without moving for a good minute, and then his lips began to twitch and he shouted, "Whoeee! The morning folks are coming! Yesiree! I can feel it in my bones!" He worked unsuccessfully at clearing the phlegm from his throat, spit in the coals and repeated himself. His bony, protruding chest heaved from the effort.

He appeared to be returning to his trance when Camel tossed a clean bone into the fireplace. "Who are the morning folks, Bones?"

The old man's face assumed a whimsical expression, but he said nothing. Camel started to repeat the question when Bones turned his skeletal-like head toward him. His eyes appeared to be bright red orbs, as he stared at Camel as though he was seeing him for the first time. An odd feeling that Camel could not describe descended on him like a wet fog and made the hairs on his neck stand erect. Perhaps it was because dark was descending and the flickering light from the coals cast eerie shadows about the tiny cabin. For the first time, Camel observed how emaciated the face before him was. Looking at Bones was like looking at a dead man. All flesh on the face and skull was taunt, pallid and exposed skeletal-like features.

The whimsical expression faded, the tired face collapsed into itself as the bony skull turned again to the crackling and sizzling embers.

Camel wanted a drink of whiskey so bad he ached from head to toe. Did he hurt more from wanting a drink or from the beating and the stabbing pricks of the cactus? He guessed it was the former. Drinking spring water from a battered tin cup did nothing to quench his desire for alcohol. He would check every nook and cranny in the cabin for a bottle when Bones left him tomorrow to fetch water. Closing his eyes, he felt like he would jump out of his skin. *Damn! I need a drink!*

CHAPTER 5

Under President Grant's Peace Policy, missionaries were assigned to teach civilization and religion to the Indians held on reservations. Indian children were not allowed to speak their native language.

Maggie smiled, placed her palm over the top of her glass and refused anymore wine. She looked at the thin Mexican girl who held the bottle and whose eyes darted to Hiram. Hiram had instructed his maid to keep her glass full. The girl stood there as though paralyzed.

"Our guest doesn't want any more wine, Juanita. Thank you." The girl's eyes appeared fearful to Maggie as she disappeared into the kitchen.

Hiram owned the nicest house in Angel Valley. It was the only two story dwelling in town. This house begged attention, being large and square, unlike most of the other houses, which were dog-run types. They were long and rectangular with an open porch separating the kitchen from the rest of the house. The remainder of the dwellings in town were stick and wattle with a few boarded shotgun houses mixed in.

Hiram's house was originally built by Orin Wister, first cattle baron, or cattle thief, depending on who told the story. Losing his fortune in the war, he died penniless. Hiram bought the house and land for a song from a nephew in San Antonio who desperately needed the money. Its new owner extensively renovated it. A high roof porch with an elaborately carved cornice, frieze and architrave, supported by massive white columns smacked of prewar southern affluence. Arches, gables, and dormers, were incorporated into the structure and it was capped with whitewash making a statement by it's owner that here rested the ultimate power for the territory.

Maggie admired the Victorian-style furniture filling the rooms. It was constructed of black walnut. The table and chairs were heavily ornamented with pineapples, the symbol of hospitality. The house held several expensive, ornamental clocks that all chimed in perfect harmony. Though she heard at least three clocks chime, the only one she could see from her chair in the large dining room was a beautifully ornate Connecticut lyre clock mounted to the wall. It had a mahogany case and produced a deep, melodious sound.

She was not the least bit surprised that Hans Stuts and Reverend McKenzie could not come to the meeting.

Hiram sat with his dark hair slicked back and wore a white shirt with ruffles down the front. He smiled at her as he made small talk. She responded with nods and slight smiles. She had to cooperate with him to a degree, but he was such a strutting, arrogant bore.

Maggie had decided months ago that Angel Valley offered no suitors that would make her a good husband. Camel had initially excited her, but she soon realized he demonstrated the maturity of a fun-loving sixteen year old.

And then there was Hiram. She pushed her plate back leaving some of the tender t-bone to indicate her vanquished appetite, though she could easily have eaten all of it. Smiling and nodding, she saw his lips moving, but tuned his voice out.

Her mind drifted again to Camel. Where was he? At first, like most people, she had not thought much of his disappearance. He was so foolhardy, he could have caught a train to New Orleans. But, it had been several days now, and she found herself worrying over him more than she should.

Hiram's voice broke into her thoughts. "Maggie, I apologize again for the mistake in scheduling tonight. It's no excuse, but I've had so much on my mind the last few days. I don't know if you have heard or not, but the Sweats are in deep financial trouble. I have . . . or the bank I should say, has lent them far more than their place is worth, so I have had the unpleasant task of foreclosing on them this week. I hate having to foreclose on a poor farmer or rancher. I guess it's my fault though for being too generous and unable to say no to a needy person" A heavy silence hovered between them. Hiram continued, "Even when the borrower makes poor decisions and exercises no discipline regarding fiscal matters." He paused, eyeing her over his imported crystal wine glass, trying to determine if he was impressing her. Fingering the silk napkin, he tried a different tack. "I've been pushing our sheriff to find Camel. We're all concerned about him."

She felt his eyes burning into hers. She maintained a neutral expression and voice, "Yes, we are all concerned over his disappearance."

Their conversation lulled.

Her crystal goblet was half full. Hiram lifted his, "Let's toast a successful year of teaching for you and may there be many more to come."

Their goblets clinked, Hiram drank the remainder of his wine, while she sipped hers and said, "I too regret that Mr. Stutz and Reverend McKenzie couldn't come tonight. Our school has many pressing needs, and I was hoping to share those with the group. We're in desperate need of more McGuffey's readers, Ray's arithmetic and . . ."

A flicker of scowl passed across his face. He interrupted, "Don't worry yourself over those needs, I'm sure we can deal with them to your satisfaction at our next meeting."

Her expression was a blank.

Pushing his chair back, he said, "I've seen you looking at my imported china and crystal. You obviously appreciate beauty and elegance. I want to show you the rest of the house."

Dabbing her lips with her napkin, she said, "I do admire the way you've furnished your house, Hiram. But, I have a numbers test to grade and need to plan lessons for tomorrow. I really need . . ."

"Nonsense, I can show it to you in a few minutes and have you home in no time. Here, let me get your chair." He placed her arm through his, leading her to the sitting room.

The massive Chesterfield couch with upholstered ends and the Chippendale chairs with elaborate ornamental cornucopias, leaves and pineapples carved into the wooden arms elicited a compliment from Maggie. However, she thought the green satin drapes and plush red carpet made for a horrid color scheme. Again the chiming clocks caught her attention. She admired a grandfather clock with mahogany veneer that displayed second and minute hands, a calendar, and the phases of the moon.

She removed her arm and stepped toward the clock. As she observed it, she felt Hiram move closer to her. His hand touched her shoulder. She quickly stepped away, turned to face him, and said, "Hiram, you have such beautiful furniture, it would impress anyone, but I must insist on going. I have so much work to do. Reverend McKenzie doesn't seem to mind my working late, but Mrs. McKenzie says she can hear my every movement, and she cannot sleep as long as I have a lamp burning. She says that even the shuffling of paper or book pages turning keep her awake. She's not well, you…"

Hiram was angry. The heat in his face reflected it. "I wanted you to see the rest of the house. Don't you think you could . . ."

"No, I'm sorry, but I can't tonight, perhaps another time."

"Alright, I'll see you home. But, Maggie, there was some other business that the Reverend and Hans wanted to discuss with you." He paused. "Would you like to sit down?"

"No thank you."

He shrugged and crossed his arms. "This is a small town, Maggie, and talk spreads like wild fire. Rumor has it that you've been seen courting Camel on a week night unescorted. It's awkward for me to discuss, especially with Camel's disappearance, but when he returns, as your friend, I strongly recommend you use discretion in selecting your suitors. Many of the folks have been very upset and talked of dismissal, but I have defended you. They point to your contract, which states you may go courting one night on the weekend, provided you go to church on Sunday. You know, Maggie, there were some on the council who wanted to include some other requirements in your contract, such as requiring you to whittle each students' pencil to meet the students' needs. They wanted you to be at the school house . . ."

"I am familiar with the contract that I signed, Hiram, and . . ."

Raising his voice, Hiram said, "I just want you to know I am your biggest supporter and I plan to continue to do so. I have stood up for you, but I can only . . ."

Maggie was angry. "I live up to my contractual agreement, and if the community has concerns regarding my performance or morality, or any improprieties on my part, then the council..."

Smiling condescendingly, he said, "Allow me to handle things, Maggie. I'm sure..." He was talking to her back. She reached for the door, and he said, "Maggie, let me walk you home. A young lady should not be seen out at night like this." She was gone.

Facing the door, his face was red and his breathing deep. He was livid. The tinkle of dishes made him turn. Juanita was cleaning off the table. He raised his voice, "Leave the wine bottle there. I want another drink."

"Si, Senor."

He picked up the bottle, emptied it into his glass. Staring into the glass, he said, "Go into the bedroom, Juanita. You have some more work to do tonight."

Camel jumped as Bones came alive with another, "Whoeee! It's getting dark in here. Where are the morning folks and some of that medicine man's concoction?"

"Who are the morning folks?" Camel's eyes brightened, "What kinda   concoction?"

Bones stared at him, his breath rattling. Camel thought he was going under again, but the old man coughed, spit, wiped at his mouth with a sleeve and said, "The Morning People led by Father Pollen will probably be here any time. Ya never know. Course I could be wrong, but my innards tell me they about to show again."

Both men stared into the flames. Each seeing his own life in retrospect. Bones rested on his cot, back against the wall, laboring to breathe. He saw himself as a young boy climbing a tree, a teenager following a plow, traveling with his parents and many siblings, striking out on his own, working a variety of jobs.

He saw the faces some of the whores he had laid with, some were pretty, most either average or downright ugly. Some men found a woman to settle down with, but not Bones. As he grew older and lived far away from towns, his encounters with women dwindled to nothing.

Then came the bone picking years rushing by as old age set in. Always on the move, always searching to fill the emptiness he'd felt all his life. The licking flames now showed him an old man defeated by heartache, time, and a lifetime of smoking.

Camel leaned forward on the stump, holding the tin cup with both hands, elbows on his knees. The cup kept shaking and he fought to keep it still. The flames painted an eerie picture of him as a sad little boy. His mother died giving him life. His only mental picture of her came from a faded old daguerreotype atop his father's bedside table. He saw himself playing with his older brother, Jessie. His father's weathered features appeared and his words rang clear as a bell, "Matthew, you're a problem while Jessie is a pleaser." His father's eyes held the look that Camel knew so well...the look of disapproval...or was it more? Something stronger?

The next flame that sputtered and spit revealed him taking his father's horse and riding away. A series of pictures encapsulated within the black, smutty fireplace ran quickly by him. He saw himself a slick young gambler who sometimes won but just as often lost. He glimpsed his mentor who taught him how to win at cards: bottom deal, angling, peeking, false cutting, culling, hand mucking, cold decking, but much more important-- how to read a man. It was all there to be read if the reader was astute: eyes, set mouth, skin color, nervous tic, rapid breathing, the way he held a winning hand instead of a losing one.

The blackened firewall was a screen showing him Deadwood, where his mentor taught him his final lesson...trust no man. He saw himself awaking at midday to find his mentor had vamoosed during the night with their winnings and horses. He saw again and even felt some of the deep ache he'd experienced as he lost the last remnant of faith in mankind.

The flames reflected a successful young gambler on his own, dressed in the attire of the trade, a black Stetson, white ruffled shirt, string tie, black silk suit, and polished, black boots. The pictures moved rapidly from the Dakota Territory, Montana, California, Arizona, New Mexico and back to Texas, where he sat now.

He saw himself clearly as he entered Texas, making few mistakes and winning lots of money. A kaleidoscope of faces rose and flickered out with each flame. He saw faces of pretty prostitutes, not so pretty ones, fellow professional gamblers, losing ranch hands and farmers who could not afford the luxury of loss. There were lawmen, some honest and straight, running him out of town, but others who were willing to look the other way as he plied his trade for a few bucks exchanged in an alley. It occurred to him, as the fire crackled, that he had known many men and women in his travels; yet, he knew no one and was known by no one.

He saw himself riding onto his father's ranch, after ten years, finding that his older brother had died almost a year earlier from a horse kick to the stomach. His father's eyes held that same old look of contempt for him. The look was different though...fiercer, wilder, angrier. Either the bewitching flames, or the moment...whatever, Camel recalled his thoughts during that time. *Was it because of Aaron's death? Did his presence remind his father that he lost his wife for this problem child who grew into a bigger problem with each passing year? Did Camel remind his father that God had taken his good son and left him the bad one? My father seemed so much smaller than I remembered him. He was like a peeled apple that's sat in the sun and shriveled up. It sure hadn't made him any easier though.*

The flames revealed him smiling in a surly way as his father chided and insulted him for his laziness and drunkenness. It was during this time that he became known as Camel rather than Matthew. The colorful view within the fireplace depicted him sitting in Stinky's saloon winning money from suckers. The fire's crackle became his father's voice yelling for him from outside the saloon. He again saw the tired, weathered old man atop his horse in front of the saloon. The flames were magic that lent him crystal clear vision and hearing as he saw his father's face crimson with rage reflected in his words, "You're a man of little consequence, Matthew. We shoulda named you Camel instead of Mathew, because you can drink whiskey like a thirsty camel drinks water."

He heard afresh the rowdy saloon crowd yelling and hooting. Camel watched his father sink in the saddle, face pale, wheel his gelding and quirt him. As the old man raced toward home, Camel heard his own words announcing that drinks were on him. From that time, everyone called him Camel.

The pictures showed him a man who drank constantly, hid bottles beneath planks in his room, under hay in the barn, and in the outhouse. He saw his father growing smaller and more silent each day. A collapsing log's exploding sparks coincided with the crash of a pistol shot and he saw his father on his blood-soaked bed with a revolver in one lifeless hand. He saw his father's fresh grave, but this picture was blurry because he'd been drunk during the funeral.

The army company wound its way through the rugged country with each man exhausted and frustrated. Captain Verlander had lost all doubt regarding the loyalty of his scouts. He was certain they were totally disloyal. He had a plan. Whenever the scouts changed directions, he would lead the company on an opposite course. *The traitorous bastards! If this plan works and I catch the renegades, I'll shoot the scouts myself.*

His hemorrhoids affected his thinking. One end of his body seemed tied to the other. The stinging in the morning became a dull ache by midday that developed into stabbing pain radiating from the center of his body to the top of his head and to the tip of his toes by day's end. Each step his horse took meant a new experience in pain for him. Standing in the stirrups, he tugged at the seat of his pants. Nothing seemed to bring relief. He hoped to hell his men did not see him bleeding from the ass.

His thoughts returned to the scouts. The more they stalled, the more his ass hurt. He thought of the scouts and his hemorrhoids as one. Since coming west with the army, he'd heard tales about some of the atrocities committed by the Comanches' and Kiowas' on their enemies. A colonel told how the Indians would take a naked enemy, stake him out face down, cut his ass with a dull antler, and pour sugar into the wound for the ants. This was what he would like to do to his scouts.

A hundred yards ahead, he saw a scout on his horse atop a bluff, pointing north. The other scout joined the first one, waved and pointed vigorously in the same direction. Drawing near them, the captain turned his gray to the south.

The small boy whimpered, wiped a tear from his chubby cheek, but did not cry aloud. The last time he cried, his mother held a blanket over his head until he stopped. He shivered in fear recalling the incident. His mother had told him that his crying would bring the white eyes down on them. He understood, but he still hated having to stop playing slap-the-ball with the other boys.

Sucking his thumb to ensure his quietness, he watched as his mother silently mashed the oscha root so he could chew it to cure his sore throat. She stopped, examined her work and whispered his name, "Chatto," as she gestured for him to come to her.

Chatto obeyed her and chewed the piece of root she stuck in his mouth as she rubbed his forehead with another piece of the root mixed with water. In the gathering dusk, he could see his friend, Mangus, taking something to eat from his mother. Chatto knew without being told they would be traveling this night. For the entire day, the adults had been packing teepees and clearing out wickiups. Parfleches on their mules were packed tight with goods. Each women had filled her home-made wicker bottles known as a tus with spring water. It had frightened Chatto when Red Deer fussed at his mother for emptying tula-pah from one of the large tus and filling it with water. Chatto feared Red Deer may strike his mother, he was so angry, but Father Pollen had intervened and told Red Deer they would need the water more than corn beer. Besides, Skinyas still had one full tus of tizwin, and that was all the alcoholic beverage they needed. Chatto continued to be concerned for his mother. He knew that Red Deer could be a bad man, sometimes, almost as bad as the white eyes.

The boy's attention was drawn back to his mother. She motioned for him to eat the baked mescal and wood sorrel before him. Chatto had learned to eat and drink plenty before a trip because there would be no time for it once they got under way.

Father Pollen patted Chatto on the head, smiled and said, "Bless you, my child. Eat plenty because we have a long journey before us." The boy's mother invited Father Pollen to eat something, but, as always, he refused and moved on encouraging everyone to eat and drink in preparation for their journey.

Chatto liked Father Pollen, but thought he was a strange looking man. Besides the hair on his arms, he walked funny. Perhaps it was because he had a hump on his back. His hair was orange, curly and there wasn't much of it. He wore glasses so thick they made him look bug eyed. His front teeth stuck out too, making him look like a rabbit. He dressed strangely, too...a black cloak, white collar, black shirt, trousers and boots with one real big sole.

Chatto worried about Father Pollen. He had heard Little Knife say he would use his big knife to cut the father's throat. The child did not understand Little Knife's hatred. He only knew Little Knife was different...he was an Apache, while all the others were Navajos. Was that the reason? Or was it because Father Pollen was a white-eye? Chatto's thoughts were interrupted by his mother who told him to pee now because once he was tied onto the travois, there would be no stopping until they reached their new home.

Father Pollen's thoughts were close to Chatto's. He, too, wondered if he may die at the hands of the angry Apache teenager. Unlike the child, the priest knew the reason for Little Knife's hatred. As a child about the age of Chatto, Little Knife had seen his mother raped and then shot by the white-eyes. A priest, who dressed like Father Pollen, had given them permission to hide in his little mission. Little Knife saw his little sister shot in the back as she tried to run away. He had miraculously escaped while the men focused on his mother. And where was the priest during all of this? Had he turned his family in to the white-eyes? Little Knife felt sure that the priest had. He also felt this little scrawny, hunch-backed priest would do the same when he found the right opportunity; whenever or wherever the most bounty was paid for an Indian's scalp.

Father Pollen was again gently encouraging Naiche to ride a travois for tonight's journey. The priest knew it was demeaning for the old warrior to ride a travois like the children who were too young to walk. But, Naiche could not keep pace with them when walking. Father Pollen had concluded the old man, whose fingers were bent and stiff with arthritis, wanted to be left behind so he could die. He had outlived his usefulness and was ready to make his final contribution by dying.

"Naiche, I need you. Your wisdom keeps all of us alive. You can lead us to water when no one else can. Please continue to help me and every member of this band by staying with us." Father Pollen was leaning close to him looking into the dark eyes, surrounded by the weathered, wrinkled face. He wanted the other to see his eyes and know he was speaking the truth.

The old Indian scoffed, gestured with his hand, but moved to the travois. Father Pollen breathed a sigh of relief. He really did need Naiche's experience and knowledge. On numerous occasions, it was Naiche who had been able to referee arguments between the young men and maintain the unity of the group. Father Pollen could not explain it and was skeptical at first, but he now listened to Naiche when he talked of his dreams and visions. They had escaped Federal troops several times based upon the old warrior's vision.

The priest stepped beside a young Navajo named Spirit Dog, who was sitting atop his painted mustang. Father asked, "Are we ready?" The young Indian nodded and nudged his mount forward. The raggedly diverse group moved out. All walked single-file. A couple of mothers carried their babies strapped into cradleboards tied to their backs with rawhide. Walking single file was an old Indian trick used to confuse the tracker. Many of the Indians instinctively stepped into the footprint ahead. It was difficult to determine the number of the party when they walked in this manner. Father Pollen took his usual position behind Naiche in the event he needed quick counsel. He had the feeling the old Indian requested he walk there so he could watch for the priest's safety. Father Pollen walked in his swaying fashion as he clutched his silver cross and chain and breathed a prayer.

He often thought of Moses leading the Israelites, but he knew he was no Moses. He carried a staff of mulberry wood like Moses, but he always pictured Moses to be a tall, imposing figure, one whose presence made men stop talking and look at him in respect. Father Pollen was the exact opposite of this picture in every way. His orange hair and freckles always provided fodder for other's amusement. His thick glasses made his eyes appear so large that as a boy the other children had called him, "fisheyes." His hunched back made him stand less than five feet tall and caused him to walk in a swaying side to side motion. Some of the teenagers said he reminded them of a duck. This comment drew subtle smiles from the adults before they chided the youngsters for their cruel remarks.

The priest allowed his mind to travel back to his days as a child in New York. He was born Donald Asbury Kelly to poor Irish immigrants. As a boy, he had been taunted endlessly by his peers for his many physical abnormalities. One older boy who was a fair cartoonist, sketched Donald's face and profile revealing the stooped posture and hump. Asbury seemed to recall seeing it on every stone wall and sidewalk in his neighborhood.

His family bordered on starvation in Ireland and lived in a ditch with a roof of logs. Rainy weather meant wading in ankle-deep water. Donald was young and his few recollections of life in Ireland showed him images of burying his brothers and sisters on an austere, wind-swept hill. His parents dug for roots when the potatoes were rotten.

Coming to America, they lived in a dank, chilly cellar in lower Manhattan. He remembered losing a sister soon after they arrived. His father was a small, bent man carrying the genetic pool that would come to fruition in Asbury. At first, his father found work with other Irishman. They were hired by a construction foremen from New Jersey to clear the swamps and lowlands for development. But, his father's health failed him and he could not keep pace with his healthier and stronger counterparts. He was fired, tried to work as a chimney sweep for a time, but soon gave up and disappeared from their lives.

Donald was a frail, pitiful physical specimen, but he was intelligent. Only his head seemed to grow to it's normal size. Indeed, it appeared overlarge because his body remained small even as he became a teenager and moved toward adulthood. At this time in Donald's life, a Presbyterian minister entered the scene. He was a tall, angular fellow who felt called to help the Irish immigrants. He encountered resistance from many of the families who were devout Catholics. Donald's family was Catholic too, but not as committed. Soon, this strange man was his ally against the bullies and encouraged him to test for the Presbyterian seminary. Donald excelled in math, English, and all the other subjects he encountered. He was on a fast-track for higher education.

He loved seminary. He even made real friends for the first time in his life. His intellect and sense of humor brought him a popularity and acceptance he'd never known before. A professor mentor encouraged him to pursue higher studies to prepare him to teach at the seminary. Another professor talked up the challenges and joys of pastoring a church. Both ideas appealed to Donald and his future appeared brighter than ever before.

Donald knew his mind until that day an elderly missionary addressed his class and told about the Native Indians and the unbelievable hardships they faced. The missionary received a chilly response from his audience when he told how the church had often worked with the army and reservation agents against the Indians. The old man's voice trembled when he spoke of the indignities and horrors experienced by those trying to survive on the reservations. Most in the audience either snickered, snoozed, or rolled their eyes at the old man's display of emotion; but not Donald.

The old man's words struck a chord deep within his soul that he was unable to ignore. Lord knows, he tried. He was ordained and sent to a small parish in southern Virginia. He tried, but the voice only grew louder and shriller with each passing day.

An elderly lady in his parish pushed him over the side. As a wealthy widow, she had spent several months volunteering on an Indian reservation in New Mexico. When Donald mentioned his interest in the cause, she saturated him with first-hand stories that corroborated his thoughts. She offered him the valid excuse he needed to resign his post and hit the rails for Oklahoma. She also financed his journey and used her influence within the hierarchy of the church to keep him out of hot water.

Donald was soon working as missionary of a small, stark, stick and wattle mission on a landscape that reminded him of pictures he had seen of the Sahara Desert. To his dismay, this did not satisfy him. It only made his frustration greater. The more he learned of the federal system and it's corruption, and the more he learned of the Indians, the more he knew something revolutionary was needed to correct a system beyond repair.

The U.S. government lied to the Indians on a daily basis, fed them rancid meat and illegally sold most of the flour, sugar, coffee and tobacco and other foods meant for them. The agents were beyond dishonest; they openly cut deals with their suppliers to fatten their pockets at the expense of the Indians and joked about doing it. One agent had been overheard by Donald as he talked how history had shown the only way to deal with the Indian was to treat him like a bad child and deny him his supper. President Jackson, known as Sharp Knife by the Indians, refused to obey the Supreme Court and forced the Indians to migrate on foot for a thousand miles. Many women and children died attempting it. Kit Carson destroyed cattle, sheep and fields of corn and reduced the Red Man along with his women and children to emaciated skeletons amidst the frigid cold. The buffalo hunters decimated the herds, taking only the hides and tongues, leaving thousands of rotting carcasses. This proved effective in eliminating the savages' food. Later, Secretary of Army, Sherman, had ordered the U.S. military to repeat in the west his successful southern Civil War strategy by destroying horses, cattle, fields of grain, orchards, and even the dwellings of the Indians.

As time went on, conditions for the Indians did not improve. In many ways they grew worse. Some turned to the white eyes' drink and most lost hope. It seemed to Donald the years hardened the whites resolve to cheat the red man and solidified the red man's frustration and hostility.

Donald wrote over a hundred letters to senators, representatives, and influential friends back in Virginia regarding his findings. His main supporter from the little parish died that year. His other supporters sent small amounts of money, but wrote him to be patient and allow God to work his will. He knew from the content of their letters they had no grasp of actual events occurring on the reservation. He tried to articulate the hardships and cruelty he found all around him, but the more desperate his letters became, the less support he received. He knew they considered him a young idealist holding unrealistic views of the situation. He came across as shrill and hysterical rather than calm and objective. His support back in Virginia soon dried up completely.

He would later conclude they were correct. He was naïve and ignorant even though he lived among the reservation agents and Indians. He perceived all whites other than himself to be cruel and vicious; all Indians to be pure and noble. He stereotyped everyone and it took over a year of intensive struggle and failure to see his error. There were some whites who sympathized with the natives plight and saw them more clearly then he did. There were some Indians who were lazy and criminal-minded who would rather steal than work.

A baby cried behind him. The sound stopped. The Indian mothers were adept at shifting the cradleboards and nursing the babies as they walked. Silence was their ally. Many times they had eluded pursuers because of their proficiency in maintaining total quiet as they moved along their way.

The missionary stumbled and went to his knees. Helpful hands pulled him erect. He cursed himself. He knew anytime he fell, it slowed them up. He felt his face warm as he thought again of how poorly he compared to Moses. *I'm no Moses ! Why do I continue to think about it?*

His followers were not like the Israelites following Moses either. His rag-tag bunch had more women and children than men. He and his followers did share a common bond though, each of them were misfits in a world that did not understand them and wanted them exterminated like so many rats or snakes. The group consisted of Indians from various reservations who had somehow managed to escape the white-eye's bullets and extermination mentality. He looked up into the darkening sky and prayed once again for the elusive promised land.

A tremor swept his slight frame as he thought of his lack of faith and spirituality. He stumbled and almost fell, but Little Sun caught him. He saw the dark trusting eyes and white teeth of the smile. They trusted him. Oh, God, their simple love, kindness and trust in him only made the pain in his soul hurt all the more.

Behind him, Little Knife's eyes burned into his neck. His eyes blazed with hatred. Jaw muscles twitched. Knuckles whitened as he squeezed the handle of his flint knife.

CHAPTER 6

Some early visitors to the west claimed seeing massive bones that were later attributed to dinosaurs. Most bones collected were buffalo bones related to the mass buffalo slaughters of 1870 to 1883. They were sold for the production of fertilizer and bone china for about eight dollars a ton.

Camel lay on the floor atop a deer hide, covered with a brightly designed blanket. Bones slept in his cot. It seemed to Camel the old man coughed and wheezed throughout the night without ever stopping. His heart raced at the thought that Bones had a contagious disease and he might have caught it sleeping in such close proximity with him. But he dismissed the thought as he recalled the many men he had known who were heavy smokers and had coughed and hacked like Bones at the end of their lives. He sat in many all-night card games with smoke filling the air in layers like leaden clouds as men smoked while losing their money to him.

The greased paper covering the window crackled and puffed inward. Several ratty holes allowed shafts of sunlight revealing floating specks. Camel sat up. Bones's rasping voice startled him. "Whoee, long, bad night. Ya wanna git the fire goin' and we'll drink the last of the coffee. I been savin' it fer sumthin special and this looks about as special as it's gonna git."

Camel stoked the banked coals, added wood to the fire and got the coffee going. Its smell ignited a deep need within him---the need for a drink of whiskey. The room was not hot, but beads of sweat appeared on his forehead and his gut gnawed for the succor of his god---alcohol. Closing his eyes, he fought the demon that was so much larger than him.

Bones spoke with greater clarity than the day before. He told how he had been a buffalo hunter on the plains for many years. Wistfulness combined with resignation sounded in the words as he told about killing a hundred buffalo a day but taking only their tongues and hides. His partner would skin them by cutting the hide in half, tying it and using his horse to slip it off like a sweater. They made a good living for many years until his friend died of consumption and the buffalo were all killed off.

Shaking his head slowly, the old man said, "I remember the time when the buffalo covered the plains as far as a man could see...for miles. When we started killin' 'em, I remember their dead carcasses as far as I could see. After a day of killin,' the sky was dark with buzzards."

He turned to collecting their bones. He called himself a bone picker. The money was not nearly as dependable or good, but it was a living. A couple of buffalo soldiers would come twice a year with two oversized wagons pulled by mules and take the bones. They brought him supplies, swapping the goods for the bones. The last time he saw them, he had found few bones and told them he'd seen buffalo tracks across the Pecos and was going to follow them. He entered the rough, hilly country and found a few bones, but hardly enough to trade for a five pound sack of coffee. The buffalo soldiers must have known and never came back.

At first, Camel felt excitement at the thought of someone coming---someone with whisky. But, as the old man rambled on, he knew there was no one coming. Bones coughed, wheezed and wiped his face with a rabbit hide. Camel squatted at the fire, fighting the pain in his gut that vacillated between nauseating agony and a deep ache that made him feel like jumping out of his skin. His ribs still ached, his vision had returned, but one eye held a deep soreness and headaches came and went, some intensely painful.

"When's the last time ya saw them fellas?"

At first he thought Bones had not heard him over his loud wheezing and whistling as he labored to suck air. He looked at Camel with glazed eyes, "I dunno. Two, maybe three years. I lost track of time. He stared at the fire, "Maybe smoking every kinda of stick, grass and weed didn't help my memory any. But when a man runs outta tobacco, he..."

Camel stared at the gaunt, frail skeleton of a man who fought for each breath and thought for the first time how he and Bones had much in common. The old man had killed himself with tobacco and whatever else he could smoke, while Camel was doing the same thing with alcohol. Or was he? Wasn't he going to quit the booze some day and settle down? *To hell and back I know the answer to that! I ain't gonna quit drinking as long as I can get it.* He shrugged off the thought. This was not the time for introspection.

He realized Bones was talking and forced himself to listen. "...though, I found a lotta bones that don't belong to no buffalo I ever seen. Some of those leg bones are taller than you are. Some of 'em are big and round as you too. I had to use Maude my mule, bless her departed soul, to fetch 'em here." A long coughing spasm ended with him spitting into a rusted tin can. Camel noticed the sputum contained bright red streaks.

Pouring two cups of coffee, Camel asked, "Do ya want me to pat your back?"

Bones shook his head, sucked air and took his coffee with two trembling hands. Camel noted his own hand trembling and again worked to close the door on the similarity between him and the dying man. But the thought was embedded in his mind, heart and soul and cried out, *Dammit, I want a drink!*

There was silence in the cabin except for the crackling of the fire and nearby dove singing his mournful, poignant lullaby. *More like a death dirge,* thought Camel. *And this coffee tastes like burnt wood. Is it me, needin' a drink, or is it the coffee?*

One sip of the coffee and Bones started coughing again. The brown liquid sloshed over the rim of the cup and Camel gently took it from him. This time he spit mostly blood and little sputum. He laid on his cot, leaning back against the wall, unable to breathe lying down and lacking the strength to hold himself up. A trickle of bright red blood flowed in a crooked line down his wrinkled face staining his white beard crimson. Camel used the rabbit hide to wipe it away.

"Is there anything I can do for ya, Bones?"

His eyes were glazed, Camel had never seen a man with the pallor of death on him like the old wheezing, ragged-breathing man before him. Bones did not look at him or acknowledge the question.

He laid without moving for a long time with his eyes closed. The only sound in the cabin was the whistle in his labored breathing. Looking at him, Camel swore off cheroots. All he needed was a drink. Alcohol did not do this to a man.

The old man had fallen asleep. Standing quietly, Camel lifted the board securing the door and worked to open it without squeaking the rawhide hinges and waking Bones. Stepping outside, he breathed deep.

All hell broke loose. An Indian charging him with a knife held low, emitted a shrill squeal. Instinctively, Camel jumped sideways and the attacker struck the cabin wall with a thud. He bounced off the wall and fell to his back moaning. Camel snatched up the crude knife to plunge it into the Indian's chest.

He raised the knife but paused as someone yelled, "Stop! Please!" The waddling, limping, man approaching him wore the black frock of a priest and a white collar. Nearing him, Camel was surprised at how small the man was. He was hunchbacked, had red curly hair, wore thick wire-rim glasses, freckles covered his round face and his front teeth protruded over his lower lip.

The prostrate figure began mumbling, shaking his head and Camel stepped away from him still holding the knife. The priest tried to talk but was gasping for breath. Behind him, another Indian approached, he was old and wizened and wrapped in a Navajo blanket.

"I'm sorry Sir, for Little Knife's behavior," gasped the priest as he studied Camel. "Please don't hurt him. He's an angry Apache youth whose had a miserable life and he naturally hates all whites."

Camel eyed the priest, "I get a little angry too when someone tries to empty me of my guts."

The moans stopped as the Indian tried to regain his feet. Camel saw that he was a small teenager with angry glazed eyes.

The priest continued, "His name is Little Knife and this is Naiche. My wise and good Navajo friend."

Camel and the old Indian exchanged nods. For the first time, he noticed several Indian women carrying something in their arms a hundred yards away. *How many Indians are there? This is 1888, what in the hell are Indians doing roaming around the country?*

*They're supposed to be on reservations. And what the hell is this
weird little elf of a white man doing with them?*

As though reading his mind, Camel would learn in the days
ahead that the tiny gnome of a priest seemed to possess an uncanny
ability to read his thoughts, the priest extended a boy-sized hand and
introduced himself. "I'm Father Pollen, Presbyterian minister and
member of a group of friends made up mostly of Navajo and three
Apache. We are in search of the promised land. We have
experienced some difficulty recently in eluding an army search team
and that's why we've returned to Bones's place."

Camel took his hand, mumbled his own name as he thought: *In
search of the promised land? This sunuvabitch must be as crazy as
he looks. I didn't think Presbyterians called their preachers father.
I thought Catholics did that.* He gripped the knife, holding it close
to his leg in case the youth or all of them jumped him. Father Pollen
smiled at him exposing more of his two protruding teeth and Camel
relaxed. There was something about the priest and the old Indian
that eliminated his unease. He did not feel that way about the teen.

Again addressing Camel's thoughts, Father Pollen continued to
grin in a lop-sided way as he said, "Sounds pretty strange doesn't it?
A group of Indians with a white priest roaming around West Texas
looking for a place to settle down. A place where we can live in
peace and dignity." He studied Camel's eyes with amusement.

Yep! He's a crazy one, alright. Camel stood dumbstruck. He
turned toward the teen who stomped away from them making a
grunt of disgust.

"Don't worry, Sir, about Little Knife. We will watch him
closely while we are here. He was just surprised by your
appearance. We have been here before and always found only
Bones." The priest looked at the knife Camel was holding and held
out a small hand for it. Camel ignored him for a long moment,
looked into the large eyes magnified by the spectacles, then placed
the crude instrument into his hand. "Thank you. He will need it for
skinning animals and sharpening our few tools and weapons. The
weapons," he added quickly, "are strictly for killing game." He
turned and looked at the cabin door, "Is Bones alright? he was
doing poorly on our last visit."

Camel nodded, "He's having lots of trouble." He lowered his voice in case Bones could hear them. "I've only been here a few days and each day I see him decline."

The priest's expression was sober. "Can I see him?"

"Of course!"

Camel opened the door, stepped back so that the priest and old Indian could enter. As the Indian moved past him, his odor of leather, musky blanket and animal fur stirred a latent memory within him--a flash of a small boy being fascinated by a group of Indians who stopped by his father's ranch to trade horses. He recalled the famiar smell.

"Whoee! Look who's here! By dang, Camel, I toldja the morning folks were comin'. I could feel 'em." He gurgled as he coughed and spit bloody sputum.

The priest crouched down, placed a small hand on Bone's shoulder, and looked up at him. Camel could hear the tenderness in the voice, "Bones, my dear friend, you are sick and I know Naiche will fix you up one of his healing potions. He will brew his medicine and I will pray for you."

Camel was unsure Bones heard much after he finished spitting because he closed his eyes and his whistled breathing was labored but paced. The little man felt Bone's forehead, turned to Naiche and said, "He's burning with fever. Can you fix him up some of your medicine?"

The old Indian shook his head indicating the hopelessness of Bone's condition, but agreeing to concoct a potion. The three walked quietly from the dark shack. Camel now saw more Indians moving about. *How many are there? Am I in the middle of an Indian uprising?*

Camel had lived with Indian war stories and rumors all his life, but had never fought them like his father. He grew up hearing horror stories of the Comanches who traveled hundreds of miles to rob, loot, burn, kill men, rape women and kidnap children. As a small boy, he had nightmares after listening to such stories. He also heard horror stories about the Apaches, Kiowa's, and Navajo. *Here I stand surrounded by people who scared hell outta me as a kid.*

Father Pollen invited him to visit with him and his group. *This little man knows I'm unsure of this situation and he's trying to reassure me. What if he's leading me into a death trap? How can he and the old Indian be sure of me? They might think I'll run to the army and report 'em.*

Glancing at the tiny man struggling to walk up the knoll toward the group, Camel sensed he was safe. Topping the knoll, the scene below took his breath. *There must be forty Indians here. I see one tepee but the rest seemed to have dug caves for themselves.* He remembered that Navajo lived in earthen structures called Hogan's, and Apaches lived in tepees.

In a quiet voice, Father Pollen said, "There are thirty-three of us in all. Most are Navajo, with five that have white blood and three are Apache. That includes three babies, two toddlers, a couple of children a bit older and myself."

A dove cooed, a hawk screeched and someone was shaking a rattle. Father Pollen and Camel sized up one another. Camel had difficulty not staring at the hump on the little man's back. *You are a strange-lookin donkey, Padre. You make Stinky look downright handsome. Yet...yet there's something about you that I can't put my finger on. You have...you have...what? I don't know.* Whatever it was, made him both easy and uneasy. He shuffled his boots in the sand and stared at them as though seeing them for the first time.

Father Pollen stared unblinking into the soft brown eyes of the big man. He stunk. He smiled inwardly as he thought how he had spent so much time with the Indians that he now found the smell of whites offensive. *Who are you? You obviously don't belong here. You have the look of both a weak man and yet, there seems to be some strength in you too. Which are you? Will you look for a chance to report us to the army? Can we trust you like we trust Bones?* The holy man lowered his gaze, stared at his people working on their dwellings, sharpening tools, skinning a rattler and going about their lives. He breathed a prayer that this man would not be their downfall. He still uncertain about him.

Returning to the cabin, Camel found Bones wheezing and whistling in his sleep. Glancing around the room, Camel felt sure there had to be a bottle somewhere. Lifting a brightly decorated blanket covering objects on a dusty shelf, his eyes blazed and his heart thumped as he uncovered jars. They had been airtight, holding canned vegetables and fruits, but all were empty. *Shit! Come on Bones, ya gotta have a bottle around here somewhere.*

Bending to scrutinize some objects in the dimly-lit dwelling, he bumped the shelf and a couple of glass jars crashed to the floor. Bones said "Whoopee! Let her rip ya rat-tailed, jar headed, bowlegged Cayuse." Camel started to say something, but heard the rhythmic breathing resume.

Another shelf held several decorative Indian blankets and even in his frenzied search for alcohol, he associated the blankets with the Morning People. He continued to rummage, but found nothing he could drink. *Wait a minute! What about the Indians? Perhaps they have something.*

His shirt stuck to his heaving chest as he walked from the cabin toward the knoll and the Indians. Halfway there, he thought of the young Indian who had tried to gut him and reminded himself to keep an eye out for the crazy little squirt. *There he is! Glaring at me like he wants to cut me from chin to crotch with a dull antler.* Maybe he should have held the knife rather than returning it to the priest.

"Hello!" Eyeing the glaring teen, Camel almost walked square into another Indian only slightly larger than Little Knife. There was a big difference. This Indian was small and slight, but showed straight white teeth in a big friendly smile. Holding a pink skinned and gutted possum with one hand and a crude knife like Little Knife's in the other, he invited Camel to enjoy cooked possum with him. "Thanks. I appreciate the offer. But the truth is, I'm not real hungry, but I'm needin a drink kinda bad."

The grin widened, "I'm Little Sun and I will show you the drinking water." As he bent to place the carcass atop a stump, Camel replied, "I'm not lookin' for water. I want something stronger. Some drink that will...put fire in my stomach and lift my spirits.

Little Sun giggled, sheathed his knife and said, "You need to see Skinyas. He has medicine. Follow me, I will take you there."

They walked among several different type dwellings. Camel was aware of eyes observing his every move. He was scared, but his craving for alcohol was stronger than his fear. He followed the young man to a strange structure of bent poles, brush and blankets.

Little Sun made a clucking sound with his tongue, said
something Camel didn't understand and then they waited. Camel
was nervous. He was about to say that there must be no one home
when a tall, thin Indian emerged from the dwelling.

Little Sun spoke again, smiled and pointed to Camel. The tall
Indian studied him for a long moment and Camel watched his hands
for a weapon. Little Sun said to Camel, "This is Skinyas. He is
Apache and he has strong drink he makes from the fruit of the
mescal cactus. He must be careful though, because if Father Pollen
finds it, he will pour it out. That's why he calls it medicine." He
giggled again.

Camel glanced down, noted his bright belt buckle, pulled it off
and said to Little Sun, "Tell him that I wish to give him a gift in
return for some of his strong medicine."

Holding out his belt, Camel looked furtively around, hoping
Father Pollen was not watching. Skinyas took the belt, rubbed the
buckle, bit it, smiled and motioned them to enter his shaded
wickiup. Camel would later learn that the Apaches of the mountains
lived in houses that were made of bent saplings covered with brush.
Apaches of the plains lived in rawhide tepees.

They sat on a blanket with legs crossed as Skinyas reached into a
leather sack and felt around. Camel recognized it as a parfleche; a
rawhide saddlebag shaped like an envelope and popular with many
Indians and Spaniards. Pulling out a lop-sided wicker jug caulked
with pinion pine gum, Skinyas pulled a wood knot plug from the
opening, grunted, and pushed it at Camel, who took it gladly.

Little Sun said, "He wants to share his special medicine with
you."

These were heavenly words for Camel who took a giant swig.
It's taste was strange, but good. It contained alcohol. Camel took
another long pull before coming to his senses and realizing he must
share it. Each one took a pull and Camel had it again. Another chug
and Camel felt himself coming back to life. The dry spell had lasted
so long, but was at an end now.

Reaching into his trouser pockets, Camel extracted one of
several coins. Offering it to his host with a smile, the Apache
grinned, accepted the coin and then did something Camel would
never have thought possible. Reaching into the parfleche, he pulled

out a stack of large-sized rawhide cards. These were not standard playing cards, but were Apache cards. Camel learned for the first time that Indians played their own version of card games. Each card contained a bold design--pictures of buffalo, mustangs, coyotes, and one depicted a swollen penis. Some were cracked and faded, but they were playing cards and Camel felt as though he had died and gone to heaven as he guzzled the lukewarm strong beer that tasted better with each swallow. *The only thing that would make this better would be if they had some hard stuff to chase it with.*

Little Sun gambled his crude knife and several colored stones he pulled from a leather pouch tucked within his breeches. The more he drank, the more he giggled. Skinyas, whom Camel assumed could not speak English, shushed him when he giggled too loud.

An hour later Camel had won his coins and belt buckle back, plus everything else in the pot. *Damned if I ain't good! I can even cheat and win at an Indian card game I've never played before. I know I should allow them to win some, especially Skinyas, since it's his beer, but damned if it ain't hard to beat old habits.*

Little Sun fell onto his back and almost immediately made loud snoring sounds. Skinyas had lost his good natured attitude along with everything the white eye had given him and also his tusk, still half-filled with beer, and his parfleche. He sat sullen. *It's the same ole trick of the weasel white-eye. Begin by giving you gifts and acting like your friend. The next thing you know, the friendship and fun is gone and the white-eye has stolen everything that you have.*

Skinyas stood, swayed, and gestured that he had to make water. Camel laughed, took another swig and waved him out of the wickiup. He continued to handle and play with the cards. They were too flexible to riff and shuffle, but he found that by watching his opponent's eyes and slowing his hands, he could still bottom-deal and cull them. One dropped and as he scolded himself for his carelessness and picked it up, he heard someone yell. Looking up, he saw Skinyas bending to enter the dwelling with a look of wildness in his eyes and carrying a large club with both hands.

Toby was furious. Someone had cut the barbed wire and by the tracks, rustled a dozen or more 3C steers. His sky-blue eyes were barely visible between narrow slits. Deep wrinkles spiraled from the corner of his eyes, swept downward and became lost in his white beard.

Dismounting, he mumbled a few choice cuss words as he rubbed his legs to restore circulation and lessen the stiffness. Holding the reins to his big brown, he walked a few feet and squatted. The tracks had roughed the ground, but he squinted at them looking for a clue. Three riders' tracks showed. Toby's experienced eye caught on something. *There it is! A chipped horseshoe. If I can find the man that rides the horse with that shoe, I'll know who's rustling 3C stock.* Squatting beside the track, he traced a chipped outline with his index finger. The track was deep; the horse was large. Walking slowly, scanning the ground, he noted several identical tracks. He squatted again studying the track. He burned every little indenture and nick into his memory.

Standing, he moaned in pain from squatting so long. His boot toe missed the stirrup twice before finding it. Grunting, he settled in the saddle and nudged the brown toward the ranch house. Tomorrow, he and Fuzzy would return and repair the breached fence.

As he rode along, his mind centered again on the whereabouts of Camel. He had to consider the possibility of him being dead. An early death would certainly be compatible with Camel's lifestyle. He over drank, over ate, used bad judgment in selecting his women and company in general, and allowed himself to grow fat and soft, inviting a sudden heart attack.

Toby slouched in the saddle as he recalled his promise to Henry Campbell. Maybe he'd over-reached with that particular promise. *Dadgummit, Camel! you sure ain't made it easy for me, or for anyone else coming into contact with ya.*

It was Saturday night and Stinky's was packed. Sounds of an off-tune piano, drunken singing, and a low roar of conversation pulsated from the saloon. Toby hitched his horse at the post in front of the stable. He was careful to remain outside the light of the lamps casting a yellowish glow from each opening. Counting fourteen horses at the first hitching post, he bent low to avoid light and methodically started checking each ones hooves. The darkness made him run his finger around the rim of each one. That was alright. It was all he needed. His back started aching, but he continued. Completing the job, he moved to the second hitching post a few feet away holding six horses. He found it! The first one. In daylight, he would have seen the horses and checked the calico mare first due to her size.

Toby stood, holding the small of his back. He knew the owner, Bryant Williams, foreman of Hiram 's Rocking H spread. *Twenty years ago, I woulda called him out and beat the manure outta him and run him outta town, but no more.*

Riding back to the 3C, he felt overwhelmed by the challenges before him. What could he do? Hiram Bishop was the most powerful man in the territory. One thing was sure, the powerful man was intent on shutting Toby and the 3C down.

Sans, the small, dark half-breed stood over Eunice. He knew she was sleeping by her light snoring. He unbuttoned his pants, pulled out his member and peed in her face. He knew this would be unacceptable in the evening before Big Boy and Jones had their romp with her, but she'd have all day to clean the piss from her face.

She sputtered, yelled, and rolled over onto her knees and crawled with the saddle blanket atop her. "You bastard! You sick, fuckin' bastard, half-breed! Hunchback!"

She'd struck a chord with him. He hated any reference to his race or background. But even more, even more he killed anyone who referred to his physique. Whipping out his knife, he whispered through clenched teeth, "I'll cut ya from ya skinny throat to your big hole, ya fuckin' whore!"

"Hold it, Sans!" Kilkenny stood, wiping sleep from his eyes with a half grin on his face. "You can't kill our cook. We'll all starve to death."

Big Boy sat up and Jones rolled over so he could observe the action. They knew Eunice belonged to Kilkenny, but he'd allowed himself to be intimidated by them and made only a half-hearted attempt to protect her. They smiled each night as he said he'd play sentry as they used her. They all knew Sans and his mustang were alert to danger and Kilkenny was simply making an excuse so he would not have to witness the act.

Sans looked through him with his deep-set, menacing eyes and with knife flashing, moved toward her. She screamed, scrambled and the blanket fell off of her. Sans reached for her with glazed eyes and a sneer showing brown fang-like teeth.

Kilkenny reached down and came up with his Colt. His voice was high with tension, "I'll kill ya, Sans!" The half-breed froze. His sneer became a cruel smile. "Are you ready to die for her, ya yellow cur? Cuz Big Boy's gonna cut you in half with that scatter gun if ya keep actin' foolish."

Kilkenny chanced a quick glance to his left and saw the shotgun aimed at his middle. He knew the two were a pair and taking on one meant taking on both. Although he knew they were both sadistic killers, he also knew Big Boy was smarter while Sans was more perverted. He talked to Big Boy now while facing Sans.

"Big Boy, ya know as well as I do that it makes no sense for there to be any killin' amongst us. I don't want any trouble, but I can't just watch while he cuts her throat. Hell, she brings satisfaction to you and Jones and she does chores, that we'd have to do ourselves if she was dead. Now, what sense does it make to kill her? And..."

"Aw right, for crise sake! Sans, the man's right. We ain't gonna kill her today. Now, when we get outta this damn place..." He paused, lowered the scattergun, smiled and said, "Then matters can be settled."

Sans slowly holstered his knife. Staring at Kilkenny with hatred, he turned his eyes filled with venom on Eunice. "I'll getcha! Both of you!"

Eunice sat there staring into the distance. Her face was drained of blood. She knew if Kilkenny had spoken a second later, she'd be dead. *But maybe that would have been the easy way out. The crazy maniac has promised to kill me. Will he torture me? What if Kilkenny's not around the next time Sans gets angry at me? Can I count on Kilkenny to keep his nerve and stand up to them? Can he do it? Will he just die along with me?*

Big Boy and Sans walked a few yards away from them. The big man rubbed sleep from his face and peed on a chinch weed. "Ya gonna take a run and see what it looks like out there?"

Sans nodded. "I'm still seein' army. I can't figure what or who they after. I saw sign late yesterday of another group too. They're mostly on foot. I'll eat some of the whore's cookin' and then take a look."

Big Boy frowned, "I just hope to hell that the Federales and the rangers are still not talkin.' If the Federales have wired the rangers and alerted them..." He made a face and shrugged.

San's husky whisper lowered to a raspy hiss as he nodded toward the camp, "I'm gonna have some fun with these two when we get rid of the bluecoats."

Big Boy grinned, "Hell yes! I'm gettin tired of the bitch's pussy and her little boyfriend too. But just..." he paused, "Let's make sure we're clear of that damn army first. We could end up needin' every gun and ever bit of help to get clear of em."

Reverend McKenzie lay his writing pen on the scarred desk-top and pinched the bridge of his nose as he squinted his eyes shut. He had completed writing seven letters to various medical doctors in other towns. Hiram had given him the list and asked him to have the letters to him by that evening. He asked, but Hiram's asking always came out a demand.

The pastor was glad to write the letters, because he was desperate for their fledgling town to attract a doctor. Even Hiram's timeline didn't bother him, or the way he asked for them. His wife continued to sink a little each day. What frustrated the pastor was Hiram's comment about the pastor's preaching subject the previous Sunday. He had preached using a text from the New Testament Book of James regarding the biblical admonition that the affluent provide help to the needy.

I knew Hiram didn't like my sermon by his red face and beady eyes. I'm amazed he heard anything I said the way he was trying to sit close to Maggie and ogling her during the entire service. But, he's a multi-talented man. I guess the next thing he'll expect me to do is have him edit my sermons before I preach them.

Standing up and stretching, he worried about maintaining his integrity with Hiram. Their relationship seemed to be on a slippery slope. Hiram was in a position to help him and his church, or hurt them. He frowned as it occurred to him that probably most of the people in the area could say the same about Hiram.

Maggie was caught off guard. Realizing all of the children were looking at her closely, she stared at Loomis who was standing holding his horned reader. She tried to recall where they were in the reading lesson. Loomis was one of the larger boys in class who had a tremendous crush on her. He now grinned at her in a manner she did not like. He was in the power seat and she had temporarily lost control. Giggles swept the class.

"Where are we Loomis?" He held his grin. She shifted awkwardly. He said, "I asked if I was to read the next paragraph and you said, "Camel."

Feeling her face burn, she answered stiffly, "You're mistaken, Loomis, I coughed as I tried to speak." Giggles again swept the room. *They know I'm lying. I've got to focus on the lesson.* "You may sit down, Loomis. Thank you. Josh, would you stand and read the next paragraph please?"

I'm surprised I didn't say, Hiram. I've thought entirely too much about that obnoxious bore lately. Why does he keep postponing the school board meeting? Is he waiting to see if I will become more compliant to his wishes before he makes his recommendations regarding the new budget and my salary?

Camel? I've hardly thought of him. Well--maybe a little. I'm angry for allowing myself to be placed in such a compromising and potentially damaging situation with him. I'm angry too for even still thinking about him. The man is of low character and I've chanced jeopardizing my career by just being seen with him, much less by what actually happened.

She became aware of an awkward silence. Again the class stared at her as Josh stood holding his book; he was wide-eyed with uncertainty. "Class, let's take an early recess today. Jeremiah, if you bother anyone today during play, you will spend a half-hour in the corner. Do you understand me?"

"Yes ma'am."

CHAPTER 7

The Indian could not tolerate alcohol. This made him an easy prey to every conniving white who wanted to get him drunk and buy his land for almost nothing.

The club came down hard and Camel instinctively laid back. The club's head swooshed by him. It struck the side of the wickiup, tearing through the brush and its knotty head became entangled. Skinyas struggled, pulled it free and raised for another swing. The delay gave Camel time to reach his feet. He had his head turned so he could see with his one good eye. This time the club was coming straight down and would have brained him, but the club-head caught on the ceiling. Camel rushed his attacker and they went through the side of the dwelling with Skinyas on bottom. Camel was aware of yelling around him, but he ignored it and drove a straight right to the Indian's chin. He felt the man go limp beneath him.

Pushing himself up, he found himself surrounded by the Morning People. He was gasping for air and thought he might puke. More Indians appeared from caves that Camel had not noticed before. *Looks like Indians comin' outta the ground.*

Skinyas groaned and shifted his legs. A young, pretty Navajo pushed through the bodies and knelt beside him. "He tried to kill me with that club!" blurted Camel as he tried to lean back against the wickiup, lost his balance, and fell backwards through the hole.

There was some grunts, laughter and then Camel heard the squeaky voice of Father Pollen. Scrambling to get up, he grabbed for the tus and holding it close to his chest as a mother would cuddle an infant, he stepped over Little Sun, bent and went through the doorway. He bumped into the priest, who toppled over. A deep rumbling rose from the Morning People, and Camel felt a fear unknown to him until that moment. Before he could move on, strong hands gripped his arms and held him in place.

Father Pollen said, "Don't hurt him. I'm O.K." Straightening his spectacles, the priest looked into Camel's eyes. "Are you alright?"

Nodding and weaving, Camel looked down with glazed eyes at the tiny man. He clutched the tus tighter and said, "I wanna go back to Bone's place."

There was silence as the priest studied him. "Why doncha let me take that jug for now, Camel. I think that you've had enough."

Camel squeezed the tus until his head hurt and his arms trembled. "No! I won this from Skinyas! It's mine!"

The arms still held him and the priest stared into his eyes. Father Pollen motioned for the Indians to release him. Camel immediately lurched forward, stumbled and fell. He heard laughter and then it ceased abruptly. Even in his drunken state, he knew it had to do with the priest's stare at his detractors.

Some beer spilled in the fall, but he clutched the tus and walked a meandering line to Bone's cabin. Inside, he thought he'd gone blind. His eyes adjusted and showed him Naiche leaning over trying to ladle a brown liquid into the old man. Bones gagged, choked and liquid ran down his grizzled face. Camel noticed that the old man's face, which was ordinarily red from the sun, was pale, almost yellow. Every breath was a squeak and whistle.

Camel looked around the tiny room in search of a place to hide the beer without Bones or Naiche seeing him. He gave up. Laying it gingerly onto the dirty wooden floor, he covered it with a Navajo blanket. He remembered he'd left his belt buckle, money, and the items he won from Skinyas in the busted-up wickiup.

Stumbling outside, he was blinded by the sunlight. Leaning against the cabin, he shaded his eyes with both palms until he could see. He was making his way toward the wickiup when he heard voices. Father Pollen appeared with several men behind him.

The priest said, "You need to stay away from Skinyas, Camel. He and Little Sun are sick." He paused, "You need to sleep it off like they're doing. You've had too…"

"To hell you say, Padre! I'm goin to get what's mine. You need to get outta the way." He weaved and glared at the men standing behind Father Pollen. "That goes for all of ya! Ya better get the hell outta here before I report you to the army. What the hell's a group of red people doin'…"

"That's enough, Camel. Tell me what belongs to you in Skinyas's place."

Camel glared at the priest. I'm getting tired of you. *You little shit, you're nosing around in my business.* "He has money of mine, a silver belt buckle, and a parfleche that I won from him fair and square. And I wanta…"

The priest raised his high-pitched voice, "I'll get your money and belt buckle, but Skinyas needs the parfleche. You have the tus of alcohol. That's enough for you. That stuff is nothing but trouble. Better that you have it than Skinyas."

Father Pollen turned to fetch his items when Camel grabbed his arm. A mountain of muscle and bone descended upon him. He heard the priest yell something, but all he could feel was the pummeling of fist all over his upper body. Darkness filled him as he slipped into a comatose sleep.

The room was smoke-filled as Hiram and a small, slender man sat in the saloon's backroom, drank beer and puffed on their cheroots. Hiram knew him only as "Winters." The small man had a high-squeaky voice of an adolescent and looked like one with sandy hair, smooth skin and freckles on his pinched nose and bony cheeks. One had to look closely at the almost invisible wrinkles running from the eyes to know that this was no teenager, but a man in his thirties, possibly early forties. He wore a black coat spotted with dust from the trail. Though small, he possessed strength that belied his youthful look and size. Beneath his coat at his hip in a polished leather holster was a Colt .44.

Hiram looked straight ahead as he spoke, "So ya didn't finish the job that I paid ya half to do."

The man in black, made an expression of nonchalance. "I got the job done. Maybe just a little different than we planned."

Hiram's face reddened. "Humph! How do I know that?"

A smirk played on the tight features. Ya ever been that far West of the Pecos in the Chihuahua?"

Hiram remained silent.

Winters chuckled in a high voice. "That's what I thought. If you'd ever been there, you'd know what I'm talkin' about. The temperature's boilin,' waters scarcer than a sainted whore, and there's no survivin' out there unless ya know where to find the little water that's there."

Hiram shook his bull-head, his face darkened, and his biceps flexed appearing capable of ripping the seams of his expensive dress coat. "I don't know if it's done or not. That sunuvabitch has unbelievable luck. You can't tell…"

The smirk on the other grew wider. Hiram forced himself not to look at him. He'd like to slap the sneer off the face of this little punk, but he'd seen the pistol and knew he was talking to a foe whose power was more deadly than his own. He also knew the answer to his next question, but asked it anyway. "I paid ya half, doncha think that under the circumstances, that makes us even?"

This time the smirk was backed with a scoff. "No! No, I don't Mr. Bishop. I've gone to great time, trouble and expense to do this job, and I expect full compensation." He lost some of the smirk, pulled on his beer and added, "If ya coulda seen the country, you'd know the man's dead. First, in order to escape me, he had to crawl away. He was already beat up bad according to the railroad dick on the cattle car. That damn place out there is nothing but desert, alkaline flats, yucca plants, creosote bushes and the dick told me there was no people livin' within miles of the track."

"Winters, I'm a well-respected business man in this town. I make deals on a daily basis and I hafta hold up my end and the other party has to do the same. I made a deal with you. You agreed to bring me the fancy belt buckle that Camel always wore. I don't see no buckle. You have not lived up to our agreement. I will pay you an additional fifty dollars, but that's all."

The smirk was replaced with a puckered mouth that appeared far too small for the narrow face. "That's fifty dollars short."

Hiram emptied his mug, lay it hard on the table and placed fifty dollars between them. Standing, he shrugged his massive shoulders and said, "That's it, Winters! I gotta get back to business.

Remember, as the book tells us, 'A false balance is abomination to the Lord: but a just weight is his delight.' Proverbs eleven, verse one." He turned and walked out without looking at the boyish face that was tense and pale in anger.

That evening Hiram left the bank and returned to the back room for a beer before going home to a hot meal cooked by Juanita. As Stinky sat the beer mug before him, he stage-whispered, "Ya buddy is in the bar hittin the hard stuff."

Hiram peeped through the cracked door and saw Winters sitting at a table with a half-empty bottle before him. His hat brim covered his face. Hiram frowned. He'd expected the little bastard to hightail it after he'd gotten the fifty bucks. *I don't like this little sunuvabitch hangin' around. What's he's up to anyhow?*

He thought of telling Sheriff Libby to check on whether there was a wanted poster out for Winters. But the gunman might talk if cornered. Another idea flashed and Hiram pictured tomorrow morning and feeling the barrel of that .44 in his ribs. The little killer would order him to open the vault and hand over all the cash. He would then shoot him and vamoose.

Something had to be done about this now. Hiram left the backroom of the bar and headed for Frank Mosley's store. It was closed. Hiram walked around the back and met Frank as he was locking up. "Let's go back inside and talk."

For the next half hour, the two men stood in the darkening store and made plans. Hiram talked low and fast as Frank listened and nodded. Hiram made several promises and ended the conversation with, "...and for God's sake, Frank, use your shotgun and keep that damn .32 in your pocket."

Both men left the building. Hiram headed for his house; Frank walked to the saloon. Inside, he ordered a whisky and casually watched Winters. After several minutes making small talk with Stinky, he picked up his drink and sauntered over to the gunman's table.

"Howdy, stranger. I hope ya like our little town." The other only stared disinterestedly at him without speaking. Frank went on, "I own a mercantile store a couple buildings away. Stop in tomorrow if you're still around." Winters took a drink and remained silent. He could tell the man standing before him was nervous and he enjoyed watching him squirm.

Frank took a quick swallow and said, "If ya planning to spend the night with us, I would recommend a place about a half mile from here on the main road headin' north. It's got a sign out front-- Birnbaum's House, and it's the best around. The hotel down the street's got bedbugs bad. They put skunk juice in tins under the bed posts, but the smell'll get ya if the bugs don't."

Winters took another drink, raised his thin face with clear hazel eyes and stared through Frank as though he were not there. Frank shifted uneasily, nodded and said apologetically, "Hope I didn't disturb ya. Jus wanted ya to know where ya could find the best place to spend the night."

Frank walked briskly to the bar, lay his glass down, ignored Stinky, and walked out. Heading back to his store, he thought, *That sunuvabitch's got the deadest eyes I ever seen.* Shivering as he saw the eyes again, he entered his store. Moving without lighting a lamp, he reached under his counter, pulled out a double-barreled shotgun, and broke it open. It was loaded. Reaching out, he grasped four more shells, pushed them into his pockets and left the building.

A half-hour later, he'd tied his horse to a saltbush about fifty feet from the north road and lay on his stomach with the shotgun extended in front of him. The moon had not appeared and the darkness limited his visibility. For this reason, he lay less than ten feet from the edge of the road.

An hour passed. His neck was aching, his arm kept going numb and he was scared as hell. Those dead eyes would scare anybody. He was about to give up when he heard horse hooves. Positioning the shotgun, he waited. The moon was peeping over the horizon now providing some light. Frank faced the east so the moonlight would provide him a silhouette. The horse was near when the rider pulled up. Frank could hear the horse snort and the creak of leather. He shivered recalling the dead-like eyes staring at him. Had he done something to tip the gunman off? There was no dust in the air because of the time lapse. He could feel sweat breaking out on his forehead. His heart pounded in his ears.

He heard the rider cluck to his mount. The clop of hooves resumed. Seconds later, he made out movement and saw the rider's silhouette against the moon lit sky.

Taking aim, he fired both barrels. The rider's body flew off the side of his horse as though he'd been lassoed by a powerful roper. The rider-less horse whinnied and thundered off.

Frank remained quiet for the next several minutes, listening for any sound. Breaking the gun open, he discarded the spent shell casings and reloaded. Standing slowly, he held the gun ready to fire as he walked to where the rider had fallen. He almost stepped on the dead body. The chest was a bloody pulp. Striking a block match, Frank murmured a profanity seeing the deadly eyes staring at him just as they had in the saloon. Fear raced through him as it seemed the eyes stared at him even when he stepped back. He almost pulled both triggers again to kill this freaky little asshole when logic replaced fear and allowed him to settle down.

The moon rose and brought light with it. Frank pulled the big .44 Colt from the assassin's holster and felt it's heft. Leaning his shotgun against the shoulder of the dead gunman, he pulled his own .32 from his pocket. Balancing both pistols, he was convinced again of the superiority of a lighter weapon over a heavier one. He pushed aside the unpleasant thought that he had followed Hiram orders by depending on his shotgun rather than using his pistol. Pushing his .32 back into his pocket, he jumped when he heard a familiar voice speak his name. *What in the hell is Sheriff Libby doin' out here?*

Sheriff Libby walked into view holding his own shotgun with both hands, the barrel angled slightly down. "What's goin'on Frank?" The storekeeper and part-time deputy picked up on the subtle suspicion in the voice.

"I'm glad you're here, Dan. This crazy bastard shot my horse out from under me and was tryin' to kill me when I got a bead on him."

"Ya usin' a scattergun these days, Frank?"

Dan's too damn observin'. The bastard doesn't miss a thing. He saw the stranger leave town and followed him.

The sheriff continued, "I only heard your scattergun. I didn't hear any…"

The .44 slug struck the sheriff an inch below the heart. The impact of the heavy slug put him on his back. Moving closer, Frank saw Dan's shotgun lying across his ankles, his hands clutching at the gaping wound. He tried to speak, but only gurgled. Frank again pointed the big handgun at the prostrate figure's chest and felt the gun recoil in his hand; his ears rang from the thundering blast.

He stared down at the dead man for a long minute. He tried to think like Hiram. Gazing at the moon, he formulated a plan, and nodded in approval of his decision. He moved to the gunman and placed the Colt in his hand. Standing over the sheriff, he lifted the lawman's gun and cocked one hammer, fired into the air, cocked the other and fired it. Bending, he placed the sheriff's shotgun across his stomach, and appraised his work. He returned the shotgun to where it first lay, across the ankles. After a long moment, he nodded again and mounted his horse.

Heavy silence filled the room. Pearl dropped her fork and asked her oldest son, Ralph, what he had just said. The nine year old stared with wide-eyed innocence. His face was turning red. "What did you just say, Ralph?"

Ralph's younger brother played with his cornbread. Pearl stood, "Ralph, if I…"

"Ginnie McCormick said you are Hiram Bishop's girlfriend." His face was changing from red to pale. He stammered on, "She said that you sleep with Fatty Hiram and that he takes care of us."

Pearl stared at her son for a long time. "What did you say to her?"

"I said that if he takes care of us he oughta do a better job cuz we don't always get what we want--things like chocolate and molasses."

"Was that all that was said?"

Ralph stared at his plate.

"Ralph?"

Looking miserable, Ralph spoke quietly, "Then Malachi Arlington said something else and I hit him in the mouth."

"What did he say that made ya hit him?"

Ralph's head hung low over his plate of fried corn, potatoes and cornbread. The floor creaked; an owl hooted.

"Ralph?"

"He said you were a...a...I can't say it."

"Ralph, you will tell me what he said. If I hear about this from one of the Arlington's, I need to know how to handle it."

"Mama, he said..."

"Ralph, we've all had a tough day; don't make it harder for me to have to whip ya to get the truth outta ya."

Ralph stammered, "He...he...said...ya...ya...ya..."

The floor creaked as she stepped toward him.

Ralph blurted it out with tears and sobs, "He called ya a whore!"

Silence continued to dominate the room with the exception of a couple more sobs punctuated with intermittent sniffing. Pearl left her place at the table and moved to him. Pulling him up, he clutched her waist and she embraced him.

"Ralph, sometimes people talk...it's called gossip and rumor. It may or may not have truth to it. Do ya believe there is any truth to this talk?"

He shook his head vigorously without speaking. "Alright then, let's finish our supper. And don't pay any attention to gossip. Remember, Ralph, I didn't hear the talk and you know there's no truth to it; so there's no need to hit big-mouth Malachi ...O.K.?"

Nodding, he said, "Yes ma'am." Separating, he sat down and she said, "Ya know boys, I still got a little of the molasses, how about some on your cornbread?" Both boys responded with broad smiles.

As she poured it for each of them, not trusting them to do it and use it all up, the younger boy, Floyd, looked up into his mother's face, "Ma, what about Camel? He was real nice to us and he said he would..."

Pearl's body stiffened, "That's enough talk for us tonight. Besides Camel has left without telling a soul where he..."

Ralph interrupted, "They say he may have been murdered! Course some say he went to..."

"I said that's enough talk for tonight. Now let's finish eating and get ready for bed." *I know where the children's talk comes from. Grandmother Stutz, the gossipin' ole' bitch just happened to have her buggy driver taking her to town and passed by both times Hiram was visiting this week.*

When Pearl missed her first mortgage payment, Hiram let her know in no uncertain terms he would be visiting her at least once more per week. At the end of their session, he told her he could not afford to continue making mortgage payments and paying for her kids transportation too. It was a matter of time, she knew, until he grew tired of her and threw her and the boys off the place. *Damn you, Hiram! Damn you, damn you, damn you! Damn you too, Camel! As my Uncle Jess usta say, neither one of ya is worth the powder it'd take to blow ya to hell and back.*

CHAPTER 8

Como Tejas, no hay otra (There's no place like Texas).

His head throbbed. Every heartbeat made his head hurt. Opening his eyes, he found he was lying in his usual place on the floor of the cabin. From the looks of the greased paper covering the window, it was daylight. He grunted in pain as he turned his head to see Bones resting quietly on his bed. Hearing no wheezing or coughing, he gave credit to the old Indian, Naiche. His medicine must be powerful. *I wonder if he has a cure for a hangover because I have a doozie.*

He laid still and quiet, hoping it would help ease the pain. His memory began returning. Lifting an arm, he felt pain shoot down it from his shoulder. *I was sore as hell from the beatin' Hiram put on me and now these red bastards beat me up again. My closed eye was just beginning to open and now it's swollen shut again and hurts like hell.*

It took a while and many grunts, but he was finally standing in the middle of the dimly-lit cabin. The rifle remained in the corner and he moved slowly toward it. *Sunuvabitches come near me again and I'll kill 'em.*

Sweat dripped off his nose and he felt like he might puke. Sitting down hard on a stump, he closed his one working eye, held his head in his hands, elbows on knees. The cabin was completely quiet. It was too quiet. It hit him that he should be hearing Bones breathe. Looking at him closely, he could see no movement of chest or stomach. His face was too pale; one eye was cracked open, the pupil glazed.

Feeling the old man's throat, he found no pulse. Bones was gone. He would get the priest to say words over him and help digging a grave. *Maybe the Indians will dig the grave. They all seemed to like Bones. Guess that's why he's got so many Navajo blankets.*

Moving outside, the glare of the sun felt like rusty knives slicing through his eye and jamming into his brain. The pain turned his stomach. He bent and puked. Spitting and wiping his mouth with his sleeve, he fell to the ground, landed on his butt and sat there breathing deep.

Getting up, he looked for the priest and the Indians. The place was deserted. He could not believe it. Holding his head with one hand and his stomach with the other, he searched the shallow caves that he had overlooked before the Morning People arrived. No one. Nothing remained of their presence. It appeared that the ground had been swept clean of tracks.

Dammit! I'll have to dig the grave alone. No help. Oh God, my head hurts and I feel like shit! Maybe if I drink a little of the beer, it'll help me feel better.

An hour later, he was feeling better. He was talking to the still form. He told Bones about his childhood; having no mother, his father and brother's attitude, and how all his life someone had made him ride the mule rather than the stallion. Bones was a very good listener. At one point he pulled the stump close to the pale face and cried. Placing his head on Bone's chest, he sobbed.

The next thing he knew, he was lying on the floor again beside the cot. Bone's corpse had changed, a little whiter, the jaws seemed to have come unhinged, and the mouth had grown into a gaping hole.

What time was it? It was daylight. His head felt larger than a barrel cactus. Crawling to the water bucket, he splashed the cool liquid onto his face. A dinged tin cup hung from a peg; he used it to drink. He used the door for support to get on his feet, then opened the door and puked. Dropping to his knees, he held to the door jam as he sank to his back. His pain and nausea blocked his realization that he was able to see through a narrow slit with the bad eye.

The sun said it was midday. Time for a drink. This day was a repeat of the prior one. The only difference was that he emptied the tus.

He awoke laying on the cot with another hangover. Peering over the side of his cot, he found Bone's body lying face down on the floor. He had traded places with the corpse. He had no recollection of doing it.

Besides the usual problems with a hangover, there was something else wrong. He lay for a time trying to clear his mind and solve the problem. He knew what it was! The cabin reeked of rotting flesh.

Stumbling to the open doorway, he puked again and again until he had the dry heaves. Resting on his knees at the entranceway, he shivered as he spit the bitter gruel. He was weak, trembling, and sick. He had to find the strength to bury the rotting corpse. But before he could do that, he must eat something.

The iron pot in the fireplace contained stinking stew. He knew from searching the cabin earlier for booze that all of the airtight vegetables and fruits had been emptied long ago. *I've gotta find his traps and get something to eat.*

He considered taking the rifle with it's three shells, but decided on a stick that was lighter than the rifle, but heavy enough to club an animal to death. Walking for what seemed an eternity, he came upon a trap. It held a possum. The animal had been dead a while. It was stiff; the mouth frozen open in a death-snarl. Ordinarily, he would not have considered eating it, but this was not an ordinary time.

An hour later, he was cooking the skinned possum over a makeshift spit he had constructed several feet from the smelly cabin. Another hour and he was digging the grave. It was rough going. The meat had really helped. Drinking fresh water from the spring had revived him and he was almost feeling human again, but the digging soon sapped his strength.

Dusk was coming down as he dragged the stinking, limp body to the shallow grave. It was only about three feet deep, but it was all he had the strength to do. Tomorrow he would lay some boulders over it to prevent animals digging up the body.

The cabin was saturated with the aroma of putrid decay. Camel slept outside wrapped in a ragged, dirty tarp he pulled from pinion trees. Bones had attached the corners about six feet high to cover something that no longer existed.

His sleep was troubled; it was filled with ghosts, screaming skeletons and poisonous serpents. His system was crying out for alcohol, but he had none to give it. Rising before dawn, he used Bone's last block match to light a fire. It's warmth felt reassuring, but he dared not get too close to it. He trembled with weakness and feared blacking out and falling onto the blaze.

He had to eat. The cooked remains of the possum carcass was gone. An animal had stolen it during the night and toppled his spit. At first light, he gathered wood, stumbling, staggering and falling several times. He threw limbs onto the fire until the flames topped his head. His objective was to build the fire up so that it would last until he found something in the traps and returned. Using small limbs, he reconstructed his spit.

Without thought, he'd thrown his club onto the fire. Searching, he found another one lighter than the first. He hoped it would be strong enough to club to death whatever he found in the traps, if it was not already dead.

He headed for the traps. Not having reset the first one holding the dead possum, he had to keep going. Nausea returned. *If I only had a drink to take the edge off. God, I hurt inside and outside. I need a drink bad.* Rivulets of sweat poured from his face. He felt weak.

The clocks were chiming precisely on the hour. The banjo clock, the lyre clock the wall regulator with the walnut case and the eight day grandfather clock with the mahogany veneer case displaying the calendar and moon phases were all sounding their announcement that it was midnight.

Hiram stood beside a Chippendale table with carved pineapples running the length of it's four legs. Atop the table rested a blue and white jasper ware lamp with a frosted glass shade. It's solitary light cast an eerie glow onto the faces of the host and his visitor, Frank.

Hiram shook his head is disbelief. "Damn, Frank, I only wanted you to rid us of that sorry-ass assassin, not kill Dan" Hiram stared at the window. It wouldn't do for Frank to be seen here tonight. The killing of the sheriff was a serious matter. Getting rid of Camel was easy. Everyone knew he was a no-good scoundrel who probably would show up drunk one night, and if he didn't...so what? The sheriff's death would really stir the town.

The more Hiram thought about it though, the more he liked it. Frank was right. Dan was too clever for his own good. If Frank set it up as he described, it would appear that the sheriff and the bad man killed each other in a gunfight. His attention focused on Frank. He was talking too fast. He was nervous and scared.

Hiram's voice was low and without emotion, "Frank, listen to me! You did what ya had to do tonight. Now, I want ya to go home, drink a big glass of clabber milk with a ladle of honey and get some good sleep. This is gonna work out fine for both of us. Don't say anything, but I think I can move the council to name you acting sheriff. Now, get outta here and don't talk in your sleep."

He squeezed Frank's shoulder and forced a close-mouthed smile. Frank appeared to wilt in relief and smiled back. As he walked through the door, Hiram trimmed the wick and killed the light. Walking to the window, he stood peering out. Both hands were shoved into the pockets of his silk robe. *Dan was becoming a pain in the ass. He was trying to act ignorant and play me along, but the wily bastard was dangerous. Frank will be a sheriff that I can count on to assist me in making this town grow and helping me to acquire what I've worked hard for. Damn! This was a sweet ending to a good day. I wish I hadn't allowed Juanita to go home. I'm ready for another romp.*

In the wee hours, no one was around to see Hiram take a ride on his prized mare. No one saw him return or saw the lone figure riding a large Missouri mule up, dismount and go inside. He obviously knew his way around the place. Inside, Hiram gripped the mahogany chair armrests and grunted as the dark silhouette brought the whip down on his shoulders and the smack of it echoed off the walls. The one appearing like death scraped up the gold coins and left quietly as he'd done so many times before.

The giant of a man had tears in his eyes. "Reverend, please come in and pray for Vera Mae. She ain't been outta the bed for three days and that jus' ain't like her."

Reverend McKenzie sat in his buggy and felt empathy for this man and his family. Big Henry Goins was a former buffalo soldier from New Orleans who remained in the area after the Indian wars. He worked a small farm and ranch and was known as a man of great physical strength. His gentle manner belied the huge hands that could straighten a horseshoe. He and Vera Mae had four children and McKenzie was looking at three of them standing close behind their father. He guessed the oldest girl was attending to her mother. Stepping down from his buggy, he followed Big Henry into the shotgun house and smelled a combination of cabbage and quinine.

The daughter, a large young lady who took after her father, moved back from the bed to allow the pastor to step near. Going to one knee, the reverend spoke softly to the slight, brown lady who lay beneath heavy quilts, though the day was warm. He could see sweat on her forehead as she shivered beneath the mound of cover.

Turning her head toward him, she tried to smile, but was so thin, it appeared more like a ghostly grin. Her eyes opened, fluttered, then dropped to half-mast and closed.

The reverend looked up at Big Henry, "I'd like to touch her as I pray for her, where can I do it that it won't hurt her?"

The voice trembled, "Anywhere, Reverend, that ya see. She ain't complained of hurting in any particular spot, jus' feels poorly all over."

Placing his hand gently on her head, he prayed for God's healing power to transform her to good health, but ended the prayer as he always did in such circumstances, that "God's will be done." *Oh Lord, I pray that I will not carry a harmful sickness back to my beloved wife.*

Riding away after promising Big Henry he would continue to pray for his sick wife and would return tomorrow, the pastor breathed a silent prayer for the Goins. McKenzie felt badly for this family and the other Negro families in the area. There were seven families in all. Most ranched and farmed except for Ben Davis who worked as a carpenter, stonemason and was recognized as a skilled artisan. It was said if you wanted a fireplace that drew the air to ensure a fire, you had Ben do it.

The pastor had invited all of the Negro families to attend church, but he knew it was a hollow invitation. The affluent families in the church such as the Arlington's, McCormick's, Grandmother Stutz, and especially Hiram had made it clear to the Negroes that they would be welcome whenever the church completed it's balcony. In the meantime, these same wealthy members made sure funds were unavailable to complete such a project.

Heading toward the Stutz Manor, as Grandmother Stutz referred to it, McKenzie felt inner turmoil. He did not want to visit her and hear about all her ailments which he had heard a thousand times before. He also grew weary of hearing how her husband, the late Colonel Stutz, was supposedly told by Robert E. Lee that if he'd had a dozen like him, they'd have won the war for sure. It was obvious that Grandmother Stutz was a self-centered old bitty who loved to gossip and make excuses how she was often too sick to attend church or perform an act of compassion for anyone else.

These were his thoughts as he turned into the wide roadway leading to her three story mansion. He hated himself for having to play the game, for having to be a political animal, for showing favoritism to someone like her because of her money and status within the community.

His mood was dark as he rolled down the drive and halted his buggy in front of the stairs that ascended to the second floor, main entrance. Rather than being here, he should be visiting all of the Negroes within the community and encouraging them to attend church.

He should be visiting Pearl Manning and her two sons. But, he had been warned by the powers that be she was a loose woman and he should not enter her place. He suggested to Hiram they visit her, but received only a disapproving frown in return.

What about the poor Beaumont family back in town? They needed the church's help, but the pastor received no support in helping them. They were that, "white trash," according to Grandmother Stutz and beyond redemption. How about the Mexican families scattered about the area? Most were Catholic, but not all. The pastor had been told that all would be welcome in church as soon as the balcony was completed.

Reverend Bilbo McKenzie sat in his buggy looking up at the large house before him. It was the only home in the area that rivaled Hiram's in size and pomp. It was built with a double staircase in the center of the structure. Visitors climbed either the east or west stairs, entering the second floor. He assumed the elderly Negro butler and his wife who served as maid lived downstairs. Grandmother Stutz had mentioned a room used for stewing and jarring fresh grown vegetables. A white ornate stable, matching the architectural design of the main house, sat behind it. A Mexican couple, who worked the cattle and grew crops, lived in it.

Lifting his arms to shake the reins and leave without going in, he heard his name called and saw the Negro maid waving to him. *Hell fire and damnation! I've been caught. I've gotta go in and see and hear the same old malarkey I've ...*

Waving and smiling back, he pulled the brake on and with Bible in hand, stepped from the buggy and walked up the steps to endure tea and gossip.

Spirit Dog's heart pounded and his nostrils flared. He stretched out on the dry sand so flat that a casual glance would not detect him. He laid in the same direction as the ripples of hard earth that ran across the spur like plowed furrows waiting for planting season. Both arms extended in front of him. One gripped a knife made from a deer antler. The handle was bound tightly with rawhide and the point had been filed sharp from a thousand strokes across a hard rock.

The young Navajo father thought of his wife and daughter, Naiche, Father Pollen and the others in their group. He hoped a baby would not cry or anyone would do anything to alert the soldiers of their presence. His horse concerned him. What if he whinnied at the smell of the other horses? The group was hunkered down in a shallow arroyo at the base of the spur less than a hundred steps away. He did not understand. The scouts had obviously been assisting the group, but now the soldiers seemed to be on them at every move. Had the scouts been threatened or paid off by the white eyes?

He knew for certain that if he was spotted by one of the riders, he stood little chance of stopping them with his knife. They rode less than forty steps away perpendicular to him; giving them plenty of time to draw a bead on him and cutting him in half with their Winchesters. That was alright. He would die running toward them, not away, and if by chance Changing Woman helped him dodge the heavy slugs, he would sink his antler into a rider's kidney up to the hilt. It would not be an instant death for the soldier like his would be when the bullet found it's mark. His victim would die a painful death.

Dusk was settling. It was becoming more difficult for a rider to sight his rifle, especially if the target came fast, low and dodging. Spirit Dog could hear their voices clearly, the tinkle of spurs, and even the squeak of leather. He could smell their dust. He thought he could smell them. The white eyes said the Indians smelled of leather and smoke while Spirit Dog always caught the scent of sweat and rancid meat when he was near a white. The closer they came, the greater his chances of killing one of them and spooking the rest.

The thought hit him. He couldn't attack. He couldn't die gloriously. If they killed him, which they would surely do even if he was able to get one of them, his presence would alert them of the group's presence. They would easily find them. Spirit Dog was convinced, as all of the others, they would be shot on sight. Although this was not discussed, it was understood by all. Wouldn't it serve the group better if he remained alive so that he could distract and stall the army and maybe succeed in pointing them in the wrong direction? The White Eyes were known to be poor torturers; he could take lots of pain and doubted they could pull the truth from him.

His soul ached. Why was it always like this? He'd much prefer to die like a man rather than shrivel up like dry corn on a reservation as he had observed his kinsmen and friends do. Closing his eyes, he relaxed and left the decision to Changing Woman. If spotted, he would not run, but discard the knife and allow himself to be captured so he could try to deceive the evil White Eyes. This would not be easy. The White Eyes were masters of lies, deceit and murder.

CHAPTER 9

A Texan's view…they did not settle Texas, they conquered it.

Camel was desperate for food. *I need something to eat and oh, God, how I need a drink of something strong.*

Checking Bones's traps, he found only a hairy paw in one. Something had devoured the animal. The next trap held a large boar coon. The creature arched his back and hissed at Camel. Finding a broken limb, Camel clubbed him and later enjoyed pulling tender meat from the carcass on the spit.

That afternoon, he lay on the ground beside the spit. The cabin still stunk too much to inhabit. A battered tin bucket of spring water sat beside him. A gourd serving as a dipper lay across the top of the bucket. Camel burped.

Remembering his promise to cover Bone's grave with stones, he told himself he would do it first thing tomorrow. Stretching back, he dozed off. He dreamed of the little priest and the old Indian who doctored Bones. He saw himself gambling with Skinyas and Little Sun. He next saw a young, pretty Indian maid moving among them. Who was she?

Opening his eyes, his first thought was his need for a drink. A drink of hard stuff! Dusk was descending. Returning to the cabin, he emerged with two Navajo blankets. He spread them on the ground and soon returned to a troubled sleep. It was the tortured sleep of a man thirsting for alcohol.

Dawn found him hunched on the ground with blankets draped over his shoulders. He stoked the smoking embers beneath the half-consumed carcass. His hand trembled as he clutched the stick. *Lord, how I wanta drink!*

He had to do something. He couldn't survive there. Bones had said the nearest neighbor was several miles away. The railroad was about twenty miles away. He would retrace his steps to the tracks and ride the rails back to Marathon.

Returning to the cabin, he found a rusty canteen and a small dusty canvas sack that would serve as a lunch bag for the remainder of the coon meat. He rinsed the canteen in the spring, filled it and looped the faded, half-rotten belt over his shoulder. He turned the sack inside out and beat on it until he felt dizzy. Placing the meat into it, he looked around the cabin, the spring and the pile of bones. He turned, with rifle in hand and headed south toward the railroad tracks.

The morning sun beat down on him. He drank often. Having probably walked no more than a mile and a half, two at the most, the canteen was already half-empty.

His boots crunched on the alkaline floor of the desert. Prickly ocatillo and creosote bushes tore at his clothes and skin.

He recalled Bone's cabin was built beside one of the few springs running alongside the wasteland. It was an oasis and the further he walked, the more he thought about it.

Topping a spur, he could see great distances. It did not inspire him. He saw only more of the same. A black-tailed jackrabbit gave him a glimpse of it's backside as it bolted among the plants. Staring at the rabbit as he walked, he stepped into a gulch and fell flat on his face. Standing on weak, wobbly legs, he sat on the edge of the dry arroyo, but the sand was too hot. Squatting on his haunches, he drank more water. Instinctively jerking as a shadow flitted across him, he peered up and saw a black buzzard circling far above him. Hefting the canteen, he figured he had a third left. He had probably walked two and a half miles, maybe close to three. At this rate, he'd never make the railroad. He gave up.

Turning back, he focused on retracing his steps to the cabin and it's spring of cool, life-giving water. His lips thinned as he tried to push aside his deep quenching thirst for alcohol. At times, he could not make out his tracks and feared losing his way, but as he lifted his head to finish off the canteen, he saw the green oasis in the distance.

As dusk neared and he rested on the ground beside his fire, he evaluated his situation. There was a reason Bones called Father

Pollen's group the Morning People; they traveled at night due to the heat and arrived at their destination in the morning. *I've gotta travel at night and pull up during the day. But, how will I know which direction to go? What will save me from stepping on a rattler in the dark?*

Tossing a clean-licked coon leg bone aside, he wished for salt to season the meat, but was unable to find any in the cabin. He assessed his situation and chances. He was still sore in several places from the beatings, but not enough to prevent him from walking. Both eyes were now open. By using the pool as a mirror, he knew his nose had been broken, a scar interrupted his right eyebrow, and another red scar streaked his left cheekbone. He now had a fighter's face. He'd probably lost fifteen or twenty pounds. His clothes were torn, ragged and hung on his slimming frame.

He still wanted booze. His system cried out for it. His greatest challenge was not hunger or the beatings, it was his need for alcohol. Resting his head in his arms on his knees, he acknowledged that he was an alcoholic. *This is my big mountain to climb. A normal man would have a far better chance to make it outta here. I'm handicapped by my need for alcohol. I'm weak. I wanta drink right now and it's the last thing I need if I'm to survive. My guess is my chances are slim...real slim.*

There was something else that nagged at the back of his mind. What was it? Something that he really wanted...what...he remembered...his hatred of that bastard, Hiram. He would kill him if it was last thing he would ever do. But first, he needed a drink.

The army captain closed his eyes and tried to focus on the renegades and block out his hemorrhoids. Holding his reins taunt, he inhaled deeply in an attempt to detect dust. He strained his ears to hear any sound that might give away the runaways. He would bet his sure-footed bay that he heard a child cry an hour ago. His heart raced with the thought of catching them. *The thieving, lying, scalping sunuvabitches ! When I getcha, I'm gonna gun ya down and leave ya for the buzzards to eat ya stinkin' guts!* While he had never fought Indians, he deeply regretted it because it would look great on his record. This was his opportunity. Dammit, he was determined not to let it slip away. A breeze touched his face. It felt good, but impaired his hearing.

A hot flash of hemorrhoid pain seared through him. Heaving himself up in the stirrups, he scrutinized the area as far as he could see. Dusk was coming down. To his left, he saw a thousand razor-sharp Spanish daggers that could well serve as cover for those not intimidated by their prickly points. Straight ahead the land appeared flat with scattered creosote and salt bushes. But, that could be misleading too. He could be overlooking a ten-foot dip in the topography a couple of hundred yards away that would provide cover for an army. To his right, the land was level with few bushes, only rows of sand, created by the wind that seemed to always blow whenever you tried to listen for sounds. When they were roasting in the unforgiving heat, the wind was nowhere to be found. He stared at the sand rows. One row seemed different ...*Aw shit! There's nothing alive there. I'm lookin' at the only place they can't hide.*

With thighs hurting from standing in the stirrups, he still stood and pretended to look. He did not want to sit on his saddle that seemed to be made of iron. The scouts, as usual, were nowhere in sight. Sounds behind him of men coughing, spitting, clearing their throats of sandy phlegm, reminded him of their impatience. Even the horses blew, snorted, stamped their hooves, and shook their heads jingling their bits and squeaking leather.

Easing slowly onto the saddle, he heard a laugh behind him. He'd ignored such until this time. His neck crunched as he turned his head to try and spot the laugher. His sergeant did the same. Reining his mount around, Captain Verlander stared with hot anger at his men. All mouth lines were grimly set, but he saw the contempt in their eyes.

He hated his men! He hated his assignment! He hated this country! He hated the people he was chasing! Most of all, he hated that his hemorrhoids hurt all the damn time!

Billy practiced his draw several times. Looking down the barrel of the silver .44, he assumed his shooting stance. With feet about eighteen inches apart, he shrugged his shoulders, turned his head as though stretching his neck muscles, and said quietly, "Throw it."

Junior Beaumont, a lanky teenager, tossed a brown whisky bottle high in the air. As it began it's descent, Billy's hand moved with ease and quickness, the gun thundered and the bottle exploded.

Junior had seen this occur so many times it held no magic for him. He wore a battered old wool hat with a brim that dipped and rose. He wore it so that glass splinters would not fall into his eyes. In a deadpan voice he asked, "Ya wanna big bottle or one of these little medicine bottles?"

"Don't matter none to me." The Colt was already in it's holster and his hand relaxed and resting in it's normal position. Junior selected a small green bottle, pulled his arm back and tossed it as hard as he could underhanded. The gun sounded but the bottle tumbled lazily and fell untouched. Following two more misses, Junior asked, "Wanna go back to the big un's?"

Billy sighed, shook his head, "Naw, I just ain't shootin' right today. Let's try it again tomorrow. You take your turn now."

Junior's eyes and expression came alive. He dropped the bottle and made for Billy. "I got my bottles already set up." Billy was reloading. Handing the Colt to the boy, he said, "Remember what ya learned. Relax and take your time before ya squeeze offa shot."

Junior looked at six whisky bottles lined up on the ground about twenty paces away. The bottles were of various shapes and colors. He tried to place his feet like Billy; aimed at the first bottle on the left end and blasted sand a foot in front of it. The flying sand toppled the bottle. Aiming for the next bottle, the slug slammed into the sand two paces beyond it.

Turning to Billy for advice and encouragement, he stared in amazement to see his mentor crying. Hiccupping, tears streaming down his face, Billy shook his head. "I...I...I'm sorry, Junior. I got to thinking about how Sheriff Dan used to brag on my shootin.' Let's do this tomorrow." Billy looked down and away from his friend, embarrassed by his show of emotion. Handing over the .44, Junior pretended all was normal by picking up and tossing rocks at imaginary villains disguised as the bottles.

Billy walked toward town slowly; too slowly for Junior. The lanky teen grew impatient, angled off, waved and without looking at him, muttered, "See ya tomorrow."

This was what Billy wanted. He headed for a spot where he and the sheriff used to sit and talk. It was on a knoll about a quarter of a mile outside of Angel Valley. Two large cottonwoods dominated the hill with a third one having fallen and provided seating for the two men. Billy stood looking up for a while, as though he was hesitant to trod on holy ground. Sitting in his usual place on the log, he looked out over the valley as he had done so many times before; only this time, he was alone. *Doggone it, I miss ya, Sheriff Dan!*

He smiled. He had an idea. He would pretend Sheriff Dan was sitting there and they would have their usual talk. "Mama's feelin' a little better now, Sheriff. She said she thought she had the milk sickness there for a while. Ya know that's what killed her ma, pa and little brother."

Scooting to the sheriff's place on the log, he lowered his voice, "Is that right, Billy? I tell ya, Son, ya got a mighty nice ma and ya need to take care of her."

The movement and role interchanging lasted quite a while until Billy faced his imaginary friend and asked, "Sheriff Dan, what in the world happened to ya out there to get ya killed?"

Changing places, assuming the demeanor of his dead friend, he said, "Billy, ya know I always keep an eye on strangers, especially those hangin' around Stinky's place. Well, I noticed this mean-lookin' little fella totin' a big iron like yours and when I saw him headin' outta town, I thought I'd mosey along behind him to make sure he left our territory. I think ya said you saw him from ya upstairs window. Then ya saw me headin' out after him."

Billy moved back to his place on the log, put his face in his hands and started sobbing. He cried, talked and hiccupped, "I did see him Sheriff Dan, but ya see I wasn't sick. Pa's been makin' me stay in and away from ya since Camel got run off. If...if I had been doin' right, I woulda been with ya that night and maybe I coulda saved ya life."

Billy continued crying and talking to his friend. He explained that in a way he had been sick. He'd felt awful ever since the night Hiram had him and Frank hold Camel while he beat him. He got even sicker when Hiram told him what he had to say to Sheriff Dan. Hiram even talked to his pa about makin' sure he did what he was told to do. It was all lies! Every day his pa made him stay in bed and play sick, he really did feel bad about the whole mess. He knew he should be out helping the sheriff rather than lying in bed and acting puny. He kept hearin' over and over what the sheriff had said about a man always havin' to do what's right even if it's not the popular thing to do.

The tears finally stopped. He sat in silence with head in hands. He had always liked Camel and knew the sheriff liked him too. He said Camel had just gotten into some bad habits and maybe one day he'd grow up. Billy never really understood that; but the sheriff often said things he didn't understand. Camel had already grown up, but Billy tried to be selective about what he asked his friend to explain. He knew from his three years in school that a teacher could grow weary of having to explain too much.

His feelings changed from sorrow to anger whenever he thought of Frank. Frank was no lawman. He only wanted to make shady deals and brag about what a good shot he was, but he would never shoot with Billy. All Frank wanted was to keep Hiram happy.

With burning eyes, aching throat and head, Billy stared out over the valley trying not to think about all of it. A mockingbird whistled a strange tune. To Billy, it sounded like a funeral dirge. The sun was nearing it's highest arc and seemed to sap the color from land, trees and town below. Across the valley, rising heat made distant mountains do a funny dance and fluffy clouds stacked against the blue sky. *It's a beautiful day outside, but inside me it's all cloudy and rainy.*

He wished Sheriff Dan were here to help him sort it all out. An hour later, he was sitting on the log staring out over the valley when he heard his ma call his name.

Maggie's eyes were tired from grading the numbers test. Rubbing them, she lay her quill on the desk and stood. Walking to the window of the room she rented from the McKinsey's, she stared out and watched the Beaumont children playing in the street. They seldom came to school. When they did, they were horrible discipline problems. She had tried to talk to their mother, Queenie, several times, but it did no good.

Maggie closed her tired eyes and thought of her home in Connecticut. Living in Texas was a cultural shock and while she felt called to her teaching, she longed for New England. She recalled someone saying upon her arrival that the west was hell on women and horses. She knew it to be true.

Hunching her shoulders with arms crossed to relieve the stress of sitting for so long, she thought of her grandmother who began the family tradition of serving as a missionary in the west by teaching school. Her grandmother, a member of the Congregational Church, had heard Catherine Beecher, the daughter of the famous minister, Lyman Beecher, speak of the desperate need for young people to travel west and carry God's light to the children there. Her grandmother had traveled to St. Louis and taught for a year in a rural school. Upon returning, she married and had children. She was always being asked to speak at missionary meetings about her experiences and ended each session by encouraging young people to pray that God would call them to go west as she had done.

Maggie's mother had heard the call and traveled to Tulsa, Oklahoma and taught in a school with a dirt floor for two years. Like her mother, she returned to Connecticut, married, gave birth to Maggie and became well-known in the American Home Missionary Society as a dynamic speaker and promoter for their cause. She wrote a circular that was published and read throughout the northern states.

For a reason Maggie could not explain, she had always assumed she would serve like her grandmother and mother before her; only she would do it for three years. Perhaps it was because as a child she had sat on hard pews and heard both her grandmother and mother speak. Sometimes, they shared the same pulpit. Maggie would stand in her backyard beneath a large elm tree and recite their speeches word for word.

Staring out the window, watching one of the larger Beaumont children hit a younger one, she was not sure at all she would remain for two more years. *Do I want to remain for one more day? No! I want to go home now!*

Returning to the battered desk, she sat with eyes closed. She was tired. This was no time to make an important decision. She knew her family would say that the question she must ask was not what she wanted to do, but what God called her to do.

She was glad her family did not know of her fling with Camel. They would not approve of him at all. She was less certain of their take on Hiram. They would probably accept him because of his respectability and success within the community.

Her thoughts returned to the young Congregational minister who had courted her back home. He had written her long letters professing his undying love for her when she first arrived, but she had received none lately. *Could Hiram have anything to do with that? Surely not! Get hold of yourself, Maggie. You sound like you're becoming tizzy in the head as grandmother would say.*

She felt absolutely certain her family and church members would be proud of her activities on Friday evenings. That was the time she was picked up a mile outside of town by a Negro family and taken to one of their houses where she taught reading and numbers to the children and their parents. The group usually consisted of eight to eleven Negro children and six to nine Mexican children. They usually met in the Goin's barn, or behind it on tables under a grape arbor. While Maggie was proud of what she was doing for these poor, second-class citizens, she worried what it could mean to the families if her activities were discovered.

A bemused look flickered across her features as she pictured Hiram learning about it. Opening her eyes, she continued grading the student's work.

CHAPTER 10

The Indian held to a different concept of land than the white. It all belonged to the Great Spirit and there was no place for private ownership and fences.

Dusk was falling when Camel began his night journey. He headed due south. He figured he could not miss the railroad track. His canteen was full and he carried Bones's rifle with three bullets in it, a home-made knife stuck in it's leather sheath, pushed into his pocket and a Navajo blanket folded over his shoulder. Walking in the dim light was far easier than walking in the sunlight. The night turned cool and he was soon thirsty, but he knew he had to discipline himself if he was going to make it. He had eaten all the coon meat back at the cabin and hoped he could either shoot game or make it to the tracks and be rescued before becoming too hungry.

Sitting on the sand, he looked up at a zillion stars. Drinking from his canteen, he noted the eastern horizon growing light. As he watched it, the moon slowly made it's appearance. The light enabled him to see better and he picked up the pace. About an hour later, he estimated he had walked three to four miles. He sat for a while and pulled deeply from his canteen. Jumping at a noise in the brush, he glimpsed a kit fox with large ears look at him and then silently disappear.

Listening, he heard sounds all about him. The Chihuahua was considered desert, but contained hundreds of plants and as many creatures. Using the rifle as a support, he pulled himself up and trudged on. The old ache returned deep within his core. He knew it well and felt a moment of panic knowing he could not satisfy it. He willed himself to walk. The thirst that no amount of water could slate, enveloped him like a wet blanket wrapped tightly about him.

Walking in the dark was not easy, even with the aid of the moon. For the first time, he appreciated the Morning People, especially the mothers who walked with babies wrapped onto cradleboards strapped to their back. They navigated the uneven terrain filled with walking obstacles. *I must have been born with a silver spoon in my mouth and have never faced the hardships so many others have. Dammit, I need a drink!*

The night grew cool and he wrapped the blanket around his shoulders. It kept slipping down. Pulling his knife from it's sheath, he squared his blanket, folded it and cut a hole in it's center, making a serape.

A white-footed mouse scampered from a small clearing into the bushes. A Coyote howled behind him and another in front of him. Soon, howls echoed all about him. Something made a sound and disappeared into a dark clump of yucca bushes. Glancing at the black sky bejeweled with twinkling white stars, he felt the impact of the beauty surrounding him, but felt more the fear of his loneliness and helplessness. He knew the pristine beauty could devour him without leaving a trace. He pictured his skeleton half-buried in the desert sands, a saltbush growing between his ribs, a peccary nudging his skull. He walked faster in an effort to push the grisly image from his mind.

With ribs and feet aching he was glad to see the approaching dawn. Looking for a place that would provide shade during the day, he figured he had walked at least ten miles, maybe eleven, though it was hard to measure.

The sun topped the horizon and he still searched for a place to hold up. His sense of balance told him he was walking downward. Leaning back so as not to topple forward, he felt the ground beneath his boots level off. He stopped at the bottom of a sloping gulch. The sides were not overhanging as he would have liked to provide easy shade, but he knew he had to stop soon.

Walking the gulch slowly, he spotted a semi-level area at the top of the slope with overhanging yuccas. The bushes would give shade until late afternoon. Unlike the stiff prickly bayonets, the yucca leaf was soft and held no stinging bite.

Spreading the blanket over the rocky earth and his rifle beside him, he drank deeply from his canteen. He did not allow himself to study its weight, but laid down and was soon lost in deep sleep.

It was the familiar troubling sleep of an alcoholic craving a drink. Demons, eerie, weird creatures taunted him by beckoning him to drink with them and then disappearing as he approached them.

She was insistent; he was hesitant. Judah had finished butchering a yearling for Pearl. It was obvious to him she could have done it all herself, only needing help with lifting the carcass onto the butchering hook. She was an impressive woman in many ways but Judah felt intimidated by her candor. He was unaccustomed to a woman being so outspoken.

She stood at the top of the stairs inviting him to come in and have a cup of coffee with her. He rubbed the back of his neck and smiled weakly. He wanted to, but something told him to get on his broken nag and return to his own place.

"I thank ya for the offer, Miss Pearl, but I gotta get back to my barn. I gotta sick calf that might not make it." He saw her face redden and it made his own do the same.

"Judah, don't call me that again. It makes no sense. Now quit makin' excuses and get in here before I hog-tie ya and drag ya in."

His face reddened more as he mounted the stairs and mumbled, "Yes ma'am."

"Have a seat at the table while I get the coffee and I want ya to tell me whatcha think I should do to improve the little bit of stock I got left."

At first, Judah was hesitant to engage in a serious conversation with her, but he soon learned she knew almost as much as he did about stock improvement and ranching in general. As his appreciation for her increased, his shyness disappeared. A half-hour later, he was calling her by her first name. They were immersed in deep conversation discussing shared ranching problems when heavy steps sounded, the door flew open and Hiram yelled, "Pearl, where the…"

He froze. Both men's eyes widened as they stared in disbelief at seeing the other. Pearl's eye's flashed in anger. "Ya forgot how to knock, Hiram ?"

Hiram's face flushed. He was unaccustomed to being chided or surprised like this. "I'm sorry, Pearl. I just stopped by to discuss that loan that you inquired about at the bank last week."

Judah's chair scraped on the hardwood floor as he rose. He did not consider himself a very intuitive man, especially around women, but he knew there was something not right here and wanted out as fast as possible. *Doggone it, if the wife was still alive and there was any gossip about these two, she woulda told me. I never talk to anyone about other folks enough to know what's goin' on.*

Pearl spoke in a sharp voice, "There's no need for ya to go, Judah. I can talk to Hiram tomorrow at the bank about our business. Why dontcha…"

Judah was already halfway to the door. "Thank ya, Miss Pearl, but I gotta get to that sick calf." Hiram stepped aside for him to pass. Pausing at the door, Judah looked at Hiram and then Pearl, "Thank ya for the coffee and if ya need help with butcherin' again, just let me know." There was a heavy silence. He was gone.

Outside, Judah saw no sign of Hiram's buggy. *It hasta be around back.* Walking into the barn where his own horse was tied, he mounted and as he rode out, he could see the back part of the buggy.

Inside the house, Pearl glared at Hiram, "You're a jackass!"

He smiled, shrugging his shoulders, "Sorry, Pearl. I happen to be in the area and thought I'd drop by. You're not being very…"

"Stop it, Hiram! What's it gonna be, ridin' me everyday until ya kick me and the boys out?"

"Now, Pearl, you stop it. No one has said anything about kickin' you and the boys out. I just want to be here with you, that's all. Can ya blame…"

"That's right nice of ya, Hiram. So how about us talkin' about how I can save my ranch instead of jumping in bed."

He grinned, "Ya know, Pearl, ya talk better in bed than any woman I've ever known. Let's do some talking right now."

Standing, she moved toward the small bedroom, removing her faded gingham dress as she went. Beside the bed, she stepped out of her homemade panties, plopped on the bed and spread her legs. "O.K., let's get it over with. I gotta lotta chores before the boys come home."

He undressed but did not move toward her.

With voice cold and hard, she taunted him. "Come on, Hiram! Dammit, I need to get to work. Whatcha think ya can do with that little shriveled piece of nothing?"

Standing nude with beefy hands on his hips, he said, "Humph! I know what you're doin'. Now ya know what I came for, and I ain't gonna leave without it. Ya wanta have the boys come in and see us like this, then it's O.K. with me."

He saw the tears well up and knew he had her. Grimacing, she wiped an eye with the muslim sheet. Turning on her side facing him, she said in a heavy laden, low voice, "Come here, Hiram."

Father Pollen shifted his position but failed to elude his constant companion---pain. Leaning against a stack of blankets, because his bent posture and weak limbs prevented him from sitting with legs crossed like the other members. He looked with admiration and frustration at the slim, pretty woman, Anrelina, and the older, frumpy, Naltzukich. He wondered if Naiche, who sat erect and solemn, felt like he did. Perhaps not. The old Indian seemed to possess a quiet strength that Father Pollen prayed for constantly, but seemed to elude him like a disappearing dream.

This meeting had been called because Anrelina and Naltzukich asked for it. *Asked...it was more like a demand than a request.* The assertiveness of the two women had surprised him. But then, he remembered what he had learned regarding their beliefs. On arriving at Fort Wingate, he had befriended a couple of Navajo religious leaders, or singers, as they were called, and found them eager to share their concepts of religion. Though they said they could not tell him certain things since he was not a Navajo, they obviously found it a refreshing change to be asked their beliefs rather than having to listen to a long-winded sermon as a white eyes holy man tried to shove his religion down their throats.

Father Pollen was fascinated to learn the Navajo version of creation was very similar to that of Christianity. The story was told differently sometimes, but the basic concept was like the Judeo-

Christian one. There was one important difference--the role of woman. Eve was subservient to Adam, while the Navajo First Woman functioned on the same level as First Man; she was his equal in every way. He had forgotten this lesson recently and relied on the men and ignored the women.

Anrelina's hands moved gracefully as she spoke. Her voice was melodious as a bell. Her words though, were direct and forceful. "Father Pollen and Naiche, Naltzukich and I respect both of you very much. We know you are carrying a heavy load for us and we thank you. But we need to be informed of decisions that affect our lives. We should be a part of the decision-making. This is the way it should be and it would take some of the load from your backs."

Father Pollen almost smiled at her political savvy. Detecting movement, he turned his head to see Naltzukich nodding her massive head. Her voice was deeper than Anrelina's, but she spoke in a lilting way that the priest found pleasing to the ear. Her message was even more direct. "Since fleeing the white eyes world, the women's blanket weaving has helped us with trading for food and goods more than anything else our group has done. We are glad to do this. It is right that we do it." Pausing, looking directly at the priest, she said, "It is also right that we share in the decisions that might mean life or death for all of us, even our children."

Father Pollen stared back at Naltzukich, his mind's eye saw past her dark pupils, he saw the half-breed, Manuelito, approaching an isolated cabin with a par fleche packed with brightly decorated blankets woven by the women. The blankets were highly popular on the frontier. Some cowboys insisted that the best saddle blanket was a Navajo blanket. The blankets provided warmth on a cold night, served as table cloths and room dividers, serapes, and met a plethora of other needs in areas where the nearest store might be twenty or fifty miles away. Manuelito usually returned with the par fleche filled with smoked hams, cleaned and gutted chickens, or even a sheep or yearling calf. Once he traded for a milk cow that yielded little milk but made a big difference to a group whose every meal was a challenge

The priest looked to Naiche whose stoic face, as always, revealed nothing. Then came the slight nod agreeing with the women. Father Pollen pushed himself up as far as his hump and painful joints would allow, "Anrelina and Naltzukich, Naiche and I agree with you.   You certainly share in all of the work, responsibility and danger.   You have a right to have a say in whatever we decide to do."

The women looked at each other for a moment. Anrelina took the lead, "We know you stay clear of the roughest trails, and that is kind of you, but we can travel anyplace we need to go to put the enemy behind us. Take the hard trails. Those who need it, will ride a travois."

Father Pollen felt his face burn. They were talking to him and Naiche, but primarily to him, since he insisted on walking. He knew he slowed them at times. They made allowances for him without word or question.

Silence settled on them. Naltzukich spoke, "We need to think longer than the next turn of the stars. Where are we going? Do we have a plan that will take us to a place of peace?   A place like you have told us about, the promised land that the great leader, Moses, led his people toward."

Again, Father Pollen looked at Naiche, but received only silence in return. The priest felt flustered but attempted to answer as best he could. "We've traveled some rough country, but you're right, we can make it rougher for the army." *And for ourselves.* We've made some friends along the way, like poor old Bones, and they continue to support us. We know for sure that the Navajo scouts heading the army have been helping us."

Naiche shifted while Father Pollen fell silent in deference to him.   The little priest grunted while trying to find a more comfortable position and when Naiche remained stoic, he continued, "Things have been a little crazy lately, though. We see the scouts point in a direction away from us, but the soldiers head in the opposite direction. We don't know if their leader is on to them, if they've been bought off, we just don't…"

Anrelina spoke, "Our greatest concern is our children. We feel sure that if the soldiers catch us, they will kill us."

Naltzukich's voice sounded passionate, "Our children are our gift and they are our hope for the seasons to come. The young mothers are fearful and feel that unless we can find our promised land very soon, we should seek safety among the churches in a town. Perhaps the army would not shoot us down like dogs if there are good white eyes helping them….White eyes like Father Pollen."

Father Pollen pondered this comment. He took it as a compliment that they were suggesting they find and depend on others like himself. His memory recalled numerous promises made to the Indians by his kind; each promise had been broken. A sinking feeling in his stomach hurt him as he remembered the callous letters filled with negative comments from his former parishioners. He had no answer for their concern regarding a quick trip to the promised land. *Am I allowing these people to hold to a false dream? Indeed, am I feeding my ego by being in a position of leadership, but in the process, likely to get them all killed?* He stared at the colorful blanket he rested on. He knew nothing else to tell Anrelina and Naltzukich.

For the first time, Naiche spoke, "Your vision is our vision. Your fears are our fears." The old Indian paused, looked at the sad little priest and said, "We must remember that all white eyes are not like Father Pollen."

The priest felt relief. Naiche was right; the father considered himself an oddity just as the Indians did. Even good whites, Christian, church-going whites held an inbred fear of Indians. Looking into the eyes of these three friends, Father Pollen felt deep anguish and foreboding. What would become of them? Would they all be shot, starved or hanged by their necks until they grew stiff with purple faces and swollen tongues protruding from gaping mouths filled with flies? He shivered at the picture. This day would be like so many others; sleep would elude him. He would spend the day praying for the group's spiritual and physical salvation.

Toby's suntanned face appeared redder than usual. He faced the bank teller as he had for many years to draw salaries for 3C ranch hands. The mousy little bank teller, A. J. Moniker, had just refused to cash a check for him. Large drops of sweat beaded the little man's forehead and his skin was unnaturally pale. He had difficulty breathing as he spoke.

"Toby, this is not Camel's signature." He gulped like a fish out of water. "We all know he's not around to sign a check. This has to be a…uh…forged check and we…"

Toby's voice was tight and husky with anger, "Ya been cashing em' for years now, A.J., and ya never refused before." He stared hard at the stooped little man who appeared to stoop more as though trying to hide behind the counter. "You've always accepted money into the account with me signin' for it , what's the difference now?"

"I'm sorry Toby, that's all I can do. Bank policy is gittin' tighter and…" He looked like he was going to throw up.

Toby glared; A.J. withered. Toby glanced at Hiram's empty desk, "Is Hiram in back?"

A.J. shook his head, "He's out on business and I don't know when or if he'll be back today."

Pulling at his gray beard, Toby shook his head in disgust, slowly turned and walked out of the bank. He wore a battered, gray, wide-rimmed Stetson with the brim drooping down like a pitched roof. His attire included a clean, faded, red and white checkered shirt, Levi's, with seat and knees white from use and boots covered with dust that made their color unrecognizable.

Toby's tall, lean, frame epitomized the image of an old cowboy. The only color about him that seemed alive was his nose and cheeks burned apple-red from years in the sun. His gray eyes and angular features appeared stark in the mid-morning sunlight. In the hours before dawn and at dusk, they lent the appearance of an apparition.

Standing on the walkway staring at his long-legged, brown mare, Toby seethed. The brown shook her head in impatience and nickered. Toby did what he often did these days. He talked to his horse. "O.K. Babs, we'll be headin' back in a little. Just give me some time to cogitate." The horse's ears stood erect; she tossed her head making her long mane flutter and nickered louder as her master turned and headed down the slatted walk.

Toby cussed under his breath. Tipping his hat to Mrs. Queenie Beaumont, he noted her wink and subtle smile. He was old, but not so much that he missed her message. Like many of the local men, he had visited her on days that her kids were not around. But on this day, he had more serious matters on his mind.

Looking through the display window of the Angel Valley Mercantile, he saw Frank on a ladder adjusting items on a top shelf. A bell tinkled as Toby opened the door and entered the store. Blinking to adjust his eyes, he nodded as Frank twisted on the ladder to greet him. Toby was surprised to see a revolver holstered to his hip.

They met at the counter. Toby was surprised again to see the sheriff's badge pinned to the storekeepers shirt. He had heard about the sheriff's death, but hadn't heard about Frank replacing him.

"What can I help ya with this morning, Toby?"

"I'm lookin' for Hiram. Ya seen him?"

Frank fiddled with an octagon shaped jar of licorice, studying it closely. "I haven't seen him this morning. Ya check at the bank?"

"Yea! Frank, I wanta ask ya one more time about Camel. Can ya…"

The store clerk's face and posture stiffened. "Now, Toby, I know Camel was like a son to ya. I'm sorry he's disappeared. The truth is I've thought, talked and burned my brain tryin' to figure it out. But I got lotsa work to do here. Being the sheriff and runnin' the store makes it kinda hard on me."

Frank returned to his ladder. Without looking back, he said, "I gotta new load of barbed wire in last week, ya might wanta take a look at the new twist."

Outside, Toby stared down at a roll of gray barbed wire and thought of how the day before he'd found another cut in 3C wire. Judging from the tracks, about twenty steers were rustled. The same chipped horseshoe was there.

Down the walk, Stinky was sweeping the rough boards at the entrance of his saloon. He stopped intermittently to lean on his broom and look up the street. Taking a few more strokes, he leaned again and looked the other direction.

Toby removed his battered Stetson and whacked it against his knee. Placing his hat on his head, he headed for his horse. Out of town, he and his horse, Babs, would have a good talk and maybe she could help him make sense of it all. *She don't talk much, just whinnies every so often, but she's the best female listener I've ever known.*

Maggie smiled at Billy. He was in love with her and she knew it. She also knew the handwriting papers before her must be graded and she needed to be working. He had cleaned her chalk board, swept the floor, sharpened pencils with his pocket knife, and now had exhausted his range of skills.

"Billy, I appreciate your help. I'll look forward to seeing you again next week."

Disappointment settled on his boyish features. "How about those corner ceilings, don'tcha think I better sweep em' agin' before the spiders build their webs?"

"No, you got them last week. Besides, I really need to grade these papers."

He shifted awkwardly, stared at his boots, but continued leaning against her desk. Deciding to ignore him, she resumed her grading. He coughed and said haltingly, "Do ya miss Camel, Miss Maggie?"

The question startled her. She felt her cheeks flush. "Yes, yes I do, Billy. I never saw much of him, but like all of us, when I did, I enjoyed his company."

Billy fidgeted with an ink bottle on her desk. "Do ya think maybe we're all better off though because he's gone." Seeing the look on her face, rattled him. He squirmed and tried again, "Ya know, some folks say he was a bad man and that the town is better off without him. Do ya think that's true?"

"First, Billy, I'm concerned for his safety. Did he leave on his own, or did something awful happen to him? Second, I think no one should judge whether someone is fit to remain in our town or not unless that person breaks the law."

"Wouldja feel better if ya knew that he was alright when he left town, or was at least alive?"

Maggie stared at Billy. She knew he wanted very much to please her. Was this a simple attempt to do that? She had come to know him fairly well during the last year and his tone and expression piqued her interest. *Is Billy trying to tell me something about Camel? Could he possibly know what's happened to him?*

"Do you know what happened to him, Billy?" She immediately regretted her direct approach.

The question seemed to awake him from a lethargic daydream. Spinning, he laughed in an awkward way she had never heard before and made hastily for the door. "I better be goin' home, Miss Maggie before Mama starts lookin' for me."

Maggie sat for a long time at her desk staring out the door. The conversation left her unsettled. Finally, she returned to grading the writing papers.

A noise made her look up at the door. Hiram stood there grinning. He looked strange. His eyes...his expression...it hit her...he was drunk.

"Good evening, Hiram."

He held his silly grin as he walked down the row of desks toward her. He tottered a bit, but remained on his feet.

"You like working late, huh!"

He reached out and gripped the edge of her desk. She could smell him and he reeked of sweat and alcohol. Her voice held a tremor as she said, "Yes, I'm working late, trying to grade some students' work." She tried to smile, but knew it didn't work. "I can't honestly say I like it, but it's necessary."

His large frame loomed over her. "It's getting late, Maggie, let's go to my place and eat some of Juanita's cookin'."

Her face wouldn't work right. For the first time, he frightened her. She knew he had to hear the tremor now, "Thank you for the offer, Hiram, but I really enjoy walking after sitting for so long. Perhaps some..."

His grip on her wrist was quick and strong. "Now, Maggie, I'm not gonna take no for an answer. Juanita's fixin' one of her Mexican concoctions and I can vouch for her good cookin'. You can't hurt her feelings like that. Come on, I got my surrey waitin' and we gonna..."

She started to utter a protest, but his grip tightened. His face was only inches from hers and he grinned wider. She stared up at him for a long moment. There was no need to scream...there was no one around. "Hiram, you're hurting my arm."

He slowly released her, but did not move or stop grinning. "Our chariot awaits us, Madam."

With great trepidation, she rose, closed her closet door, and walked toward the entrance with Hiram. The thought occurred to her to run from him, but she gave that up as she stepped onto the porch and felt his beefy hand take her arm and assist her into his carriage.

CHAPTER 11

Men dying of thirst in the desert, have been known to stuff sand and cactus in their mouths.

Two nights of walking and trying to sleep during the heat of the day, but what did he have to show for it? Out of water, no food, and being totally lost, struck fear within Camel. How could he have missed the railroad track? It was almost dawn and he still had not seen nor heard anything of a train. He had tried to walk according to the stars, but had obviously walked a crooked line or even in a circle.

Forcing himself to walk until first light, he felt sick seeing the purple mountains in the distant looking exactly as they did yesterday. The terrain was more desert-like and he felt sure he had moved further into the Chihuahua. What should he do? Looking back at his tracks, he made a decision, he would backtrack to Bone's place again for water. He would have to do it during daylight; he could not see his tracks at night. But that would mean walking during the heat of the day, without water. Could he make it back to the spring? Should he continue searching for the railroad tracks? What should he do?

Climbing a scruffy knoll, he saw his meandering tracks. His heart sank. The brilliant morning light showed him tracks that curved and zigzagged. The blazing orb rising in the east bathed him with its blinding glare and seemed to laugh at his attempt to walk due south. It's position told him he had veered to the east.

He laughed. He laughed the hysterical laugh of an insane man. *I walk like I'm drunk even when I'm sober. The only two things I can do well is play poker and drink.*

A salty tear touched his lips; he was laughing and crying at the same time.

Wiping his face with a dirty sleeve, he worked to gain control of himself. This was no time to lose it. *I gotta think clearly.*

He agonized again with decision-making. He faced two choices: correct his direction and head south to find the railroad tracks, or trace his own tracks back to the spring. He decided on the spring.

By midday, he was in trouble. Trudging on, sometime in early afternoon, he collapsed in the partial shade of a buckhorn bush and drifted into a semi-sleep. He dreamed he was playing stud poker in hell. It was a terrible hell because there was a barroom and poker to play, but no beer or whiskey.

Frank stood before the large display window of his store. It was dusk outside and darker within. He felt comfortable in his privacy. Using the window as a dim mirror, he practiced his fast draw. His revolver was empty, enabling him to snap on an empty chamber following each draw.

He was thinking about the city council meeting tomorrow evening. Hiram had already persuaded the other members to hire him as sheriff on a temporary basis, but he wanted the job to be a permanent one. Hiram had given him some notes to read and memorize. He'd gone over them numerous times and could regurgitate every word. This was his dream come true and he wasn't going to blow it.

He knew well how people looked at you if you were a stogy store clerk versus the lawman in town. He had seen it in Del Rio years ago, when he shot and killed a man attempting to rob his store. *It wasn't my fault that I shot him in the back. He shoulda give me more time to make my play. He challenged me and while I'm studying him, he turns to ride off.*

His face burned and he fumbled the draw as he recalled the sheriff ordering him to leave the territory. The lawman gave him credit for stopping a suspected murderer and known horse thief. He promised to keep it a secret about the back shot, but he wanted Frank out of Del Rio. The sheriff had said the man might have family or friends who could show up to make trouble, but Frank suspected another reason. He knew the sheriff was jealous of him and feared Frank was a threat to his own job.

Tiring of drawing practice, he reloaded his pistol, holstered it, and craned his neck down to see the badge. He pulled it up as far as his shirt would allow and blew on it. Polishing it with his sleeve, he admired it for a long moment and then locked his store and left.

Turning toward the saloon, he began his nightly inspection. He planned to make himself highly visible to the town people. The sheriff's job was about law and order, but it was also about politics. Dan Libby never understood that. He was not as visible as he should have been, nor as political as he should have been.

Entering the saloon, Frank eyeballed the room and finding only two men at a table drinking and talking quietly, he sauntered to the bar. Stinky nodded to him. *That's right ya little weasel bastard, you're lots nicer now that I'm wearing this badge ain'tcha.*

The bartender placed a clean glass on the bar and filled it with root beer. Saying nothing, only nodding, Frank sipped it. Stinky made conversation, Frank nodded in agreement without talking. Turning and tipping his hat at the men, the lawman grunted and walked out.

Moving down the walk, he heard one of the Beaumont boys yelling. The mother answered with a string of profanities. Shaking his head in disapproval, he walked quickly toward their house.

Standing at the door of the run-down house, he banged on it. Meeting only silence, he spoke in a loud voice. "If I hear any more loud talk outta the Beaumont's tonight, somebody's gonna spend the night in my jail." He liked the sound of it being his jail. He hoped several other people heard him warning this white trash family. It was obvious to him, Hiram wanted them outta town. Frank would not be as tolerant to the trash as Sheriff Libby had been.

It was now dark. Pausing at the end of the boarded walkway, with one hand resting on the grip of his pistol, and the other on a supporting beam, he turned his head to the street to see Hiram's tassel-fringed buggy pass by. The big bay was pulling it faster than usual. *Hiram must be in a hurry for Juanita's cooking or maybe Carmen's got something waitin' for him tonight.* Hiram's deep laugh sounded and Frank wondered who was riding with him.

Stepping from the boards, he walked quietly in the direction of Hiram's house. He could not see much, but made out voices. It was Maggie, the school marm. She sounded different. Her voice held a note of fear, anger, or something. *What in the hell is goin' on with Hiram and the teacher? We all know he wants her, but she hasn't exactly appeared too warm to the idea.*

Squeaking sounds followed by the sound of a slap, made Frank stop walking. It was dark, but he definitely did not want to be seen, so he squatted, making a smaller silhouette. Hiram laughed; Maggie cried. More sounds of protests and physical interaction were heard as the two moved from the buggy to the house.

Frank stood to leave. This was none of his business. Returning to the boarded walk, he headed home. He was tired. It was fun being sheriff, but it was wearisome too. He well knew that as the town's chief lawman, it was as important what he did not see and hear as what he did see and hear.

Maggie hated herself for crying. Her face stung from the slap, but the tears were the result of anger more than pain. She was also afraid. She had never seen Hiram like this. He was obviously drunk and mean.

They sat at the table which Juanita had set with a full meal of fried pork chops, baked potatoes, baked bread, and summer squash. Hiram dismissed Juanita as he entered the room holding Maggie's arm.

"Hiram Bishop, just know that I will report you to the sheriff in the morning, and if he's in your pocket, like everyone claims, than I will appear before the city council meeting tomorrow night and report your behavior. If they fail to act, then I will appear before the judge on his next visit. This is kidnapping."

Hiram grinned and drooled. Maggie stared at the crazed drunk before her. He met her stare as he missed her glass and poured wine onto the white crocheted table cloth. He held his devious grin and said, "I heard some gossip about you today, Maggie."

She sat silent, stiff and cold. The clocks chimed and she jumped. He laughed a deep, nasty sound that chilled her. She fought to remain calm and focused all of her mental and physical resources on gaining control of the situation.

He said, "A little horsey told me he saw you in a buggy with Camel. He said…"

"I don't care what your little gossipy horsey told you. If I was with Camel, it's my business. If you want to make it an issue with the city council…do it."

Hiram smirked as he sipped a drink, "Are ya gonna go back to the north with a bad reputation and be known as a quitter?" He chuckled, wiped his mouth with the back of his hand and said, "Ya gonna go back and be known as an adulterer?"

"I'll do whatever I have to do. Living in this place is not a pleasure. Connecticut is heaven compared to this backwater area. I'll miss the children and some of the adults, but, I'm…"

He leaned forward, grinning at her, "A letter from our township will be sent to your pastor and the school superintendent of your district. With that, you'll not be employed anywhere. Ya won't be welcome in a lotta circles either."

They exchanged stares; hers icy, his glazed. Hiram was confirming her suspicions. He was blackmailing her. *You bastard! There's truth in what you're saying. I was in the buggy with Camel and allowed myself to lose control. And now, someone's told you, and you're pouncing on it like a hungry cur would attack a piece of raw meat.*

His hand clamped onto her wrist. He breathed heavy as he stood and pulled her to him. *"Thy breasts are like two young roes that are twins.* Song of Solomon, chapter seven, verse two." He held her in his vise-like grip and kissed her. She struggled, but was helplessly overpowered.

Riding the fence line kept Toby from having to return to the ranch and face unpaid employees. He knew he had to do it, but he was in no hurry. *Payin' the hands is only part of the problem. How do ya run a outfit without money? I know the bank has always been lenient, allowing me to conduct business without my name on the accounts. But, dammit, everyone in this territory knows the circumstances at the 3C. They also know I'm an honest man.*

His eyes were focused on the fence and he did not see the man until he was almost on top of him. He jerked his reins in surprise and stared at Bryant Williams, foreman of Hiram's Rocking H spread. The rider sat loosely in the saddle with one leg arched over the saddle horn as he rolled a smoke. Toby's eyes took in the Colt holstered on his hip.

For a long moment the only sounds were the nicker of a horse that Toby could not spot and a quail whistling his poignant tune somewhere in the scrubs. Bryant studied his rolled smoke. His voice was low and flat. "I hear you've been checkin' out horses, Toby. Seems like ya like mine. I thought I ought to tell ya, he's not for sale."

Toby felt his voice raise an octave in anger, "I was lookin' for a certain chipped shoe and I found it on your horse."

Bryant's eyes were cold and his voice flat. With the rolled smoke dangling from his thin lips, he struck a block match against his tight Levi's, lit up, and tossed the match onto the ground. For the first time he faced Toby. "Whatcha gittin' at Old Man?"

"Somebody's rustlin' 3C steers and that track was there every time."

"Are ya accusing me of being a rustler, Old Man?"

Bryant's hand rested lightly on his pistol grip. Toby knew that it was a not too subtle threat. His own Winchester rested in it's scabbard and he could not pull it before he was shot out of the saddle.

Another long pause was broken by Toby's horse shaking his neck, fluffing his mane and snorting. Bryant smiled through the smoke that wafted around his hardened features, "I think ya better listen to your hoss, Old Man. Ya not usin' ya head. Ya slipped back to your younger days and using that old Indian style of reading tracks. That chip could be on a dozen horses and as for the rustlin', well, we had some of that at Rockin' H too."

Toby took a deep breath. He made himself relax in the saddle. His options were limited, so no need to bust a gut over it in front of this slimy hard-ass.

Bryant seemed to relax too, "I saw the fence cuttin' on your side and I found it on our east side too. They picked up a lot more steers of ours than of yours and their tracks disappeared on the hard bottom of Rondo's flat."

Toby showed no sign of acknowledgement. He sat impassive, staring coldly at the man in front of him. *Ya lyin' piece of cowshit.*

Bryant blew a smoke ring, examining it as he spoke, "You should know, Old Man, this is dangerous country. Be careful who ya accuse of rustlin' or ya could end up disappearin' like your no-count boss."

Toby lost his patience. He felt his hands tremble with rage. His horse mistook the movement in the reins and moved into a walk. Reining up hard, Toby said, "I don't scare easy, Calf-Boy."

The foreman's boot found his stirrups as he sat stiff in the saddle, "Don't be runnin' around at night touching my horse again, Old Man, or it'll be the last one ya ever touch." With that, he turned his mount and trotted away.

Toby stared at the man's back. He thought how he would be doing the world a favor by shooting him out of the saddle, but back-shooting was not in him. The nicker of the horse earlier reminded him that more Rocking H men could be in the clump of cottonwoods sighting him down the barrel of a rifle. Shaking his reins, he headed toward the ranch to tell the men he could not pay them.

Kilkenny's body swayed rhythmically with the gait of his horse. He looked to the east, but it was a ruse. He was using his peripheral vision to scan Sans who always rode drag. The half-breed was aware of what he was doing and made sure he was sharpening his knife or fiddling with his rifle each time.

Kilkenny hated this group. He made a stupid choice to throw in with these cut-throats. He was wanted in Texas and Mexico, but for robbing banks, and having to shoot a couple of people, not killing groups of people for no reason. He had robbed three banks in Sonora and never harmed a soul. After he agreed to go with them, he had observed first-hand, Big Boy and Sans shoot down poor Mexicans, eaten their frijoles, and then laughed as they burned their shacks down.

He recalled the first time he saw Eunice. At first, he had paid for her services like every other cowboy or vaquero, but after a short time, she quit prostituting and swore her love for him. They had even talked of going north, get through Texas quick and quiet, and head for the Colorado country and start over.

As they talked and planned, he was not really serious about settling down with her; he just wanted female companionship on the long ride. After they set out and he saw how determined she was to please him, for the first time in many years, he felt something for a woman other than lust and contempt.

Sighting a troop of Federales and thinking they were after them, he made the bad decision to join this group. Later, he awoke to the realization that Big Boy, Sans, and Jones were the ones being pursued.

Men taking advantage of Eunice was the sort of thing that never bothered him in the past. But this time was different. He avoided her eyes and felt terrible for getting both of them into this mess.

Eyeing the half-breed from the corner of his eye, he felt hatred, fear and loathing for the man. If Big Boy were not present, he would challenge the sick little bastard. Kilkenny had always been handy with the kicker on his hip and did not fear one man, but no way would he survive taking on the two of them. He racked his brain to figure out something for he and Eunice or they would not make it out of this one alive. The hairs on his neck raised hearing Sans laugh quietly in his wheezing manner as though he were reading his thoughts.

CHAPTER 12

For gunfights, Texas was the most violent western area. Roughly 160 shooting incidents occurred there during the gunfighters' era.

The stars sparkled in the indigo sky. They were beautiful and they were dry. Camel struggled to his feet, using the rifle as a cane, and wished he had died in his sleep. Staggering and stumbling, he cussed in a hoarse whisper when it felt like a mountain fell on his back, driving him to the ground and knocking the wind from his lungs. He couldn't breathe. A tight band around his throat cut off his air. His fingers clawed at it, but the leather strip was buried in his throat.

He heard a grunt and realized he'd been attacked from behind. With all his strength, he heaved himself up, feeling two bodies slide off each side of his back. The garrote tightened. He felt himself blacking out. His right elbow shot back and struck ribs. A grunt of pain sounded in his ear. The noose loosened. His left elbow shot back but found little. The pressure increased; he felt himself slipping into unconsciousness. The dark figures were grasping his arms when he heard what sounded like a voice from far away say, "Stop! Stop! It's Camel! The white eye at Bones's."

Camel rubbed his stinging throat and took giant breaths. His heart felt like it would explode in his chest. As his vision improved, he surveyed the scene before him. The moonlight showed him two small Indians and a larger one. Leaning forward, he recognized Little Sun's smiling white teeth. He didn't recognize the other smaller one, but was glad it was not Little Knife. The larger Indian,

Spirit Dog, tied the strip of rawhide around his waist and said, "Come, Camel."

Little Sun held his rifle and Camel fell in behind Spirit Dog. A large clump of Spanish bayonets became a horse which Spirit Dog led. A walk of a hundred or so feet and the lead Indian stopped and howled like a coyote. Camel felt a shiver run up his spine as the clumps of barrel cactus and Spanish bayonets came alive.

Indians gathered around him; their silence was unnerving. He was relieved when he sighted Father Pollen's humped figure leaning on a limb. "Camel! What are you doing here?"

"Tryin' to make my way to the train tracks so I can get outta this desert and back to Angel Valley."

Someone spoke the priest's name. Father Pollen paused and then said, "Excuse me for a moment, Camel."

The little man disappeared into the lump of dark figures. Camel worked to stay calm. Someone said something and several giggles were heard. The Indians surrounding him, appeared to draw closer. In a minute, the faces parted and Father Pollen reappeared. "We've got to be moving! Come with us!"

"But are ya headed south toward the tracks?"

A sound and then another one from the dark, made the little man step closer to Camel, his voice held fear, "There's no time to talk now, we gotta move. Follow me."

At that moment, he felt something jabbing his side and he automatically grasped the stock of his rifle which Little Sun gave him. Camel started to protest being forced to accompany them, but the shadows thinned and in the next moment, he was walking single-file behind the priest. If he walked too slow, someone behind him stepped on his heels. He turned once in pain and saw a familiar face. It was his former drinking buddy, Skinyas, the one whose tus he won. The thought of the strong tasting beer made him hurt just thinking about the wonderful taste and effect.

The speed of the group amazed him. He focused on walking in the footprints of the hobbling priest. He became aware of a strange sound and realized it emerged from Father Pollen. Every step produced a high-pitched whine. The man must be in pain and reflected it in a sound that he was oblivious to. Camel tried not to think of what his presence meant to this group. What would the morning bring? Would Skinyas and Little Knife lead other braves to kill him? Would the little priest banish him and leave him in an area even more remote and removed from his destination? Another sound emerged from behind him; he concluded it was Skinyas grunting each time he aimed his foot for Camel's heel and missed.

Maggie and Reverend Bilbo McKenzie stared at one another. He was thinking he should not have gotten out of bed and confronted her as she entered, but it was too late for that now. "We've been worried about you, Maggie! I'm relieved to see that you're alright."

He had not lit a lamp leaving her face lost in a shadow. But he could sense by her breathing that something was wrong. She had never come home this late on a week night before. "Are you alright, Maggie?"

Her voice was tremulous, "I was grading papers at the school and fell asleep. I'm fine, thank you."

The pastor's wife called from their bedroom, "What's wrong, Bilbo? Is she still not in her room?"

"She's here, Dear, and she's fine."

Maggie brushed past him, entered her bedroom and closed her door. He frowned. Something was definitely wrong. Was it alcohol he smelled on her? There was another smell, he knew it-- Hiram's cigar smoke.

His wife called again and as he shuffled toward her, he felt uneasy about the incident.

"Where in the world has she been at this hour?" his wife asked.

Her accusatory tone irritated him, but this was no time for an argument. Faking a yawn, he rolled away from her and said in his sleepiest voice, "She fell asleep at the school grading papers. I figured that would happen sooner or later."

"Won't you have to report her to the board for this? She's not supposed to…"

The glee in her voice angered him; he could not restrain the anger in his own. "For heaven's sake, she fell asleep working for the community's children. Would you please allow us to go back to sleep?"

Both lay awake for the next half-hour. Whenever he finally heard her even breathing, he slipped quietly from his covers and tip-toed to Maggie's door. Placing his ear to it, he heard her soft crying. Retreating to the small sitting room, he sat in the dark and stared into the blackness of the fireplace.

Camel slept; Father Pollen shivered. He made sure Little Sun was sleeping a few feet behind Camel so as to watch his back. He knew both Skinyas and Little Knife had their reason to hate the white eye. The priest now huddled beside a waist-high rock several yards away from Camel and the remainder of the group. He was one of four hunched figures who had met to make plans. A desert breeze tousled his thin hair. He pulled at the wool blanket around his humped back and narrow shoulders. The eastern sky lightened with a pink glow. The sun would appear anytime.

Anrelina's large dark brown eyes touched briefly on each one, then settled on the priest. "This man, Camel, is a threat to all of us. He has already shown us that." The men were silent. Naltzukich huffed with anger, "He is a weak and bad man, the worst kind. The first time the soldiers get close, he might signal them and cost us all our lives. We had to leave him once before because of the trouble he caused us. We must do it again. Only this time, we cannot allow him to follow us."

Anrelina said in her soft, lilting voice, "The direction we will go, trying to cross the desert, will take all our strength, skill and water. We will do well to have enough water for our children."

A quail sounded its three notes, the last one weak, typical of the desert species. Father Pollen knew they were right. Camel was a scoundrel who demonstrated a desire only for alcohol. The priest was shocked at how different the man looked--shaggy, thinner, but eyes that still reflected the sickness of alcoholism. Deprivation and difficulty had not seeded any improvement in the man's character. The priest was sure of that.

This was no time for a sermon. It was decision time. He looked directly at the old Indian, Naiche, "I agree with them. What do you say?" The old man nodded in agreement.

The priest scowled, "I agree we cannot allow him to accompany us, but I will not agree to harming the man in any way in order to insure that he will not follow us."

Naiche said little, but when he did speak, his words found receptive ears. He lifted his hand slightly; all looked at him. "I will do it." Turning to his friend, he said, "I will not harm him."

No one dared ask how the old stooped Indian would do it. His presence and demeanor eliminated any questions. Naiche endured their gazes, staring ahead stoically.

Camel smiled in his sleep. His dream transported him to the Blue Diamond Saloon in Carson City where he once won over four hundred dollars in a poker game. The owner of the establishment, a sexy woman in her early forties, had invited him into her luxurious suite where they drank high-priced booze and made love for a week.

The mood in the bunkhouse was tense. Toby had just informed the five ranch hands he did not have their pay. They had cleaned up and were prepared for a big night at Stinky's and maybe a romp in a feather bed with Queenie Beaumont when they received the disappointing announcement.

Olsen, the youngest hand and the largest, at six foot four and well over two hundred pounds, stood with hands on hips facing his weary foreman who sat on a wooden bench with his back against the wall. "When will we get it, Toby?"

Toby was chewing and rolled the wad around in his mouth, appearing not to hear the question. Silence settled over the group. Olsen shifted, his face reddened, he opened his mouth to repeat the question when Toby responded, "I don't rightly know when I can pay ya. Maybe next week, next month, maybe never. I don't know."

August, a seasoned ranch hand, frowned and said quietly, "I've always found ya to be more than a fair boss, Toby, but a man can't be expected to work for nothing."

Toby made the bucket ring with a spit of brown tobacco juice. He stood, seemed to come alive. "Ya right about that, August. I suggest we work a settlement and ya look for work elsewhere."

Olsen asked, "What kinda settlement?"

"Ya rode in here on a broken down nag, the horse ya planning to ride to town is a 3C smooth ridin' mare. I suggest ya leave your nag here and ride away on that mare. The same deal is offered to each man who wants it."

By noon the following day, only Fuzzy, almost as old as Toby, was still riding for the 3C. The others had packed their gear and rode off on their newly acquired horses. Olsen had been the last one to leave. He surprised Toby by giving him a bear hug rather than shaking his hand like the other hands had done. Toby thought he saw tears in the young giant's eyes as he tried to speak, "You've been like a father to..." Shaking his head, he turned suddenly and rode away.

The two men leaned against a corral. Toby chewed while Fuzzy rolled a smoke. Neither man spoke for a long while. The noon day sun made the distant horizon ripple and dance with heat. Fuzzy spoke first, "Seems to me, ya gotta puma by the tail. The powers that be, and we all know who that is around here, is jus' gonna squeeze ya like a chicken snake coils and chokes a quail."

Toby nodded and spit. Fuzzy blew smoke, coughed, and said, "Hiram Bishop's hands are gonna cut our fences, rustle our steers until there's nothing left here."

The foreman stared straight ahead. After a long minute, he spit again and said in a low voice, "I guess we'll hang on as long as we can. When there's nothing left, then we'll go too. In the meantime, you and me gotta watch our backs and each others back."

Hiram sat on the side of his bed with his face buried in his hands. Moonlight cast eerie shadows through the room. Standing, his fists trembled as he shrieked the cry of a banshee. He dropped to all fours and sobs racked his massive frame.

After a while, he grew quiet. He knew what he had to do. His voice was deep and wracked with guilt. "Be not wise in thine own eyes: fear the Lord and depart from evil. Proverbs, chapter four, verse seven."

Less than a half-hour later, Cholla scooped the gold pieces from the table and pocketed them. "How many?"

Hiram shook his head and mumbled, "Until you get tired, Cholla."

Later, Hiram laid in bed on his stomach. He spoke to his feather mattress in a monotone, "I try to make the world a better place. I work hard at maintaining law and order and stability in this town. I lend money to those in need. I chair the council. I look after the widow women and even their children. I 've done everything I know to do to make Maggie see that she should submit to me and become my wife." He sniffed, grunted in pain, turned his head and continued, "Maybe I'm trying too hard. Maybe I'm too good for my own good. Is that the lesson the Lord's trying to teach me? Maybe I..." He entered a restless, tortured sleep.

CHAPTER 13

Whites encountering Indians for the first time often reported they smelled of smoke, fur, and wild tanned leather.

A fly buzzed his nose. Camel shifted and ignored it. The insect landed on his upper lip. He swatted at it, but felt his hand stop short. Opening his eyes, he saw that his wrists and ankles were tied and staked with rawhide. The rawhide seemed to tighten each time he stressed it. Squinting up at the sun, he estimated it was late morning.

A small tus rested on the blanket beside him. Reaching carefully within his range of motion, he lifted the rough-hewn container and found it to be full. His heart raced, but a sip told him it was water, not Indian beer.

Lifting his head as high as possible, he saw only bayonets, yuccas, various cacti and tumble weeds atop sun-scalded sand. There was no sign of the priest or the Morning People. *Looks like they've done it to you again, Camel old boy.*

He was glad he lay within the partial shade of a scrawny madrone tree. His rifle lay close beside him. For what it was worth, he figured he had enough motion to use it if necessary. *I can use my rifle. I probably should use it on myself.*

Forcing himself to think positive, he assessed his situation. He was confined to this spot, but enjoyed a range of motion that allowed him to drink water and fire his rifle. Staring at the tus, he knew he should be grateful, but he wasn't. He was mad as hell. He wanted a drink that would quieten the demons deep within him.

His eyes brightened with thought. Slowly, he reached for his knife in his back pocket. His fingers fumbled with the leather sheath, but the knife was gone. In hot anger, he jerked both hands up with all of his might and was rewarded with stinging, throbbing wrists.

He lay back on his blanket listening to the ebb and flow of sounds around him. Everything was free except him. Desert quail, mockingbirds, the thump of a running black-tailed jackrabbit, a screeching hawk, all reflected the myriad of life enjoying movement, and all he could do was struggle to free himself. Camel lifted his head and ran his eyes along the scruffy desert horizon. He saw something. His heart raced. He yelled. Another couple of minutes and two lean, dour-faced Indians stood above him. Camel thought of the little priest and figured he had persuaded them to return and free him. They made no move to do it. One spoke in his native language; the other nodded and knelt beside Camel.

"Who did this to you?"

The Indian's English was good. His question surprised Camel. *They're not the Morning People.* He felt a pang of fear. *Are they dangerous?* Stories he had heard all of his life about Indians torturing whites flooded his mind. Straining on the rawhide without appearing to, only made it tighten and hurt more.

An Indian picked up the rifle and examined it. Camel felt a surge of fear. Would he be killed with his own weapon? He told them his story. Again they spoke in their own tongue. Camel pleaded, "I'd appreciate it if you'd untie me. I uh…" He stopped and stared as the Indian who had spoken to him, bent down and tied a grimy bandanna around his mouth. Camel twisted, violently rolled his head, strained every limb, grunted and growled like a wild animal, all to no avail. The dirty cloth bit into the sides of his mouth and he tasted blood.

The Indian's disappeared behind him. He heard a couple of thumps, horse hooves moving away. A little over an hour later, he had succeeded in chewing through the bandanna. Both wrists were bleeding, but he felt the stake binding his right arm give a little. Another hour and he had freed himself entirely.

It was getting dark. The western sky was turning rosy pink. Drinking from the tus, he contemplated his next move. He was ravenous for food and alcohol. He knew there was no chance for the latter, but he would begin hunting for the former. Then he saw it, a small rawhide bag close to the bayonet. It contained something dried, smelled spoiled, but his ravenous appetite kicked in and he began chewing. He was thankful for strong teeth. The dried meat of unknown origin was tough, but tasted better the more he ate. Washing down a swallow of it, he forced himself to limit the amount he ate. He would need it later.

He knew these were gifts from the Morning People and not his last visitors. He was surprised and pleased that the two had not taken his rifle, food and water. In the distance a coyote, barked, yelped and howled mournfully. The creature repeated the cycle for as long as Camel was awake.

Laying down on his blanket, he blew on his stinging wrists and wished he had ointment to doctor them. He began to formulate a plan. In the morning, he would head south again. This time he must succeed. What about the two Indians? What were they doing? Why did they gag him? He felt sure they were not part of the Morning People. But who were they? He gave up trying to figure it out and his mind, as usual, returned to drinking, card playing, drinking, women, drinking, bluffing his way out of tight spots, and another night of tormented sleep.

Captain Verlander scowled at his scouts. They were telling him the renegades had headed straight into the desert. This did not make sense. He studied them for a long moment, but then gave up on reading them. Their expressions were totally passive and told him nothing. Were they telling him this figuring he would give up and turn back?

He had taken to viewing the scouts as much as possible with his spy glass. The problem was the uneven terrain. He would follow them visually while they were a couple of miles out, but they would disappear into a draw and either reappear an hour later, or, approach him from behind.

"Show me the sign."

He had started insisting they show him evidence of the renegades. The trouble with that was he was convinced they faked it sometimes. A broken saltbush might have been smashed by the foot of the runaways or by one of the scouts. The captain now insisted on seeing more than one sign. He was beginning to learn to track himself. He dreamed of the day he would become a proficient tracker and then he would look for a tree tall enough to hang both of the scouts.

In the meantime, he must play the game and outguess them. *What if the lying bastards are telling the truth this time? What if the renegades have become so desperate they're willing to risk their asses in the desert? What do I do?* Returning to Fort Stockton in failure would mean the end of his career. He realized he was standing in the stirrups for relief. Easing himself onto the rock-hard saddle, he motioned for the scouts to lead him to the sign that indicated the runaways had headed into the Chihuahua Desert.

Following them, his mind conjured up some of the horror stories he'd heard about the desert. The Chihuahua Desert had a notorious reputation for swallowing people up who had the audacity and stupidity to tackle it head on. The Captain was a newcomer to these parts, but he'd been here long enough to hear numerous tales of the danger of the hot, dry, drifting sands that robbed a man of his water and then his strength, resolve, mind, and finally his life. The heat of the desert was supposed to be the closest a man could come to the fires of hell, according to a frontier preacher he had heard back at Fort Stockton.

The captain squeezed his temples with one hand as he struggled with his physical problems. He struggled internally even more with the mental challenge of decision-making. Did he make a wise decision leading his men into the desert to catch these ragamuffins who were led by an insane, religious fanatic whose reasoning was totally nonexistent? Twenty minutes later, he stood staring at the tell-tale signs. Even he could read these tracks and determine their direction. They were moving southeast, straight into the heart of the desert country. *Maybe they're playing with us. Are they trying to make us think they are going to cross the Chihuahua so we'll turn back and then when its safe for them, they backtrack?*

The captain and the two scouts stood holding the reins to their mounts, while the company of soldiers behind them dismounted, tightened cinches, pulled sweet life-giving liquid from their canteens and groused among themselves. The captain's head pounded, his ass hurt constantly, and to make matters worse, he'd had diarrhea for the last two days.

Wiping his forehead with his sleeve, he made a decision. "I'm sending men back to the old timer's spring for water and another group to hunt game." He squinted and spoke harshly to the scouts, "You two will split up. One will head north with an escort and one of you will head south with an escort. You'll skirt the desert for twenty miles to see if they head back. If they don't, within two days, we'll have enough food and water to go after 'em."

Holy shit! I can only pray that they pick up signs of the bastards heading outta the desert. Maybe after a couple of days dealin' with the conditions, they'll decide to give up and gent their asses back to the fort.

The captain had given up trying to employ logic to the renegades. When logic told him they would take the easiest route, they took the more difficult one. When they should have encountered starvation a month ago, they had found food. When local residents should have been reporting a group of Indians roaming the territory, hardly a peep was heard. The captain stood in his stirrups, dug at the seat of his pants, and became aware that he was frowning and shaking his head at the bizarre actions of the renegades.

Dismounting, he motioned the lieutenant and sergeant to do the same. He spoke sharply, "Men, we will succeed. The sooner we catch these dangerous animals, the sooner we'll all be back at the fort lookin' for some liberty, whisky and women." He paused, stepped forward with his sweaty, bearded, sun-crusted face inches from the scouts faces, "Catch these people or we will all die out here. And I promise you, I will personally gut shoot each one of you before one of my men dies. Is that understood?"

The stoic faces stared back at him. He glared, determined to win the contest. After a long minute, he said in a high, tension-tight voice, "Now get the hell outta my sight."

Judah lifted the wagon bed while Pearl slipped the wheel onto the axle. He kept glancing at the barn door. After the look Hiram had given him, he didn't want to repeat the incident. Judah was a simple man. He only wanted to work, care for his children, and enjoy the warmth of a good woman. He had given up on the latter following his wife's death. Lately though, as he worked his ranch, he often thought of Pearl. *A man don't have to be too smart to see that the river runs right through both our lives. But if she's Hiram's woman, then I could be askin' to have him call the note due on my place.*

A half hour later, they sat together on the front steps sipping Sweetwater. Pearl knew he liked her. She sensed him eyeing her when he thought she was unaware of it. Judah was a good man; she was a good woman. She knew that according to big city eastern standards, theirs was hardly an ideally romantic situation, but this was not an eastern big city. This was the Pecos region of west Texas. She desperately needed a good man to help her run the ranch and raise the boys. By his comments, she could tell he was struggling with raising his own children.

Judah was not a handsome man by any criteria. She remembered the first time she saw him. She thought he was almost comical the way his neck drooped from his shoulders and his expression appeared like he was sleep-walking. But she saw him differently now. The eyes that seemed to hold no depth of thought at first, actually reflected an intelligent and sensitive man who held to simple values and ethics, who wanted only to love and be loved.

Which is exactly what I want. But he's jittery. I guess he's concerned that Hiram might come bustin' in any time. Hell, I'm concerned about the same thing.

An hour later, they were still yakking on the steps when the wagon dropped her boys off. Judah shook their hands and treated them with polite dignity. Pearl wasn't sure how they would all hit it off, but it brought tears to her eyes to hear Judah ask the boy's questions and the way they answered; bashful at first, but soon losing their shyness and enjoying his company. She and the boys stood in the yard waving him off. The boys were excited because he had promised he would bring each one a black and tan hound puppy when they were weaned in a couple of weeks. His eyes found Pearl as he told the boys if they worked with their dogs, they would more than feed themselves by the rabbits they caught and quail they flushed. The boys grinned wide as he told them he would help them train the dogs.

As Pearl and the boys entered their slatted house, she felt giddy with happiness for a moment until she thought of Hiram. She spoke too harshly to Floyd when he playfully pushed Ralph. She knew the boys had relished the attention that Judah had heaped upon them. It made her ache all over to think how they were all starved for a solid relationship with a good man.

"Doggone it, Babs, I wish ya would stop lookin so pretty and frisky and tell me what I'm gonna have to do to save..." Toby stopped in mid-sentence when he smelled dust. Reining up, he peered through Cottonwoods to see two riders driving a dozen or so 3C steers. Pulling his Winchester from it's scabbard, he nudged Babs through the trees to a rise where he dismounted. From this spot he saw four riders at work driving steers through a cut fence.

By dammit! There he is--Bryant Williams, Hiram's foreman, rustling 3C steers. Leaning against a tree, he watched as Bryant Williams yelled and waved a looped lariat. The rider's were less than a hundred yards from him. Toby felt the heat rise in his face and his heart pump faster. Raising his rifle, he sighted Bryant's chest. He couldn't do it. *There was a time when I coulda laid all four of 'em out before they could get outta sight. But no more. Last year I had to take the trigger guard off my rifle cuz my arthritis has my finger joints so swollen, my finger couldn't fit in it. My eyes ain't so good either like they once was. And I hate to admit it, but I just can't kill a man like I once could.*

Studying the scene before him, Toby knew what discretion dictated--sit tight and let them go. He couldn't do that. He couldn't shoot the men. What could he do? As he anguished over his plight, a steer bolted and ran for the trees where Toby stood. The foreman was nearest to the steer and gave chase. Toby found himself looking at Williams riding straight toward him. He knew that the shade and thickness of the trees would hide him, and he saw an opportunity to stop this craziness.

Taking sight, he did something he hated, but had no choice. He aimed for the center of William's big brown gelding's head. His rifle thundered within the canopy of the trees. The slug entered the skull of Bryant's horse just above the right eye. The animal collapsed instantly, sending Bryant tumbling off. The foreman was stunned by the impact for a moment, shook the cobwebs from his head, snatched his hat and scampered up. Toby's next slug kicked dust an inch from the cow thief's boot. A half dozen years ago, he'd have shot the hat from his head, but he was no longer confident of his vision or steadiness of hand to attempt the shot.

For a moment, Toby thought there might be a gunfight as the riders pulled their six shooters and looked toward the trees. Bryant's command made the rider closest to him holster his gun and ride in a gallop toward him. Bryant jumped on the back of the horse and riding double, they disappeared in a cloud of dust.

As they rode away, Toby leaned against a tree, realizing he was panting. His heart pounded in his temples and chest. It had been many a year since he'd fired a gun in anger. He knew he had won today; he'd saved some steers. He also knew the conflict between he and Bryant had been moved up a notch. He had begun the shooting and Hiram's henchmen would welcome the opportunity to finish it.

Maggie avoided the eyes of the pastor during breakfast. She knew he was observing her closely and she worked to appear as though everything was normal. Maggie prepared the eggs, grits and ham for Bilbo and herself. Nausea welled up within her and she fought to contain it.

Bilbo's wife laid in bed. In the beginning of Maggie's contract period, the wife had fixed breakfast, but soon said she was too ill to do it. Maggie had her doubts about the woman. At least twice, Maggie had come home earlier than usual and caught her standing, singing and acting normal. Each time when she saw Maggie, she acted sick and retreated to her bedroom. Maggie thought the woman's problems were mental rather than physical. Of course she could not share her ideas with the pastor. *Is she unable to shoulder the load of being a pastor's wife? Is she mentally ill? Is she jealous of me? Could she want attention? Does she simply want to get out of this town? If it's the latter, I can relate to her. Hiram raped me. HIRAM RAPED ME!*

The thought had no impact upon her. She knew she was in shock. Images of the night before flashed before her. It was like she was watching someone else; it could not be happening to her.

Noting a bruise on her wrist, she turned her arm so that Bilbo would not see it. She hoped the powder adequately covered the dark bruise on her cheek where Hiram had slapped her. Last night more than confirmed everything she had ever thought about him. *He's a wretched bastard!* Camel came to mind. What a difference! He might be a scalawag, but he was a man who knew how to treat a woman. He was gentle and sensitive where Hiram was coarse and rough. She found herself thinking if Camel had been around, Hiram would have not done such a terrible thing to her. Deep within, where she could not go right now, she knew she was kidding herself.

Bilbo was speaking to her. "I'm sorry, Bilbo, guess I was thinking about the number of children having difficulty learning their alphabet."

He lay his fork down, "I was just saying that I have several house calls to make this morning and that I would be happy to give you a ride to the school."

"That's kind of you, but no thanks, I always enjoy the walk."

He did not move to pick up his fork, but stared at her. She felt uncomfortable under his scrutiny and though she tried, she could not stop the color from creeping into her face and throat.

"Is everything alright with you, Maggie? You seemed upset last night. Is there anything going on that…"

"I become emotional and frustrated when I teach as hard as I can and my students still fail a test."

He did not move, but continued to look her directly in the eyes. She remembered her mother telling her that with her fair skin, she would never make a good liar because her color always gave her away. Maggie hoped that was not true at this moment. *What can you do, Bilbo, if I told you that Hiram raped me? Would you even believe me? Isn't Hiram one of your primary supporters in the church? Would you risk your position and all you have and go up against him? Will anyone in the town do it?*

After what seemed an eternity to her, he resumed eating. It was then she became aware she had been pushing her food around on her plate and had eaten almost nothing. Feeling strangely apart from herself, as though she were watching from the ceiling, she excused herself. Tying on her bonnet, she lifted her cloth carrying case holding students' work and headed for the school. Walking the slatted walkway, she prayed she would not encounter Hiram. She gasped for air. Only after leaving Bilbo did she realize she'd felt like she had been suffocating under his watchful eyes. The air did little to stop the thudding pain behind her eyes, the ache in her chest, and the nausea in her stomach. Leaving the walkway and entering the worn path to the school house, she stepped behind a large live oak, leaned against it, and vomited.

What if he shows up at the school today? What if he plans to do today, tomorrow and every day from now on what he did last night? Wiping her lips with a white handkerchief she had pulled from her cloth purse, she tried to tell herself she was being irrational. She was allowing her fears to dominate her. She must carry on. She must carry on for the good of the children. Walking on, she could not lose the nagging worry and fear that at any moment Hiram might appear from behind a tree and rape her again. She heard someone move in the thick woods to her left. Terror froze her and a chill ran down her spine. Maybe it was one of the kids coming to school early. She turned and stared at the woods, but saw or heard no one. Lifting her dress to her knees, she ran awkwardly with the carrying case bouncing off her thigh until she reached the school house.

CHAPTER 14

The desert is a harsh environment and each living species must fight for its survival. Each plant protects its own turf as reflected in its name...prickly pear, Spanish dagger, crucifixion thorn, catclaw, whitethorn acacia, etc.

Eerie silhouettes of Yucca and Spanish Bayonets rose around Camel against the night sky like vapors escaping their graves. Some were clumped and leaning like a mob of attackers. Some appeared to possess claw-like limbs reaching out for him. Camel fought back fearful thoughts. He reminded himself they were only plants. Plants did not attack.

His craving for alcohol had morphed him. Years earlier, he held no such irrational fears. But the sickness at his core twisted his thinking, wrecked his emotions and liquefied his resolve. If he had a bottle of whisky, he'd be fearless. Without the aid of alcohol, he flinched at each rattle in the brush. He told himself his trembling was the result of the night air, but deep down, he knew better. Dawn was still an hour or so away, but he stood, stretched stiff muscles, retrieved his gear, and began walking.

The sky birthed bright orange, predicting another dazzling hot day when he rested on a drift of sand and drew from his canteen. Eating two pieces of jerky from the sack, he figured this was his final chance to locate the railroad tracks. He could not depend on his luck holding out, not in this god-forsaken country.

He was walking briskly, staring at a mountain rise in the distance when he heard a yell. A bullet whizzed over his shoulder. Dropping to the sand, he heard another yell and the drum of horse hoofs. Discarding his items, he slowly raised himself above a saltbush and tumbleweed that had married and squinted at the approaching figures. He'd lost Bone's hat and held his hand above his eyes as he counted five riders coming hard.

Another bullet whistled past his ear. He saw three soldiers coming directly toward him and two Indians a distance behind them. Another minute and they would be upon him. Raising his rifle, he took aim and fired over the head of the lead rider. It had no effect. Another bullet tugged at his torn sleeve. He had to stop them. Aiming, his next shot tore into the soldier's shoulder, followed his upper arm and exited at the elbow. The impact of the hit twisted him from his saddle and sent him spiraling over a barrel cactus and sprawling on sand that enveloped him in a dust cloud. He would bleed badly, but live to receive a medical discharge.

Camel's shot had it's desired effect on the other riders. They pulled hard on their reins; made controlled falls to the sand and wished they had followed their Indian scout's lead and approached the renegade more carefully.

Peeping above his cover, Camel saw only milling horses. His heart leaped as he saw one standing only a couple of yards from him munching on a clump of buffalo grass. Talking softly, he walked in a crouch toward the animal. He heard a yell and then another one. They would be shooting at him any moment now. The horse raised his head as Camel neared and started to shy away. Camel continued his soft talk as his hand grasped the reins. Leaping onto the horse, a soldier stood with rifle raised, Camel fired a quick shot making him drop to the ground. Kicking his horse hard in the side, he raced away. There was more yelling and then the blast of two rifles. He expected to feel a bullet smash into his spine at any second. Leaning as low over the horses neck as possible, he rode as fast as his mount's long legs would carry him.

He rode over a drift of sand and down into a deep gully. The firing stopped. He rode hard, remaining in the gully for another couple of minutes. The low ground gradually slanted upward and he was riding atop a drift of sand again. The firing resumed. Dropping down into another dip of the desert sand, the firing stopped. His horse was gasping and he pulled back on the reins. If they pursued him, he would need to discipline himself and not run his mount out in the first few minutes.

As his horse started up another rise, he reined up, dismounted, and led him toward the top. He peered over, looking for the soldiers. There were none. No dust was visible to indicate a pursuit. He led the horse over the rise and heard no firing.

Mounting up, he became aware his attackers had come out of the southwest. They were between him and the railroad tracks. He was heading straight into the heart of the Chihuahua. He reined up and studied the terrain before him-- killer desert. Turning in the saddle, he observed patches of sand interspersed with brown ground cover that became greener in the distance.

Dismounting, he held the reins with one hand while using the other to scoop sand and bury the empty rifle. Without ammo it was a hot, heavy and useless burden. He assessed his gear. He'd lost his canteen and poncho when he fled. Relief flowed through him as he lifted a half-full canteen hanging from the saddle by a leather strap. A rolled tarp behind the saddle contained no food or other gear. *What do I do? I can't head south because of the soldiers; I can't go north and take on the desert. What if I head east for the rest of today and tomorrow turn south and get outta this hell-hole.*

The next day, he turned south and was in sight of a green strip running beneath what he guessed were the Chisos Mountains. His horse had not had any water and was growing weaker every hour. Camel was feeling optimistic when he spotted a dust cloud. Dismounting, he squatted on his heels in the hot sand and watched. Sure enough, it was moving and coming nearer to him. *What the hell are they chasing me for?*

He shook his head in disgust; he figured they were probably searching for the Morning People and he'd gotten in the way. Now they thought he was one of them.

Reluctantly, he mounted up and headed into the desert. His canteen was almost empty. Ahead of him was death by thirst; behind him was death by a bullet. He slunk in the saddle as he thought that if he had any real guts, he would choose the quick death rather than the prolonged one. Pushing the thought from his mind, he prodded his weakening mount forward across wind-rippled sand dunes. Occasionally, he'd turn in the saddle and find the dust cloud smaller. When the sun was blazing directly overhead, there was no sign of his pursuers.

By late afternoon, his animal was wheezing and stumbling. Camel dismounted and led the horse. The sky was streaked with orange bands that illuminated high dry clouds when his horse fell. Camel knelt and stroked the head with the white mark resembling a lightning flash. The horse's large brown eyes stirred a deep emotion within him and he realized he was crying. The dying animal struggled up, uttered several deep gasps, shivered and dropped again. Convulsive shudders racked his frame; his eyes rolled back and he was gone.

Camel sat there for an undetermined amount of time. He envied the dead animal; at least he was out of his suffering. Standing, he held his canteen high and drained the last few drops from it. He started to toss it into the sand, but he didn't. Adjusting the strap on his shoulder and heading across the sand, he knew he would not die as quickly as the horse. The sun, burning sand and dry wind would make a half dead skeleton out of him before he breathed his last. As dusk descended, a wind kicked up and he felt the grains of sand stinging his face, throat, hands, all exposed flesh. Dropping to his knees at the base of a dune, he dug into the side and leaned back into the crevice. With knees to chin, he wrapped his arms around his head and prayed to die.

The tiny cemetery with faded wooden grave markers sat atop a sandy spur of sand nurturing a lone Cottonwood. The tree appeared to be dying; a poignant symbol of it's surroundings. The dying tree reminded Maggie of a macabre skeleton etched against the gray sky. She felt as though she would never stop crying. The simple wooden coffin rested beside the open grave. Piles of sand on the opposite side of the grave appeared to be restless visitors waiting to be returned to their natural sanctuary.

Other than Reverend McKenzie, Maggie was the only white person attending Vera Mae's funeral. She eyed the minister and pondered his actions toward her. He had been so attentive lately, but had acted strangely aloof when she informed him she was attending today's funeral. *Why did he appear so reluctant to even give me a ride?*

A child's sobbing pulled her back to the present scene. All seven of the black families were present. A baby cried. A year-old child pulled at his mother's ear and made occasional squeals at each new discovery. Big Henry and Vera Mae's offspring alternated sobbing quietly and wailing loudly. The saddest of all for Maggie, was Big Henry. His giant shoulders convulsed as he cried quietly like a child.

Maggie noted three wooden crosses; she figured these were children stillborn or died very young. This was characteristic of the frontier. This was a part of her environment she loathed.

Closing her eyes, she visualized this tiny woman who had given her all to her family. She had always been impressed with Vera Mae's infectious smile and positive attitude. She knew this mother of five could not read, but she always assisted Maggie whenever she taught the children by monitoring their behavior and bringing fresh cold milk and cookies at the end of each session. When the weather was bad and Maggie taught the children in a barn, it was Vera Mae who kept the lamps burning and a constant vigil to ensure that no white locals caught them. When they met under an arbor, Vera Mae would walk among the children with a fly swat made of horsehair, swatting intruding insects and pinching an ear of any student who failed to be doing his best.

The Reverend was reading scripture and trying to talk above the mournful sounds. His voice and body stiffness revealed his uneasiness with the task. As Maggie watched him, she wondered again if she should leave the area and return to Connecticut.

Hiram had raped her; would he do it again? The judge was due to arrive tomorrow, but was she going to report the rape to him? She felt a nauseating fear in the pit of her stomach as she saw again Hiram's drunken leer and him telling her that if she said anything about their, "little affair," he had several witnesses that would testify that she had been seen having sex with Camel, a no-good drunk and gambler who had disappeared. It was also reported, said Hiram with a wide grin, that Camel had caught a cattle train while drunk in order to escape her demands that he marry her.

Then there was Camel. She had felt anger at herself many times for missing him so much since his disappearance. Her feeling for the no-good scoundrel had surprised her. *But when the only other suitor is Hiram, I guess it's understandable that I would miss the only man who knew how to treat a lady.*

She corrected herself; there was Bilbo McKenzie. Since the rape, Bilbo had been so attentive to her. It was as though he knew what had occurred and was trying to help her through it. His attention to her was creating more tension in their household. *Could that be why he's so distant toward me today? Is his wife jealous?*

She wiped a tear and asked herself again if she should leave Texas as soon as possible. *Why is it even a question? What's wrong with me? Surely, reason and logic dictate that I go home and try to put all of this behind me. But...I'm not a quitter.* She was making a difference to the children. She was making a difference to these children right here. Hearing a noise, she looked down to see she had torn her handkerchief.

Bilbo appeared to be in a hurry to leave this grieving family and their friends. The neighbors had brought in lots of food and Bilbo ate his share of it while she pushed hers around on the plate. Since the horrid incident with Hiram, she had no appetite or zest for life.

Spotting Ben Davis, the carpenter, she made her way to him and asked about the reading sessions with the children. He smiled warmly and assured her that they would want her to continue with them. Together they agreed they would skip this week and lessons would continue the following week.

Riding back in the buggy with Bilbo, he seemed unusually quiet. Maggie assumed he was thinking about the Goins family and how they would fare without Vera Mae. His voice sounded strained when he spoke. "You know, Maggie, our attending the funeral today will not make us very popular in town."

She looked at him and saw the struggle going on within him. She started to respond that it mattered not at all to her what others thought, but she held her tongue.

After a long pause, he said, "Would it surprise you to know I was approached by three of our most affluent church leaders and warned about conducting this funeral?"

Faces and names appeared to her: Grandmother Stutz, Mrs. McCormick, Mr. and Mrs. Arlington, and of course, Hiram. "That's terrible! What kind of..." the pained look on his face forced her to stop.

"I was warned that if I conducted the funeral, I might be fired. They felt that, "those people," as they referred to them, should take care of their own. They said I could run off prospective members if the news got out of my involvement with those people. I felt the need to tell you because my wife and I might be leaving this congregation. You will need to seek other housing accommodations." He paused, slapped the reins and said, "Of course, my leaving the church would not ordinarily affect your situation because the town people would find you housing, but since you attended the funeral, your position might be jeopardized also. I thought you should be prepared to encounter some disapproval."

The old, tired rider rode ramrod straight but leaned at times, appearing about to topple over. His horse would shake her head and snort; Toby would correct his seat in the saddle.

"Thank ya gal. Ya gotcha self an extra shovel of oats tonight. Course that's probably why ya done it, ya can't handle that shovel very well. If ya get so that ya can open the bin, you'll probably get too ornery to keep my skinny butt in the saddle."

He stood in the stirrups to stretch and try to exorcise sleep from his weary muscles. He wondered how long he and Fuzzy could continue to run a spread that ordinarily employed a dozen hands for spring branding and half that many for the remainder of the year. He and Fuzzy were old men trying to do the job of six young men. He frowned as he thought how Fuzzy had slurred his speech over supper last night. Years ago, he'd have known his partner had gotten into the juice, but not now. He knew Fuzzy, like himself, was mentally and physically exhausted.

Reining up, he studied the ground which contained a myriad of tracks. Several steers had been driven through an area between a stand of pines and the fence line he was checking. Grasping his Winchester, he levered a shell and scanned the area for movement. Seeing nothing, he closed his eyes and listened, still nothing. He clucked and moved out slowly, scrutinizing the woods to his right and the fence line to his left. Another grove of mixed hardwoods stood a couple of hundred yards beyond the fence.

He talked quietly to his horse, "Careful, Babs. These tracks are no more than a couple of hours old. The rustlers coulda left a rider hidin' in those woods to cover their backs." He paused, continued, "Especially since I shot Williams' horse."

He squinted. There was something on the fence line a quarter of a mile away. He moved his horse to a fast walk as he held his rifle at ready. Was it a Rocking H rider serving as a backup for the rustlers? His squint grew into a grimace as he strained to see. He recognized a man's figure that was leaning against a post. *Is that a rifle he's holding? The wire's been cut there. Is it a lookout that's fallen asleep? Watch out!*

A wave of shock and revulsion engulfed him; it was Fuzzy. Fuzzy leaned back against a post, held there by strands of barbed wire wrapped tightly around his face, throat and torso. Toby charged his mount ahead and stopped a couple of feet from his friend. Caution was forgotten. His own voice sounded strange to him, "Fuzzy, I'm here! I'll getcha outta there! Hold on!"

Dismounting, he saw that his riding partner of over a decade was dead. His eyes were open, but viewed a scene beyond Toby's vision. A large fly was resting on one eye and another appeared on his tongue, emerging from the gaping mouth. Toby shooed them away with a wave of his hand. Fuzzy's pale face was streaked with blood; his clothes ripped, revealing bright red lines. His shirt and pants were saturated with dark blood. Toby examined a split board leaning against Fuzzy's still chest. It was half of a sign that had been nailed to an anchor post showing the ranch's name and brand. Rough hands had split the board and with a knife carved a message, "Rustler and Fence-cutter."

Toby swore as he slung the board away. His arthritic hands trembled and a lone tear ran down a wrinkle as he gently unwound the sharp barbed wire that left lines of blood where it had pierced the flesh. *He was gut-shot and alive when they wrapped him. The murdering bastards.*

"I'm sorry my compadre! I'm so damn sorry!"

Pearl stood in the doorway of her bedroom listening to the sounds of Hiram's surrey disappear. He was coming almost every day now. She stared at the old antiquated double-barreled shotgun leaning in the corner. She had thought more than once how she could enjoy cutting him in half with it as he entered her room with his evil, sneering grin.

Closing her eyes, she focused on breathing deeply and forcing the thought of killing Hiram from her tortured mind. She was naked. Grabbing up her sack cloth slip and faded gingham dress, she moved outside to the well to wash up. No matter how hard she scrubbed her body with the rough homemade soap, she continued to feel dirty.

Less than an hour later, she was milking in the barn when she heard a familiar and welcome voice. Judah stood there with a shy grin on his face holding a sack at his side. She knew it was a ham or a slab of ribs, or something she and the boys needed and would enjoy.

He leaned against the rough-hewn boards as she finished the milking. He would adamantly argue, but she would insist that he return with some of her fresh milk. Making small talk, Pearl was worried. She was certain that three days before when he visited her, he had almost asked her to marry him. What could she do? She knew from their conversations Hiram held the note on Judah's property just as he did on hers. If she agreed to marry Judah, what would Hiram's response be?

Judah had surprised her with his tenacity. She assumed after the first incident when Hiram had burst in on them, Judah would disappear. She had not seen him for two weeks and accepted the fact everyone knew she was being used by Hiram and not worthy of anything else. She was shocked to see him ride up one day with a bag of seeds for fall planting.

Their relationship had grown quickly over the weeks and she had been pleased with his warmth toward her sons. The boys loved his attention; she knew they were hungry for male bonding which she could not give to them.

What about his children? Will his children accept me as a stepmother? What kind of stepmother will I make? How will my boys get along with his kids?

She smiled at Judah as he rambled on about dealing with a steer infested with screw worms. Her mind returned to Hiram and how she could be rid of him so that she and her boys could live a normal life. She thought about asking Judah's help in killing Hiram, but as she observed his tired face and posture, she knew the gentle eyes and voice were not those of a killer. Again she forced herself to push the horrid wish aside and laugh at one of his comments. The laugh did nothing to relieve her of the burden of worry and fear she possessed for herself and her children. *And Judah. I'm fearful for him too. Will Hiram have the sheriff serve eviction papers on Judah if he knew he was a competitor for my affections? And yet, Judah has always treated me like a lady, making no indecent demands.*

Pearl felt trapped. She felt it when her husband died. She allowed herself to hope for better times when Camel showed interest in her. But he was only a scoundrel who the boys loved and she reluctantly admitted having fallen in love with him. *What a dummy I was! Camel only wanted sex, like Hiram. I tried to be smart and use Hiram to make Camel jealous, but he never was. Camel disappeared and left me with only ugly Hiram to show up almost every day to ride me like I was a horse.*

She and Judah had moved into the kitchen and he was unwrapping a salted ham. She felt hot tears running down her cheeks and hugged him hard for his generosity. She knew the tears reflected her feelings for him, but they were more. They also reflected her loss of love and hope in Camel. They were expressions of her frustration with her situation. A part of them contained her hatred for Hiram. As she hugged Judah and felt the roughness of his coarse beard on her neck, she stared at the shotgun in the corner.

Captain Verlander stood silent as the corpsman tended the private's wound. He couldn't admit it, but he felt a certain satisfaction over the incident. It was the first time they had actually encountered the renegades. He would have liked for it to have come out differently, but the cavalryman wouldn't die, and the rest of the company saw how dangerous these savages could be.

He scratched his butt and spit onto the hot sand as he scanned the horizon for his scouts. He didn't expect them to catch the renegade who had escaped on one of their horses, but he was anxious to hear their report. *Hear their latest bullshit!* His heart pounded over the prospect of finally catching these trouble makers. *There was only one of them, but it means they are still around here. I think they are just acting like they're going into the desert. Tomorrow will be a new day, and regardless what our worthless scouts say, we're going to be on their asses.*

Some distance away, both scouts stood looking at the earth and its signs. One pointed to a smooth spot and the other bent and started scooping sand aside. The scout standing, cradled his rifle and watched the horizon. Their relaxed manner reflected no fear, but they were instinctively vigilant. The one digging, grunted and pulled Camel's rifle from the sand. He shook the weapon and blew on it's lever base to clean it of grit. Working the lever several times, the two smiled at each other as they saw that the rifle contained no bullets. They talked for a minute and then buried the weapon again. Mounting up, they walked their mounts slowly, neither in a hurry to face the angry, red-faced, butt-scratching captain.

Billy frowned. He stood on the train platform with sheriff Frank and two rough looking drifters. A slight west wind rocked the lantern, making weird shapes and shadows dance across the rough planks of the platform. A feeling of deja-vu swept over him. The next feeling was nausea. These two unkempt bums had drifted into town and made trouble. Both of their horses were sad creatures with exposed ribs and curved spines. One of them died while tied to the hitching post outside of the saloon. The men were broke and panhandling drinks in Stinky's when he sent for Frank to run them out of town.

Frank had sent word for Billy to meet him at Stinky's. One of the drifters was a small, slight fellow whose face possessed a perpetual sneer. The other was large, grizzled and appeared as happy-go-lucky as his partner was surly. Frank was forcing them to leave town in Cholla's wagon with their one bony mare tied to the back of the wagon..

The little man's voice was as nasty as his expression. He snarled at Frank, "Whatcha arresting us for, lawman? Ya can't do this shit to us. We ain't done nothing. If we broke the law then…"

Frank barked, "You shut the hell up! I don't like ya looks and if ya keep talkin,' I might just change 'em for ya."

The big fellow laughed, "Yeah, Wiley, why doncha shut the hell up like the…"

Frank turned to him and bellowed, "Both of ya shut up! Ya give me a headache and I ain't gonna take any shit tonight, so just…"

Billy blinked. Light reflected off of a blade in the little man's hand. Frank had his back turned to him and didn't see it. Billy instinctively drew and fired. He aimed for the hand, but this was not target practice, it was not a small medicine bottle, it was a man's hand. He missed.

The blast of the gunfire shocked the knife's owner into an automatic reflex, he dropped the knife onto the rough planks. Frank yelled, pulled his pistol and backed away from the drifters and toward Billy. Seeing the knife at the feet of the sour-faced drifter, Frank exploded.

"Ya bastard! Ya back-stabbing little... I'm gonna show both of ya what happens when ya try to kill the sheriff in Angel Valley."

Billy stepped back as Frank's gun spit fire in the darkness. Billy could not believe his eyes. Frank was gunning them down. Frank fired several times; first the small man screamed, grabbed his knee and rolled onto the planks. Next, the big man grunted and grabbed his leg above the knee as he dropped to the platform.

The stench of gunfire burned Billy's nostrils. He took another step back as he heard both men crying and groaning in pain. He was stopped by Frank's voice. "Hold on, Billy! I need ya to help me put this trash into the wagon. It oughta be here any time now."

Frank stepped forward, picked up the knife, examined it and stuck it behind his belt. "This is whatcha gotta do to riff-raff like this, Billy. Ya watch and mark my word; the word will go up and down this country from New Orleans to San Francisco to all the trash to stay clear of our nice little town."

Billy felt weak. He holstered his pistol and rested on one knee, trying to catch his breath and clear his swimming head. He heard the deep voice of the big man who was squeezing his leg above the knee with both hands, "Sheriff, if ya don't get me some help here, I'm gonna bleed to death."

Staring down at the growing dark brown circle around the man, Billy knew he was speaking the truth. Billy's eyes widened, he whispered to Frank, "Want me to go get our new doctor?"

Frank's answer was in his look. The small man was cussing and crying as he rolled and tossed and clutched his knee. The big man was calm and didn't show any anger. His face was lifted so that the lantern light showed large, soft brown eyes pleading for help. "I'd be much obliged to ya sheriff for some medical help. I don't wanta bleed to death here in west Texas. I promised my mama I'd see her afore she dies and…"

Frank hissed, "Ya shoulda thought of that before ya hooked up with this killer here. Ya run with killers and ya die with killers."

Billy wanted to move away from the bleeding, suffering men, but he did not have the strength to do it. He sat heavily onto the planks leaning on his arms, trying not to hear their voices.

It seemed to Billy an eternity had passed before Cholla pulled up with his wagon and stopped. The small man still cussed and groaned, but the big man was now silent. As they pulled each one onto the wagon bed, Billy saw that the big man's eyes were open and he was alive, but barely. Billy worked to avoid the eyes that had pleaded earlier, but now reflected dull acceptance. The blood on the platform seemed to Billy to have been enough to keep an elephant alive. Pouring pails of water to wash it off, Billy refused to look at Frank and after the task was completed, he ignored Frank's parting words and walked away from town.

CHAPTER 15

In 1857, Secretary of War, Jefferson Davis, introduced 75 camels to the Texas Desert. The experiment was abandoned after a short time, but for many years, scared travelers reported seeing giant, shaggy beasts.

He was dying! Blackness surrounded him and sucked all life out of him. Camel gasped, spit, kicked and flailed his arms. Standing, he choked and found himself knee-deep in sand under a starry sky. He had fallen asleep during the sandstorm and was covered with fine grains of sand. Shaking grit from his head and upper torso, he pawed his face to rid it of the little pellets that seemed to invade every niche of his body. Blinking and spitting, he pulled his feet from the sand and stared at the dunes around him. He'd lost one boot, or what was left of it, so he squatted and felt for it in the silica-like specks. Extracting a tattered sole and rotten tarp strips, he gave up on trying to put it on his foot. He struggled to create foot covering from the other battered boot that was wrapped with the same rotten canvas. It was an impossible task. Giving up, he tossed it aside.

His only possessions now were a tattered shirt, torn pants and the empty canteen that hung from his shoulder. Staring at the stars, he struck out in what he hoped was an easterly direction. He could not go south to look for the railroad tracks; the Calvary was looking for him there. Due to his running from the Calvary, he no longer trusted his ability to find his way back to Bone's spring. His only hope was…what? Did he think he could cross the Chihuahua?

His mouth and throat felt raw and stinging from the dry granules. He was already hurting from thirst; what could he possibly do but die in this God-forsaken place?   Forcing himself to stand erect, he plodded forward. Daylight was breaking in the east.

His heart jumped with hope as he spotted dull green objects ahead.   Nearing, he saw several Cholla cactus amidst a patch of wheat-colored, dried brush grass.   If there was any water nearby, his eagerly searching eyes could not find it.

He had to find shelter.   Plodding through the wind-rippled sand, he gazed dully as the eastern sky transformed from bright orange to a light blue that welcomed the dazzling sun and sent its rays of molten heat onto everything in it's path. He searched for shelter, but saw none.   In the distance he spotted a patch of dark brown and headed for it.   Almost an hour later, his feet were burning and his canteen was becoming scorching hot.   The dark brown spot was a series of dunes, some providing shade on their western sides.   It was weak shade, but it would have to do.

Sitting at the bottom of a dune, he closed his eyes and enjoyed the difference in the temperature of the sand.   This beat walking in the sun, but barely.   Every breath felt like he was standing over a blazing fire, inhaling deeply.

His tongue was swollen in his cottony mouth.   He could not remember the last time he peed. Wallowing out a bed in the sand, he laid back and tried to sleep.

Sleep, if that's what it was, brought no relief.   It meant only more pain and terror.   His body jerked and convulsed as his mind slipped into a world where the sky was made of red and orange burning sand and clouds of sulfurous smoke burped from volcanic abysses.   There was no horizon is this world.   The pulsating scorched sand enveloped him.   It formed a gaseous bubble of searing steam that held him prisoner.   This was a world of agonizing thirst and misery.

During sleep, his body moaned a constant death dirge whose rhythm was found in his pounding pulse, popping ears, and growling, protesting organs.   One word dominated his dreams.   The eerie voice would not be ignored.   It grew louder and louder until he woke himself whispering the word through dried mouth and throat-- "die!"

Maggie saw Hiram's buggy coming as she peered through the open school house door. Sitting at her desk, grading papers, she glanced at Billy sweeping the wood floor with a cornstalk broom. As always, he immediately smiled sheepishly at her. Anytime he was around her he was watching her, even when he appeared not to be. She found his presence comforting. Lately, she'd stopped sending him away and he'd responded as she knew he would by showing up every day after school. He was fixated with her; it was obvious in his eyes, voice, and increasing presence.

"Billy, stop that for now and write your letters for me." She held out a slate board and chalk. He looked at her and grinned. She responded, "I have confidence you've not forgotten how to do it, but you haven't written them for me lately."

He beamed. He loved to impress her and here was an ideal opportunity. He didn't tell her he'd been practicing at home each evening since she taught him his letters. He'd been waiting for just such a moment. He took the board and chalk, sat at a battered table, contorted his face in concentration and began writing.

She heard the sounds of the buggy stop, the horse blow and Hiram's heavy boots on the front porch. Entering, he grinned his biggest smile until he saw Billy. Before he could order the young man out, she said, "Hello Hiram. Billy is working on his letters for me and then I'll check them." He opened his mouth to protest, but she hastily continued, "Let's step out on the porch so we do not interrupt him."

Walking toward the door, she could feel Billy's eyes on her. She stopped outside the doorway, remaining in view of Billy, giving Hiram just enough room to step out. His face was red as he stepped around her, turned and whispered in anger, "The community's not paying you to teach Billy to read!" As he spoke, he reached for her elbow to move her out of the doorway and Billy's vision. She avoided his grip, stepped back and said in her sternest schoolmarm voice, "Hiram, I was called by God to come west to teach the illiterate regardless of their sex, age, race or any other difference. If that is unacceptable to the community, than my services are not needed here." She didn't care how she sounded; she was determined to control the situation.

He paused, closed his eyes, and rubbed his mouth in frustration. "Maggie, I'm here on business!" He leaned forward, scowled at her, "Did you attend the nigger funeral?"

She felt her face grow hot, "I attended the funeral of Vera Mae Goins, a lovely, woman and mother. Is that whom you're referring to, Hiram?"

His face was red and a vein stood out on his massive neck. "Humph! Damn right, that's what I'm referring to, Miss Yankee know-it-all. Don't you realize that…"

He'd raised his voice, so she stepped into the doorway and said, "You're yelling, and name-calling, Hiram. I'll not stand for that. As I've told you before, if the community does not want my services, then dismiss me. It's that simple. In the meantime, I will uphold my contract and teach whomever I please on my own time. Excuse me now, Billy needs me to grade his paper."

She realized she was trembling and her knees were weak as she walked toward Billy. Forcing herself to smile at him, she said, "Let's see how you did with your letters."

He beamed as he handed her the slate. Standing, he began to sweep again as she looked over his letters.

She jumped with fright hearing Hiram speak her name. He was standing in the doorway with an expression of fury on his face. "Maggie, would you step here again please? We need to talk."

Giving him her coldest stare and hardest voice, she said, "I'm busy now, Hiram."

He frowned, his face reddened again, he opened his mouth, paused, turned quickly and left.

Maggie felt relieved as she looked down at the slate. Her eyes grew wide with thought, standing up abruptly, she walked quickly toward the door. *I'll tell him about teaching the Negro families. Let them address all of the issues and then do what they will about it.* Just before she reached the door, she heard Hiram yell at his horse and the sound of horse hooves. She yelled at him, "Hiram! Wait!" Too late; he was gone in a cloud of dust.

She turned to see Billy staring at her with his mouth open and a look of total confusion on his face.

Realizing she held the slate, she said, "Billy, this is very good! Your handwriting has greatly improved, too. You've been practicing, haven't you?"

He giggled awkwardly and swept harder as they listened to Hiram's buggy race away

Toby cussed as he hit his thumb with the hammer. The pine box he was building for Fuzzy was almost completed. He leaned against the box, wiped sweat from his forehead with his sleeve and struggled again with the question of whether he should report Fuzzy's death to the sheriff. *What about some of the folks around here who knew Fuzzy? Shouldn't they be invited to his funeral? Should a man of the cloth say words over him?*

His horse nickered from her stall where she munched oats. "I know Babs, I know that Fuzzy could be an affable man at times, especially when he was drinking, and lots of folks around here liked him." Toby stared at his bruised thumb, sucked it, trying to extract some of the pain. Examining it, he continued slowly, "But ya see, Babs, we gotta bad situation here. First, I know it's a waste of time to report this thing to our new so called sheriff. Second, something tells me the quieter I can be about things, the better chance I got to hold on."

Babs shook her head and pawed the stall floor. Laying the hammer down, turning and holding his lower back with one calloused hand, he walked over to the stall and scratched his beloved horses' head. "Baby, ya eatin' too darn much." He removed his battered Stetson and scratched his tousled gray hair. "The real problem is I'm feedin' ya too much ain't I?" Babs extended her large head and nuzzled his ear. Toby grinned, "Doggone it, Babs, ya make a fella do things he knows he shouldn't but can't help himself. You just a young filly takin' advantage of an old man." Reaching for the pitchfork, he tossed two tufts of Timothy hay into the stall.

Returning to the coffin, he picked up the hammer and spoke aloud, "Course what am I holdin' on for? With Camel gone, it's a only a matter of time before Hiram gobbles this spread up like he's gobblin' everything up in the valley." Staring at the pine box, Toby knew for sure Hiram had done something terrible to Camel. He had suspected it all along, but now the idea assumed new clarity. It was as though a fog had lifted and he saw fifty steers the fog had concealed. Amongst the stable smells and sounds, Toby realized for the first time how greed-driven Hiram was and to what lengths he would go in order to steal a man's possessions and take his life, if necessary.

Babs whinnied, shook her long mane and stomped her hoof as she did when strange horses entered the area. Toby listened for a moment, heard only Babs, but trusted her keen sense of smell and sound. He glanced over to the beam holding his saddle with the rifle still in the scabbard. Laying the hammer down, he moved to the kerosene lamp hanging from a ceiling beam and turned the wick down until the flame sputtered and went out. He walked gingerly in the pitch black stable and felt his rifle stock. Pulling it to him, he levered a shell into the barrel and listened.

Thinking he heard a voice outside, he felt his way to Babs and stroked her head. His presence quietened her so he could listen for noises. He heard it. A horse nickered somewhere and then there was a couple of minutes of silence. This time he heard the squeak of leather. That meant a rider was very close.

Hurry up, for God's sake, Hiram. Pearl's hands were behind her head. She hated every spot of her body that came into contact with the heaving, grunting, sweating man that lay on her. During these moments, she concentrated with all her might on anything but what was happening to her. She thought of the boys and what she would cook for supper. She mentally grappled with the challenge of how she could repair the broken handle on the sulky plow her dead husband had broken the last time he used it. *Where can I find the money to buy another mule?*

Today, nothing worked. She could not place herself anywhere but where she actually was. She feared that Judah might appear and learn the truth about her. Her feelings were a combination of fear of discovery and hatred of Hiram. Turning her head, she focused on the shotgun and dreamed of how it would feel to use it on the one who made her a whore.

Finally, Hiram rolled off of her and lay breathing hard. He laughed lightly, "Judah soft on ya, huh." It was not a question, but a statement. She rolled away from him and continued to stare at the shotgun.

She remained silent. He took a deep breath. "Judah's gotta passel of kids. You'd make a nice size family if ya put them together."

There was silence between them. Hiram's voice assumed a different tone, low and menacing, "It's your business what you do about Judah, Pearl, just don't let it interfere with our business. I'm having a tough time at the bank balancing the books cuz I'm tryin' to help too many people like you and Judah."

Pulling strands of red wavy hair between her teeth, she closed her eyes and said nothing. Even with her eyes closed, she still saw the shotgun.

This was the first time in his life the captain had thought of using his revolver on himself. He succumbed to his depression and allowed his mind to consider the advantages of death. His hemorrhoids pained him constantly, he feared the thought of dying of thirst, his men were showing signs of rebellion, and most significantly, he'd lost confidence in himself.

This was their third day in the desert. He had heard there were water holes if you knew where they were located. As usual, he suspected his scouts knew more than they were telling him. He was now checking their canteens each evening to see if they had been refilled.

He was desperate. He was pursuing an elusive enemy across a desert and he had no experience in desert-fighting. The horses were acting strange; they didn't like this country either. The wagon hauling two barrels of water for the men and horses kept bogging in the sand.

The captain was learning that the color of the sand sent a message to the reader smart enough to interpret it. The light-colored sand may be like quicksand and a horse stepping into it, was up to his belly in an instant. While his scouts claimed they were unable to read the desert signs, he noted they had not led their horses into any of the soft sand.

He was ignoring derisive looks and comments from his men. The looks were growing meaner and the comments growing louder with each passing day. How long could he continue to overlook all of it? When he faced them, would they obey or rebel? He would rather face death at his own hands than having his wife, children and especially, his father, learn he'd allowed his men to mutiny on him.

A voice aroused him from his morbid thoughts. He saw dust ahead and his spirits lifted. In about half an hour, his scouts appeared. For the first time he noticed a different look about them. They appeared excited. Perhaps they were coming around. Maybe they had come to believe him when he said they would cross the desert if needed to catch these killer renegades.

The lead scout spoke clearly and looked him in the eye, "They are about three miles east, held up and sleepin'. They have no one on watch."

The captain straightened in the saddle and turned his horse to face his men. "Men, it looks like we are about to get what we came for. Lieutenant, have the men dismount, check their horses and weapons and be ready to ride in five minutes."

Dismounting, he urinated, tightened his animal's cinch, and checked out his revolver. His heart thumped in anticipation. It did not surprise him that no sentries were posted. He'd heard many stories from Indian fighters who told how cunning and efficient the Indians could be in conducting warfare, but then return to their villages and depend on their dogs to alert them of intruders. This group had no dogs, so they had nothing to alert them of approaching danger. *Damn! It's about time something went our way. I just want to get close enough to put a bullet in that cussed, traitorous, asshole who calls himself a priest and any Indian that gets in my gun-sight.*

The scouts stood beside their mounts and observed the captain and his men. One looked at the other, they exchanged knowing looks though to any observer, their expressions were as stoic as always.

Three miles away, the four men and a woman half-slept in the heat of the day. As one of them tossed and turned beneath a torn, dirty tarp stretched between two madrone trees, a folded paper slipped from his shirt pocket. A hot draft of air caught it and opened it as deftly as any nimble fingers. A cartoon-like drawing depicted its owner with large letters above it--WANTED: DEAD OR ALIVE. The list of crimes ranged from petty larceny, to rape and murder. Anyone familiar with the man's riding partners, would have smiled at this because he was actually one of the more affable and least dangerous of the group.

The wind flipped the paper end over end until it came to rest on the face of another man whose mouth was open and eyelids half-shut. The vellum-like poster formed around his inhaling mouth and cut off his air. Choking, gasping, he clawed the paper away and sat up. He was lying in the small shade of two Spanish bayonets and cussed as one pricked his hand. He studied the large, dirty hand and delicately plucked out the black prong. Squinting up into the blue sky, he glanced down to the horizon and saw a cloud of dust.

"Yee-haw!" He yelled. "Company's comin' and we better git gone fast!"

The other men were on their feet in a heartbeat and moving toward their horses as they grabbed only their canteens and rifles. Four of the five carried a sidearm and each one boasted a knife strapped to his belt. The woman dragged behind. Sans spoke to her in his raspy, low voice that speeded her up.

CHAPTER 16

Apache boys were taught to run for miles in desert country holding water in their mouth.

Camel felt a new pain. His experiences with thirst in recent days had introduced him to a swollen tongue. Now, he felt his tongue shrinking. It even flopped from top to bottom in his mouth with each step. His ears continued to pop and he heard music at times. Looking in the distance, he saw it--water! A shimmering lake danced in the heated air and he felt drunk with elation. He tried to speed up his gait, but weakness was now his constant companion, second only to his thirst.

Looking at the lake in the distance, made him want to pee. He unbuttoned his ragged pants and held his penis with one hand and cupped his other beneath it. He knew water was ahead, but he also knew that distance was deceiving in the desert and the lake might be a day's march away. He strained and concentrated on peeing. He finally felt a burning sting and a few drops of orange urine leaked into his palm. He sucked it into his mouth and it tasted warm and wet. It helped his hurting tongue, but did little to relieve his maddening thirst.

He was walking at midday. He no longer cared whether it was day or night. He was going mad with thirst and he knew it. Wind-swept dunes surrounded him except for a patch of scrawny Spanish daggers amidst some dry weeds a couple of hundred yards to his right. He wanted to continue to walk directly toward the lake, but he veered toward the greenish-gray daggers. Approaching them, he tried to peel a shaft from the trunk. He felt himself being stuck by the needle-sharp points, but he continued to work. His breath was rasping and his tongue now seemed to be lodged to the roof of his mouth and he couldn't move it.

He finally pulled a shaft loose and sucked the torn end. He could taste nothing. Trying several times, he gave up. His arms held several black dagger points and he pulled them out. One had cut a deep groove the length of his arm and he realized he was not bleeding. He pinched the throbbing areas, but produced no blood.

Staring at the shimmering lake, with dried tongue stuck to the roof of his mouth, he concluded that his body did not have any liquid, even blood, to give up. This had to be near the end for him unless he reached that lake.

Plodding forward, he was struck like a hammer with a chilling thought, what if he was seeing a mirage? Blinking and shaking his shaggy, sand-encrusted beard, he could not test it. The only thing he knew to do was tromp forward.

There was something else. Tossing the empty canteen into the sand, his skin felt ablaze so he ripped the torn shirt from his skeletal-like torso and removed his pants and underwear. He stood naked, a swaying, bearded, gaunt ghost-like of a man. He was no longer the soft, overweight alcoholic he'd been when he arrived in this country; he was now a scrawny underweight alcoholic.

The only sound he could make now was a high-pitched squeal. He felt the desire to laugh and giggle, but could manage only a series of squeals and grunts as he staggered toward the crystal, shimmering water.

Maggie leaned over Micah Beaumont to help him with his numbers. She frowned as she saw the large red sores on his arms and neck. It was not the first time. Bedbugs had often been a problem for this family. She whispered, "Micah come to my desk."

He was the youngest of the family and the one who attended school the most. She pulled him close to her so she could whisper to him without alerting the others students. "Micah, are you getting bitten again at night?"

He was a tow-headed, seven year old, and Maggie's heart went out to him. He looked at his feet, his face reddened, and at first he said nothing. Maggie gently squeezed his arm, "Micah?"

Slowly he raised his face and his light blue eyes were wide with embarrassment and fear. She could barely make out his words, "Yes ma'am. They was bad last night."

She smiled gently and whispered, "I will write your mother a note. Will you give it to her?"

He nodded agreement and then said, "Yesterday, the preacher's wife came over for the first time ever. Mama said she's a queer duck. She asked to catch some of the bugs and carried 'em home in a jar. She said she was going to perform a speermint."

That night, Maggie learned firsthand about the experiment. She tossed and turned, and scratched burning spots on her body until she finally rose and lit a lamp. She saw several black bugs scampering over and under her feather mattress.

Rising before dawn, she pulled all the cover from her bed and piled it onto the back porch. Lugging her mattress outside, she hung it over a rope clothes line. Hauling water from the well, she filled the black-smutted wash pot. Next, she lit a fire beneath it and after the water became warm, she used some of the home-made soap sent to her as a gift by Pearl Manning and began scrubbing the bed linen.

Later, at the breakfast table, Bilbo asked what she had been doing. She acted nonchalant and told him she had just felt like washing her linen and airing out her mattress. As they talked, his wife entered. She held her stomach as though she were ill and he helped her into a chair. Her appearance this early was unusual. Bilbo commented on it, but she smiled weakly at Maggie and said she heard them talking and wanted to join them.

"How are you, Maggie? Is everything O.K. with you? Are you sleeping alright?" Her voice held a sarcasm lost on Bilbo, but not Maggie.

Maggie held a stoic face. "I'm sleeping fine, thank you."

Toby peeped through cracks of the barn but it was too dark to see anything. Instinctively, he pulled back as he heard the crunch of horse hoofs. A rider was setting his mount directly outside the barn. Toby thought he heard whispers, but could not make out what was said.

He had an idea. He moved as quickly and quietly as possible toward the ladder leading to the loft. Climbing it, he stepped to the open window at the front of the barn. Each board seemed to squeak and he felt certain he had been heard.

Peering down, he made out the outline of at least three riders setting on their horses. They moved apart some and he saw one strike a match and light a limb soaked in pitch. Without thinking, Toby raised his rifle and fired over the heads of the men. He heard several cuss as the torch was dropped and the riders rode away hard.

He remained where he was for several minutes. The blazing torch was a couple of feet from the barn wall, and he didn't worry about it at first. After a few minutes, a stream of fire caught a strand of hay and made its way to the wall. Toby climbed down and extinguished the blaze with a bucket of water from one of the stalls.

That night, he did not light another lamp. He sat on the porch with his rifle in his lap. He didn't even roll a smoke. He chewed a little and spit into the dark. Intermittently, he would stop chewing, listen for a long while, and then resume his chewing.

He wondered how long he could live like this. Fuzzy was right. Hiram's crew would keep twisting the rope tighter and tighter until it broke. He was the rope.

Tomorrow, he must bury his old friend. *Wonder how long before somebody is digging my grave.*

Pearl hid behind the base of a giant live oak tree and watched Hiram. He had yelled, knocked on the door and even shot a little pistol into the air. She thought she could hear him cussing. Finally, he returned to his surrey, pulled a book from the seat and began writing. After a couple of minutes, he stood, walked up the steps and stood by the screen door for a while. Pearl couldn't see what he was doing, but another minute and he was gone.

Breathing a sigh of relief, she moved to the door to see what he had done. Wedged between the door and jamb was a hand-written note. Pearl did not read very well, especially handwriting. She tried, but finally gave up.

When the boys ran into the yard from school, she handed the note to the oldest one and asked him to read it aloud. He struggled, but plowed ahead, "Pearl, I must have payment on your uh...a big word, Mama, uh...and then, note." His face paled as he looked up at his mother. She said, "Go ahead, Ralph, I gotta hear what it says.

He stammered and read slowly, "The full amount of two hundred and twenty-four dollars is due by tomorrow, July twelfth, eighteen hundred and ninety-one."

Pearl tried to keep her emotions from the boys, but couldn't. When they saw her tears, each wrapped their arms about her waist and cried with her.

Captain Verlander kicked his horse and ignored the animal's wheezing. There would be time to rest later; now, they had to finish their business and get out of this Chihuahua Desert hell-hole. He ignored the scout's advice to approach the camp slow and quiet. *To hell you say! We're gonna kick these bastards hard! I wanta see some of their blood instead of seeing my own from these damn bleeding hemorrhoids.*

Holding his revolver ready, he pulled hard on his reins and his horse came to an abrupt stop. A blanket staked to madrone trees swayed and the captain drilled three shots into it. Several other soldiers did the same. This volley of shots elicited another volley from soldiers arriving on the scene and imagining seeing dangerous renegades firing on them from bayonets and saltbushes.

The captain held up his pistol for the firing to stop. There was silence except for squeaking leather, a horse's whinny and hooves stomping the hot desert floor. A dust cloud of their own making enshrouded them. The camp was deserted. There was no one here. The lieutenant pointed to the horizon and the moving dust cloud.

Captain Verlander turned searching for his scouts. As usual, they were far in the rear and out of any danger. He kicked his tired horse and raced toward them. "What the hell is that?" He asked, pointing to the dust cloud. "If these people are on foot, how can they move so fast?"

One of them said, "Some on horses. We know this all the time. Maybe they have split up."

The captain's face was beet red. "And where did they do that?" He yelled the question at the top of his lungs, "Where did they do that? And if they did, why didn't you spot it and tell me?"

The scouts looked at one another and shrugged. One of them said, "We track... report to you."

The captain knew their horses were exhausted and could not give serious chase at this time. "Yeah! You follow them and you damn sure better not lose them." He yelled again, "You damn sure better report back to me too."

The scouts turned their mounts and moved out in the direction of the fading dust cloud. The captain, shouted, "Rest your horses, men. We've almost got 'em now. We'll move out in fifteen minutes."

Stepping down and pulling at the seat of his pants, he had no confidence in his words, and doubted the men believed him. Again he thought of using his pistol on himself.

Spirit Dog sat his horse and by his expression, Father Pollen knew he had something important to say. He, Naiche, and Anrelina moved close to the scout so that their conversation would not be overheard.

Spirit Dog nodded toward the south, "We gotta dying man coming this way, unless he don't make it."

"How far away?" asked Anrelina.

The scout pursed his lips. "About a quarter mile. He's dying of thirst. He's naked, almost blind, and making funny noises. And...and I'm not sure, but it might be the white eye, Camel. He looks so bad, I can't be sure."

The three on the ground traded looks. There was silence between them. In the distance, a dust devil writhed and danced across the blowing sands. Father Pollen looked southward and said, "I'll go after him. We can't allow a man to die of thirst."

Anrelina interrupted him, "We've already agreed that we cannot allow this man to bring death on all of us. Why does he keep following us?"

Naltzukich said, "I say we push on. If Camel or whoever this man is catches up with us when we camp, then we decide what to do with him."

The priest shook his head in disagreement; the other two were adamant. Spirit Dog scanned the dry horizon as he spoke, "We are losing time as we talk. I am still seeing two dust clouds at times." He shrugged, "I don't know the meaning of this unless there are two groups of white eyes following us."

A few seconds later, Anrelina ended the conference, "Let's move now and it is up to the evil man whether he catches us or not."

CHAPTER 17

"I am weary of being cheated, treated like a dog. All the promises given to me have turned out to be lies. I am weary of seeing my people hungry and sick." Geronimo

The sidewinder coiled, arched his triangular head back, and vibrated his rattlers. Camel staggered directly toward the deadly snake because he neither saw nor heard it. He saw only the crystal line on the horizon; cool, life-sustaining water that seemed to remain stationary, regardless of how long he stared at it or struggled to reach it. The snake's rattlers shook violently. The large head holding the flicking, forked tongue, deep-set viper eyes, and pulsating poison sacs, lifted almost a foot from the hot, desert sands as it prepared to deliver its lethal dose of death. The plodding, reeling figure was almost within its striking range.

Camel stopped, the crystal line he thought he was seeing changed to stars that shot upward and then spiraled downward. He shook his shaggy, bearded, head and pounded the side of his temple trying to restore his vision. Like a drunken sailor, he swayed and weaved as he looked upward, directly into the ball of fire that bathed him. Slapping both ears with his palms, he shook his head to try to rid it of the popping and snapping sounds that reverberated throughout his skull.

He appeared to look down at the coiled reptile; though, in fact, he saw only stars and lightning bolts that confused and befuddled him. His trembling hand touched his bearded face, dry parched skin stretched over his facial bones.

He lurched forward; the sidewinder's head shot out like a bullet. Camel's faltering steps offset the deadly serpent's timing. The hypodermic-like fangs flew past Camel's shriveled calve missing the target by less than an eighth of an inch.

A hot wind kicked up tiny grains of sand which pelted his nude body. Like a reed in the wind, he swayed, responding to its strength. He possessed few human characteristics: rational thinking, logical choice-making, sight, hearing, taste, smell and the few he retained, he was losing fast.

He had not urinated for several hours. The last time he tried to pee and catch it with the cup of his palm, he produced nothing. It hurt bad.

Moving with the pressure of the wind, he stumbled to the bottom of a miniature valley surrounded by sandy dunes. He couldn't walk up the dunes. Falling to his knees, he began crawling. He didn't see or hear anything, but a few feet in front of him a small boy ran away screaming in fear, while another one dropped a spear that had been made especially for him...small and light. He yelled in fear as he ran toward a larger boy. "Little Knife! Little Knife, come quick! There's a wolf-devil coming after us."

Maggie squirmed on the hard wooden bench and compared this town council meeting to those she had attended in Connecticut. This one was orchestrated from beginning to end. Rather than the meeting providing a forum for free speech, it was a mockery of the real thing. She wondered how many of the people attending the meeting realized what a farce it was.

New England town meetings were famous for their intellectual and fiery rhetoric. People attending the meetings came informed and ready to share their opinions. She recalled some dandies when men rose and spoke of lofty constitutional rights, often associating those rights with the most mundane problems such as horses soiling the streets.

Here in Angel Valley, people were not informed, but blissfully ignorant. She thought it horrid that the town had no newspaper. The best one could do to elicit information was engage in gossip at Moseley's Mercantile. The problem was that the talk usually centered around the weather, stock prices, or who Pearl Manning was courting.

She did not like thinking of herself as an intellectual elitist snob, but the "angels," as many referred to themselves, were uninformed, uneducated, and the only time they spoke out was when they became angry and began cussing and threatening one another. She guessed that most of them didn't know enough to ask a meaningful question or comprehend the agenda of the meeting.

She found it interesting that a Texas saying had it that, "Texas was not settled, but conquered." She knew the early pioneers had to fight the elements, Indians, Mexicans, each other for land and water rights, and general hardships; but this group of Texans she sat with had little fight for the right, only for what interested them and served their personal welfare. There were many good people living in the area, but they did not attend the meetings, and some, the Mexicans and Negroes, were not allowed to participate.

She knew she irritated people, especially those on the council, but she came to each meeting as informed as possible and asked relevant questions. Reverend Bilbo McKenzie gaveled the meeting to order. They met in the church and the council, made up of Bilbo, Hiram, his bank clerk, A.J. Moniker, who was the puppet mayor for the council, Grandmother Stutz, Ira McCormick, and Benjamin Arlington sat behind a wooden table before the pulpit.

Maggie resolved to say little on this night. She did not want to make matters worse for Bilbo. She used to walk to the meeting, unafraid of the dark, but now, she rode with the reverend to the chagrin, she knew, of his wife. It was apparent to her, Bilbo's wife was mentally unstable and terribly jealous. While the entire town believed she was physically ill due to some mysterious, undiagnosed malady, Maggie was convinced that the woman was a hypochondriac who enjoyed poor health.

A. J. gave his usual nervous, stammering account of the council's financial standing. Grandmother Stutz reported on the problem of loiters and drifters in town and made a motion the council authorize the sheriff to remove them, forcibly if necessary, from the city. The motion was agreed upon, and Hiram moved that Frank Moseley be named permanent sheriff. This too was agreed upon, and then Bilbo asked Maggie to report the school's needs and general status.

Maggie stood ramrod straight before the group. She avoided Hiram's eyes. She shared a progress report regarding the number of children attending, their grade-levels, and then the needs of the school. Along with telling about the need for additional desks, more reading primers, pencils and dictionaries, she quoted the cost estimates for each of the stated needs.

The discussion that ensued, showed her quickly she would receive nothing. Grandmother Stutz smiled sweetly as she told Maggie how much she appreciated her professionalism, but the money was simply not available for the numerous items she was requesting. Ben Arlington commended her and then repeated the same lines. Hiram's oily smile gave her goosebumps as his speech reiterated what had already been said.

At first, Maggie was disappointed Bilbo did not come to her aid. But then she could not expect him to go against everyone else. What would it have gained? Despite her little self-talk, she still felt a touch of regret that Bilbo was going along with the others. A motion was made by Ira McCormick to deny her request but note that the council would reconsider it whenever funds became available.

Maggie tuned out discussions regarding the need for additional street lights and board walks. She sat, fighting back tears. Eager for the meeting to end, she strode for the door as Bilbo banged his gavel closing the bureaucratic charade.

For the first time since her rape, she walked alone in the dark. She was furious at the council for denying her every request, but especially livid with Bilbo for his silent acquiescence. She heard her name called, but walked faster, almost running.

She beat Bilbo home. She was under her covers when she heard him enter the house. The floor squeaked outside her door, and she knew he was standing there. The talking floor told her that he moved on to his bedroom. She heard the mumble of voices and then all was quiet.

She was too angry to sleep. Recalling her report to the council members, she didn't know what she did wrong. It was concise and accurate as all of her reports had been. Again she found herself analyzing her call to teaching and whether she was in the right place or not. Her mind raced with questions and doubts and it was late when she heard noises outside her door again. This time the sound was quieter, but she knew for sure that someone was there.

She was gravely disappointed in Bilbo. He was a man of the cloth; he knew better. Turning over away from the door, she began silently quoting memorized scripture as she always did when having difficulty sleeping. She never heard him leave her door.

Toby leaned back against the shed wall and sucked on his unlit pipe. His rifle laid across his lap. The shed was located roughly twenty yards northwest of the cabin and positioned so that he could view both the cabin and barn from here. It was early night and the moon had not risen. Laying his pipe aside, he pulled a strip of jerky from his shirt pocket and chewed on it. Luckily, with age he had retained good teeth. A foot away a wooden bucket filled with well water and a gourd dipper floating atop it served to quench his thirst.

Chewing the jerky and holding the rifle, ignited a myriad of memories. He remembered fighting the Mescaleros. No one in the area knew it, but he'd been a squaw man one time in his early years. He'd taken up with a tiny little Apache squaw who was as good a wife as any man could ever ask for. She was a good farmer too. While he was killing and skinning buffalo, she grew corn, pumpkins, squash, melons, onions and chili peppers. He remembered for the first time in a long time how she counted the years by the harvest seasons. He smiled as in his mind's eye he saw her pulling firewood using a tumpline, a leather strap around her head, leaning her small, lithe, strong body into it. She hated the Navajo and Comanches and would tell him stories of the vicious acts of terrorism committed by the other tribes.

He would argue with her just for the fun of it and remind her that Apaches had some of the same beliefs as the Navajo. Each feared death. The deceased were buried quickly and their dwelling and possessions burned. The men would do the burying and then cleanse themselves with sagebrush smoke. They feared catching the ghost sickness.

She was frightened by many things…the dark, lightning or the sight of a crow. She always begged him to carry only four bullets in his guns. Four was the luckiest number. At first he kidded her about her many superstitions, but finally out of love for her, he would allow her to watch him place four bullets in his magazine and then when out of her sight, he would load his guns. She was also afraid of bears. She believed bears were the reincarnated ghosts of people who had been bad in their former life. He'd been stung by a centipede and she was hysterical. She told him later she had been taught a person stung, had one day of life for the number of legs on the insect.

Once when the weather was extremely dry and her garden was dying, he found her killing a lizard. She turned the body of the reptile skyward and said it would bring rain. He was surprised when it rained three days later. He shook his head and smiled in the dark; he still hadn't figured that one out.

He sighed. The moon was peeping over Bear Hill. He had lived a good life on the Texas frontier. He fought Indians, killed buffalo, run horses, and finally, worked cattle. He had known quite a few whores in his day, but his only love had been the little Apache squaw. His weathered hand gripped the gourd, one that she had hollowed. It reminded him how she was adept at so many things, like making a great tasting beer from the fruit of the Mescal cactus.

Sorrow, like a deep canyon, ran through him. He had ridden a lot of trails and seen a lot of things, but now it all came down to this. Camel was dead! He had suspected it for some time. Camel would often disappear for a few days or even a week, but he always showed up laughing and telling how a pretty widow almost screwed him to death, or how he got drunk and caught the cattle train west until he sobered up enough and came home.

No, Camel was dead. Killed no doubt by Hiram or one of Hiram's hired hands. Toby felt anger…anger at Camel, at Camel's father, Camel's brother, Hiram, and finally, anger at himself. Why was he sitting on this place risking his life for it? For what? Sighing again, he guessed he knew he had always stood up for what he thought was right. He had lost lots of fights, but he had won a few too. And in the end, isn't that all a fella could do? Give his best to a right cause?

Something caused him to sharpen his eyes and ears. What was it? It came to him. The crickets, whippoorwills, everything was quiet. Something had disturbed them. What was it?

He jumped when a brood mare in the barn whinnied. The mare had smelled a stallion. The closest stallion he knew about was over a mile from here. Someone was out there. Stuffing his pipe into his shirt pocket, he stiffened in his chair, cradled his rifle and waited.

Pearl gave up on Judah making the first move. He'd brought a Rhode Island Red rooster to service her hens. A possum ate her last rooster just before she caught him with a single-spring steel trap and she and the boys enjoyed stewed possum. For the last month, her hens were squatting on the ground whenever a person came near to them. They were horny and as Judah's rooster made his way from one to the other, Judah gave his nervous little laugh and looked toward the barn. He asked about the boys, but she ignored the question and kept her eyes on the rooster.

"Come on in, Judah. I wantcha to try my honey bread."

Entering the kitchen, he stood as always with his dusty, worn Homburg twisting in his fingers. She took his hat, tossed it on the table and kissed him hard. At first, he was rigid with uncertainty, but a second later, he was holding her and kissing her harder.

Kissing and grappling, they made their way to her bedroom. She pulled her faded gingham dress over her head when he asked, "Pearl, forgive me but I gotta ask, do you have feelins for Hiram?"

Her eyes flashed. "Yes, Judah! I hate him!" She looked at him and her voice softened, "I care for you, Judah."

He reached out and caressed her suntanned cheek with his calloused hand. "I care for you, Pearl. I wanta do this with you mighty bad, but I'm willin' to wait for the preacher if that's what would make you happy."

Laughing, she slipped off her homemade underwear and stood naked before him. Removing his pants, his desire was obvious. He uttered a hoarse whisper, "You're the most beautiful woman I've ever seen, Pearl. I wantcha so bad, it makes me feel weak."

She laughed again lightly. It was wonderful to make love to a man who cared for her. Unlike Hiram, Judah was gentle and breathed his love for her into her ear several times during their lovemaking.

When it was over and she laid in his arms, she stared beyond his rising and falling chest at the shotgun in the corner. Closing her

eyes, she buried her head in his throat and focused on the sweetness
of their lovemaking, but could not keep the image of the shotgun out
of her mind.

Something was bad wrong. The captain rose in his saddle by
standing in his stirrups. Peering into the desert, he could make out
two puffs of clouds. They were each several miles ahead and
appeared to be about three miles apart. How to explain it? Had the
renegades split up? Which group should he chase? Should he split
his men?

The men were grumbling again. Morale had sunk to a new low.
It didn't help any when one of the men fell off his horse and went
into convulsions the day before. The limestone flats they had been
riding for two days were like a blazing fire. Their horse hooves
made a hollow sound on the white slate sand which made a man
wonder if he was riding on top of hell and he and his mount would
break through and fall into the fiery abyss at any moment.

He had not seen his scouts for two days and this both angered
him and scared him. Did his constant haranguing drive them off?
Could he lead his company out of this hell-hole of a desert without
them? For all of their faults, he now admitted they had the Indian's
natural ingenuity to find water. In another day, they would be
running out of it. What should he do? Should he turn his company
around and backtrack out of the desert before the wind wiped clean
their tracks? What about his career in the military? *Now, that's not
a question, Captain. You know the answer to that one.*

Pulling on the reins of his horse, he turned around to face his
men. Shoving his military training aside, he had made the decision
to split his company so they could pursue each band of dust.

Little Knife pulled his weapon and marched forth to slay the
wolf-devil. He stopped short when he saw the creature before him.
Chatto was right…this was a real wolf-devil. The creature moved
on all fours and had long gray stringy hair hanging down over his
face. It was the face that frightened Little Knife more than anything
ever had before. The creature's eyes were deep-set in his head and
red with blood. His nostrils were pulled back, revealing black, dried
skin; but the scariest thing of all was his mouth. He had no lips. His

mouth was frozen into a death-like grin exposing large teeth and black gums. His arms and legs were like sticks containing no muscle, only bones and ligaments. Each vertebrae was visible with parchment skin stretched tight. Each rib was identifiable.

The creature kept crawling toward him and when Chatto cried out and ran, Little Knife did the same. The wolf-devil made a rasping screech with each breath. Even as he ran, Little Knife could hear the thing breathing fire and glanced back to ensure that it was not catching him.

Manuelito, the half-breed, was the first to reach Camel. In less than a minute, a crowd of Morning People surrounded the wheezing creature. People stepped aside so the old, withered Navajo, Naiche, could see it. With one glance he knew it was Camel. He had seen a half-dozen Indians in this condition before, and most had died. Studying the white man who seemed to be on the verge on death, Naiche thought, *Should we waste our precious water on this white eye who has caused us only grief?*

As Naiche gave thought to the question, Father Pollen, Anrelina and Naltzukich arrived to stare at the wheezing, pathetic dying man. There was a moment of silence. Naltzukich snorted and asked in an angry voice, "Is this the same white eye who's followed us and made such trouble for us?"

Anrelina answered, "Yes! And we must act fast to save his life!"

Father Pollen agreed. He was the only one to kneel down by the scary-looking man, stroke his bony back and talk soothingly to him, though Camel couldn't hear him.

Naiche said to the crowd, "You need to rest now. Go to your blankets, drink and be ready to walk." The group had continued to walk at night, but lately, with their pursuers, they had been forced to move also as much as possible during the day.

Naiche didn't want an audience as they discussed Camel's plight. As the last of the reluctant spectators moved away, he said, "We must think of our water supply. With age my nose does not always smell water as it once did."

Naltzukich agreed. "We have our children to look after. This man is no good! He does not deserve our water."

Father Pollen shook his head, "We can't allow a man to die of thirst when we have water. He can have my share until we find more."

Camel continued to crawl, though he moved like a sloth in slow motion. Anrelina shook her head, "I agree with both of you. But I...I..." She paused, looked at each one and continued, "I believe that we must have the faith Father Pollen talks about. I believe as long as we do right, we will be safe like the children of Israel led by the one called Moses."

Father Pollen had tears in his eyes, "Thank you for that, Anrelina."

Naltzukich shook her fat jowls, "I am against it!"

They all looked at Naiche. He had a faraway look in his eyes. A long pause and he spoke to Anrelina, "Get a blanket of rawhide and one of wool. Bring them to me along with two skins of water."

Manuelito helped her. Anrelina laid the rawhide in the shade of a saguaro cactus that had its fruit removed by Skinyas earlier. Manuelito, Anrelina and Father Pollen carried Camel to the shade. They were amazed at how little he weighed. Camel's arms and legs continued to work at crawling, even when he was lying on his back on the hide. His limbs moved slowly and he was completely helpless.

Naiche directed Anrelina to spread the bright red Navajo blanket over Camel. His limbs continued to move, but not enough to throw off the blanket. His breathing sounded like a whistling tea kettle. Next, Naiche had Anrelina pour water very slowly onto the blanket...all over it. Once the blanket was soaked, Naiche had her moisten her hand and wipe his face.

Manuelito went for Spirit Dog and his painted horse. A travois was hastily put together and Camel with his wet rawhide and blanket were strapped to it. Naiche said, "We must give him water, but very slowly and very carefully." He stared into the distance and back to her, "Even so, he will probably die before another moon passes."

CHAPTER 18

The sidewinder eats the kangaroo rat. The roadrunner kills the sluggish snake and walks around for several days with the tail of the snake protruding from its beak.

"Is he dead?" Spirit Dog stepped back wide-eyed as he asked the question. He greatly feared death. Would he have to abandon his horse if the white eye was dead? Surely he was dead; no man could look like that and be alive.

Holding to the travois for support, Father Pollen placed his ear over Camel's face and listened intently for a long moment. The priest said quietly, "I think he's gone, Spirit Dog."

The young, lean Indian turned abruptly and walked away. Naltzukich approached, but stood several feet away. They did not want to have the evil white eye's ghost enter them. Regardless of Father Pollen's ideas, most of the Morning People still held to many of the superstitions of their ancestors. She scowled, "Now we will have to take time to bury him. I say we cut the travois free and leave him here for the big birds, or let his own kind bury him."

Anrelina neared. "Is he dead?"

Naltzukich nodded and her expression grew more pleasant with the thought.

Anrelina slowly walked to the side of the travois. The priest could see her hands trembling; she was defying all she'd been taught about death and spirits. She looked up to see Naiche coming. Without looking at the withered, lifeless figure, he said to Little Knife who was standing back scowling with his hand on his knife, "Bring me a tus of water."

Little Knife's frown deepened, but he did as Naiche told him to do. Pouring the water on Camel, Naiche said, "Bloom, my fellow creature, bloom like the desert plants and grass that come alive when the spirit sends the rains."

A gasp arose from the bystanders as Camel opened his eyes and looked at Naiche as though responding to his command. Several stepped back in fear. Naiche turned to Anrelina, "The same spirit made us all and we all need the rain to bloom. There is no magic here." He looked again at Little Knife who was scratching the horses neck. It was no secret that Little Knife envied Spirit Dog and his horse. He wanted to ride and be a scout, too. "Go get Spirit Dog and tell him I need to see him." Speaking to the priest, Anrelina and Naltzukich, he said, "We need talk."

They moved a few yards to a patch of brush grass growing among a bunch of Soaptree Yucca. White clusters of flowers topped each Yucca and crinkled brown seed pods split by the baking sun served as a backdrop for their council meeting.

Spirit Dog appeared, whispered something to his horse which was munching bunchgrass as they all looked at Naiche. In the desert, he was their natural leader due to his ability to lead them to water. He said he could smell it and that it talked to him.

He looked at Spirit Dog, "Do we still have two groups after us?"

Spirit Dog responded quickly, "Yes! We have two groups, one larger than the other and we still have the scouts from the larger group that I cannot understand." He shrugged, "They are of our people and follow us easily. They seem to be trying to help us by leading the group away, although the last couple of moons, they...they..." He shrugged again and yielded to Naiche.

Naltzukich crossed her arms and asked him, "Is it the same group who have split up so they might trap us?"

Spirit Dog looked at the dark beady eyes and heavy jowls and looked down and pulled the top off a blade of buffalo grass and examined it, "I believe that it is two different groups. I would have seen them when they split if it was the same group."

Anrelina spoke, "They get closer each day. What can we do?"

Naltzukich blurted with anger in her voice, "We can leave this one to the bird spirits! It will slow the white eyes to bury him." She glared at Father Pollen, prepared for his response.

Naiche waved the comment aside and said, "Stop looking at the gopher and see the bear. We are making it easy for our enemies. We are leading them to water. I have a plan."

Father Pollen felt his handicapped body trembling, and said with urgency, "Let's hear it, Naiche. We must do something and do it quick."

Naiche's weathered, wrinkled face scrunched even more and he raised his head and breathed deeply. "The Great Spirit sent a tiny bird to fly over me so its wings stirred the air and brought the smell of water. It is not far from here. If we go to it, our enemies will follow us and find it too." He paused, scanned the horizon, and nodded his head. "Do you see the Greasewood running that line in the distance?"

Father Pollen wrinkled his nose and squinted his eyes, but saw only fuzzy shapes. Naktzukich shook her head, her jowls swinging, and said, "I cannot see it. Are you sure that you do?" Anrelina and Spirit Dog said at the same time, "I see it!"

Naiche allowed a moment to pass. A baby cried and a grasshopper jumped from a creosote bush to Naltzukich's shoulder. She grabbed it, bit its head off and chewed as they all waited for the old Indian to continue. He said, "I smell sweet water there. This is my plan: we move north as we're doing, but small groups begin to break away and go to the water and hide out. We will sweep the trails. When everyone is there with the water, Spirit Dog will ride on with his travois making a dust cloud for the enemy to follow. After some miles, he will drop the travois and double back to us. The enemy may be fooled, they may not, but..." He shrugged and made an expression that said, maybe it will work, and I think it's worth a try.

Everyone nodded in agreement with him. Naltzukich, with large, brown arms still crossed, looked at Camel and said, "We cannot keep him. Our children are too important to..."

Again, Naiche waved her aside. But she would not compromise this time. She seemed to puff like an inflated toad, "Let Spirit Dog use him as weight on his drag to make a dust cloud."

Father Pollen's back and legs burned with pain and irritation crept into his voice, "That's not the Christian thing to do, Naltzukich! I can't..."

She was angry. "Tell me, Father, how do we get him to the water without making dust and giving ourselves away? He cannot walk."

There was silence except for a swishing on the sand as a Gopher snake spotted them and crawled for the safety of the Yuccas. Naltzukich noted it and would find it and kill it for food after the parley.

Anrelina said with sadness, "I think Naltzukich is right, Father. We have no way to save the white eye without giving our plan away. He will have to take his chances with Spirit Dog."

Naiche agreed. He looked at the forlorn priest and said, "We will soon have all of the water we need. We will have those going with Spirit Dog to pour water on him. Maybe...maybe your God will see that he lives. But, it does not..." His voice trailed off as they all moved out, all except Naltzukich, who began searching for the Gopher snake.

Captain Verlander blinked in amazement. Shaking his head, he removed his hat and looked back at his men. *It's the sun and heat! I'm going mad! I see a group of riders in the sky. To make it even crazier, they're upside down.*

He felt great relief whenever his lieutenant said, "Looks like one of those mirages we've heard about, Captain."

The captain had pulled up and his company did the same. They studied the mirage. The captain wondered if this weird phenomena could somehow be a help to them in catching their prey. *Am I looking at the savages that...hell no, that's white people. Looks like four men and a woman. Where are they? What in the hell are they doing out here?*

He stood in his stirrups and scanned the horizon for what he was seeing in the sky. He saw only desert sand, cactus, salt flats, all radiating dizzily in the oppressive heat. He sat there for another full minute staring and then motioned for his lieutenant to move the men forward.

His hand rested on his pistol butt and he moved it to his saddle pommel. *I'll kill myself before I lose my company in this cursed desert. What kind of record will I leave behind for my son if I lose my men on this half-assed venture.*

The captain was a descendent of a long line of military men and he was aware of his dismal rank and status as compared to his father and grandfather, each of whom were generals. It seemed that at every step in his career, bad luck had dogged him. At Fort Dodge, a fire had been started by a drunk sergeant in his command and it had gone onto the captain's record. On an assignment in Oklahoma, he had the misfortune of losing two men to a gang of scalawags who then disappeared as soon as they had shown up. He couldn't fail on this assignment. It was unacceptable. He would die before he returned to the fort empty-handed.

Less than two miles away, his two scouts sat their horses. They were hidden behind a clump of yucca bushes. They watched as most of the Morning People settled into a wallow beside a spring. A horse carrying a lone rider and pulling a travois with a man on it went on. The rider was obviously trying to make a dust trail for the Calvary to see.

One of the scouts pointed to another cloud of dust less than a mile away. It was the group of four men and a women. They each stood in their stirrups and pointed to the cloud that belonged to their foul-mouthed, angry captain and his men. The three groups were very close together. What would happen when they met up? The scouts had already agreed that when that time came, they would return to their people. The white eyes were mad with the evil susto, or spirit, and this group of their own people were following the white-eyed priest. The scouts thought all of them were crazy.

Captain Verlander kept his lips pressed tightly together. He focused on breathing through his nose. Opening his mouth allowed the fine, silt-like sand to get in and grind between his teeth. His horse acted strange, tossing his neck and straining at the bit, he knew that in the past, this meant they would soon come to water by trailing the savages. The captain hoped with all of his heart this was true today. The cook had informed him that morning they had enough water for only one more day.

He hated the situation he found himself in. He and his company could survive only by following the Indians who obviously knew where the water was.

Sometimes, they muddied the water and he had thought of the possibility of them poisoning it. But, they had no choice; they drank the water, muddy or not.

His horse now tried to resist the reins and turn in another direction. *Cussed desert! It makes everyone, including the animals, crazy as hell. I can see the dust cloud ahead marking the savages movement. What in the hell is wrong with you, Boy?*

Deep down, he felt more scared than any time since they had entered this dead man's zone. Something was wrong! The Indians were still moving, there was no evidence they had stopped for water and rest the last couple of days. How was that? Were they able to store more water than his company? Were they so desperate because the army was closing in that they were carrying on without water? Had they accepted their fate, knowing they were going to die in the desert so they would take a company of army men with them?

Viscously yanking on his reins, the captain spurred his gelding and forced the dumb animal forward, toward the dust cloud. His hand rested on his pistol butt and he gripped it so hard his fingers were cramping. Placing both hands on the reins, he thought of his wife and son and tried to forget his thirst and what the future held for him and his men.

Hiram's booming voice echoed off the hardwood boards of the school house walls, "Poverty and shame shall be to him that refuseth instruction: but he that regardeth reproof shall be honored.' That, my dear children, comes from the Lord's word found in the book of Proverbs, chapter thirteen, verse eighteen."

Maggie stood frozen. She could not believe her eyes and ears. She was bent over a table helping Myrtle with an arithmetic problem. She slowly straightened and started to rebuke Hiram for interrupting her lessons when he announced, "Children, we are blessed to have someone of Miss Pickett's stature come all the way from Connecticut to teach you readin', writin', and numbers." He paused, grinned, and continued, "And teaches you morals and the importance of living a sanctified life of working and saving. The city council, at my suggestion, has decided that Miss Pickett should have proper transportation. That little show of gratitude is sitting outside. Children, as chairman of the council I assume the authority to give you the rest of the day off. You can see Miss Pickett's gift as you leave."

There was chaos as the kids ran for the door. Hiram stood in the middle of the room grinning. "Well, Miss Pickett, aren't you going to see what the council, in its wisdom and generosity, has decided to award you?"

Her expression and body language were rigid. Her voice was iron. "This is my classroom, you cannot and will..."

"Now, Maggie, Maggie. Stop it! It's time that we put the past behind us and carry on with the future. Keeping mercy for thousands, forgiving iniquity and transgression and sin, and..."

"Stop it! Don't you dare quote scripture to me, you grinning, fat, baboon of a hypocrite!" She would have continued, but her anger sucked her breath away. She stood there trembling, taking big breaths, fists knotted at her sides.

He frowned. "Be careful, Maggie. They'll be locking you up for going mad. Ya know some of the fine ladies like yourself that come west from the fancy northeast can't handle the harsh conditions of the west. They go crazy and have to be locked up and shipped back east in chains. Now, I know that I may..."

"You pompous ass! You're the one who's crazy! Your religion reflects your illness! You..."

His face was red, a vessel pulsating on his forehead. With eyes that seemed to grow darker and beadier by the moment, he stepped forward, stopped, and they stared in silence at one another. There's no telling how long the staring duel might have lasted, but it was broken when her active little student, David, sang out from the doorway, "That's a mighty pretty surrey Mr. Hiram brought ya Miss Pickett. And that little mare's got mustang in her and my pa says a mustang can pull more than twice their weight."

The anger in Hiram's eyes dimmed. Turning, he said to David, "You're right about that, Son. I was just trying to get Miss Pickett to look at her new possession. Your pa's a smart man. Ya better get on home now and maybe ya can help him with his chores." He turned back to Maggie, "Barney Womack will stable your horse. This will..."

Maggie took a breath, fought back her own anger, and said in a voice still racked with emotion, "You mean I receive a horse and surrey rather than the teaching supplies and materials I need to..."

Hiram said, "The council didn't pay for this. I did. Maggie, I'm trying to..."

"Hiram, I will not accept your gift and will have nothing to do with you. Don't ever come into my building again, interrupt studies and dismiss my students. You might run your bank, the town and all of the territory, but this school is mine."

As she hastily gathered papers from her desk, he said quietly, "Maggie, I'm trying to apologize for my actions the other night. Please don't bother to threaten me. You're an intelligent woman and know I can have ya fired like that." He snapped his big fingers and it angered her even more that she jumped at the sound.

Brushing past him, she said, "That's fine, Hiram. I'll return to civilization where murder, rape, mayhem and missing persons are not the order of the day. A place where the town bully can't make people disappear by snapping his fingers."

Hiram erupted. Moving quickly, he rushed forward, grabbed her upper arm and said, "Whatcha talking about? Explain yourself."

Fighting not to show him he was hurting her arm or reveal her fear, she met his stare, "What's wrong, Hiram? You quote lots of scripture for a man who cannot face the truth."

He squeezed her arm and it took her breath, but she retained her impassive expression. Leaning closer to her, he growled, "Whaddya mean I make people disappear?"

Forcing a smile of derision, she said through clenched teeth, "Everyone knows that if anyone causes you trouble, they just disappear. You going to make me disappear too, Hiram?"

He stared at her a long while and then said in a low monotone that made a chill run up her spine, "Ya just might disappear, Maggie. But there won't be any mystery about it. Everyone in the territory will know you're an immoral woman unfit to teach our little ones. There'll be damn few people grieving ya too. Ya can count on that."

He was gone in a second. She stood there listening to him ride away. Collapsing onto a hard wooden bench, she began trembling and sobbing.

Pearl rocked atop Judah and when he rolled his eyes back in pleasure, she fell off of him laughing. As she shook with laughter, he lifted on one elbow and said in his usual quiet drawl, "And I thought I was really doin' ya some good there." His dry wit made her giggle.

Pearl had never known such happiness with a man before. Judah was thoughtful, sensitive, caring, and a hard worker. Thanks to his help, she had a crop in the field, three calves nursing in the barn, a pen with a sow and four piglets squealing as they followed her around, and a smoked ham hanging in the now completed smoke house. Every Sunday, they alternated between her house and his by putting the kids together and all eating dinner at one table. Her boys loved Judah. His three daughters seemed as taken with her.

He grunted as she rolled back onto him. "You were doin' me some good there, Sweet Judah. I just gotta keep my eyes closed so I don't see you roll yours back like a stallion when he's mating."

As they worked in unison to meet their mutual needs, she reflected on their relationship. Hiram had reduced his visits to once a week since he saw Judah's plow horse in front of her house so often. He visited her on Wednesdays. She had told Judah she needed one day to herself to clean and do womanly chores. Did he know Hiram visited her on that day? It was still a sickening ordeal for her. She tried to force Hiram from her mind. She was making love to a wonderful man, but Hiram still invaded her thoughts.

Judah's lean, muscular body quivered in ecstasy as he reached a climax. She kissed him and rolled off. Sitting up, she eyed the shotgun for the thousandth time as she imagined blowing a hole in fat Hiram's stomach. *What if I stay still while he gets undressed and gets in bed. Then I jump up and blast the mean sunuvabitch. I bruise my face and tell everyone he forced himself on me.*

She knew why she didn't do it. She might hang. Lots of people knew Hiram visited her place often. Did about everyone know it except Judah? Thinking of her situation made her face suddenly change from happiness to dread.

"What's wrong, Pearl? Ya look like ya just saw the devil. That don't bode well for me."

Standing, stretching, holding her lower back, she stared at the firearm leaning in the corner and said, "It's not you, Judah. I was just thinking that I better get at my chores before the boys get home. You gotta do the same before your girls get back, too."

Toby cracked the back door of the cabin and peeped out. Nothing moved. He opened it further and closed it quickly. He was trying to draw out a shooter if one was nestled down out there behind a saltbush just waiting for him to appear.

He felt silly and embarrassed for his fears. *But dammit, I know my feelings and there's been somebody snoopin' around here the last few nights. I might not know jackrabbit, but Babs damn sure does and she's been telling' me about as loud as a lady can talk that there's some kinda scoundrel out there.*

An unusual whinny from the stable froze him. *Babs! If some sunuvabitch hurts my lady I'll...*

Clutching his rifle, he ran out the front door, tripped on the steps and fell as a rifle shot breezed his hair. Scrambling up, he ran, bent at the waist for the stable. Another bullet whizzed over his back. Toby heard Babs whinny again and then a loud, crashing sound as he felt a giant hand slam him to the ground. He laid on his back and tried to get up, but a familiar voice sounded over the rushing thump of his blood against his eardrum. He looked up into the dead-like eye's of Bryant Williams. Bryant held his rifle over his shoulder. Pushing his Stetson back, his lips curled in a crooked grin.

"I toldja to watch yourself, Old Man, but you're hardheaded. Ya remind me of my mean-ass pa. I shot that sunuvabitch, too."

Toby could muster only a hoarse whisper, "Take care of my horse. Don't hurt my Babs, she's..."

Blackness enveloped him and his voice sounded like an echo. Like all echoes, it faded into silence. Toby knew the first rest he'd felt in a long, long time.

CHAPTER 19

In desert country, camels are sometimes called "ships of the desert."

Camel could hear someone dismounting from a horse and walking toward him. There was a moment of quiet, then a sound he didn't recognize. Water caressed his parched, shrunken lips. He licked it and heard someone say, "Ahhh, you like it." A trickle of water struck his chest, stomach and legs. The feeling was muted by some type of cloth that covered him. Now he felt not a trickle, but drops on his lips. He opened his mouth to allow the sweet nectar of life to soak into the dried fibers of his tongue and throat.

He didn't know if his eyes were open or not. Was he blind? Why couldn't he see? Then he remembered. He'd heard that extreme thirst could bring on blindness. Straining to open an eyelid, he felt a sharp sting as one lid cracked open. He saw a shape standing over him. The person was fiddling with something, a popping sound, and then the shape disappeared. Camel felt himself moving. With his hands he could feel that he was on a travois.

They were moving fast and a hard bump told him he was tied to the travois. Good thing. The alkaline flat they were riding over was rippled with drifts of salt and made for a bumpy and wild ride.

Sometime later, he heard his name being called and he opened his eye again. This time he was able to make out Spirit Dog offering him water. He opened his mouth, but received only a few drops. It angered him that the Indian was pouring it over his body rather than allowing him to drink it.

Spirit Dog spoke as though he'd read his thoughts, "Naiche said to pour it on you and if you did wake up, to give you only a little of it. He says that if you drink very much now, it will kill you."

Camel tried to speak, but nothing came out. Spirit Dog disappeared and after a moment, returned to bend over him, "Now, Camel, you evil, drunk, white eye, we will see if you have the stuff to live or not. To live, you must help me get you on my horse and hold on while we ride back to my people. Naiche said if you cannot do this, I am to leave you here. Maybe the army will find you and save you; maybe they will not find you and you will die here. It is up to you."

The Indian pulled a knife made from a sharpened deer antler and Camel felt a pang of fear. Spirit Dog used it to cut the rope holding him to the travois. He reached under Camel's armpits and said, "You are very light, but I will need your help to get you up and mounted. Hold onto me."

Spirit Dog lifted Camel with ease and thought how he was as light as a feather. Sitting on the horse, Camel looked like a stick of saltbush and wavered, but he didn't fall off. Spirit Dog cut the leather thongs tying the travois to his horse and threw it into a pile of creosote bushes clumped against a patch of Banana Yucca. The dull brown travois disappeared into the natural fauna.

Spirit Dog turned the horse and began to backtrack to the wallow where the others waited. He expected Camel to fall off, but was surprised to see him grasping the horses mane and remaining on even though he swayed badly at times. The wet blanket was about to slip off of Camel's bony shoulders and the Indian held it, aware it could give them away if found by the army.

Spirit Dog could see the two clouds of dust in the distance. He would need to make good time to avoid encountering the army. If Camel fell or did anything to delay him, he would leave him behind.

Guiding his horse through waving Tarbushes with their yellow flowers, the rider nudged his mount forward. The cloud made by the army was getting closer fast and he could not be caught too close to the wallow. If he saw he couldn't make it, he'd head back into the desert; he must not lead the white eyes to his people.

The two clouds of dust were growing closer. Were they going to join up? The Indian kicked his horse again; would Camel be able to stay on a galloping horse?

As the horse galloped into the wallow, Camel fell off. He bounced on hard sand and flopped into the shallow spring. The blanket lay crumpled on the sand and he laid face-down in the water. He lifted his head, it trembled, he was too weak to hold it up. His face disappeared into the water again. The Morning People sat in clumps watching. Manuelito lifted him as Anrelina placed the blanket over his naked, bony frame. They leaned him back against the wallow's edge.

Naiche reminded everyone to stay low so they would not be spotted by the approaching army. Spirit Dog along with several others laid on their stomachs and stared at the dust clouds. The women sat on the edge of the spring and nursed their babies or talked quietly to their children.

Camel had both eyes open now. He could not believe the skeletal limbs he was staring at could belong to him. He wiggled his fingers to assure that they were his. The water tasted so good, but it made his stomach hurt. He saw someone coming toward him and made out Anrelina. She had pressed a skin into the spring and filled it and now poured it onto the blanket covering his body.

He tried to thank her, but made only a croaking sound. She moved away without saying anything, just looking him in the eyes. Across the spring, he saw a large woman frowning at him. His vision was impaired, but he could see well enough to know this woman was not his friend.

"Doggone it, Sheriff Dan, I got a big problem on my hands and I need ya help. Everybody knows I ain't too dang smart, but even I know things aren't right around Angel Valley."

Billy stared into the face of his friend who smiled back. Sheriff Dan's face seemed to be fading lately. It bothered Billy. "And another thing, Sheriff, doggone it, ya face is getting so I can hardly see it. I don't understand it."

The sheriff looked down at his boots, and up into the eyes of Billy. "That's cuz I'm dead, Billy and you're forgettin' how I looked. Now, don't go getting' riled up about it, Son, that's just natural."

Billy felt tears welling up. "But I don't wanta forget you, Sheriff Dan. Ya the best friend I ever had. In fact, to tell the truth, ya the only friend I ever had."

"I"m still here. I ain't left ya. What's botherin' ya, Son?"

"A lotta things. Your death for one thing. There's sumthin' not right about the whole thing. I keep seein' ya lying there with ya shotgun across ya ankles and somehow there's sumthin' not right about..." Billy's eyes widened, and he smiled, "I'll be doggone if I ain't uh skunk's cousin. That's it! Now I see it! I see it!

The sheriff smiled back, though Billy could barely make him out. "Ya see, Son, ya ain't dumb. Ya heckuva lot smarter than that thing they got for a sheriff now. And there's plenty more for ya to learn; just keep your eyes and ears open like I taught ya."

Billy became aware that he was standing. He looked up into the white clouds stacked over the horizon and felt better than he had in some time. He smiled and looked back and started to say something, but stopped. His friend was gone. This seemed to be happening more often and it worried him that Sheriff Dan might not return someday. Deep down he knew it would happen, but he wasn't ready to face that fact yet.

Pearl and Judah sat on her back steps saying nothing. A big Rhode Island Rooster chased a hen and caught her a few feet from them. Pecking her head, resting on top of her, his tail feathers trembled as he fertilized her eggs.

Judah spoke quieter than usual, "He's called the note in on Ephraim too."

Pearl spoke with bitterness that concealed hatred, "That man deserves to be shot by somebody."

After another long silence, he responded, "I guess there's always a Hiram around, Honey. Ya can't kill all of 'em."

"I don't wanta kill all of 'em, just this one."

A rider could be heard in the distance. Pearl figured it a good chance it was Sheriff Frank Moseley serving her papers as he had on Ephraim and Judah. As the hoof beats receded, she breathed a sigh of relief. *But for how long? Hiram was here yesterday to collect his payment. I guess if Ephraim and Judah were women, women who would get in bed with him, they'd hold on a little longer. But, hell, I ain't foolin' myself. Hiram has to be getting tired of me. I'll get a visit from the sheriff any day now.*

She wanted to cry...cry for Ephraim and especially for Judah and herself. It bothered her constantly that she was unfaithful to Judah. He had asked her to marry him several times. She had considered it. But what would it mean? Would it make Hiram act faster in running them all off of their land? Was she thinking of land when she should be thinking of their relationship?

He heard a voice. It sounded familiar although he could not place it. It sounded like...like Olsen. The young giant of a cowboy who'd been Toby's protege for over three years. Toby tried to greet him, but no sound came out. He tried again but managed only a squeaky whisper.

He opened his eyes, but when he did, it made him dizzy. Olsen's soothing voice had a calming effect, "Take it easy, Toby. You just relax now and let me take care of you. The new doctor from Angel Valley's been here and wrapped ya all up in bandages. He says it's a miracle that ya not dead. He said the slugs..."

Toby lost the voice and found himself drifting back to another life. A life when he was a young shirttail and rounder. He was riding a gray sorrel in the high country of Colorado. Cutting through a rocky niche, he heard the thunk of a rock and looked up to see Indians topping the canyon walls above him. He spurred the sorrel as he felt the first bullet breeze his chaps. He reached for his Winchester...next, his dream-like state found him frying a trout he'd caught in the Canadian. The pan was sticking and he burned his hand reaching for the handle. Boy, did he love a good fried fish. Wiggling his hands into his leather gloves, he lifted the pan off of the rocks he had used to rim the fire and worked his Bowie knife to scrape the tasty filets from the scorched pan. Hearing a sound, he looked up to see his gray gelding had slipped his hobble and galloped toward a thicket of agave. Damn! He whistled but the horse only shook his head making his mane flutter and continued running. Toby knew he would have to...next, he was raising his boot to put it on when a scorpion fell out. He dropped the heel of his boot on the pesky insect, only to feel something on his finger and saw another one latched onto him. He yelled in pain as the...

Olsen sat in a wooden chair beside the bed of his old friend. He placed his hand on Toby's arm as he jerked and moaned. The young man squinted his eyes closed and muttered a simple prayer, "Lord, the doctor says he shouldn't be alive. He says that he most likely won't make it. I ask ya to help him. Amen."

CHAPTER 20

"In the entire history of the Untied States, Congress has failed to honor one single treaty made with the native people of this land."
Senator Inouye

Camel leaned back against the sand wallow and listened as Naiche reminisced over his youth. As a youngster, he had lived in the territory of New Mexico. The army led by Kit Carson defeated the Apaches and Navajos at Canyon de Chelly. His soldiers slaughtered Indian horses and cattle and forced the survivors to walk three hundred miles to a terrible place called Bosque Redondo in East New Mexico. There, the Indians found only a barren wasteland. That's where Naiche learned to find water. Like now, his survival depended on it.

The old warrior looked away from the small fire that burned in a hole within the wallow. Camel, who sat behind most of the others, felt like Naiche was staring at him as he spoke, "I learned to watch the way the birds flew, the sky tells a story also, the type of plants that grow, the lay of the land, they are all telling us the way to water if we know how to read them."

He shook his head and looked down, "If I were younger and my eyesight and smell better, we would have had much more water." A unison response arose disagreeing with him and several comments were made how he had saved their lives with his skills. Their comments had no effect on him. Naiche was not seeking approval or confirmation. Camel looked at the deep crevices running the old Indian's face, the clear eyes, strong jaw, and thought he reminded him of his father.

Naiche went on, "We were forced to live beside the Mescalero Apache, sometimes our friends, sometimes our enemies. In that place we shared a common enemy...starvation by the white eyes."

Camel was weak and on the verge of dozing, but he was certain now the old man looked directly at him. Naiche paused and took a drink from a small tus handed him by Anrelina. He cleared phlegm from his throat and continued in his deep, baritone voice, "The white eyes told us we were to farm for our food." He smiled now and wrinkles built around his eyes and down his face as he looked at Anrelina. "We told them farming was woman's work and we men were to hunt the buffalo. But...the white eyes had already killed and butchered all of the buffalo for their hides and tongues. So, they told us since there were no buffalo to hunt, we would learn to farm.

Naiche paused and stared into the small fire as it crackled and popped. His voice assumed a poignancy as his eyes saw scenes no one else around the fire saw. "We Navajo did do some farming. My spirit fathers told me the Pueblo taught us to plant corn, weave, and sand painting. But, in our hatred of the white eyes, we refused to do even what we knew to do. A proud people forced to give up all of their ways and do only what the white eyes order them to do is a people who fight back the only way they can...by doing nothing or running away." Shaking his head in sad remembrance, he said, "Some turned to the white eyes firewater and..." he fell into silence, staring into the night.

A long silence followed. Camel dozed, but woke to see women carrying their children to bed down for the night. He dozed again and this time he heard Father Pollen's squeaky voice, "...didn't agree with the government's treatment of the proud red people. Another holy man, an Episcopal priest, Bishop Henry Whittle, wrote a plea asking our men in power to deal fairly with you. He criticized the reservation system for forcing you to have to depend on the white eyes for food. But, our leaders didn't take his suggestions. Other white eyes rose up to plea for you, a woman named Helen Hunt wrote several books telling about the bad things happening to you, the same things that Naiche spoke of, but again, the leaders did not hear her."

Camel tried, but could not keep his eyes open. He dozed off listening to the tenor voice of the priest. When he opened them again, he heard Naiche's deep voice, "Then, like now, they opened a school for our little ones and made them speak and dress like the white eyes. They cut their hair and beat them if they heard them speak anything but their language. They ripped them from their mother's arms and took them away as the children cried and reached for their parent's. Next, the white eyes..."

In that interlude between sleep and awakening, Camel laid and listened to the sounds of quiet talk and someone sharpening their knife. The morning sun hurt his eyes. He watched silently as people dipped their tus into the small spring and filled them. He spotted Little Knife staring at him. The youth turned away after a long moment. Hearing footsteps, he turned his head to look up into the cold, hard eyes of Skinyas, his old drinking buddy. Skinyas stuck his tongue out at him, blew hard, and turned away.

Camel watched him walk away. He understood the man's anger. His gesture of disrespect was understandable. Camel recalled what he remembered of his association with the Morning People and thought it a miracle they had taken him in. He was stoned much of the time when with them and some of his memories were fuzzy. He recalled enough to know like always when drunk, he had shown his butt.

Lying still, observing the people preparing meals, dipping water, working leather, and sharpening tools, he knew a deeply strange sensation. *What is it? Am I still about to die? Is my body so wasted away I'll never have any more energy than right now?*

Something was very different, but he couldn't pinpoint it and it bothered him. He lost the thought as Anrelina bent over him with a small tus. He reached up with trembling hands, held the rim and drank deeply. She pulled it away. He tried to hold onto it, but she was too strong for him. She turned away without speaking.

He heard scurrying behind him and tried to turn and see what it was, but lacked the strength. A figure came into view cackling with delight and he saw it was the frumpy, mean-looking woman named Naltzukich. She held a prairie dog by a back leg. The lifeless body swung loosely as she squatted, reached for a knife and began skinning the carcass.

Another sound of quiet glee went up and Manuelito, the half-breed known for his blanket trading, held a long, writhing, diamond back rattler. The head had been cut off, but the body arched and stretched its knotty muscles.

Naltzukich skinned and gutted the rattler and placed it on a spit above a low-burning fire. A skinned jackrabbit was already cooking and smelling heavenly. Naltzukich had killed it with a well thrown rock. The wood was extremely dry and gave off almost no smoke. Even so, there was a heated discussion over making a fire. Naiche was opposed to it, but Naltzukich convinced everyone else that the children needed cooked food. She was a worthy adversary and Naiche finally gave in and sulked off. Father Pollen tried to negotiate a compromise but failed.

As discussions and movement occurred around him, Camel alternated between wakefulness, dozing, and somewhere in a twilight zone. A voice woke him and he looked into the pretty face of Anrelina. She held a wooden ladle to his mouth and said, "Eat!"

Why? I've never felt so dead in my life. I don't have enough strength to lift my head. I'm dying! Shouldn't your limited food be given to your own people?

When he failed to respond, she said, "You must eat so you get strong. So open your mouth."

He mumbled, "Give it to your own people. I...I don't need it."

She eyed him curiously for a moment and then for the first time called him by his name, "Camel, you must eat. Naiche said he has seen many die in the desert and only one as bad as you make it. But he says you will live now if you want to. Besides, you need to be able to walk when we leave here. We cannot carry you."

He turned his face from the outreached ladle, closed his eyes and ignored her voice. About to doze off, he felt himself being shaken roughly. Opening his eyes, he looked into hers. Her voice combined strength and compassion, "Camel, eat!"

Naltzukich's gruff voice blurted, "We must leave him. The white eyes will save their own. We cannot..."

Father Pollen's head seemed overly large for his deformed, stunted body and now it was red with anger. "We will not abandon him to die in the desert. We have talked about God's word and it..."

Naiche lifted his brown, wrinkled hand and all fell into silence. He said, "Why fight? If he's able to walk when we leave, he can go with us. If not, he will stay here. God will decide for us."

Camel drank his fill and whispered a weak thanks; but, if she heard him she didn't respond and was gone in a second. It was dusk. Wondering where the day had gone, he fell into a deep sleep and woke to bright lightning dancing in the sky above him. At first he thought he was dreaming, but as the dazzling light flickered in crooked lines, he decided it was no dream. Thunder clapped and the earth shook. Voices sounded around him and he saw figures scrambling during the long moments of eerie daylight. The sight and sounds filled him and he stared open-eyed at the beautiful display of natures work.

A bolt of lightning struck a shaft of a rotten cottonwood that exploded into a thousand pieces of yellow bits that glowed and then dimmed into darkness. Camel found the strength to push himself into a sitting position so he could admire the storm. He felt no fear, only a calmness and peace that had eluded him so long he hardly recognized it.

The next lightning strike pierced a yucca plant and lit a crucifixion thorn within a half-dozen yards from Camel. The yucca plant glowed and then dimmed but the wiry crucifixion thorn burned brightly.

It burned on and on and Camel was transfixed by the sight. Behind him, the Morning People viewed his silhouette before the burning bush. The plant seemed to burn an unusually long time and he raised his weak arm up and looked through his spread fingers at the thin stems of the brightly burning plant.

Juanita wrung her hands wrapped in her apron. Standing in the kitchen doorway, she waited while Hiram gave thanks for the steak, smoked corn, squash and cornbread on his plate. She was nervous about the cornbread. He'd grown tired of her Mexican bread with jalapeno peppers and demanded some American cornbread.

Completing the blessing, he fiddled with his steak, chewed a piece, followed with a fork full of corn and then bit into the cornbread. Her heart pounded. She crossed herself and breathed a prayer that St. Bartholemew would keep her from Hiram's wrath. Her prayer worked.

"Now, that's cornbread, Juanita. I hope ya saved the recipe because I'll want some more of that."

She smiled and retreated to the kitchen. Every few minutes, she would move to the doorway to allow him to tell her if he wanted anything else. The third time she stood there, he belched, and motioned for her. "I need to see Carmen! Go tell her to come over right away."

"Si, Senor!" In the kitchen, she banked the fire in the wood stove, removed her apron and hung it on a hook behind the door. Walking quickly down the back stairs, she headed toward her stick and wattle house. She both loved and hated Hiram. He could be kind and gentle at times; at other times, he was cruel and vicious. But, she and her old father, brother, two children and sister, all ate very well because of Hiram Bishop.

Hiram stood on his front porch waiting and listening to hear Juanita close the back door. Looking down the only street of Angel Valley, he puffed on a long, expensive cigar, put one foot on the porch railing and studied the far end of the boarded walkway. Watching Queenie Beaumont strut her stuff in a frilly dress, he wondered why he allowed her and her rough-neck sons to remain in their God-fearing town. *I guess I'm soft-hearted. I don't mess with common whores like her, and some day soon I'm gonna invite her to church. Maybe she'll come, repent for her sins and we'll have a victory dinner at church on me. I know Bryant and several of the hands would be pissed off if I change this Jezebel into a Mary, but...aw, the Lord will handle it. Turn it over to him, Hiram.*

Next, he saw Stinky sweeping the walkway in front of the saloon. Stinky seemed to be seeing worse and stinking more every day. He wondered if the bartender had seen the new doctor about trying to close that open wound in his ass that carried the bad odor. He'd have to remember to ask him about that.

The only other person on the street in the midday heat was the black carpenter, Ben Davis, driving his wagon filled with his tools. Hiram glanced down at the railing he was leaning on and reminded himself to tell Ben to fix it. Hiram frowned as he thought of the carpenter. He was a likable man...too likable. There was something about him that Hiram didn't like. He couldn't put his finger on it, but sensed that beneath the smiling expression, was a man of defiance. Hiram couldn't take that in a black man. The Bible clearly...*oh well, again Hiram, you're a big man and try to give every man, regardless of the color of his skin, every opportunity to lift himself up. I just wonder where he got the money to buy that place of his and to make it without borrowing any money from me.*

Hearing a sound within the house, he flipped his smoke into the yard, turned and entered. He heard Carmen's voice and giggle and he felt a pony ride up his spine, over his shoulders, down his chest, stomach and rear up in his pants.

Billy tugged at the collar of his nut-colored shirt. He had buttoned the top button preparing for his second meeting with the judge, but it bothered him---almost cut off his air. With hair slicked back, he closed his eyes and mentally repeated for the hundredth time what he was going to say to the judge. The last time he spoke to the judge, Billy knew something was wrong with the sheriff's death, but he was unable to articulate it. But now he knew exactly what he would say.

He shook his head and a sort of smile covered his features. Darn, it was good to see things clearly. Billy enjoyed few such moments. He was slow and he knew it. Everything came hard for him. And people didn't make it any easier for him. He was keenly aware that no one was impressed with a dullard. That word had stuck with him for many years now. A teacher from the East had used it on him in school one day and his mother refused to make him attend after that. She tried to teach him what little she knew about letters, reading and numbers, but she knew so little and allowed Billy to cut his lessons short most days so he could practice his shooting.

Billy ran his hand over his shiny Colt Army .44. He started not to wear it since he was going to see the judge, but somehow the gun gave him confidence. It was the only thing in his life he'd ever excelled at and received praise for his skill. But, just before heading out, he decided to follow his mothers advice and placed his gun, belt and holster onto the peg beside the door.

He hoped he didn't encounter Hiram or Frank on his way. Taking big strides, he licked his lip nervously and kept turning his head looking for anyone who might be watching him. He saw Junior Beaumont down the street doing something like whittling or whatever, but saw no one else as he slipped into the building where the judge held court. Breathing a sigh of relief, he realized his heart was racing wildly and he felt the need to pee. That always happened when he got stressed, he had to pee. Sitting on an old oak chair, he crossed his legs and tried to remember what he would tell the judge.

A deep, gurgling voice called his name and he nervously rose, pulled at his choking collar again and marched straight-backed into to see the judge. The prune-faced old man began asking Billy questions and Billy felt his shirt collar getting tighter and he kept tugging at it as he tried to think clearly so he could answer the questions. He must remember what he came to say, but the judge scared the living hell out of him and his questions made Billy's thinking fuzz up and his head started to really hurt.

The army's scouts were the only people who knew what was occurring in the desert. They didn't know the parties, or circumstances, but they knew that there were two groups of people running from the jackass, Captain Verlander. One group was mostly Indians, half-breeds and a couple of whites, while the other smaller group was three white men, a half-breed, and a white woman. They knew the large group was lightly armed, treated each other with respect and kindness; while the other was armed to the teeth, and hateful to their own, especially the woman.

They also knew the half-breed with the smaller group was as clever and sharp-sighted as they were. He had spotted them at least once, maybe more, they knew for sure.

The scouts knew, too, that a lone white man was wandering in the same area. He was a question to them. Had he been kicked out of one of the groups or was he on his own?

They knew more. They knew the ones that seemed to be led by the old Navajo, were hiding in a wallow by a spring. They knew that up until now, both the army and the small group had been led to water by the old Indian. The old Indian's plan was obvious to them. They had observed as the one scout worked to raise dust and then hide his backtrack to the spring. Their only initial confusion was the man riding in the travois who needed help getting on the horse to ride back to the spring. Was he the lone wanderer or just one of their own who rode the travois to give it added weight? Why did they need a man to do that? They could have tied some yucca onto it to add weight and make more dust. They concluded it was the lone white man.

The scouts admired the cunning of the old Navajo. They hoped he could pull it off. So far, the others were riding deeper into the Chihuahua Desert and getting only dust and thirst for their efforts.

The scouts had agreed early on that if given the opportunity, they would avoid the large group and lead the crazy-ass captain and his men back to safety. Both scouts had also agreed that the captain was possessed by an evil spirit that had eaten his brain and heart and was now eating on his ass. Who could say what such a man might do?

Meanwhile Captain Verlander sat his mount and scanned the landscape from one horizon to the other. Alkaline flats, cactus...every type known to man was visible, dried, yellow brush grass, dull-brown creosote bushes, thickets of yucca without any nearby water, saltbushes, an occasional madrone tree, it was all the same everywhere the eye rested. Everything but water!

His horse stepped sideways, whinnied and he almost fell from the saddle. On the ground was a coiled rattlesnake. The captain cussed, drew his pistol and fired six times at the snake and missed as many times. His lieutenant drew up a couple yards away, aimed his Army Colt and the blast made the rattler's head disappear.

The red-faced captain stared at him. "Good shooting, Lieutenant," he said through gritted teeth. *This makes me look like shit in front of my men. I almost get my ass thrown off and then I can't hit the damn snake.*

The lieutenant rode close to him and said, "Sir, may I speak freely?"

Hell no! You insubordinate sunuvabitch! I'll court marshal your ass if you keep trying to make me look bad.

The captain spoke loud enough for the sergeant to hear, "Take a rest and tighten those cinches!"

Nodding to the lieutenant, they rode twenty yards beyond and pulled up. "Speak freely, Lieutenant." He stood in the stirrups and pulled his bloody pants from his itching ass.

The young officer hesitated, glanced back to the stern-faced sergeant who was looking at him and said in an anguished voice, "Sir, the men and horses are just about to drop. I don't think they can go much further. *And unless you give 'em a good reason, they're not going to follow you much further. You mean, crazy bastard! Everyone of 'em, including me, hates your guts.*

"I'll be the judge of that. In the meantime, I expect your full support, Lieutenant. Let's move out!"

He spurred his horse unnecessarily hard and galloped across a salt flat. He thought it important that the men see their captain demonstrate leadership and he felt he was doing this as he forced himself to ride the saddle with his behind screaming in pain. Reloading, he holstered his pistol. Riding through a clump of creosote bushes reaching up to his horses fetlocks, a kit fox scampered from the dark, security of his den. It startled the captain's fine quarter horse, causing it to jump and twist like a rodeo mount. The captain lost his seat, sailed through the air, heard himself yell and then his mouth filled with sand as he bounced and then slid along the dry lake bed.

Olsen drew water from the well and was pouring it into a pan that he kept beside Toby's bed when he heard horse hooves. A group of three men rode toward him. The big Swede squinted and held his hand to his forehead as he tried to make out his visitors.

In a minute, Bryant Williams rode in with two Rocking H hands. Olsen stood, and contrary to the big man's nature, he gave no greeting. He had heard the talk before he left about the Rocking H and Bryant Williams. He studied the foreman's hard eyes and had no trouble believing he might well be looking at the man who shot his friend.

The foreman said in a flat voice, "I thought all ya 3C hands vamoosed a while back. Whatcha doin' around here?"

It was obvious Williams did not expect to find him there. If he was the man who shot Toby, would he shoot him now too? The Swede worked to make his voice sound matter-of-fact, "Toby got in the way of a .44 slug sent to him by a bushwhacker and is bad off. I'm tryin' to give him some nursin'." He felt the sudden urge to add, "He's not gonna make it though." Pausing, he lowered his voice to a stage whisper, "The doc gives him no chance at all. I guess what I'm doin' is watching him until he croaks and then I'll bury him and be on my way."

Williams grunted and said, "This place is bad luck for everyone. After he kicks off, I'd bury him and go to better country." He started to move his mount when, as an afterthought, he said, "We're just cuttin' cross to get to our spread. Adios."

The three rode away. Olsen watched their dust and saw again the deep-set eyes and flat voice. He thought how Williams never expressed any sympathy for Toby or interest in who might have shot him. Olsen figured he and Bryant knew the answer to that one.

CHAPTER 21

Crooked Indian agents abounded. They grew wealthy by serving as middlemen selling foodstuffs and clothes meant for the Indians. Meanwhile, the Indians suffered an extremely high mortality rate due to inadequate housing, clothing and too little food.

The storm had brought only wind, sand, lightning and thunder, but no rain. The morning showed Camel a golden ball of fire rising in the east and people moving about. He heard voices behind him. Turning slowly, he saw several figures standing in a tight, circle. He wondered what was going on and then heard Father Pollen's voice, "No, no, it's not the same thing. It's what we call a natural phenomena, not supernatural."

A sound made Camel turn back to see Anrelina. She bent down and prepared to feed him again. He held up his hand and said in a squeaky voice, "I can hold it."

She looked doubtful, and he was too, but he managed to take the wooden bowl and spoon and feed himself. He saw pieces of meat in it and whatever it was, tasted wonderful.

He was still weak, but he felt himself growing stronger. He dozed a short time and then got up to walk a short way into the bushes to relieve himself. He was beginning to urinate without pain. Walking slowly back to his place, he became aware of something strange. *What is it? I thought before it was death taking me but I'm getting stronger and feeling like a human again.*

Resting on the ground, he watched children playing. Something about them was different and then it hit him...they played silently. They had learned to function without making sounds. Camel thought it sad that little children played like that. He remembered the names of the two boys before him, Chatto and Mangus. It surprised him he could recall their names. Things were different for him since his near death experience. Everything looked and felt different somehow. He wondered about it, but lost the thought as he watched the boys scamper silently after a horned toad.

He looked with interest at his wardrobe. He wore home-made leather boots, beige pants without buttons, a dark hand-woven shirt held together by leather thongs, and his long, unruly hair held in place by a bandanna. Except for his beard, he looked like an Apache warrior. A wool blanket draped over a chinch weed nearby. He didn't need it during the scalding days, but found it comforting at night when the desert temperature dropped. Wondering whose clothes he was wearing, he hoped they were not Skinyas, who might demand them back.

Recognizing Little Knife, he watched him skinning a rattler Camel estimated to be at least six feet long. The young Apache glanced toward him but showed no sign of emotion as he focused on his work. Naiche and Father Pollen sat on wool blankets ten or so yards away and talked quietly.

A shadow covered him and looking up, he was startled to see a man standing over him. It was the smiling young Navajo, Little Sun. Another young man stood slightly behind Little Sun. Little Sun introduced him as Chee, but the handsome, unusually tall Indian only smiled and nodded at Camel. It surprised him when Little Sun squatted before him and stared at him without speaking. Chee did the same.

Camel tried to return a smile, but his cracked lips would not allow it. Little Sun said, "You gave us a scare when you came to us. I did not know it was you."

Camel nodded. "I don't remember any of that."

There was silence between them as another shadow flitted across Camel and he looked into the blue sky to see a black buzzard circling. Without looking up, Little Sun smiled and said, "I think he better give up on you."

Camel nodded and watched as his visitors moved away. The nagging unreal feeling was strong and again he tried to figure it out. He was puzzling over it when Anrelina brought another small portion of food…grilled rattler, a portion of ground corn mixed with chili peppers and a rough-textured bread. He gulped it down.

When Anrelina returned to get his wooden dish, he asked in a voice that still squeaked with hoarseness, "Where's the army that's been chasing us?"

Her face grew dark and she said, "Our scout, Spirit Dog, told us a short time ago the soldiers are coming this way and we must be ready to move anytime." She eyed him for a long moment and then asked, "Can you walk? Do you want to? The soldiers will find you when they come here for water. Maybe that would be best for you."

Their eyes locked for a time and he said, "I've met them already and I don't like them and I kinda think the feeling's mutual." He paused as her large dark eyes stared at him. He said, "I can walk. I want to go with you…" He paused and added, "to go with your people if you will have me."

She nodded and he tried to read her as she turned and walked to the center of the group. Her expression had been impassive, impossible to read. *She'd make a great poker player. I wonder if they will let me go with them. I caused real trouble for them more than once. Even so, they saved my life. I certainly can't blame them if they tell me I gotta wait for the soldiers. But what will that mean? Did the soldier that I shot die? They might hang me on the first tree they find or just leave me behind to become buzzard bait.*

A few minutes later, he saw Naiche, Father Pollen, Anrelina, and Naltzukich coming toward him. Their expressions were somber. He braced himself for the worst.

Maggie, the reverend, and his wife ate in silence. Maggie thought of the two options open to her on the four evenings she did not teach the Mexican and black children; she could avoid the cold atmosphere of the McKenzie household by remaining at school and working, and be terrified she might encounter Hiram, or she could come to her residence and feel the hostility of the reverend's wife.

The woman's irritation was obviously moving to rage, directed toward Bilbo, but meant for Maggie. Bilbo cleared his throat, and tried again for civil conversation. Maggie wished he'd forget it and allow silence to prevail. It was better than the wife's apparent fury.

He said, "Well, Maggie, are the children behaving these days? I hear the last schoolmaster could not control them. I've never heard you complain about that."

Maggie's peripheral vision showed her the wife rolling her eyes in disgust. Seeing the gesture, gave her insight into her own mental state. Maggie had dealt with melancholia or depression ever since the rape. She had no appetite, trouble sleeping, and found herself short-tempered with the children for no reason. Her thoughts were dark and ominous. Concentration was almost impossible. A long awkward silence followed when she realized her dinner mates were staring at her expecting an answer.

Feeling her face flush with embarrassment, she smiled half-heartedly and asked Bilbo to repeat the question. She answered him, excused herself and headed for her room. He would have to clean up tonight by himself if his sickly wife could not help him.

In bed, she tossed and turned. She felt miserable. When sleep did come in short spurts, it brought the smell of Hiram's breath and body odors. She would awaken to find her heart pounding and once, she'd wet herself.

Tonight, she prayed for the thousandth time to know God's will for her life. Should she quit and return to Connecticut? It would be difficult lying to her family, but that was not her greatest concern. What bothered her the most was quitting and running away. She'd been taught to stand and fight injustice. She wondered for the umpteenth time how her grandmother or mother would have handled the situation. Would they have been too wise to select Angel Valley for their service? Her face burned with anger and anguish as she wrestled with the demons of guilt. Did she do something to lead Hiram on? Did she send conflicting signals to him? What about her fall from grace with Camel? Did she ruin her reputation with him, and Hiram was not to blame for his actions?

Turning over in the bed, she sighed deeply. She knew Hiram was wrong. Dead wrong. She'd heard how women blamed themselves for rape. Her rational thinking reminded her how wrong he was and how innocent she was, but it did not resolve the conflict and torment within her.

A creak outside her door, told her Bilbo was standing there as he had done every night for the past couple weeks. Had she somehow inadvertently sent him a wrong signal too? Turning onto her back, she stared at the dark ceiling. For the first time since the rape, she admitted her deep need within just to be held gently. The idea of sex was too ugly to contemplate. The idea of a person wrapping their arms around her and holding her would help heal the deep gaping mental and emotional wound that Hiram had inflicted upon her.

It was as though her body was not her own as she slipped from the bed and tiptoed to her door. Holding her breath that the leather door hinges would not squeak, she opened it slowly to see Bilbo's silhouette standing there immobile. They stood without moving for a long moment. She held out her hand and felt him take it. He cupped her hand in both of his, but did not try to enter. She pulled him gently to her and they embraced. Feeling his hardness pressed against her, she reached down and squeezed his member with all her might. He grunted in pain, leaned against the door jamb as she whispered in his ear, "You may come in and be my friend. I need to be held, but nothing more. Is that understood?"

His hoarse whisper confirmed his agreement to her proposal. She led him to her bed and they laid atop the covers and held one another close. Each one knew if his wife caught them, it would matter little, if at all, that sex was not part of their arrangement.

He 'd never felt so weak before, but dang if he wasn't still alive. Toby looked around the sparsely furnished room, the old oak chifforobe, several battered hats dangling at precarious angles from the slightly leaning hat tree, and an old oak rocker covered with cow hide made up his room. It hurt, but he lifted his head enough to see if his rifle was leaning in the corner. It was not there. Every breath felt like a knife wedging between his ribs.

He felt a cough coming on and did his best to smother it, but failed and winced in pain. The house shook with heavy footsteps and he instinctively closed his eyes as someone entered his room. There was a moment of silence and then the squeak of his chair as someone's weight pressed into it.

Toby peeped through one eyelid but could see only a man's leg and boot. Turning his head slowly a little at a time, he made out the big Swede, Olsen. He looked like an overgrown boy sitting there staring at him.

Olsen jumped in surprise as he saw Toby open his sky blue eyes. The young man moved swiftly to his mentor's side and said in a hushed tone, "It's O.K. Toby. Ya gonna be alright."

Toby's voice was a hoarse whisper, "How's Babs?" Hearing Olsen assure him that she was fine, he slipped back into a deep sleep.

Olsen remained on his knees listening to his patient's even breathing. He sure sounded better than before. When Olsen first found him, his pulse had hardly been detectable and his breathing ragged and shallow. Olsen had sat at his friends bedside for two days and nights expecting him to die at any moment. He'd even dug a grave. When he could sit no longer watching his patient struggle for life, he'd take a break by going to the hill where the owner, his wife, and son were buried, and dig for a while.

Olsen's face beamed with joy and he wiped a tear with the back of his beefy hand. By dang it looked like he wouldn't need a grave after all.

Returning to his rocker, his expression became somber as he realized there were still big problems. Whoever had shot Toby, and Olsen figured it was Bryant or one of his men, would be gunning for the old man again when they learned he was still kicking.

Billy sat on the log crying. Sheriff Libby had not shown himself. Billy wiped mucus from his nose with the back of his sleeve and said between sobs, "I tried, Sheriff Dan, to tell the judge that you was murdered. I kept tryin' to tell him but he kept askin' questions and confusing me. That mean old man got me all fuddled up. I don't know if I ever told him what I went there for."

A sound made Billy turn. Junior Beaumont stood there fingering something. He stared at Billy's red eyes and said, "Whatcha doin,' cryin' like a baby, Billy? I could see ya all the way from town up here talkin' and motionin' to yaself." Junior smiled, showing a missing front tooth, "Damn, Billy, people gonna say ya crazier than ya really are."

Flipping a coin and catching it, he looked again at Billy who stared at his feet. Junior and Billy each knew that Junior was the smarter of the two. The only thing Billy could outdo him in was shooting. For that reason, Billy enjoyed giving Junior shooting lessons. It was nice to feel superior at something even if for a short period of time.

A hawk screeched overhead as Junior flipped his coin and slapped his palms together each time he caught it. Billy looked up at him, wiped his nose with his sleeve and said, "I gotta get back to town."

Junior appeared to focus on his coin as he said, "Better be careful down there. I saw our new sheriff aiming a rifle atcha on my way up here. Ya must be agitatin' folks somehow or other."

Billy's eyes widened as they did sometimes when he was confused. Did the judge tell the sheriff what he said? Fear, fear that nauseated him as it enveloped him made him stand and face Junior as he unconsciously gripped his pistol butt.

Now, Junior's eyes widened in fear. He dropped his coin and said in a high-pitched voice, "The sheriff was probably just sightin' his rifle, Billy. I'm sure he was not really aimin' it atcha."

Suddenly Billy wanted to be close to his mother. Since Sheriff Libby died, his mother was the only one to comfort him. Junior's jaw dropped as he watched Billy run awkwardly toward town holding his revolver to his thigh.

She sweated as she used a broken iron spindle from a wagon wheel to grind the glass. Blowing a swatch of red hair from her face, she paused to evaluate her handiwork. It had to be clear glass or he would see it. Satisfied with her work, she scooped the glass particles into a crock bowl and emptied it into a pot of chicken stew on the wood stove.

Pearl was a woman with a plan. She couldn't shoot Hiram without hanging or going to prison for life and then what about her boys. No, this plan was hatched after much thought on her part. She'd invite Hiram for dinner and feed him the stew spiced with broken glass. Whatever he did not eat, she would send home with him and prepare her and the boys something else for supper.

Dinnertime would mean the boys were at school and it would be no problem luring him into bed for a romp and then cap it off with a hardy meal. She smiled faintly to herself as she went through the plan again.

Along with the meal, today's sex would be different too. She'd been a lousy lover she knew, but not today. Today, she would be a hot filly panting for her stallion.

An hour later, Hiram shook his head, pushed Pearl's hand away from his tired member and said, "Whoa, Pearl. Damn if ya ain't gonna kill me if ya keep lovin' me like that. Is that your plan, to kill me with ya love?"

She leaned on one elbow, smiled down on his red, sweaty face and rubbed his hairy, heaving chest. Damn! Now there was a thought. Hiram was big and fat and if she could get him to go enough times, maybe his heart would bust like she heard a man's did one time while he was loving his slave girl.

He blew hard, like a winded stallion and said, "Pearl, honey, I hope ya don't think this is gonna change anything, cause I gotta do what I gotta do as far as the bank is concerned. Business is business and..."

She felt fear at her core, but would not give up easily. She placed her finger over his mouth and said, "Hiram, I understand. You're right, business is business. I guess I just feel like you've been so good to me and the boys and I've given you diddly-squat in return."

He turned to look at her closely. She had makeup on today and damn if he didn't have to admit she looked pretty good. Pretty damn good. Perhaps he had been a bit hasty in serving her an eviction notice. Hell, what difference would another couple months make? She was mighty...he felt himself falling into a deep sleep.

Opening his eyes, he stared at the rough-hewed boards of the ceiling and wondered where he was. Pearl called his name again and he remembered. She appeared at the door wearing that tight, green dress and looked as fresh as when he'd first arrived. She said, "Come on in here, Hiram. I'm starved after that romp and I bet you are too."

An hour later, Hiram sat in his surrey holding the reins, looking down into Pearl's face. He smiled at her and said, 'That was good, Pearl. I mean all of it." He burped loudly and said, "Look, I gotta do what those damn mean-ass bank directors order me to, but I'm gonna go back and talk to 'em. No promises, mind you."

She smiled and said, "I understand, Hiram. Why dontcha plan to come back next week at the same time and ya can tell me what the directors say."

"I'll do that." He looked down at the crockery bowl resting on the surrey seat beside him and said, "And thanks for giving me the rest of that stew. That's some of the best damn eatin' I've had in a long time. It puts my cook to shame."

The army troop walked their horses, leading them over dry alkaline flats and scrubby hummocks of sand. Each man dealt with his own inner demons as he contemplated death by thirst. The line of men and horses was ragged and uneven. The lieutenant had given up maintaining an orderly row. He now uneasily watched the enlisted men with his peripheral vision. He feared a mutiny. It would take only one thirst-crazed soldier to fire at him or the captain and the rest might go berserk.

Captain Verlander was not oblivious to the realities of their ordeal. His neck and back tingled every time the terrain was level enough so the entire unit was visible and every man could see him leading them. He'd placed his lieutenant at the rear and sergeant in the middle of the chaotic line to monitor for danger; but hell, the way things had gone lately, one of them might be the one to shoot him in the back

The captain hurt with hope the scouts were telling him the truth about a water hole just a few miles to the east. He'd ordered them to stay close until they reached the water and it irritated him that they now rode a quarter mile ahead of him. It was obvious the scouts and their horses had drunk recently because they showed none of the effects of thirst that everyone in the unit felt. He sometimes lost sight of them and it made him uneasy until they reappeared. But the land was deceptive. With the rolling, waving, tilting landscape, a thousand Indians could be waiting a hundred yards out there and he wouldn't know it until he was looking at their war-paint.

The scouts rode with a dread of their own. They didn't fear dying of thirst, they could locate water when they needed it, but they anxiously hoped the group fleeing before them had seen their dust the day before and abandoned the hole. The scouts had decided they had no choice but to backtrack the army to the waterhole or they would all die. They hoped the Indians had spotted their dust and moved on, but had they?

They were leading the Calvary in a roundabout way to the hole, but would be there in another hour. They had to be. Some of the men and horses were on their last leg. The scouts wore heavy expressions, each wondering if they had cut it too close. Too close for the army and the fleeing group. What about the other group of wanderers. Where were they? The scouts prided themselves on being skilled scouts and trackers, and yet they had lost the other group. What if they showed up at the same time as the army? What if the smaller group had attacked the larger group which the scouts had grown to respect and had tried to protect.

A rifle shot from behind made them rein up and look back at the scraggly line of followers. Were they about to see the men turn on their leader, Captain Hurting Ass?

The two men stood just below the crest of a gentle hill. Their horses stood twenty or so yards behind them, out of sight. Big Boy stood with his weight primarily on one leg, hands resting on his narrow hips. His bearded face was burned and he pressed the middle of his dried, peeling lower lip trying to stem the trickle of blood flowing down his chin.

Sans stood a few feet from him. His face was darkly tanned, but held no hair. He didn't burn regardless of the sun and heat. He even spit, which Big Boy envied. Damn, he couldn't spit if his life depended on it. He had put a pebble in his mouth an hour ago, but he'd had to blow it out. It produced no spit and only hurt his sore mouth and dried tongue.

Big Boy turned to Sans and said, "Whatcha make of it?"

The half-breed scanned the horizon with his spyglass. Lowering it, his eyes narrowed until Big Boy could hardly see the light brown pupils. He didn't speak for a minute and Big Boy looked at the horizon again and waited patiently. He well knew his life depended on San's judgment. He also knew they were in a desperate spot. Only a few times before could he recall Sans using his spyglass. Each time had been when a posse, band of Texas Rangers or

Mexican Federales had been hot on their trail and about to catch them. But each time, under Sans quiet leadership, they had escaped capture. At times like these, Big Boy relinquished decision-making to this small, wiry man who seemed to hate everything and everyone.

Big Boy's eyes took in the man whom he considered one of few worthy adversaries. Although Big Boy outweighed him by more than a hundred pounds and stood almost a foot taller, he'd seen Sans whip the leather-handled knife from his belt and empty a man's entrails before the other fella could pull his revolver and get off a shot.

Sans finally spoke softly, "The group the army's chasin' found water. They been laid up at it while the army and us have been running after our tails. The army's movin' to the water hole now and the others have vamoosed."

Big Boy rubbed his grizzled chin. "What we gonna do? We gotta get water or we're dead."

Sans said, "Unless we wanta fight it out with those troops, we better find that other group fast. They'll have water with 'em."

Big Boy grunted, "Ya gonna track 'em?"

Sans didn't respond to the obvious. It always amazed him how tough Big Boy could be in dealing with others in a fist fight or gunfight, but how weak he became when the going got really tough and his brute strength or pure meanness was no longer an asset to him. Sans mounted his horse, Big Boy followed and they rode off. A half mile away, they reined up where Kilkenny, Jones and Eunice each squatted within a narrow band of shade created by overhanging Yucca. "Get mounted. We're gonna track that group the army's been after and get some water," barked Big Boy.

Sans rode ahead, the only tracker in their band. Big Boy ordered Jones to follow Sans, Kilkenny came next, with Eunice riding ahead of Big Boy. They didn't worry about dust now because they knew the army was focused on one thing only---the water hole. Just as they were intent on only one thing---finding the ones with water.

CHAPTER 22

The old West could be rough in lots of ways. Fleas and bedbugs were a common problem throughout the frontier. One trick was to place a devoured ham beside the bed to attract the vermin. Another ploy was to place each bed leg into a can of skunk juice.

Camel felt like he was floating. As he walked behind Manuelito, he expected the walking to be difficult, perhaps impossible. His bravado before Anrelina had been feigned. He only knew he wanted to throw his lot in with this group rather than with the soldiers.

Why wasn't the walking more difficult? Was he simply beyond feeling? Would he collapse any moment and the group have to leave him behind. He knew several who would like that---Skinyas, whom he'd cheated out of his beer, Little Knife, whom he'd pushed into the side of Bone's shack and cracked his head, but he knew his most powerful enemy was Naltzukich. She was an accepted leader and hated his guts. Every time he caught her looking at him, her face held a frown or worse, a look of disgust. All things considered, he didn't blame her at all for her feelings.

That was another thing. Where were his feelings? He'd been angry his entire life and now he felt no hostility toward anyone.

And how to explain that strange feeling he'd had ever since he became conscious after almost dying in the desert. Had Anrelina fed him some type of Indian potion that was killing him? Was it a drug that made him feel like this?

Thinking of Anrelina, he could not believe she would do anything to hurt him. He again saw her large, soft brown eyes with the long eyelashes. He'd never seen an Indian so beautiful before.

Maybe it was just that he had not seen a pretty white woman in a long time.

A soft voice behind him alerted him to the present. It was Father Pollen asking how he was feeling. Assuring the priest he was alright, it occurred to him that his own position in the line was by design. The priest could monitor his condition and if a problem, Manuelito could assist him.

Camel's thoughts wandered as he took measured steps to maintain the pace. He was a small boy again slipping behind the corral to avoid his father and the directions to work that would follow. August Campbell was always working and he expected his sons to do the same. Why couldn't he have made his father happier? Was his father too harsh on him? Was Camel just lazy? He was unsure about the first question, but knew the answer to the latter.

Memories of him leaving home and becoming a gambler washed over him. In a new and starkly clear manner he saw how he wasted so many good years. His only concern for all those years was a pretty woman who was ready to give herself to him without any commitment on his part, a challenging, rewarding card game, and whiskey. Whiskey. Camel almost lost his walking rhythm as the thought cascaded around him like a waterfall. He had lost his desire for alcohol. It held no allure for him. Would he change his mind if Skinyas offered him a drink of his beer from his tus?

The thought weighed heavy on him. If given the opportunity, would he resort to his old self? Trudging along, stumbling often, the idea nagged at him.

Camel glanced back to see Spirit Dog disappear into the dark shadows made by the Yucca. Perhaps he'd heard something and was checking it out.

Spirit Dog urged his horse through a gap in the Yucca but pulled at the reins when he smelled dust. Too late. He saw movement to his side and then Sans razor-sharp knife pierced his neck muscle and slashed through the jugular vein. Spirit Dog's last thought was how dark everything had become despite the full moon.

The three men stood alone beside the corral, each leaning on a timber, puffing on a long cheroot. Hiram wore his usual dark suit and with the afternoon sun bearing down, he removed his coat and tossed it across his broad shoulder.

Bryant Williams wore his usual working garb, Stetson, dirty bandanna, sweat-soaked shirt, faded Levi's, riding boots with spurs and completing his outfit, was a large-handled silver .44 Colt holstered to his thigh.

Bryant had a severe case of smallpox as a child, almost dying from it and the story was written on his face for all the world to see. Some of the women in Angel Valley, those bold enough to say it, acknowledged that after Camel, Bryant was the best looking man in the area. They also readily admitted that neither were prospective husbands. They all knew what Camel was about, but not so with Bryant. They sensed a dark side to the man that scared them beyond dreaming up any fantasies about him as they sometimes did with Camel.

Sheriff Moseley, was the third man. Wearing his store apron, which in his haste he'd forgotten to remove when he left the store, he had remembered to strap on his holstered .32 Colt.

The three men were a study in sharp contrast. The one common trait they shared was their personal greed and ambition. Hiram blew smoke in the air, studied it and said, "Is the Swede still there?"

Without speaking, Bryant nodded his assent. Frank spoke with boyish eagerness in his voice, "Maybe he needs a little visit from the sheriff to persuade him to move on."

The other two ignored the remark. Bryant looked at Hiram and said, "From what the Swede tells me and the doc tells you, old Toby ain't gonna make it anyhow. I figure we just wait until he kicks off and then we tell the Swede good-by if he don't take off when Toby dies."

Hiram stuck out his bottom lip, nodded, and said, "Makes sense to me."

Frank's face was red with embarrassment at being ignored. He tried again, looking directly at Hiram, "I can get rid of him quick if ya need me to."

Bryant smiled and his voice was filled with contempt, "The Swede see ya wearin' that pretty little apron and he might wanta propose marriage to ya."

Hiram chuckled, Frank's face reddened more. He looked at Bryant for the first time, "Ya think he'll laugh when this pretty little filly loads his belly with lead?"

Bryant stepped back from the corral and blew smoke toward Frank. "Ya talkin' about that little pea-shooter ya carry? It's a pretty little thing, but I imagine that big ole Swede might mistake it for sumthin' to shove up ya ass."

Both men's hands gripped their pistol butts as they stared belligerently at one another. His bluff being called, Frank dropped his hand, looked away and mumbled, "I'm hired to enforce the law, not get into gunfights."

Hiram chuckled, winked at Bryant and said, "Boys, I damn sure don't pay ya to fight each other. Ya gotta do that on ya own time. Right now we got plenty to do without this bullshit." Turning to Frank he said, "Get the surrey, Frank, we need to get back to town before dark so ya can make ya rounds."

Frank welcomed the opportunity to remove himself from the volatile situation. Hiram said to Bryant, "Take a ride over to the 3C tomorrow and see what's goin' on. Let me know whatcha find."

The soldiers laid on the ground, put their faces into the pool of water and drank deeply. Some laid between the forelegs of their horses who were also drinking. Captain Verlander had forced himself to hold back and allow the enlisted men to drink first. He'd expected his lieutenant to follow his example, but he didn't. This demonstrated the lack of respect toward him and his leadership.

His gaunt, sun-parched face lifted to the slight rise of the land and he viewed his scouts sitting their mounts watching the scene before them. For some reason this bothered him. It was like he was allowing them to watch his wife bathe. He nudged his horse to turn so he could ride to them, but to no avail. His mount would not leave the water. A space opened up so his horse stepped forward, bent and slurped the liquid of life into his parched throat. The captain mentally cursed the scouts as he dropped to all fours to drink like his horse.

I don't even have control of my horse. How can I expect...stoppit, dammit! I've gotta get hold of myself. Gotta talk to the guides.

After talking with the scouts, he felt better. At least he had not lost his company to the desert and the scouts had good news. They said the runaways they were chasing were only a days ride ahead of them. The captain spoke civil to them for the first time in a long time. He even thanked them and told them they would resume the chase early in the morning...giving the men and mounts time to regain their strength.

Sliding off his horse, the captain thought even his aching ass didn't hurt as bad. Maybe it was the water and good news. Whatever. It was damn sure time to hear some positive news and feel some relief from his hurting hemorrhoids.

The scouts watched the captain urinate on a tumbleweed and exchanged glances. They were concerned for the runaways because they knew the other group seemed to be tracking them. Were they simply following for water, or did they mean harm for the group made up mostly of old men, women and children?

Sans led the group. Big Boy rode drag, keeping an eye on everyone to ensure no one slipped away, although it was doubtful any one would try it in the middle of the desert. Sans knew they were all depending on him to save their asses. Actually, other than Big Boy, he'd like nothing better to gut each one of them, especially the bitch, wrap their entrails around a devil's head cactus and leave them to the sun and sand.

Sans reined up, looked at the half-moon, and dismounted. Tracking during daylight was so easy for him, but night time was a challenge, especially with these damn Indians. He was thankful for one of the walkers in the group who must be crippled or club-footed. He made a helluva track, dragging his foot more than lifting it.

San's horse-hooves and his own boots told him he was standing on stone. That was the reason he was having trouble seeing the track. Dammit it to hell! Maybe Big Boy was right. Maybe they should move in and take the water from the Indians and see which one was even better than Sans at locating water in the desert. They would take that one captive and either kill the others or just leave them to the desert.

But Sans had not survived this long by being reckless. He was extremely cautious. Killing didn't faze him. In fact, he enjoyed it sometimes.   But if possible, he always knew his victim and his chances against him.   Like the Indian whose throat he had just cut. He'd observed him on several occasions and knew his only weapon was a knife.

Actually, the knife was Sans favorite weapon.   Unlike a gun, a knife was always loaded.   It meant feeling the killing of a man, too. And most men, Sans knew were no match with his skill with a sharp blade.   He felt his knife handle in its leather sheath.   His other hand felt the knife he'd taken from the dead Indian.   It was made of deer antler.   Sans had never seen a knife he didn't like.

Leading his mount a couple of yards, he spotted where the rock ended and the sand began.   There was that line in the sand made by the clubfoot.   Sans mounted up, glanced back at the others and headed out. He sighed. Big Boy was right. Regardless, they would have no choice but to move in on this group real soon.   Their horses were hurting for water.   The dead Indian's water-skin had slated the thirst of the men but there was not enough for the horses.   And Kilkenny tried to give Eunice a drink but Sans had stopped him.

"Let the slut die of thirst," growled Sans.   Sans did have some respect, if just a little, for Kilkenny.   Sans was sure Kilkenny would have challenged him and fought him if Big Boy had not been behind him.   Well, that was alright and probably good for Kilkenny.   When the time came, Sans would make his death quick and easy.   But as for the bitch, he felt himself grow hard just thinking about the fun he and his knife would have with her.

CHAPTER 23

The Bureau of Indian Affairs resettled Indians with promises of annual funds, goods, food and guarantees that they would hold their new land "as long as the grasses grow and the waters run."

Dawn was a sliver of pale sky on the eastern horizon when Camel looked up to see Skinyas standing before he and Father Pollen. The priest clung to Camel's forearm, receiving the help he needed to keep walking. Both men breathed heavily and at times Camel felt light-headed, but he had spoken words of assurance and encouragement to his bent, crippled walking partner.

Skinyas stood before the lightning sky, providing only a silhouette to them. His voice gave his expression away. "Naiche needs to see you now, Father. He is very...very...he needs you now."

Camel paused and looked down at the panting priest. "Do you need me to give ya a hand there, Father?"

"Please. I know you are weak, Camel and I shouldn't be taking advantage of you, but..."

Camel interrupted him as he stepped forward, the priest on his arm. "I consider it a privilege, Father."

They walked past knots of whispering groups, and the priest said, "I sense a new man in you, Camel. I think, like St. Paul's life-altering experience on the road to Damascus, you've been struck by a blinding light that was God speaking to you."

Camel paused as Father Pollen rubbed the head of a young boy and said, "You're a good boy, Mangus. Go back to your mother, she is calling you."

Moving on, Camel said, "I don't think so, Father. The only thing that happened to me was almost dying of thirst."

They came upon Naiche, Anrelina, and Naltzukich talking quietly. Camel stopped, expecting the priest to move ahead without him so the four could conduct their business in private. But the priest tugged at his arm and said, "Come on, Camel. Whatever it is, perhaps you can help." Coming close, Naltzukich's expression did not appear to reflect the thinking of Father Pollen. The priest ignored her. Looking at Naiche, he said, "What's wrong?"

Dawn was breaking fast and Camel could make out deep lines of worry etched like a map across the old Indian's face. "Spirit Dog has not come back. When we are traveling at night, he always comes an hour before dawn and tells me where we will camp unless he is depending on me to find water. We agreed earlier that we have plenty of water for the next two days and he would lead us to the best camping place." The old Indian paused, raised his head, took a deep breath and spoke quietly, unable to disguise a note of anxiety in his deep voice. "I fear that all is not well with Spirit Dog. I felt in my heart earlier that something was wrong and now I think I know what it is."

There was a long moment of silence. Finally, Anrelina spoke, "Day is here. We must find a camp. Can you find one for us? The women and children must rest. Then we can decide what we must do. Maybe then..." her voice took on a sound of resignation that collided with her words, "Maybe Spirit Dog will be here soon."

Camel thought of the sounds he'd heard earlier and how like Naiche, he'd felt uneasy throughout the night. *Could the soldiers be closing in on us? Will they come riding in here like hell-fire any minute and shoot us all down?* He was aware that he had thrown his lot in with the Morning People and could expect no allowances for being a white man. Indeed, many soldiers would consider him a traitor and rather shoot him than an Indian because he had joined up with them. His having shot one of the soldiers would not encourage a special break for him either.

Looking back from where they'd come, Camel wished he had the strength and a weapon so he could check out their trail. But he was spent and needed to rest his tired, spindly frame.

Naiche pointed to a clump of mixed catclaw and saltbushes and said, "Let's find shade there and wait for Spirit Dog." He sounded no more optimistic than Anrelina.

The scouts stood at a distance staring at the corpse of Spirit Dog. Both men were part Apache and part Navajo and highly superstitious regarding the dead. When a family member died, they took great measures to avoid the dead body as much as possible. They believed in ghosts and that those spirits often invaded the bodies of wild animals that were determined to harm humans. Each man had been preached to by white missionaries, but none of the preaching had obliterated their learned behavior.

They were close enough to recognize the man who had served as scout of the pursued. The dark stain in the sand around his throat told how he had died. Their eyes met and each shook his head. They had observed the tracks of the vigilantes and the scout merge. The signs were easily readable. The small group had caught the scout off guard and slit his throat. Someone was handy with a knife to do it while both were mounted on horseback. Someone expert with a knife and a killer's instinct.

Maggie bent over the small, thin, black girl as she scratched out the letter 'A' on a slate-board. She glanced over at Bilbo as he guided a small boy's finger over the words of a page in a McGuffey's Eclectic Primer. She noticed Bilbo kept glancing up and surveying the area. Being here, assisting her, required strength, and she knew Bilbo was taking a big risk doing it.

Reading a sentence haltingly, the child looked up at Bilbo, his face split with a wide grin of satisfaction. Bilbo squeezed his shoulder and said, "I'm proud of you, Jeremiah. Now, let's look at the next page."

Maggie stood and felt her head touch a vine of the arbor they worked under. There were about nine children in attendance today. They ranged in age from six to seventeen. Watching Bilbo, Maggie could not help but smile with pride the way Bilbo was such a natural as a teacher. She felt he was a much better teacher than preacher, even when he was nervous.

She pushed aside her conscience regarding her personal relationship with him. He still came to her bed at night and they held hands, sometimes gently rubbing the other's arm until he would return to his own bed.

She shoved aside her fear of what they were doing right now. Lately, she was bringing slate-boards and McGuffey readers from the school for the black children. If Hiram or any of the elite families got wind of this, she knew she and Bilbo would be run out of town immediately. Shouldn't she be afraid? Shouldn't she be ashamed? She was certainly not living up to the expectations of the community. More importantly, she knew she was not living up to her expectations of herself.

Hearing Ben Davis's deep voice say, "Yessir!" She turned to see Hiram standing there with a look that could kill. His face was red and his eyes more beady than she'd ever seen them.

The big Swede sweated as he shoveled sand over the pine box. He didn't stop until a mound of sand stood as a final monument to Toby's grave. He was handed a slab of pine nailed to a sharp post. With the shovel, he hammered the stake into the sand. Standing back, he read aloud the message burned into the wood, "Toby Smith, Rest in Peace."

Turning to the man behind him, he said, "Well, whadda ya think?"

Toby leaned against a forked crutch the Swede had cut from a cottonwood for him. He grinned, though he was so thin, the grin showed teeth which seemed to have outgrown him. "Mighty good, Olsen. Durn if it don't make me wonder if all this is a dream and I'm really dead."

Olsen frowned, "Ya gonna be if ya keep up this fool idea of yours." He turned and faced Toby, "Why don'tcha ride with me and let's git..."

Toby waved a thin, veined hand and Olsen went silent. Toby leaned on his crutch, stepped closer to the young giant of a man, placed his hand on his shoulder and said, "Olsen, ya been like a son to me and I can't tell ya how much I appreciate ya. But now it's time for both of us to ride outta here."

Olsen shook his head and headed back to the house. Toby followed, limping along with his crutch. Inside, each man packed his gear without talking. Less than a half-hour later, Toby held a saddlebag filled with supplies and a rifle. It was too heavy for him so he dropped the saddlebag and leaned his rifle against the wall. He heard Olsen say from the next room. "I'm gonna saddle 'em up."

Toby sat on the side of his bed and took deep breaths. He didn't dare do this as long as Olsen was around. His arms, bracing his torso, trembled and he looked at them with disgust. "Come on, dammit. Don't peter out on me now." Glimpsing his thin face and body reflected in the milky mirror, he looked away. He knew he looked like a damn skinny fence post that had been trampled by a herd of steers. Filling his lungs with air, he forced himself to stand and used his crutch to make his way to his rifle leaning in the corner. Pulling the lever an inch down, he saw Olsen had loaded it after cleaning it. On the floor was his saddlebags loaded with supplies and ammo.

Damn, he hated not being able to do things for himself. *If I'm having this much trouble now, how in the devil am I gonna make it out there on my own?* Hearing Olsen slam the front door, he pushed the thought aside and hobbled through the door holding to his rifle. Olsen stepped around him, lifted his saddlebags and said, "Why don'tcha let me carry that rifle?"

Toby looked ahead, not letting the Swede see the strained look on his face as he said, "I got it." The horses were tied to the hitching post at the bottom of the steps. He smiled as he spotted Babs and she nickered and tossed her head as he stroked her mane. "Okay, Babs. It's me and you, baby. Ya gotta look out for me and ya gotta do a durn sight better than ya did before."

Toby pushed his rifle into the scabbard and the effort left him breathing hard. He stood beside his horse preparing mentally to lift his foot to the stirrup. Olsen tossed his saddlebag over his saddle skirt, rounded the back of Babs and with no apparent effort gently placed Toby in the seat of his saddle. Toby placed both palms over the saddle horn and fought the nausea of weakness and pain.

He had to fake it or he knew he'd never get rid of his friend. He watched Olsen sit his saddle and said, "Olsen, remember to keep it short and sweet in town and then start ridin' and don't stop until ya at least a days ride from here. And whatever happens, my friend, remember ya helped me do what I wanta do. And, by durn, ya can't do more than that for a friend."

Olsen sat slouched, looking like he was sick. Toby said, "Now get the heck outta here before an old man starts blubberin'. Go on!"

The young cowpoke nodded, reined his horse away from the hitching post and moved into a trot. As Toby watched him fade into the distance, he wiped the moisture from his eyes, turned Babs in the opposite direction and prodded her into a trot. It was too painful. Slowing to a walk, he said, "Whew. That's better sweetheart. Let's head for cougar country slow and easy."

A little over an hour later, Olsen stood at the bar drinking a beer and talking to Stinky. *Damn! Stinky really smells like shit today. The guy must walk around with his pants full all the time.*

Stinky leaned over the bar and said, "I hate to hear that about old Toby. He and old Fuzzy usta come in here most every Saturday and drink a beer. I ain't seen either of them in a while, especially Fuzzy. I think Toby often came in just to check up on Camel. Many's the time he carried that sorry-ass Camel home sloppy drunk."

Olsen gulped down his beer. He had to get out of the place before he puked. Setting the mug down hard, he turned and said, "Well, Toby's pushin' up daisies now out there in the graveyard with Mr. Campbell and his son. There's nothing here for me now, so I'm takin' off. See ya sometime, Stinky."

Watching Olsen leave, Stinky headed for the front swinging half-doors. Looking up and down the street, he spotted Junior Beaumont. With fingers in his mouth, he whistled and gestured when Junior looked his way. As the teen neared him, Stinky flipped him a gold piece, "Run over to the bank and tell Mr. Bishop I need to see him as soon as possible."

Judah and Pearl stood in the dark outside her house. Inside, the boys talked and laughed. Judah had brought presents for them as usual. Floyd played with a flexible wooden snake that Judah had carved from a cottonwood tree and Ralph was trying to master tying a Hondo Knot with a short lariat made of horsehair that Judah and his daughters had worked on over the light of their fireplace before going to bed.

Pearl stood close beside him, holding onto his arm as though he might disappear at any moment. He sighed, shook his head, "I gotta go, Pearl. My times almost up and I know Hiram ain't gonna give me any breaks. I'm glad he's treating you and the boys different. He should have some mercy on a widow woman and..."

Pearl's voice was tight and louder than she meant it to be, "He should have mercy on a widower with three daughters, too. The cruel-hearted bastard."

He patted her back and said soothingly, "Now, Maggie. There ain't no use in..."

Twisting and removing his hand from her back, she said, "Ya know, Judah, I've thought a hundred times or more about takin' that shotgun in there and just killin' that..."

Squeezing both her upper arms tightly, his face was close to hers as he said, "Maggie, that's no way for a decent woman to talk. Now, you're a God-fearin' woman and I'm proud to know ya, like to make it more than that, but I can't. But, I also can't listen to that kinda talk from ya. Now give me a big hug and kiss and I'm gonna be on my way. Me and the girls are workin' to clear our gear out and make our way back to Arkansas. Oh, I'm leavin' ya one of my best Missouri mules, somethin' to remind you of me."

Pearl felt tears filling her eyes. "Ya can't leave me, Judah. Ya know we care for one another deeply and the boys love ya and I love ya girls. We gotta..."

His voice was deep with hurt, "Don't say those things, Pearl. It only makes it worse for both of us. If there was any way I could marry ya and make a livin' for you and ya boys, ya know I'd do it faster than a lightning strike. But..." He shrugged, pulled her close, kissed her wet lips, wiped tears from one cheek with a calloused hand and then was gone.

Pearl listened to his horse's hooves as they faded into the night. She saw the shotgun again, clenched her fists, and went to the barn. It was dark inside, but she knew the contents and what she was after. Feeling for a moment, she found it. Taking the demijohn over to the shelf, she searched next for a sack. Finding one, she placed the jug into the sack, and reached for the hammer. Taking it, she placed one hand over her eyes and then smashed the jug. She hit it several times, alternated between feeling tentatively for jagged pieces and then bringing the hammer down on them with all her might.

Finding a sack, she filled it with the smashed pieces and entered the cabin. The boys looked up from their fun and saw her standing there with blood dripping from her hand. Ralph stood, dropped his half-finished knot, "Ma, ya bleedin'."

She turned away and said, "It's just a scratch. You boys get ready for bed."

Later, as Floyd slept, Ralph peeped around the patched cowhides and watched his mother grinding glass chunks into small particles. She hummed something beneath her breath, but he could not make it out.

CHAPTER 24

By 1890 the buffalo had been exterminated from the plains and fencing ended the open range and cattle drives.

Camel woke with a start. He was sleeping against a sandy hummock and sat up as he heard strange voices and made out white men and a woman standing nearby. The Eastern sky was announcing daybreak.

Father Pollen, Naiche, and Naltzukich was standing together in a knot as the group passed around a tus of water. Camel studied the group. The man talking and who Camel assumed to be the leader, was a giant of a man with a dark beard, greasy, black hair and spoke in a deep voice.

He passed the jug to a half-breed who was half his size and said, "We appreciate the water. We have to have some for our horses too or they gonna die." He turned and stared as Anrelina approached. She rubbed sleep from her eyes and returned the stare of the strange man. Naltzukich reached out with a quick hand and pulled her close to her. The big man grinned and said, "Hello!"

Father Pollen stepped forward, squinting through his thick spectacles up at Big Boy. "We're glad to share with you, but we have a limited amount of water and we have children we must care for."

A skinny man wearing a rumpled Homburg, sandy hair reaching his shoulders and red freckles across his cheeks and nose stepped closer to Anrelina. "I gotta get to know this sweet thing. Honey, my name is Jones and I'm one helluva find for any woman. I can kill, gut, and skin a bear before breakfast and..."

Big Boy's deep voice silenced him, "Git back! Folks, we need water for our horses. Where is it?"

Jones pushed his homburg over his eyes and slinked back to his horse. More Indians gathered, women holding children, and men scratching sand flea bites, all with eyes wide. The word had passed that Spirit Dog was missing and these strangers didn't ease their troubled minds.

As the sun topped the horizon and flooded the dry land with its brilliant rays, Camel looked at their horses and felt a stab of fear as he recognized the brown mare ridden by Spirit Dog. They had removed saddle blankets and everything belonging to its owner, but he knew the horse.

Looking back at the knot of Morning People, he saw Naiche staring at the mare while everyone else followed his eyes. Father Pollen stepped closer to Big Boy, making the contrast between them even greater. "Where did you get that horse? He belongs to one of us, Spirit Dog."

Big Boy glanced back at his group and then lowered his head and said, "I'm sorry to be the one to tell ya, Padre, but we met the Indian who owned this horse. He'd been shot. He lived to tell us it was the army who did it. We tried to nurse him best we could, but..." His voice trailed off and he looked at his boots like he'd just lost his mother.

There was silence for a long moment. Now, they knew for sure. Spirit Dog was dead. Camel thought if he was still a gambler, he'd bet all he owned that not one soul among the Morning People, himself included, believed the story they'd just heard.

Father Pollen said, "Did you give him a Christian funeral?" As soon as the sad little priest asked the question, he recognized its absurdity. Turning away from the big man, he seemed bent more than ever as he used his walking stick to limp over to a hummock of sand and dropped onto it.

Big Boy's response was too quick. "We sure did, Padre. Kilkenny said words over him and the misses here quoted from memory several verses from the good book."

A young Navajo woman picked up her son, Mangus, and walked to a limestone rock and sat on it. She was a small woman and the boy seemed almost as large as she was. The woman spoke something to the boy who looked down with her and then Camel recalled that Spirit Dog had a wife and child.

Camel turned and watched the half-breed. After drinking, he'd mounted his horse again, ready to ride from danger at the slightest provocation. His elevated seat provided him the advantage of watching all directions and monitoring the Morning People. Balancing his carbine across the saddle, his deep-set hazel eyes never stopped roving, probing every niche and cranny for possible danger. Camel and Sans locked eyes and the half-breed seemed to squint and sneer at him. In a moment, Sans' eyes continued their constant search and vigilance.

Naltzukich said in her rough voice, "We don't have enough water for your horses. We can only allow you to drink."

A coyote howled and was answered by a mourning dove. Big Boy stared at Naltzukich who met his stare, head-on without blinking. Big Boy's voice got louder, "I hear ya, Mama, but we got no choice, we gotta have water for our horses or they die and we die with them."

The tense silence was broken by a screeching Red-tailed hawk that flew over them. Another man spoke up. Big Boy frowned and turned back to look at him. The man nodded in acquiescence of Big Boy's leadership, but said, "Let me try to help, Big Boy." His face was burned beet-red making his pale blue eyes stand out in sharp contrast. Stepping forward, he looked directly at Naltzukich and Naiche as he spoke. "Good people, we really appreciate you givin' us some of your water. It's sure precious stuff out here. Maybe if ya know us and our situation, you'll feel more like helping us."

Camel glanced at the half-breed and was sure there was a sneer on his face. His eyes alternated scanning the horizon and the immediate area.

The sun-burned man went on. My name is Kilkenny and this here is Big Boy. I guess ya can see why they call him that." He smiled, paused, met silence and continued, "That's my woman there, her name is Eunice. Ya can tell she's sick and feelin' poorly. That's Jones and the man on his horses is Sans. We were on business in Sonora. On the way back, we got hit by Mexican robars and they almost got us all killed. The Federales got into it somehow and got mixed up, thinkin' we were the robars. So we been on the run, my wife's bad sick and we gotta get to a town with a doctor. That's why we gotta have water for our horses."

Naltzukich's stern expression remained the same. "We gotta give water to our children. You can see for yourself how many little ones we..."

A sharp cry cut her short. Everyone turned to see Skinyas clutching the side of his head and screaming. Blood, lots of it flowed down his neck and down the front of his shirt. He'd been standing on the fringe of the group and while everyone focused on Kilkenny, Sans had quietly rode his mount to within a few feet of Skinyas. A groan went up from the group as Sans held Skinyas bloody ear up for all to see. The Indian cupped the wound with his hand and whimpered.

Sans wiped the blade of his knife on his pants and sheathed it. He nodded toward Big Boy who shouted, "Alright, Folks, quieten down! My friend, Sans, is telling ya how bad we need that water for our horses. Now, he's a gentle soul, Padre, but he's a desperate man. We all are. Now, where's the rest of ya water?"

Father Pollen's eyes appeared enormous with outrage through his thick spectacles as he preached him a strong sermon on the spot. But as he did it, the Indians brought their skins and tuses of water so the horses could drink. Anrelina led the whimpering Skinyas away to doctor the severed skin where his ear had been attached.

Naiche said nothing, but with crossed arms beneath his blanket, ambled over to Camel. Naltzukich followed him and Father Pollen joined them after delivering his stinging theological treatise on Sans's horrific action.

As he preached to Big Boy, Camel noticed Sans sitting his mount sneering. It was obvious to Camel that Big Boy wasn't listening to the priest and he wondered how long the giant would tolerate this gnat of a man who chided him.

Naiche's presence was powerful, but he said nothing. The others watched him and waited for him to speak. He glanced back once to see the newcomers watering their mounts and talking among themselves. They were aware that only the half-breed still watched them like an eagle who sees a rabbit jump or a snake coil from a half-mile away.

Maggie felt miserable sitting in the hard straight-back chair. She'd read about the Salem Witch Trials and thought how each of the accused must have felt much like she did now.

A special meeting of the town's elite, known as the council, was held in Grandmother Stutz's large, fancy house. She appeared to be about seventy to Maggie, but that was only a guess. A thin, narrow-faced woman, her thin white hair was piled into a tight knot atop her bony head. Her eyes were deep-set, her nose a tight stretch of skin across the bone, her jaw and teeth apparent beneath the yellow vellum of aged skin and in the flickering lamp light, it all came together to lend her a look of death's mistress.

Maggie pushed a wisp of hair from her eye for the hundredth time and told herself to calm down and not let her imagination run away. Beside Grandmother Stutz, sat Mr. McCormick. He was a short man with a bald pate and paunchy gut. Rumor had it that in his prime he was a young Hiram. *Meaning he was a sociopathic liar and unscrupulous wheeler-dealer. But he's here to judge me tonight so try to be polite to him regardless what is said. I must not allow myself to sink to their level. I must act with truth and honesty.*

Looking across the room at Bilbo that thought dissipated. He was obviously as uncomfortable as she. He kept his face down for the most part as though he were studying the expensive rug.

Mr. Arlington appeared to be in his early sixties. He carried himself with an air of gentility. His white hair, fair complexion, with suntanned cheeks made him a handsome older man. He stared at Maggie with unblinking eyes. He'd always appeared to be one of her primary supporters, but now his countenance held the look of a prosecuting attorney about to pounce on a feeble-minded, weak-willed habitual criminal.

A.J. Moniker, Hiram's bank clerk, was secretary. He was partially bald, and looked through thick spectacles too large for him, reminding Maggie of an owl.

Of course Hiram was there. He'd reported back to the council that he'd observed them teaching Negro children to read out at the Salt flats under an arbor. So this unscheduled meeting was called.

Sitting in a corner, wearing a dark suit too small for him, Sheriff Moseley tugged at his necktie and held an expression of solemnity.

He carried a two-shot derringer stuck in his belt because the tight, ill-fitting suit wouldn't accommodate anything else.

Mr. Arlington, the chairman, looked at Maggie and then the reverend. "Miss Maggie Pickett do you deny doing any of this?"

Maggie had thought of so much she wanted to say, but now she bit her lip, looked down and shook her head. There was a long moment of silence, broken by Grandmother Stutz's stage whisper, "Help us Dear Lord."

The chairman looked at the other accused and said, "Reverend Bilbo McKenzie, do you have anything to say for yourself regarding this matter?" He emphasized the title, reverend, and Maggie heard a strange sound come from Bilbo.

His shoulders shook uncontrollably as he wept. He stood with tears running down his cheeks and tried to speak, but couldn't get the words out. He tried several times, but each attempt ended with hiccups and deep-breathing.

The chairman appeared embarrassed and flustered at how best to proceed. Hiram intervened. "Mr. Chairman, may I make a recommendation to the council?"

The chairman nodded and Hiram stood. Unnoticed to everyone, he winced ever so slightly as his shirt pressed against an angry red welt on his back. *Cholla is hitting too hard. I gotta talk to him about that.* Hiram cleared his throat and began, "In talking to the Negroes, they said the whole thing had been pushed on them by this woman," He pointed at Maggie, as though he didn't know her name and she were a piece of garbage. It is my belief that our beloved pastor was led astray by this...this Jezebel, and he was trying to prevent her from getting in trouble as wrong as that may be. He's told me, when he was not as upset as today, that he thought that with his assistance, they could complete what they were doing quicker and he could get her away from there and try to talk some sense into her." Hiram paused, looked at the sniffling reverend and indignant Maggie. He turned again to the council, "I know that we all highly disapprove of what has happened. However, forgiveness is a top priority for me in my dealings with others be it personal or professional. As scripture reminds us, "Be ye kind to one another, tenderhearted, forgiving one another, even as God for Christ's sake hath forgiven you."

Hiram paused in a dramatic fashion, took a deep breath and continued, The Apostle Paul also wrote, "Let all things be done decently and in order." So we must be prudent regarding this matter and implement a workable plan that will be best for our loving, Christian community. I make a motion that our pastor be forgiven and we only ask his word that he will never be engaged in such an enterprise as teaching the Negroes to read ever again while in our employment. I make a motion that our school marm be forgiven and the same requirement be made of her. Also, in order to keep all of us above reproach, I suggest that Miss Pickett move from the reverends residence and reside in the home of a man who, although is a Mexican, I hold in high esteem. He has worked for me on numerous occasions and has always performed his tasks in a timely manner. He goes by the name of Quiermo and lives in a clean adobe less than two miles from the school house."

Bryant Williams sat his calico mare, one leg lying over his saddle horn. The other hand rested on the cantle of his saddle as he studied the mound of dirt and read the marker atop Toby's grave. Three more riders sat their mounts a couple yards behind him.

Dismounting, Bryant tossed the stirrup and fender over the seat of his saddle and tightened the cinch. Holding the saddle by the horn and cantle, he adjusted it, walked around the front of his horse, holding the reins and looked down at the grave. "Boys, this is what happens when a man loses his good sense. I hear Toby was a good horseman and a damn good shot in his day." He looked up at the men with a slight grin, "I'd like to have crossed trails with h'm back then."

The cowboys laughed and one said, "I'd bet a month's wages he'd been in a hole lots sooner if ya had." The comment was followed with more laughter.

One asked, "Ya want us to burn the house and barn?"

Bryant studied the house, barn, corral, smoke house, outhouse and shook his head. "Nah, I better talk with Hiram before we do that. He might have plans to use it.

Mounting up, Bryant said, "Let's find some steers."

A half hour later, the sun stood low on the horizon as Bryant searched for the man who'd never appeared at the agreed meeting place. Bryant had ordered the other two men to drive the fourteen steers through the 3C cut fence and to Hiram's Rocking H spread.

Leaning over to avoid a pine branch, he watched the ground for tracks. The man had been driving three or four steers, making it easy to track, but a ways back, the steers began to spread until now he followed only the horse tracks, and it was not his man's horse tracks. *What the hell's going on here?*

Backtracking, dusk was fast approaching when he spotted something unusual. Dismounting, he tethered his horse to a madrone tree and walked slowly, staring at the ground for clues. He almost stumbled over the body. It scared him and in a flash of fear, he palmed his revolver. Casting his eyes about for signs of danger, he saw nothing and heard only a whipoorwill singing his melancholy tune.

Dropping to one knee, he examined the body. It was his man alright. It was ugly. He'd been hit over the head and then had his throat cut. Bryant again looked carefully around him. *Who the hell did this?*

He prided himself on his courage in the face of death, but now the hairs on his neck stood up and he felt fear run down his backbone. Holding onto his pistol, he stood, took one more quick glance at the corpse, looked around, jumped on his horse and sank his spurs deep into his horse's sides.

Toby leaned against a cottonwood tree less than a hundred yards away. Scrub madrones and a variety of cacti concealed his position. His gray eyes appeared like flint in the waning light as he watched Bryant high-tail it away from there. Knocking a man in the head and cutting his throat had never been his style, and he'd never have done it if he were thirty years younger. But, he wasn't a young man and he was up against the worst bunch he had ever encountered. Lowering his head, he shook it sadly. He was not proud of what he had done, but he was doing the best he could. In the end, wasn't that all a man could do?

It was almost pitch dark when he rose shakily, clutching his rifle and made his way through the scrubs to Babs. "Well, ole girl, I guess it's gonna get more interesting from now on. I don't know how long we'll last, but we'll darn sure give 'em a run, won't we?"

Patting her neck as they rode, he wished he could make out a will and leave his few belongings to Babs and ensure she be put out to pasture. By golly, she sure deserved to be taken care of in her old age. Next to his wife, she was the nicest, gentlest female he'd ever known; beat hell out of that whore he'd shacked up with one winter outside Fort Griffin.

Pearl sweated as she cooked over her wood-burning stove. Hiram was on his way and she prepared for him. Her objective was two-fold, persuade him to not evict Judah and to poison him with the ground glass. Today she had the powdered glass in every dish. She pulled the vinegar cobbler from the oven and set it atop the iron stove to stay warm. Lifting the lid to her largest pot, she stirred the sunuvabitch stew. It was one her husband had taught her to cook. He'd been forced to assist the cook on a cattle drive once when his horse had stepped into a gopher hole, threw him and sprained his wrist. The cook had showed him how to make the stew and it was a hit with the cowpokes.

Pearl made a mental note to make sure she'd not left anything out...lean beef, half a calf heart, calf liver, sweetbreads, brains, marrow gut, salt, pepper and Louisiana hot sauce. Moving the pot to the back of the stove, she hurried to her bedroom to fix herself up for Hiram.

An hour later, they laid in bed. Hiram snored, Pearl lay on her side staring at the shotgun. She'd had to use every trick she'd learned as a woman to entice him to promise to give Judah another three months before he had to abandon his place.

Hell, I don't even know if that'll be enough to convince Judah to stay. I started bargaining for a year but Hiram was about to come so I had to settle for what I could get.

Later, they ate her stew but Hiram was too full to eat the cobbler, so she sent it home with him. She was happy that he had to use her outhouse after eating.

I hope you shit blood and lots of it, you bastard pig.

But he emerged from the outhouse without showing any ill effects of the meal. He bragged on it as usual and took all of it home since she couldn't feed it to the boys or eat it herself anyway.

Waving goodby as his surrey pulled away, Pearl began to think Hiram had the stomach of a goat and hog. She swore to herself that he appeared to be getting fatter and healthier on her cooking.

The shotgun would be so much faster and easier.

CHAPTER 25

In 1892, the government made it compulsory that all Indian children attend schools. In 1896, the government issued an order that all male Indians would wear their hair short like Anglo men.

Stars speckled the purple dark sky like falling confetti. The silhouettes of agave plants, yucca, madrone trees and jagged rock formations stood against the same sky. The only sounds were an occasional yelp or howl of a coyote, the squeak of leather, or a mumbled curse as Jones's arm or legs caught hold of a crucifixion thorn, devil's head cactus, or one of a dozen or so other plants that rewarded the unwelcome touch with a sharp prick.

The Morning People and their recent unwelcome visitors moved in a line without any conversation. Big Boy and Sans had quickly decided that Naiche was to lead them. His orders were to lead them away from the pursuing army troops and to locate water. Big Boy ordered Anrelina to walk behind the leader and he rode his horse behind her. This way he could watch the old Indian to make sure he didn't try anything funny and he could watch the sexy Indian squaw's ass at the same time. Members of the visiting party were interspersed among the Indians. Camel was near the end of the line. He walked directly behind Manuelito who'd helped finance their journey with his salesmanship of Navajo blankets. In front of Manuelito, rode Jones who cussed and whined about the hardships of the desert. Behind Camel rode Sans who was the last of the line. Camel focused on placing his steps to match Manuelito; one misstep and Camel felt Sans's horse breathing down his neck. Once, when he stumbled, the horses head struck him between the shoulders and pushed him into Manuelito. Both almost crashed to the ground. Sans hoarse, squeaky voice laughed.

They had wiled away the day seeking shade and lying quietly. Camel had watched the way the men in the group kept eyeing Anrelina. Their intentions were obvious. Soon after they arrived and consumed most of the water, Big Boy had announced to the Morning People that his group would ride along with them until they had lost the army for good.

Camel noted how Sans observed everyone and then whispered in Big Boy's ear. It was obvious to Camel that the half-breed with the cruel eyes and sneering expression was the brains and the most dangerous one of the group. Sans had taken a special interest in him. As they laid quietly waiting for night to travel, the pint-sized man with a hoarse whisper for a voice sat beside Camel in the shade of a clump of agave plants.

Sans studied Camel, one of two white men with these Indians. He looked carefully at Camel's long hair that was now mostly white and his shaggy beard that was completely white. His hard eyes took in the leather and skin dress Camel wore. His words were more accusing than questioning, "Whatcha doin' here, Squaw Man?"

Camel met his eyes, pulled at his beard and said, "Tryin' to survive, like you."

Sans snorted, "Who runs this group?"

Camel rested on one elbow, making himself not look at San's rifle which he held loosely across his knees or the knife handle which protruded and leaned in his direction. He wondered if Sans was hoping he'd grab for one and have an excuse to kill him. Although he felt for sure this man didn't really require a reason.

Camel repeated the question, "Who runs this group?" He continued to tug at his beard. He recognized the Evans carbine. With that, he might be able to make a difference and...*stop it! If this were a poker hand, I'd be holding all jokers.* "It's like family, and like in all of them, the women have their say."

Sans's eyes constantly scanned the movement of everyone around them. A toddler broke from his mother's arms, took a few quick steps and fell before the mother could grab him up and pull him back into her lap. Sans's hands tightened on the rifle, then relaxed.

With eyes on his surroundings, he said, "Ya not telling me anything Squaw Man. Whose the leader?"

Camel was being evasive and the cunning half-breed knew it. Again Camel fought the urge to grab the handle of the knife. It appeared to have moved closer to him and he could imagine ramming it to the hilt in the stomach of this cruel, sadistic man and then grabbing the rifle and begin taking care of each of these uninvited guests.

He had to give Sans an answer. "They pow-wow over decisions. They've even allowed me into them lately." He watched the profile of Sans as he told him what he already knew. "The white priest, Father Pollen, the old Indian you chose to lead us, Naiche, and the older woman, Naltzukich, usually have the most to say and they make final decisions."

Sans turned to him and his deep-set hazel eyes bored into Camel, "Ya left out the pretty squaw. Don't lie to me again or I'll gut ya and ya'll die slow and hard."

With that, he rose effortlessly and moved away. Throughout the long, hot day, he would appear out of nowhere, sometime behind Camel, beside him, sometime Camel would see him eyeing him from among yucca plants several yards away.

The day passed uneventful except for one occurrence; Anrelina walked across the dry riverbed they camped in to get some water from their last tus to doctor Skinyas wound. Jones saw her and moved toward her. He began saying something to her that Camel could not make out. They were obviously arguing and when Jones took her upper arm, she snatched it away. He grabbed her with both arms and the Morning People, appearing to be lifeless rags in the torpid heat, came to life. Camel was on his feet and moving toward the cluster of people surrounding the arguing couple when Big Boy's deep, booming voice sounded, "Jones, git the hell away from her. And the rest of ya, go back to your places."

No one moved so Big Boy said, "Jones, git ya ass over here I said."

Camel saw a ripple in the crowd as Jones made his way out of the mass of Indians and sauntered by him. His hat was pushed over his eyes in a cocky type of way and he mumbled something unintelligible.

Big Boy stood on a dried stump of a cottonwood, making him appear even larger than he was. With hands on hips, he said, "Go back to ya places, People. No harm is gonna come to ya or to the little lady as long as ya do what I tell ya."

As the day wound down, Camel concluded this group was a disunited one. Kilkenny and the woman rested together beneath a rock formation, but her expression was tense and Camel thought he overheard her voice once or twice, each time sounding angry. A couple of times Sans appeared near them and each time, she looked at him with terror. Jones kept to himself. He appeared to sleep soundly most of the day between two large wax plants. Big Boy resembled a panting bear with his dark, curly hair and massive body that was not built for this type heat.

At dusk, Big Boy gave the word and everyone lined up to his and Sans satisfaction. Camel held no allusions regarding this group of vigilantes. They were cruel and merciless, and no one was safe in their presence. It was for sure that in time, Jones would get to Anrelina, Big Boy would deal with Father Pollen, and when Naiche was no longer useful, he would be cast aside like a worn boot. Naltzukich's temper and mouth would get either her throat cut by Sans or choked by Big Boy. And Camel? For some reason, he sensed Sans took a special disliking to him.

There was something else. It had nagged him ever since the vigilantes had appeared, but only now did it become clear to him. He was no longer concerned only for himself; he worried for the Morning People. Dread and fear filled him when he thought of Anrelina, Naiche, Father Pollen, and even the foul-tempered Naltzukich. As though the sun had risen and the morning's, clear, crisp air enabled him to see for miles, he now saw the women and children whose lives depended upon someone saving them from these killer vigilantes.

If the Morning People and Camel were to survive, something had to be done and done fast. But what? The vigilantes had the guns and horses and the upper-hand. *Where's the weak link in the group? How can I get one of their guns? I'm still a scarecrow...probably weigh no more than a hundred and forty or fifty pounds. Am I strong enough to do anything? Can I match Big*

Boy's strength or Sans's craftiness? What about Kilkenny and Jones? How about the...

Stumbling over a hedgehog cactus and feeling a burning sting in his calf, he struggled to regain his balance and gait. Behind him he heard the hoarse whisper, "Hold us up Squaw Man and I'll use my knife on ya."

Maggie packed her clothes, books and papers and felt like she was watching herself from afar. Mr. Arlington and Hiram waited for her outside. They sat in Hiram's surrey, talking about the town and its future while waiting to transport her to Quiermo's house. *Shouldn't I be leaving town at last? How much humiliation am I willing to take? Will I be safe at this man's house? What about Bilbo? Why didn't he speak up? Why didn't I? For some reason, I can't understand, I feel that I have to hang on. Why? Does it have anything to do with Camel? He's been gone for weeks. In all probability, he's dead. Never to return. Am I stuck here because he's the only man I've ever really loved, though its taken his disappearance and some time for me to see that?*

Hearing a sound, Maggie turned to see the doe-eyed pastor's wife standing at the doorway watching her. Maggie turned away and continued her task. The wife's scolding voice filled the room, "You're nothing but a common whore, you know. You think ya could move in here and rob my man with what you have between your legs? I saw the two of ya in here. I know he never did anything but lie with ya because he felt sorry for ya. He told me he could hear ya crying at night and reached out to you in Christian love. He said ya tried every trick a Jezebel like you has to lure him into sin, but he resisted ya, you disciple of the devil. You common whore."

Maggie locked eyes with her and each held her place until the woman turned away, "Get outta my house you she-devil from hell!"

A half-hour later, Hiram halted his surrey before a large adobe house. Grass grew atop the roof and the few small windows held bars of wood. Chickens roamed the yard and two large hogs slept in the shade, nestled against the side of the dwelling. A couple of mongrel dogs rested in the shade of a leaning cottonwood a few yards away. The heat seemed to have sapped their energy and they showed only a passing interest in the new arrivals. A woman worked with a hoe in a large garden and three children had been playing in the yard, but scurried into the safety of the house as the surrey neared them.

A man appeared at the door. He was middle-aged and wore a white cotton shirt that hung over beige trousers. His smile showed white teeth except for one missing at the corner of his mouth. His white beard and mustache stood in sharp contrast to his brown, tanned skin. "Buenos dias. Welcome to our adobe. Can we get you a drink of cool well water?"

Maggie noticed his greeting and question was directed to the men. He had not looked at her. Mr. Arlington touched the brim of his black Stetson and Hiram said, "No thank you, Quiermo. I have your new renter here. Our school marm."

The woman in the garden had laid her hoe down and now stood beside the door, her hands lost behind her apron. She was younger than Quiermo and though she didn't speak or smile, her expression was pleasant.

Hiram lowered her trunk from his surrey and Quiermo helped him take it into the adobe. Mr. Arlington stepped stiffly from the surrey, reflecting his age, and held Maggie's hand as she descended to the sandy yard. Mr. Arlington's face reddened with embarrassment as he pointed to chicken droppings and said, "Watch your step, Ma'am."

Maggie wanted to cry more than anything. She wanted to cry, then leave this awful place forever. Instead, she held her head high, ignored the warning about the chicken droppings, smiled and greeted the lady of the adobe.

Bryant Williams, foreman of the Rocking H, returned with a small army to reclaim the body of their slain comrade. Each man had been ordered to carry a sidearm. Those who didn't own one were lent one. Bryant sat his saddle studying the surrounding terrain as several of his men wrapped the swollen body in an old army blanket and tied it to the back of a mule.

Even with seven armed men present, Bryant felt the hairs on his neck rise. This was not like him. Dammit, he knew somebody or something was watching them. He had romped around Oklahoma and the Texas panhandle for several years, often less than a day's ride from a hanging. He had been jailed five times and broke out the last two times. He had killed four men, two in fair fights and the rest he'd shot in the back. With all that, he didn't recall the feeling of being spooked that he felt now.

He nudged his horse toward a clump of mesquite and a meadow lark sprang up before him. He drew his revolver and fired in a heartbeat. He missed the bird which disappeared behind a cottonwood tree; his men drew their weapons, too.

Dismounting, he wrapped his horses reins around a juniper stump and walked forward cautiously, gun held at the ready. Pausing, he stopped several times to bend and examine the ground. He could see tracks. Somebody had walked in this direction to their horse, mounted up and rode away.

Bryant returned to the group, ordered two of the men to return to the ranch with the body while the rest went with him. They followed the horse tracks for half a mile but lost them when they left sand and found themselves on hard rock. They made a half-mile circle, but did not pick up the trail again.

Bryant felt confused and angry. Dammit, something was not right. Made no sense at all. Sitting astride his horse, he looked steadily at each wooded and rocky area, especially the niches and crannies capable of hiding a man for a long while. His men eyed one another, but said nothing, just tried to hold their restless horses in check. As the group rode away, a bush trembled and moved back in place; no longer held down by an aged, veined hand.

The scouts were in a quandary. The tracks of the two groups had become one. They had worked diligently to lead the captain and his band of soldiers away from the fleeing Indians, but now, the Indians were with the angry ones and that could not be good. What should they do? They had talked many times about abandoning old ass-scratcher.

They had observed the Morning People, at first, with mere interest, then familiarity, and then genuine concern. After some discussion, they decided they would lead the army to the angry group. They might be saving their own, or at least some of them.

Captain Verlander stared at the backs of the scouts and for the thousandth time wondered how their minds worked. Now, the scouts were staying within range and actually encouraging the captain to order his men to travel faster. *What in the hell is wrong here? Do I simply not understand these people and how they think? Yep, that's for damn sure. But why would they suddenly become so energized and motivated? Have they finally decided that I'm a man of principle and will not turn back regardless of the hardship? Perhaps their asses are beginning to hurt too and they're ready to catch these runaway bastards and go home. Maybe they've developed hemorrhoids.*

Staring into the distance, the shadows of mountains danced and seemed to melt into dark blobs as the hot waves of heat emanated from Mexico. The dazzling heat whitened and bleached everything it touched. The sun scalded the few cactus and anything green that attempted to survive here. But, they did survive and the captain was amazed at the patches of color that scattered across the areas: the gold and orange black-eyed susans, yellow and white daisies, goldenrod, lavender and white wild phlox and many more. The captain felt things must be looking up if he were able to appreciate the little beauty found in this arid hell-hole.

But serious problems remained, constant fear of running out of water and not finding any, supplies running dangerously low, and finally, horses growing lame. The rocky, irregular ground covered with more types of cactus than he ever dreamed existed, wore down their horses hooves or penetrated the shank and soon the horse was lame. Three men were reduced to leading their horses on foot and the other men sensed it was only a matter of time before they would be doing the same. *Dammit it to hell! No wonder morale is so low. Being on foot in this hell hole, never knowing when a rattler is going to strike your leg or you're going to trip and fall into one of these damn cactus and blind yourself is enough to drive a man crazy.* Turning again, he yelled and waved his men forward.

The scouts knew they were taking a risk by traveling during the day rather than the night, but their spirits told them they must hurry or all the red men would be dead at the hands of the ruthless whites.

Judah's girls played with Pearl's boys as their parents sat on the steps and talked. He shook his head forlornly, "Not goin' to make any difference, Pearl, three months, six months, maybe even a year, I won't be able to repay Hiram. My stayin' another three months just prolongs the agony for us."

Pearl shook her head in disagreement. "That's not the way I see it. It gives you and me another three months together. And who knows what might happen in that time? Judah, we care for one another, and look at our kids. They laughin' and playin' and that's what kids are suppose to be doin'. Lord knows, the boys love ya. And I get along real fine with ya girls. I can't ever take the place of their mama, but I can be a woman who loves 'em and provides a woman's touch."

The children were playing tag, being silly and laughing without care as only children can do. Pearl and Judah sat in silence for a long while watching them. He turned to her and said, "We just puttin' off what we gonna have to do. But, ya right. Even if we hafta leave, which we most likely will have to do, it will give us three more months together."

Pearl massaged his neck and said, "We'll find a way, Honey, just wait and see." *Hiram's comin' tomorrow and I'm gonna have a wonderful surprise waitin' for him.*

CHAPTER 26

Secretary of War, Sherman, waged the same burnt soil war with the Indian tribes as he had in the South during the Civil War.

Naiche walked slowly, stiffly, staring down at the rocky, alkaline, arroyo floor. Everyone else stood watching him. The old Indian stopped, held his hands straight out, closed his eyes and allowed his arms to drop to his side. Camel heard Jones mutter, "Crazy old Indian damn sure better find some water fast or we all dead."

Camel's skin felt clammy, his tongue thick, reminding him of his earlier brush with death from lack of water. Looking around him, he felt sorry for the others. The children were lethargic and the adults quiet. Camel's arms were weary because he had carried the small child, Mangus, for about half a mile when his mother had no more strength to do it. Another small boy, Chatto, leaned against his mother and stared unblinking at Camel.

Naiche pointed down and said, "Water here. Must dig for it."

Sans said, "Hey, Squaw Man. Use this." He pulled a short handled shovel from his saddle roll and tossed it to Camel.

Camel walked to where Naiche was standing. Naiche stepped back, pointed down and said, "Dig here. Water!"

It was hard work. Camel had to break through the limestone and dig into the rocky earth. A quarter-hour later, he was breathing hard and his arms were trembling with every thrust. Naiche motioned to someone and Manuelito appeared. Naiche said, "Give it to Manuelito, Camel."

Camel had to be helped from the two foot hole. Manuelito worked clumsily with the shovel and within a few minutes was gasping for breath. Next, Skinyas took a turn. Camel was beginning to worry that Naiche had been wrong when Little Sun took his turn. His head was barely showing above the hole's rim as he worked. But now, Camel noticed the earth being removed was dark and damp. A few minutes later, Little Sun uttered a cry of joy. Camel peered over the side and saw water slowly seeping into the bottom of the hole.

Sans and Big Boy rushed forward, pushing Camel, Naiche and Manuelito aside. The rest came forward, the women in the rear. Big Boy said to Little Sun, "Here's a canteen, fill it up!"

Father Pollen stepped up beside Big Boy, his head coming to the big man's waist. "The children and women should get the first drink. That's the..."

Big Boy ignored him. Little Sun handed up the canteen and Big Boy threw it up and drank deeply, water running down his black whiskers. He handed it to Sans to finish off as he tossed another canteen to Little Sun.

Father Pollen spoke again, his voice squeaky as usual, only more so from dryness and indignation. "Big Boy, I must insist we allow the children and women to have the next one. We must..."

Big Boy said, "Get the hell outta the way, Padre. We all thirsty and unless we get water in these horses, they gonna die on us."

As though on cue, several horses whinnied, smelling the water. One broke from Eunice's grip and ran for the water hole. Little Sun scrambled out of the hole which was filling with water.

Big Boy shouted to his gang, "Hold em! We'll let 'em come one at a time and you drink ya fill along with ya horse."

Eunice walked forward to drink with her horse, but Sans squeaky voice halted her, "Women last!"

Father Pollen put his hand on Big Boy's wrist, "Our children must have..."

Big Boy swatted at the pesky voice and didn't see Father Pollen fall over backwards. Sans held his horse in check, allowing Big Boy to drink. He looked at Jones and signaled for him to be next.

A strange sound made the hair on Camel's neck rise. He turned to see Naiche swaying and wailing a warbled chant. His hands rose with his voice and fell in a lament that sounded to Camel like something the red men had been doing for a thousand years.

The sound had the same effect on others. Big Boy's deep voice shouted over the mournful dirge, "Shut the hell up old man or Sans will cut ya throat."

Camel rested against a limestone rock that vaguely resembled a buffalo, he said, "Ya kill him and who's gonna find water for ya?"

Naiche continued his caterwaul, oblivious to his surroundings. Father Pollen, helped up by Manuelito, limped toward his old friend. Taking his arm, the hunch-backed priest spoke low to Naiche. This continued for a long minute, each man doing his own thing, until finally, Naiche stopped howling and Father Pollen continued his quiet talk for another minute or so. Naiche allowed himself to be led to a rock hummock where he and Father Pollen sat together.

As Eunice, the last of the vigilante group to drink stood, Big Boy turned to Father Pollen and said, "Okay, Padre, your people can drink now."

Camel watched as the women carried or led their children to the water hole. Feeling someone close, he looked up into the dead-like eyes of Sans setting his mount. The half-breed grinned, showing teeth that looked like fangs to Camel.

Sans said, "Ya a smart squaw man ain'tcha."

Camel shrugged, spoke in a monotone, his dry throat allowing nothing more, "Don't make sense to kill the one man who can find us water."

Sans's grin widened, "Ya right. But it might scare the hell outta of 'em and make 'em really jump if they watched as I worked on you with my blade."

Camel stared ahead, wondering if he was about to die. If this was the time, he'd make his play even though he knew it would be a futile one. Eyeing Sans's knife with his peripheral vision, he worked to prepare to move into action while appearing calm and relaxed.

Sans whispered in his squeaky voice, "Ya ever seen a man skinned?"

Camel took a deep breath, looked up at the smelly, ugly face and said, "I was already thirsty, now ya gone and made me hungry too." Sans made a strange sound Camel read as a laugh. Turning away, Camel moved to the water hole for a much needed drink.

As he kneeled like a dog and drank, he caught a distorted reflection of himself. It startled him. Gazing at a strange, unfamiliar face, he noted long dark hair streaked with gray; a beard gray and shaggy. A right eyebrow held a blank space in the middle, scar tissue as a result of the beatings and a nose that was bumped and crooked, obviously broken. It was a fighter's face.

Drinking his fill, he knew he would have to act soon. This was the most dangerous man he had ever encountered. During his years as a gambler, working saloons throughout the Dakotas, Wyoming, Colorado, and New Mexico, he had met some really bad men and women, but nothing like Sans. He thought of Hiram. It struck him that this was the first time he had thought for a while of the man he had sworn to kill. Hiram was not the immediate threat. This group was. Either they would be killed or they would kill everyone in the group. He had to develop a plan and fast or these good people who had saved his life would be killed along with him.

Hiram saw blood in his stools. His face was pale and he took deep breaths as he stared down into his chamber pot. He didn't really feel that bad, but seeing the strings of blood in his stools shocked him into sickness. *Eatin' that damn Juanita's red-hot, spicy food is killin' me. The bitch has gotta stop feedin' me like I'm Mexican and feed me like I'm a white, Christian anglo.*

He fell onto his bed so hard, the slats broke and the head of his mattress went to the floor. He laid on a sharp angle and groaned. *Oh God, I'm gonna die from eatin' hot chili peppers and all the beans and onions she feeds me.*

He paused and listened. He became aware he'd been hearing a tapping on his back door. He held his stomach, though it didn't really hurt, just the thought of whatever made his stools bloody gave him phantom pains in the gut.

Holding his stomach, he opened the back door and Carmen entered. She looked so sexy in his favorite dress, the one with large red, yellow and black flowers that clung tightly to her curvy figure. It always amazed him how well-endowed Carmen was, in contrast to her sister, Juanita, who was flat chested and straight as a board. Carmen's eyes were large with dark, black pupils where Juanita's eyes were small and beady. In addition, one eye often drifted, especially when she became flustered.

Carmen deftly avoided his clutching hands and said, "You ready for your bath?"

He grimaced, "I think I'll skip the bath tonight, how about just a rub down with a little oil. My stomachs not..."

She rolled her large eyes and pouted. "Hiram, I have told you before, you are a big, strong man and your manliness makes you stink. Now, you know it will make me sick to rub you if you are not clean."

Taking his hand, she pulled him forward, "Come on, I know Juanita drew your bath so let's wash you while the water is still warm and then I will rub you."

Looking at her, he forgot his problem, removed his robe, and stepped into his over-sized tub that the black carpenter, Ben Davis, had built to accommodate his large physique.

Later, as Carmen rubbed him with sweet oil, he found himself recalling the day's events. It had been a bad day. He had mistakenly thought his bank assistant, A.J. Moniker, was stealing from him. He had gotten the little, short, fat man in his back room and whipped him with a razor strap. In the melee, A.J. had cried like a baby, dropped his glasses which Hiram had accidentally stepped on and crushed. Later, he found the error and apologized to him.

Dammit, the whole day has been a bastard. The only good thing was my visit to Pearl and her good lovin' and chicken and dumplins. I gotta get her and those kids off the place, but why be in a hurry when she works so hard to please me. I know she's gotta thing for old Judah, and I'll let him hang around awhile too. It's good publicity since A.J. got up in church and, without calling names, told how I've gone the extra mile to help widows and widowers. Hell, he didn't have to name Pearl and Judah, everybody knew who he was talkin' about.

Carmen's voice brought him back to the present. "Oooohhhh! Senor Hiram, You and your dragon are someplace far away tonight. It is not ready for Carmen's sweetness."

Hiram pulled her to him and said, "It'll be ready as soon as you mount the old stallion, Carmen, sweetie." And so he was.

But after lovemaking he did not find the usual solace waiting for him. As she prepared to leave, he said in a flat, emotionless voice, "Send Cholla over, I got business with him that won't wait until morning."

Cholla appeared less than a half hour later. Pocketing the gold pieces from the table, he asked, "How many tonight, Senor Hiram?"

Hiram's voice broke with sadness, he sniffled and said in a tiny voice, "Until ya get tired, Cholla. As Job said, Is not thy wickedness great? And thine iniquities infinite?"

The crushing of his little bank assistant's spectacles had been no accident. Perhaps that's why there had been blood in his stool. Punishment was due.

Billy rubbed the back of his neck, grimaced, and a tear squeezed from the corner of one eye. He sat on his favorite log with his best friend, Sheriff Dan Libby. He could see through the sheriff, but he was much clearer than the last time Billy saw him.

Billy was elated to see his friend, but torn by the scolding his mentor delivered. Looking at his friend's transparent boots, he could not look him in the eye. To anyone listening, there was no voice on the wind; only the woeful, melancholy sound of the mourning dove that matched Billy's mood.

The crying, agitated young man stood and faced his accuser. "I know it. I know I've done some sorry things that would hurt my ma, Sheriff Dan, but, but..."

Sitting on the log again, he blinked through his tears as his fear mounted. The sheriff was fading out. His voice seemed far away and another second there was no sight or sound, only the dried, sun-bleached wood of the dead Cottonwood and the somber lament of the mourning dove.

A sound made Billy turn to see Junior Beaumont coming near. Billy hastily wiped his eyes and stood. He wished he'd seen Junior so he could have avoided him but it was too late now.

Junior grinned wickedly and said, "Why ya cryin', Billy? Is it cuz the town council decided that whore of a teacher was about to screw the preacher to death and moved her down to the Mexican quarters? I betcha mad cuz ya didn't get any of that."

Billy felt all the frustration, embarrassment, and dead weight of recent events descend upon him. He sputtered, stammered and tried to disagree with Junior, but he couldn't get any of it out.

Junior went into hysterics. He was barefoot as usual, wearing the same old pants that were cut-off between the knees and ankles, and a butternut shirt with one sleeve badly torn. He was beginning to grow long, light hairs above his lip and around his pimple-pocked face. He wore a gray, crumbled Homburg atop his long, uncut chestnut hair.

Billy could not talk; but he could communicate. Fast-drawing his .44, he snapped off a round into the hat Junior wore at a cocked angle. The hat went flying. Junior screamed, grabbed his head, dropped to his knees, and Billy could see blood streaming between his fingers, blackening the sand.

Panic seized him. Junior was dying. He had meant to shoot his hat off his head, but had missed and killed him. Holstering his revolver, he ran for home. Half-way there he stopped. Pressing both hands against his temples, he tried to push clear thought into his head. Why did thinking come so hard for him? Why did a thought that Junior would have on Monday not come home to him until Friday? He thought slow, but under pressure, his mind was even fuzzier.

He could not go home now. He must not disgrace his mother like this. He had to...had to... *What should I do? Where should I go? Sheriff...oh God, no, I don't want Sheriff Dan to know about this. I shot an unarmed man down in cold blood. That means I hang.*

Overwhelmed by the magnitude of his actions, he stumbled and fell, sitting Indian style in the dirt. He wanted to cry. He wanted to bury his head in his mother's lap, but he had to be a man and he had to decide what to do on his own.

He had a thought! He couldn't go back to his father's place where there were several horses in the corral; he had to steal one and ride out of the territory. He must put lots of distance between himself and Angel Valley. He stood, wiped his eyes, took one last look at Junior who had collapsed face down and headed for the south side of the main street to see what horse he could take.

The man standing before Bryant shook his head and pushed his boots in the sandy soil. Bryant spit tobacco and said, "Tell me again what happened and don't leave anything out."

The man held his hat in one hand and like all of his type, sported a suntanned face except for an inch of pale skin below the hairline, protected by his brown, weathered, hat. He looked at his shuffling feet and began, "Me and Worley did like ya said, and rounded up about a dozen head of 3C steers. We herded 'em into a gully and Worley threw a line between 'em and a high rock. Each of us went for what sounded like a bellowing group of 'em over a low hill. Well, when we topped the hill, there was no sign of any steers so we headed back to what we already had, but the rope was down and the steers had scattered."

Bryant looked up in frustration, "Sounds like Worley's sorry-ass lark's knot to me."

The hired hand shook his head, "I watched him tie a bowline knot, Boss, and it was a good one."

Bryant's eyes darkened. He stepped closer, "Whatcha telling me?"

"That knot wouldn't untie itself and unless one of those steers did it, then somebody untied it and scattered those steers."

Bryant rubbed his chin, "Tomorrow, I want you and Worley back over there and we'll send another man along. We gotta get those steers on our side of the fence."

The hired hand shuffled off as Bryant stood there staring at him. Something was not right. Had he spooked the hands by his own reaction? He knew the talk in the bunkhouse. The 3C spread was bad luck. Everyone associated with the place was dead or missing. There was talk now of ghosts haunting the place. One of the hands even claimed to have spotted Toby at a distance riding his same old nag.

CHAPTER 27

Whites were convinced of the importance of having Indians farm and produce their own food. But Apache men felt that farming was a feminine task. Their role was that of the hunter. White farmers were hired on some reservations to teach Indians agriculture, but the plan was soon deemed a failure.

As the vigilantes rested and talked among themselves, except for Kilkenny and Eunice who separated themselves from the others, Naiche, Father Pollen, Anrelina, and Naltzukich stood around Camel and talked quietly.

The priest looked at Naiche and said, "I'm wondering if we're better off with this group or would it benefit us to be caught by the army?"

"Humphhh!" Naltzukich grunted. "If the army catches us they will probably kill all of us, including the children."

Camel watched Sans from the corner of his eye and saw him watching them as he talked with Big Boy and Jones. Anrelina spoke, "At least with this group we might have a chance if all goes well, but with the army..."

Camel realized Naiche was eyeing him and waiting for his observation. He swallowed, licked his dry lips and said, "I gotta agree with Naltzukich. I think our chances are better with this group, as bad as they are, than with the army. But..." He paused and seeing Sans standing and staring at them, he quickly added, "These are dangerous people and we've gotta be ready to act if the chance presents itself. And Anrelina, you need to stick close with Naltzukich or..."

Sans came close and said, "Havin' a pow-wow, huh? What's the thinking of the group?"

All were silent. Sans stared at Camel. "What's goin' on, Squaw Man? Whatcha telling 'em?"

Camel said, "We were trying to decide whether our chances are better with your group or the army." He smiled, felt his lips crack and tasted blood, but went on, "We decided we like your group best. Guess it's your affable personality."

San's eyes bored into his own for a long moment and then he grinned, showing his yellow teeth and walked away. Camel watched as he said something to Big Boy, who looked over at them, focused on Camel and nodded. Sans mounted his horse and rode off.

Father Pollen said, "I think you're right about these men, Camel, they're highly dangerous. They're using us only..."

Big Boy's deep, gruff voice interrupted him, "Let's stop the pow-wowing over there. Ya better be resting up cuz if Sans comes back and says that army's still on our tail, we gonna be movin' again."

In less than half an hour Sans returned and told Big Boy, "The army's still comin' though they in worse shape than we were in. If this water was ten miles away, they'd never make it." He shrugged, "We gotta move."

Big Boy shouted for everyone to get in their positions to move out. But there was a problem. Mangus, the five year-old, and his mother, were unable to stand. The child was lethargic and laid beside his mother on a spread blanket. Both were pale and their breathing shallow.

Skinyas, Camel's old drinking partner, stood beside them and said he was not going further and would wait with mother and child. The bandage wrapped around his head was dirty from working in the well and the red stain showed the wound had been reopened. Anrelina and Naltzukich knelt beside the mother and child and tried to encourage them. Anrelina said, "We can carry Mangus and we will carry you, if we need to. Come on, let's go."

The mother whispered something in Anrelina's ear and then closed her eyes and refused to respond any further. Big Boy yelled, "I said, let's go, dammit! If anybody wants to wait on the good ole

U.S. army, they can. But the rest of us are movin' out now. Naiche, I need ya on lead to find us more water."

Father Pollen, Naiche, Naltzukich and Manuelito formed a protective circle around the mother and child. Skinyas was pushed outside the circle but stood close by.

No one moved. The circle stood in defiance of Big Boy's orders. His face reddened and he raised the scattergun. Sans voice behind him sounded quietly so only Big Boy heard it. He lowered his gun and Sans nudged his horse around and close to the circle. He raised his carbine, pointing it at Father Pollen. "His voice was a harsh, grating, whisper, "On three I kill the priest. On four I kill fat mama, on five..."

Camel raised both arms, stepped in front of Father Pollen, and said, "We're going, Sans, right now." With that he pushed through the group, bent down and lifted the limp woman. He was surprised how light she was. Holding her, he said, "Anrelina, you carry Mangus and trade off with Naltzukich. Skinyas, if you choose to wait here for the army, that's your business. The rest of us are going..." He glanced at Sans's rifle leveled at his mid-section and said, "Now!"

Naiche nodded and everyone moved. All except Skinyas. He looked sullen and angry and scratched his black hair above the bandage. As everyone tramped off, he made a face, kicked the alkaline sand and took his place in the moving line.

Big Boy growled, "Anybody don't keep up, gets left behind. Let's go!"

Dusk found the line moving along a rocky fault line with purple mountains rising in the distance. The setting sun gave them a hazy hue that somehow made them seem unreal. The prickly pear that stabbed Camel in the calf was real enough and the pain shot through his entire leg, but he didn't dare pause, knowing what the result would be.

In no time, Camel was breathing hard and wondering how long he could continue to carry the young woman and keep up with the others. His arms trembled and she was gradually dropping lower on his body. He knew if he faltered or lagged behind, Sans, who was riding directly behind him, would either leave him and the woman in the desert to die, shoot them, or cut their throats.

He bumped into Manuelito, who scooped the woman from Camel's arms and assumed the duty. Feeling Sans's horse blow down his neck, Camel worked mentally to make a plan. He decided the weak link was Jones. He was the loner in the group. Big Boy and Sans were a team and Kilkenny and Eunice stuck together, but while resting, Jones most often kept to himself. He didn't seem to enjoy acceptance from the others. Camel tried to figure a plan to get one of Jones's weapons. He carried a revolver in his pants belt and a Sharps lever action in his scabbard. He wore a knife like all the men, but Camel didn't want the knife, he must get hold of one of the guns.

*I gotta take his revolver or rifle and...*A gasp went down the line, carried like a message transmitted from one post to the next. Camel squinted, trying to see what was going on, but saw only the column knotting at the front with the vigilantes setting their horses.

Camel caught his breath when he saw Father Pollen lying on the ground and Big Boy towering over him. The priest was on his back and struggled to right himself. Big Boy held his scatter gun with one hand and with the other, pulled his revolver from his waist belt and pointing it at the struggling priest...he fired.

Maggie knew the three children were watching her as she hung her washed clothes on a roped clothesline. Shaking out a petticoat, she heard giggles and smiled herself. She stared into the distance, at the surrounding craggy country and wondered anew how'd she'd overlooked the Hispanic children in this area. Thinking back, she realized she became aware of the Negro children first by prying information from the colored carpenter, Ben Davis, when he repaired her desk and built a new student's bench. Going to the home of the former buffalo soldier, Henry Goins, to visit his sick wife, Vera Mae, had given her a first-hand view of the blacks and their living conditions.

She now realized she had completely overlooked the Mexicans, living like the blacks, apart from the town of Angel Valley. There were a half-dozen adobe homes in sight and each one appeared to have several children. How could she have been so blind? She had heard someone mention Adobeville, but did not pick up on it.

The Sanchez home was not so bad. The house was cooler than the reverend's framed home. The one large room was divided by brightly woven blankets, and mats. One partition was made up of various animal hides. Maggie's room was spartan, housing a hard single bed, a large wooden trunk and a small table holding a stone basin and gourd dipper. A roughly-hewn three-legged stool provided seating.

The woman of the house was named Estefania and Maggie immediately liked her. She laughed easily and obviously enjoyed Maggie's company. She was in her early twenties, attractive, though her curvy body was fast turning plump. She'd had five children, one still-born, one died at three, leaving three boys, aged four, five, and nine.

They were very shy at first and continued to be so, though they were coming closer each day and allowing her to see their interest in her. They spoke mostly Spanish, intermingled with English. Quiermo and Estefania spoke fluent Spanish and fair English. Maggie and Estefania made a pact, Estefania would teach Maggie Spanish while she taught the mother and three children English.

One thing Maggie learned right away was that Hiram's name was not to be used in the home. Maggie wondered the reason, though she had no trouble accepting it. These simple, sweet people possessed a wisdom that the more sophisticated and wealthy town's people did not command.

She resumed her teaching duties at school, though several of the children dropped out. She overheard a rumor that another teacher was coming to Angel Valley to tutor those students, all for the more affluent families, and she had no doubt if the teacher was acceptable, she'd be appointed to replace Maggie for the coming school year.

Maggie now taught the white children during the day, the Negro children two nights per week and did the same with the Hispanic children. She noted that all the children she taught, regardless of race or culture, were poor.

Maggie was an idealist, but a realist too. She knew her days were numbered as schoolmarm for Angel Valley. She was being unceremoniously dumped.

Lying in bed reading, with everyone else asleep, she heard a knock on the door. The second series of thumps, initiated

Quiermo's shuffled feet and grumble in Spanish. A chill of fear swept over her as she heard Hiram's voice at the door, "Send the schoolmarm out here, Quiermo. I've got school business to discuss with her."

Reverend McKenzie stared at the page of the Bible and tried for the third or fourth time to comprehend it's meaning. Giving up, he leaned forward, placing both hands on his forehead. He knew no peace. He was miserable. Standing, he stared out his window down the street of the town. A woman left the store with a sack of groceries tucked under one arm. She was one of a new family in town and ordinarily, he'd grab his hat and coat and rush out to greet her and invite she and her family to church on Sunday. But now he only turned and stared down at his feet. Seems he'd done lots of that lately.

Looking up, he gazed into the eyes of his wife who stood at the doorway. Guilt, remorse, anger and hatred all mixed together within him at the sight of her. As usual, she wore her nightgown although it was almost noon.

She coughed, cleared her throat and said in a small, whiny voice, "I feel so bad, Bilbo. Could you wipe my forehead with a wet cloth and quote scripture like you used to do?"

He nodded meekly as she plodded back to bed. On the back porch, he stood over a metal basin and wrung out a white rag. Sitting on the bed beside her, he pushed her mousy brown hair back, folded the cloth and laid it over her forehead. Her eyes were closed and she breathed deeply. Looking at her, he started to quote a psalm, but the words would not come. His memory went black. For the first time ever, he thought about choking her. He hated her. God, how he loathed her.

She opened her eyes and said, "Quote to me, Bilbo. Its always made me feel better. Makes this headache ease up a bit, makes the pain in my stomach hurt a little less. Helps me all over."

He tried again, but the words would not come. Staring at her thin face, he thought how disappointed he was that the new doctor could not help her. Bilbo was convinced that her problem was not in her body but in her head. Standing abruptly, he said, "I got to get some air. I'll be back in a few minutes." Putting on his summer coat, and black hat, he felt her eyes boring into his back."

Her voice was flat, but steely, "Don't ever see that Whore of Babylon again, Bilbo. If you do, I will leave you and go home to my folks. You know that no church will ever call a divorced preacher."

He stood holding the doorknob. More than ever he had to escape before he said or did something he would regret. Out of habit, he heard himself say, "Take care, Dear. I will be back shortly."

A half hour later, he surveyed the schoolhouse from behind a large oak tree, less than a hundred yards away. Pulling his pocket watch out, he studied it for a moment, returned it and leaned against the tree.

Almost a half-hour later, yelling children, several barefoot, ran from the shingled building to play crack the whip and tag. Bilbo straightened when he saw Maggie. He looked to see that no children were watching and waved to her, trying to get her attention. If Maggie saw him, she ignored him. A couple times, he was convinced she saw him, but each time looked away. In only a few minutes, she rang the cowbell for the children to line up and enter the building.

Bilbo stood beside the tree for a long time after the yard was empty and the door of the building was closed. That told him she saw him because the door was open when he arrived. Turning away, he walked slowly toward town. He knew what he'd just attempted was stupid. What if Hiram or any of the people on the council had seen him at the school?

The scouts sat their mounts staring at the lagging troops. They were all but used up. As the captain neared them, the scout who always did the talking said, "We are almost at the water hole where they camped a few hours ago."

The captain, lifted himself from the saddle, relieving his buttocks, and said, "Good, our horses can't go much further. A couple of the men have had it too. After we water up, I'm sending five of them back. One of you will have to escort them back to the fort." He looked straight at the scout who did not speak and said,

"You will need to get them back safely. One of them will have a message for the colonel. It's important that he gets it."

Almost two hours later, they drank from the water hole dug by the Morning People. It was obvious they would not travel anymore on this day. One of the soldiers stood after lapping water like a dog and said, "Damn! Ya gotta chew that before ya can swallow it."

Captain Verlander conferred with the men returning to the fort and their scout. It was agreed that those returning would camp there for the night and then move out in the morning. The scout remaining with the army, advised the officer that they must return to traveling during the night and hold up during the day. The captain had learned something about the desert and concluded the same.

Standing before his men, he said, "We will rest here until dark, then we'll move out again."

He ignored the groans of the men. A few cuss words were heard, but he acted like he didn't hear them. He'd made a decision; two nights more and if they didn't have them by then, they would turn tail and return to the fort. The captain knew his career would be finished. He'd be the laughing stock of the fort and the entire army when the story got out. He was the captain who could not catch a ragtag group of Indians made up of women, children and a crippled white preacher.

He could see the headlines in all of the eastern newspapers. His heart gripped his throat when he thought of his wife and mother seeing those headlines.

He realized his hand was resting on the butt of his pistol. That was still an option. But shouldn't he at least make sure his men got back to the fort safely before he did that? Walking between prickly pear cactus, he kicked at a creosote bush.

CHAPTER 28

The Apache and Navajo each practiced the shared cultural taboo of mother-in-law avoidance. A man must not look at or even speak to his mother-in-law.

Camel and the other Morning People rushed forward at the shot. Camel breathed a sigh of relief when he saw that father Pollen was unhurt. In frustration, Big Boy had fired between his legs. Manuelito and Chee helped him to his feet. The tiny priest looked up defiantly at Big Boy, "Kill me if you like, but the women and children need rest and we will stop now."

Big Boy held his revolver an inch from Father Pollen's forehead. He spoke quietly but with steel in his voice, "I tell you when we stop and when we walk and I'm getting' tired of ya ugly face, Padre."

Naiche stepped forward and said, "If you kill him you will need to kill me, because I will not lead you to water anymore."

Big Boy swung the barrel of his revolver into the old Indian's wrinkled face, but Naiche's expression remained stoic and his unblinking eyes met those of the man who threatened his life. The light of day was almost gone, only an orange streak on the horizon remained but it was enough to give Big Boy's face an orangish hue as he glared at everyone who circled him.

After a long pause, he lowered his pistol, shook his massive head and spit the words out, "To hell with it! Ya wanta break, take one. But when I give the word, everyone of you bastards better be ready to move."

The Morning People slowly dispersed as they realized Father Pollen and Naiche were safe. People slumped against rocks and squatted on the rocky soil as they passed the water skins around.

Camel saw Sans and Big Boy talking; Sans rode out. Camel figured he was going to scout out the army.

Big Boy stepped beside a tall cactus and peed. Looking back at his horse chewing on dried chinch weed, he slung his shotgun over his broad shoulder and headed off into the darkening night. In a minute, Camel could not make him out. Kilkenny and Eunice drank water and sat leaning back against one another.

The one Camel was most interested in was Jones. The outlaw tied the reins of his horse to a stunted madrone tree and peed. Buttoning his pants, he took a tus of water from Little Sun, drank deeply and handed the skin back. He carried his rifle loosely in one hand; his revolver was stuck beneath his broad leather waist belt. Camel watched his every move as he wandered over to a sandy hummock and laid back against it. Removing his battered Homburg, he swatted it against his knee to shake off some of the dust and then placed it back on his head. He looked toward Camel who looked quickly away to see Anrelina bending over Skinyas, doctoring his wound.

Glancing back at Jones, Camel strained his eyes to make out what he was doing. In the growing darkness, it was impossible to see if the man's eyes were closed. If they were...*no, this is not the time. I don't know where Big Boy and Sans are right now. What about Kilkenny? His big .44 was always at hand in its holster. No, this is not the time, but I gotta find it and soon. Next time, Big Boy or Sans will kill one of us.*

Little Knife asked Naiche if he could build a fire, but the old Indian only shook his head and motioned for the young man to stay put. It was completely dark now, the only light being the stars; the moon was not out yet.

Camel drank water from a tus and wondered about something to eat. So far the Morning People had amazed him with their skills in finding food in the desert. It was not always for the weak-stomached, but when you were hungry, grilled rattler, peccary, even desert mice tasted fine. Tonight, they all sat quietly in the dark, hungry and unsure what the vigilantes would demand of them next. Everyone's hunger was reflected in their lethargic posture and quietness.

Camel tried not to doze; tried to focus on Jones's shape in case an opportunity presented itself. He thought he was awake, but a noise startled him, making him aware he had dozed off. Hearing Big Boy's voice and something he couldn't make out, he concluded it was Sans's hoarse whisper. The moon had appeared and Camel made out the two men standing and talking. Sans held the reins of his horse, turned and moved off. Big Boy looked around at the dark figures and said, "The army's been resting, but they're getting' ready to come after us. Get ya gear together cuz we're movin' out."

It surprised Camel to see Skinyas approach Big Boy. At first, the big man pointed his shotgun at the Indian's stomach, probably thinking he might have a knife. After a few words, Big Boy lowered his gun and stepped nearer to Skinyas. They talked for a long minute and then separated.

Camel tensed as he half saw and felt someone approach him. It was Anrelina. She moved close to him and her hair smelled like a flower Camel could not name. She whispered, "Jones keeps looking at me. I see you looking at him. At the first chance, I will distract him so you can get his gun."

Camel smiled, though he knew she couldn't see it in the dark. It was as though she'd been reading his mind. She impressed him. Two working together could be more effective than one, especially when dealing with enemies as vicious as these.

He whispered "I agree. We've got to move as quickly as possible."

She knelt over him and her hair brushed his chest, as she watched for danger. Her smell, voice, presence, all reminded him of her femininity. She said, "The one called Big Boy wants to take Naiche with them and leave the rest of us. He keeps telling Naiche that when the time comes, he and the one called Sans will kill Father Pollen and...and..."

He completed her sentence, "And me."

Her silence confirmed it. She turned and was gone in a second. Camel inhaled deeply, trying to get a whiff of her again.

His heart skipped as Sans appeared out of the dark. He stepped close, bent down and whispered, "I gotcha, Squaw Man." He wheezed a laugh that sounded like a hiss and turned away.

What did he mean by that? Did he overhear me and Anrelina?

Maggie took a deep breath, laid her book down and moved to the doorway. Hiram stood scowling at the hogs that grunted a few feet from him. Seeing Maggie, he said, "I need a word with you in private, Miss Pickett."

Maggie turned back and saw all of Quiermo's family sitting at the table frozen in place. She smiled at them, pulled a lock of hair from her eye and stepped outside. This time she did watch the ground for animal feces.

Hiram's black buggy sat a few yards away. He pointed towards it, "Would you like for us to ride as we talk, Miss Pickett?"

"No thank you. We can talk here."

Hiram made a sound of disgust, he'd stepped in chicken crap. Rubbing his boot heel into clean sand, he checked to see if he got it and then looked up at her. He lowered his voice and said, "Maggie, Maggie, Maggie. What in the world would the good people back in Connecticut think if they saw you now?"

Maggie looked for a long moment at him, smiled faintly and said, "They would be proud that I'm living with the poor and downtrodden and teaching the little children to read. Sound like scripture, Hiram?"

Hiram scoffed. "I've asked Mr. Arlington to write a letter to your pastor back in Connecticut. He's going to tell him what you've been doing here and persuade your folks to ask you to come home. Of course..." He kicked at a hog that had come near him, "Of course, you could just go ahead and resign and go on home and that letter won't need to be written."

Fear made her heart race, but she would have died before she allowed him the satisfaction of knowing he scared her. She smiled sweetly, "Why Hiram, I think the letter's a great idea. I'm proud of what I'm doing here and perhaps such a letter would persuade some of my family to come here and see for themselves what Angel Valley's like."

His face darkened, "Ain't you got any pride about you? You smart-talking Yankee hussy!" His face quivered in rage, "Repent or else I will come unto thee quickly, and I will...I will..." He sputtered, anger blocking his memory.

She held the smile because she saw it enraged him. "Now Hiram. Name-calling is for children, very young children. But then you often act like a spoiled, arrogant, self-indulgent child when you don't get your way, don't you? We must work on that."

Whirling, his coat tail slapped at her hand as he stalked to his surrey, shook the reins hard and let out a roar, making the big brown almost stand on his hind legs and then take off in a cloud of dust.

The ranch foreman, Bryant Williams, was furious. He threw his hat to the ground and got right in the tall, thin cowboy's face. "What in the hell is wrong with you girls? Do I hafta personally drive every one of those damn 3C steers over to our side? I'm tired of ya bullshit excuses! Now, tell me again what happened and don'tcha leave a thing out, ya hear me?"

The cowboy's face was splotched red and white. The other two ranch hands looking on, figured the red was embarrassment and the white was fear. His Adam's apple bobbled, his lips trembled and he stuttered, "Me, me, and Ike split up. And I was chasing a couple cows and calves and he was driving a dozen or so head out of a deep draw. When he d...didn't show up, I went lookin' and found him sittin' on the ground. His horse had run off. He was rubbin' his throat and workin' his m...mouth like a frog. He said he was ridin' along real good when a rope caught him and knocked him off his horse. He said he about blacked out and couldn't see, but he could hear somebody movin' like they was untyin' the rope and ridin' off."

Bryant rubbed his grizzled chin and looked off into the distance. The heat made the mountains on the horizon dance a jig and distorted the open range. Oaks, Cottonwoods, Yuccas, all moved in a hazy, swaying motion that made him use his bandanna to wipe sweat from his brow and wish he had a bucket of cold beer. It all looked unreal. A feeling of deja vu swept over him. This seemed so familiar somehow and yet so strange too.

Snatching his hat from a cowboys hand, he pushed it down on his head and strode away. The ranch hands stood in place looking after him. The tall one turned to the others and said, "I know what I saw and you fellas know Ike. He's not a story-teller. He's getting his gear outta the bunkhouse right now and gonna high-tail it outta here. He'll hafta hurry to beat me outta this country."

Later that night at Stinky's, Bryant sipped a beer as he leaned against the bar. He took a deep draw, wiped foam from his upper lip and said, "Stinky, tell me again what the Swede said."

Stinky clouded over, "Aw shit, Bryant, we done been there..." He stopped in mid-sentence as he saw Bryant's eyes harden. "Okay, here we go again. He walked in here, ordered a beer jus like you did and..."

At one of the wobbly tables in the corner, three more hands from the Rocking H talked quietly so Bryant wouldn't hear them. One said, "Ike and Josh left today and I hear they looked like they saw a ghost. I ain't getting paid enough to herd ghosts or to lose my life. That moons gonna find me ridin' out tonight."

The other two nodded in agreement.

Billy had hobbled his horse and laid with his head on the saddle. He was in a deep draw on the east side of the 3C spread. Since everyone heard Toby had died and the ranch was deserted, he figured it was the best place to hold up until he could figure out what to do next. But with the sun sinking fast behind the mountains, he wasn't sure he'd made such a wise choice. Sitting up, he held his Colt in his hand. Had he heard a noise? He remained completely still for a long while, as though immobility was synonymous with invisibility.

Standing, he looked around in the growing dusk and felt more scared than anytime in his life. He wanted his mother. He wanted to cry. An idea struck him and he looked around for a fallen log. If there was one, he could not see it in the dimming light. It occurred to him that if he could find a log to sit on, perhaps the sheriff would join him. He would know what Billy should do.

Holstering his revolver, he sat back down and leaned against the saddle. He hadn't seen his friend lately and he was afraid he would not appear to him again. Of course the sheriff might not visit him again because of his shooting Junior Beaumont.

He wanted to cry again when he thought what the lawman might say to him now. What if the sheriff arrested him? Yielding to his emotions, Billy sank his head in his hands and cried like a baby.

He had never been away from home at night in his life. His mother tucked him in every night after they knelt beside his bed and said their prayers. What would his mother be thinking right now? How did she take it when she heard her Billy boy was a murderer?

Would his mean father beat his mother? Would he take his anger for Billy out on her? Wiping his eyes, he looked up at the darkening sky and said a prayer like his mother had taught him to do.

Should he saddle up and return home? Then he imagined the eyes of Hiram and the new sorry sheriff, Frank Moseley, staring at him. What if Frank tried to pull his wimpy .32 on him? Would Billy shoot him like he'd shot Junior? For a second, the idea appealed to him, but then he thought of his poor mother. And what would Sheriff Dan say to him? It was too much for him and he began crying again.

He sobbed; his shoulders heaved. Because of his own noise, he didn't hear the footsteps walking away or the grunt of the gaunt figure heaving himself into the saddle.

The scout sat his horse and watched the camp of the Morning People and the vigilantes who had joined them. Both groups had returned to traveling at night and resting during the heat of the day. Something made him uneasy and he knew to pay attention to it. A glint of light flashed from thick trees that climbed a mountain to his right. Kicking his horse, he raced down into a deep, rocky draw and urged his mount forward as fast as the craggy ground would allow.

He didn't look back. He focused on his riding as he tried to ignore the burning sensation in the middle of his back. He'd been in enough close scrapes to know he always had this feeling when danger was near. It was rough country to run a horse in; a fall could mean a broken neck, but the scout's gut told him he was near death and his survival depended on the spirit being with him and him riding as hard as he could. His horse labored up a limestone gully and he saw the troops resting a couple hundred yards in the distance.

Only now did he whip his horse around and scan where he'd been. He patted the neck of his mustang and spoke soothingly to her as she blew hard. He couldn't see anything but he didn't have to. He knew someone was out there. Someone who had skills as good as his own. This someone wanted very much to kill him.

He knew who it was...the little, hunch-backed half-breed. The scout remained there for some time, not expecting to see or hear anything, but to thank the spirit who'd been with him and given him warning. He would have to be more careful. This man was dangerous. He thought again of his people with this man with the evil spirit and how they must be faring.

Turning his mount, he rode into the army camp. Most of the men were asleep in the shade of hastily-erected canvases or the couple of Cottonwoods that sprang from the rocky earth.

The captain approached him. His beard was shaggy like his men, his skin had browned, and his clothes hung on him. He said, "You stood there for a long time, like you were seeing someone. Did you find them?"

The scout ignored the question and said, "If we ride at first dusk and do not stop, we can catch them."

The captain looked him in the eye for a long moment, "Alright. We do it. We gotta do it now, or..."

He turned and walked slowly back to his stretched tarp. The scout looked up and saw an owl fly overhead. He shivered. To see the bird of prey during the hot daylight meant bad things. Bending, he closed his eyes, tossed sand over his head, and hummed a quiet chant. The bird meant death was nearby. But whose death?

Sans shook his head in frustration. If he could kill that Indian scout, he figured the army might not even be able to backtrack and save themselves. But the scout was good, he had to admit. Sans almost had a bead on him with his rifle when the scout spooked and ran. Sans thought he could catch him and if he'd ever stopped to check his back out, he would have. He sought solace in the knowledge that only one scout was now tracking for the army. That most likely meant one led some of the men back. Perhaps if they could avoid the army for another day or so, they would all turn back. In the meantime, Sans would watch for another chance to eliminate their tracker.

CHAPTER 29

An old log hut.
A new log hut.
Is it for me?
Is it for you?
Why do you ask?
    McGuffey's Eclectic Primer

The Morning People and vigilantes continued to march single-file. They had started earlier than usual this night. All of the vigilantes stayed close except for Sans. When he wasn't riding close behind Camel, he was scouting and keeping tabs on the army.

Camel often found himself exchanging looks with Anrelina as each observed Jones and the overall situation. Camel hoped she didn't make a bad move, because it could be disastrous for all of them. But he had confidence in her. His gut told him he could trust her to play it smart. He noticed Chee watching her and understood. Both were young, attractive Indians, but he hoped romance would not get in the way.

After an hour of walking, and darkness had descended, Big Boy had them crowd together so they could hear his directions. He sat his horse and addressed them, "We're gonna split up here. I'm takin' a group with me and the rest of ya will go with Sans. We'll meet up a few miles from here." He paused, "I hear it's a trick ya been using with lots of luck and we gonna try to throw that group of soldiers off with it."

Camel didn't like it and was not surprised when he learned he would be part of Sans' group. Anrelina would be part of the other group. At least it was a relief to know that Jones would not be in her party.

He felt sure it was Skinyas who'd alerted Big Boy to their previous tactics to confuse and stall the army. Camel and Manuelito continued to take turns carrying Mangus. The mother was walking with the help of Anrelina and Naltzukich. The mother cried out in being separated from her child but was encouraged by the women to go along and allow the men to care for the child. The mother was too weak to resist.

Manuelito carried the child and Camel noted how the small arms dangled and swayed with each step. When his turn came to take Mangus, he was completely limp. Camel asked, "Is he alive?"

Manuelito said, "I don't know. I don't think so."

Even though the group had divided, Camel continued to walk directly ahead of Sans who sat his horse. Stepping aside, he looked up into the partially darkened face of the half-breed, "I need to lay him on the ground and check to..."

"Ya keep movin' or you and the kid will be dead."

Camel heaved the dead weight up to chest level and picked up the pace. As he walked, he lifted the child's face to his own but felt no breath. His skin felt cold and leathery. Several minutes later, someone fell and the line came to a halt. Camel heard Sans utter a hoarse curse and spurred his horse forward to deal with the problem.

Camel and Manuelito took the opportunity to lay Mangus on the ground and determine if he was still alive. Camel felt his throat for a pulse but detected none. Manuelito rested on all fours and placed his cheek against the child's nose and mouth. They agreed he was dead.

They heard Sans' horse returning so Camel quickly lifted him as again they began their march. Sometime later, they stopped again and Camel realized the groups had come together. But there was to be no rest as Sans left and Jones took his place. Camel felt sure Sans was scouting again to determine the location of the army. It was obvious they would not rest until they felt safe.

Camel was weak from not eating and still thin as a rail from his desert ordeal. He and Manuelito swapped the limp chilling body often between themselves as weakness made them gasp, weave and trip.

After an eternity they halted and were allowed to rest. The water tus was passed around and Mangus's mother came looking for him. She wailed as she held the cold, stiffening child to her breast. Anrelina and Naltzukich appeared and tried to comfort her.

Father Pollen joined them in consoling the sobbing mother. The priest moved to Camel and said, "Would you help me in burying the child?"

Camel stood and said, "I'll ask Sans to lend me his shovel."

Naltzukich stood close to him and blocked his way. He took a deep breath and waited for her wrath on whatever he might have done wrong. Instead, she smiled showing a dimple he had never seen before. She said, "Camel, you have turned into a good white eye."

How about it Camel? You have won over one of your biggest detractors. Skinyas and Little Knife still hate my guts, and I can understand the teen's hatred and Skinyas is just a sorry scoundrel like me. But Naltzukich. Naltzukich demanded respect and gave it only where it was deserved.

As Camel moved forward in the dark, the quarter moon cast a dim light, aided by a zillion stars, making bushes and trees look like people. The Morning People were sitting and lying in small knots, all weak from hunger and exhausted from the long forced hike. Camel passed Kilkenny and Eunice standing beside their mounts; they stared at him in silence as he walked past them.

 He spotted Big Boy's and Sans's silhouettes, each juxtaposed against the starry night sky. Nearing them, Big Boy's deep growl stopped him, "Whatcha want, Squaw Man?"

Camel told them of Mangus death and the need for a shovel to bury him. Big Boy looked at Sans and said, "Give it to h'm Sans, but if they ain't ready to move when we are, take the shovel and leave 'em for the army."

As Sans threw the shovel at his feet, Camel knew Sans would not leave anyone alive to talk to the army about their members, number, water supply or anything else.

When Camel returned, Father Pollen was holding the child. He could see dark shapes and hear loud crying and knew Anrelina and Naltzukich had their hands full trying to comfort the distraught mother.

Camel followed the limping priest for a couple yards. Twice, he thought Father Pollen was going to fall with the difficulty of walking on the uneven terrain in the dark, weakness, and the fact that the dead child was almost half as large as the priest.

Stopping, turning and breathing hard, the priest said, "Let's bury him here." Laying the body down gently, he placed his hands on the still head and prayed.

Digging, Camel felt rivelets of sweat run down his face. Weakness made him feel light-headed and he feared passing out. *If I do, old Sans will just cut my throat along with the priest's and leave our bodies here for the buzzards. I don't know if it is the hard ground or my weakness, but I'm not making much progress here.*

The sound of creaking leather made Camel look up and see the silhouette of Sans sitting atop his horse. Wiping sweat, he continued to dig furiously, ignoring the hoarse whisper, "Times up."

He stopped when Sans urged his mount closer to them. "Gimme my shovel, Squaw Man, now!"

Father Pollen said, "We're almost through, Sans, all we need is a couple more minutes to bury him and say a short..."

Camel couldn't see the face, but knew what Sans was capable of doing. He stepped forward and handed the shovel up to him. Sans half-turned and secured the implement atop his saddle skirt and whispered, "We're movin' out, don't hold us up."

He urged his horse forward as Father Pollen tried to protest, but Camel moved close to him and cupped his palm over the sputtering, struggling, minister's mouth. Camel jerked his hand back as he felt the pain of a bite.

Camel glanced back to see that Sans had moved off. Bending, as Father Pollen continued his verbal bomblast, he placed the dead child's body into the shallow grave and scooped dirt over it with his hands.

Feeling nauseated and weak, he heard the vigilantes lining up the Morning People to begin marching. He grabbed the clergyman who had bent to help him cover the body and dragged him along until they came to their place in the line. Behind him, Camel heard Sans's wheezing laugh.

Hiram stood at the bottom of the steps and stared at his feet. His face was pale and drawn. Pearl's heart leaped with joy. Standing on the porch she looked down on him, both hands on her hips and said, "Hiram, you devil, I was beginning to think you were not coming to see me today."

He shook his head, turned and plopped down on the stairs. She walked down and sat beside him. It was difficult for her, but she managed to feign concern, "Are you alright, Hiram? You look a little peaked."

He shook his head, rubbed his neck and said, "That damn Mexican cookin's about to kill me, Pearl. I'm gonna hafta fire my cook and have you come and fix my meals."

Her heart raced. Was he serious? She'd never planned for this. Her anxiety disappeared when he smiled weakly and said, "I'm just teasing, of course, it wouldn't look proper for you to be living with me and there's your boys for you to care for. I might getcha to come in though and show that cussed little skinny Juanita how to cook some good old American vittles."

Standing, wiping her hands on her apron, she said, "I cooked your favorite---chicken and dumplings, field peas and cornbread. The table is set, you ready for it?"

A hen cackled from somewhere in the yard as if in protest of the menu. Hiram rubbed his stomach and shook his head. "I don't know, Pearl. I feel so cussed bad I don't think I can eat a thing today."

She reached down and squeezed his upper arm and said in a husky whisper, "You gonna need your strength for later on so you better eat my cookin'."

He smiled grimly, shook his head, as he rose and turned to her. "Well, maybe just a small helpin'."

A few minutes later, Pearl smiled inwardly as he started on his second helping. She knew if she got him to the table, he would eat an enormous amount. She jumped as he yelled out and pushed back from the table, knocking his chair over. Pulling something from his mouth, he stared at it, moved it closer to his eyes and squinted at it. Her heart thumped in her throat and she felt a cold fear wrap its arms around her as he bellowed, "This is a damn piece of glass!"

She put on her best face of shock and said, "Omigod, Hiram, lemme see it."

He handed it to her. As she looked at it, he squeezed the dumpling on his plate and rubbed the cooked dough between his thumb and index finger. He stopped, examined particles in his hand, and said in a quiet voice that scared her even more, "This dumplin' is full of grit. Only this grit is crushed glass."

Their eyes met and she reflected feigned sorrow mixed with genuine fear. "Hiram, what in the world happened to my..."

He pitched the table aside. Dishes and food splattered onto the walls and floor as he gasped, "You slutty bitch! You feedin' me glass and then screwin' me!"

She made a break for the shotgun in the corner of her bedroom, but he was on her. He slung her into the door jamb, breaking her nose and shoved her across the room, crashing her into the wall where she slid down and shook her head trying to clear the buzzing bees that hummed in her ears. Dropping to his knees beside her, he clutched her throat with both beefy hands and squeezed. Her legs thrashed wildly and she gripped his wrists with her hands but was helpless as his face, dark with rage, appeared to turn to black and white and then slowly fade to blackness.

Billy looked around cautiously, like a deer or antelope wary of possible danger lurking behind every cottonwood, cactus or rock. Survival was his chief goal. How long could he avoid being captured while remaining in the area where he committed his heinous crime? He wondered why he had not been pursued by a posse. Had he just been lucky so far? If so, how long could his luck hold out?

He stood in a crouch like a mountain lion ready to pounce or run depending on the circumstance. Standing at the log where he hoped to meet Sheriff Dan, he could see no movement in the street of the town. He thought he glimpsed Stinky step from his saloon and then disappear back inside.

Sitting on the log, he focused on seeing his old friend. He had misgivings. What would Sheriff Dan say to him? Scold him? Order him to march down to the new sorry excuse of a sheriff and turn himself in? Or would he have advice for him that he sorely needed?

Billy sat on the log for the better part of an hour but his old ghost of a friend was a no-show. Billy initiated conversation numerous times, hoping to flesh his mentor out, but all to no avail. Spotting A.J. emerge from the bank and lock the door, Billy stood and headed for the trees where his horse was tethered. Mounting up, he saw the sheriff, Frank Moseley, leaving his store and heading for the saloon. Billy kicked his horse in the sides and quickly rode away.

Some time later, he stood beside his mount and looked down on the deserted buildings of the 3C ranch. After several minutes, convinced no one was around, he rode down and drank for a long while from the well pump. Pumping water into a half-barrel for his horse to drink, he felt the hair on the nape of his neck stand up. The place was spooky. He had heard the talk. This was a ghost ranch. With Camel long gone and undoubtedly dead, all the ranch hands gone or dead, like Fuzzy and the foreman, Toby, the place was haunted by their ghosts.

As soon as the horse lifted his head from the barrel, Billy rode away, glancing over his shoulder as though he heard the hooves of a ghost posse chasing him. Dusk found him sitting among Cholla cactus, as though their spikes could hold off any foe, alive or ghost. He roasted a jack rabbit over a spit, using dry wood that made little smoke. As he cooked the rabbit, he half cried and talked to himself. He talked about how much he missed his mother and how he wanted more than anything else to see her. He sobbed as he spoke of Sheriff Dan and how he missed him. The sun was a thin line of gold on the rocky horizon when Billy felt a presence. Looking up, he gasped in fright. Toby stood holding his rifle, leaning, angular and thin. A wisp of an apparition. Billy thought he could see through him as he could Sheriff Dan.

Billy jumped when Toby said, "That rabbit smells mighty good, Billy. Think you could share a bite with a ghost?"

Captain Verlander stood on a graded slope facing his troops. "Men, I want to commend you on your vigor and perseverance. Each of you will receive a commendation from the colonel when we get back to the fort." He pretended not to hear the low voice that came from the back of the group, "If we get back to the fort."

He went on hurriedly, "Our scout tells me we are closing on the renegades. I am convinced that we will catch them within the next two days. I am aware of the hardships that you are being subjected to and the status of our supplies. Let's ride hard tonight and tomorrow night; lets catch these bastards and make them pay for their crime of escaping their reservation. Now, let's ride!"

In the saddle, he saw the scout move out without waiting for his command. *The sunuvabitch.* Behind him, he heard the sergeant give the command. Captain Verlander's face and neck burned with embarrassment and anger, but he ignored the slights to his authority and looked straight ahead.

Maggie stepped through the school house door and almost collided with Reverend McKenzie. He held his hat in his hand and a sheepish grin on his face. Maggie looked around, but all of the children had gone home for the day.

Bilbo's voice pleaded, "Maggie, please allow me to apologize to you and to..."

Her palm caught him square on the jaw and made a loud smacking sound. The force and sting of the blow stunned him into silence. Maggie said, "Bilbo McKenzie, you are a sorry excuse for a man, husband, friend, and certainly, you are no pastor. I demand that you turn and leave from this place this moment and never speak to me or come near me again."

She stared at him with a coldness that shocked him. He started to speak and she slapped him again. Whirling around, she strode to the corner of the room and came back carrying the broom that Billy had made for her. The handle was made of hickory and the children complained of its weight; but Maggie figured it would make an excellent weapon. Nearing him, she lifted it high and said, "If you remain here, Bilbo, I will beat you soundly with this broom. I find it handy to sweep trash from our school and I'm about to use it for that purpose again."

He turned and left, his body language screaming rejection and remorse. Maggie stood at the door until he disappeared from view. Returning the broom to its place, she sat on one of the student's benches and took deep breaths. Glancing outside, she knew she should be on her way. She had a longer walk now that she lived with Quiermo, Estefania and their three boys. The first day, Quiermo had brought his donkey for her to ride as he led it. She thanked him profusely but refused to allow him to do that for her. Besides, she did not like the picture it formed in her mind.

But rather than leave for home, she carried her satchel filled with papers to grade to her scarred wooden desk and sat down. She thought again of first coming to Angel Valley and the innocent, wide-eyed optimism that filled her. Did she retain any of it?

Her thoughts turned to Hiram, his cruelness and total self-centeredness; she pushed his picture aside and replaced it with that of Camel. Why did she continue to think of him? He told her he loved her once, but she knew at the time it was only to have his way. Yet, she still recalled that night and her hope that this romantic, funny, handsome man was her dream come true. Was it part of the naiveté that she brought with her from Connecticut? That was understandable, but why did she still think of him so often?

And Bilbo. She shook her head and sighed silently. She knew she was not without blame in their platonic relationship. Once again she had employed poor judgment in allowing him admission to her bedroom. While they had not had sex, her actions were completely inappropriate.

She didn't know how long she sat there, but was alerted when she heard a whippoorwill sing his lament and it was followed by Quiermo calling her name. She stood abruptly when she realized the door opening had changed from yellow sunlight to gray dusk. She apologized to Quiermo for being late and disagreed only mildly when he insisted she ride his donkey as he led them home.

Swaying to the rhythm of the donkey's rough stride, she thought of how many enemies she had made in the Valley. She knew she was the prime object of viscously whispered town gossip. It was understandable.

CHAPTER 30

Indians reported that the first time they saw whites, they were surprised to find them not to be as white as they thought they would be.

Camel had tried to eat as little as possible from the bowl of soup that the women cooked up. The children and women needed nourishment desperately. He smiled to himself as he gulped it down, thinking about what it contained. He had seen Naltzukich skin and butcher a six-foot rattler for the pot along with several desert rats and a jack rabbit. Naltzukich's throwing arm had saved them from starvation once again. She also dropped mesquite beans into the pot. He devoured the soup and the tasty corn meal cake. Resting against a boulder and closing his eyes, the food felt heavy but good in his stomach. Sensing a presence, he looked up into the face of Anrelina. She held another bowl filled with the liquid for him with a slab of bread laying over it.

He shook his head, "I've had something. The women and children need it more than me."

Pushing the bowl into his chest, she said with intensity, "You and I will need our strength so we can save their lives."

Sometime later, he burped and it sounded strange to him. It was mid-morning and the objective was to rest until nightfall when they would walk again. The sun went behind a fluffy gray cloud and it brought a respite from the intense heat. Something rustled in the brush and Camel smiled to himself as he thought if it was alive and moving, Naltzukich would have it in her pot for soup.

Looking down at his body, he was amazed again at the loss of weight. At first he had appeared to be a skeleton and it depressed him, but now muscle had replaced the fat. His arms were muscular, but his ribs still showed through his tanned skin and he wondered if he had the strength and stamina to handle a showdown with this group of killers. It had surprised him that he was able to carry the mother and then her child, but that was far different from whipping a man.

The sun appeared like a flash and then dipped behind another cloud. He saw Jones sleeping on the other side of a narrow arroyo. He laid on his back with his battered hat covering his face. One hand held his revolver resting atop his stomach and the other wrapped around his rifle that snuggled to his side.

Big Boy laid on his side with his head in the little shade that a madrone tree provided. He snored loudly. His scatter gun rested beside him, partly visible. Camel could not see his revolver, but knew it was someplace close to him.

Kilkenny and Eunice laid close together as usual. He laid on his saddle blanket; revolver in hand. She laid on her blanket with head propped against her saddle for a pillow. Sans was nowhere to be seen. No one had ever seen the little crippled monster sleep.

Camel yawned. The food had made him sleepy. He started to lean back and get some shut-eye when he jolted awake. Anrelina was walking directly toward Jones holding a tus. The look she gave Camel told him all he needed to know. This was it! But where was Sans? He wanted him in his sights when they made their play, but too late now.

He stood, made himself stretch nonchalantly and took a couple steps toward Jones. She began humming as she neared the outlaw. Stopping beside him, she said something unintelligible to Camel, but Jones's hand left his rifle and lifted his hat. He squinted up at her and then smiled as she knelt and offered him the tus. Laying his revolver onto his saddle blanket, he took the tus and drank from it. Camel lunged for the revolver. He palmed and cocked it as Jones reached for his rifle. Camel's bullet struck Jones between the eyes and he collapsed like an accordion. Where was Sans?

Big Boy made a sound of rage as he scrambled for his scattergun. He brought it up as Camel fired the first round into the big man's chest. The .32 round had no impact on him as he cocked both hammers and leveled his weapon at Camel. Camel's next round caught him high in the chest and pierced his heart. The giant of a man leaned forward clutching his weapon. His convulsing finger fired buckshot into the ground a couple of feet from Camel's legs. Camel ignored the sting of sand and rocks on his legs and wondered where Sans was.

Turning toward Kilkenny, Camel saw that the killer had the drop on him with his big.44. Each man held their weapon on the other. Somewhere a child cried and a woman wailed.

Kilkenny smiled. "I'm packing lots more wallop than you are, Camel. Drop the little shooter before I make a hole in ya big enough to ride my horse through."

A figure appeared in Camel's peripheral vision, but he dared not break the deadly stare with Kilkenny. The shadow made its way almost to Kilkenny when he turned and his .44 bucked in his hand. It was Little Knife. The big slow moving slug caught the skinny, angry teenager in the chest and catapulted him backwards, causing him to do a flip onto his stomach. Camel fired at Kilkenny. The bullet struck him in the ribs beneath his raised firing arm. Clutching his side, he grimaced in pain and turned back to Camel, a snarl covering his handsome face. Camel cocked and snapped the trigger. Nothing. He knew he had fired four times. Jones had only four rounds in his pistol, not six.

A smile flitted across Kilkenny's face as he aimed the big barrel at Camel. A rock smashed into his face dissolving the smile and leaving a streak of blood across his cheek. Stumbling sideways, he turned to face his new adversary.

Camel leaped for Jones's rifle. He levered a shell into the barrel as Kilkenny's gun sounded again. Kilkenny twisted back to face Camel when he felt the impact of the slug from the Sharps repeater rifle tear through his guts and exit his spine.

He fell backwards and didn't move. Camel looked to see who had thrown the rock and saw Naltzukich lying on her back one arm twisted awkwardly behind her and the other arm over her face. Levering another round, Camel searched among the yelling, crying, and scrambling crowd for Sans. Where was he?

The Morning People split into two groups, one encircling Naltzukich and one around Little Knife. Camel scanned the rocks and crannies for Sans and then turned his attention to the one

renegade remaining in their midst---Eunice.   She knelt over
Kilkenny's body and sobbed.   Camel could hear little, his ears
concussed by the gunfire.   Everything sounded tinny and distant.
That bothered him.   He would have to see Sans coming; he could
not hear him.

Holding the rifle at ready, he stood over her for a few minutes,
allowing her time to say her goodbyes.   When she glanced up at
him, he said, "Come with me."

He spotted Manuelito and gestured to him.   They tied her hands
behind her back as she protested with most unladylike terminology.

Camel kept his eyes peeled for Sans as he went to see about
Naltzukich and Little Knife.   The young Indian still clutched his
knife in a death-grip.   Naltzukich was alive, but barely.   The bullet
had entered low in her massive stomach and the ground was soaked
with her blood.

Anrelina wept as she rested on her knees with Naltzukich's large
round head in her lap.   Father Pollen kneeled beside her and held
one of her hands as he prayed that God intervene and heal her if it
was His will.   It was not.   In a few minutes, blood gushed from the
mortally wounded woman's mouth as she convulsed and died.

Constantly scanning the area for Sans, Camel strapped on
Kilkenny's gun belt and holster.   He reloaded the .44 and held it for
a moment to gain some familiarity with it.   In Jones's saddlebags, he
found a small sack of bullets for the Sharps rifle.

He gave Big Boy's scattergun to Manuelito.   Skinyas wanted
Big Boy's .36 caliber revolver, but Camel gave it to Little Sun after
showing him how to work it.   The young man kept laughing and
insisting that he already knew how to shoot a handgun, but Camel
had his reservations.   He could find no ammo for Jones's .32 so he
asked one of the women to put it away for him.

At least he was well armed now as were Manuelito and Little
Sun. But he knew the Indians were not proficient with their weapons
and he feared they might shoot themselves or one of their own
people.   He knew the burden of responsibility of dealing with Sans
would be up to him.   He would need all the luck of the best poker
game he ever played when he faced Sans.

Pearl dreamed she was a young girl again sitting on her father's shoulders. The fiddler was playing a bouncy tune. It was Turkey in the Straw, followed by Betsy from Pike. She relished the attention she received from onlookers. But then a loud, deep sound overrode the fiddle music. It was a crashing, ugly, painful sound and she placed her hands over her ears and began to cry. She heard her father calling her name between the crashing sounds. Then gradually, the voice changed from her father to someone else. Her heart thumped in her painful throat and chest.

She recognized the voice. It was Hiram. She cringed and tried to back away from it but it followed her. It came even closer. Cold water splashed on her made her open her eyes. She stared up into the dark, tight-lipped, face of Hiram.

He spit out the words, "If you tell anybody what's happened here, bitch, I'll kill your boys before your eyes and then kill you. Do ya understand me?"

She laid crumpled against the wall and tasted blood in her mouth. She tried to speak, but only moved her lips. Her throat had shut down and felt numb where he had choked her. His face came closer until she smelled his breath. He hissed, "Ya understand me?"

She nodded in agreement and felt red hot pain shoot through her neck and down her spine. He stood and wiped his face with his handkerchief. Stuffing it into his coat pocket, he said, "We'll tell people that a drifter came by and tried to rape you. You fought him off but got beat up before he got away."

She laid without moving. Staring up at him, she thought of the boys and how she did not want them to see her like this. He seemed to read her thoughts. "We gotta get you up and clean you off before the boys come home. I'll tell 'em I saw a stranger riding outta here too fast, stopped by to check on ya and found ya like this. You got that?"

She raised herself with one elbow and managed to nod her agreement. He reached down, yanked her by her dress which she heard rip and said, "Come on, there's time before the boys get here to do what ya planned to do." He held to her upper arm and pushed her roughly, "For true and righteous are his judgments: for he hath judged the great whore, which did corrupt the earth with her fornication, and hath avenged the blood of his servants at her hand."

He pushed her toward the bedroom and onto the bed. As he ripped her clothes off and lowered his pants, she turned her head to look at the scattergun. Her eyes never left it as he had his way with her. When he stood and walked out of the room, buttoning his pants, she heaved herself up to get the gun. Her bruised throat emitted only a squeak as pain shot through her arm and shoulder. Falling back onto the bed, she felt warm saliva in her mouth from the pain. Nausea swept through her and she thought she would puke. She knew she had a broken collarbone. One eye was swollen shut and she whistled as she breathed. She feared her throat might close up and she would suffocate.

After a long while the sickness went away and she tried again to get up, this time very slowly and gingerly. She couldn't do it. She was laying there nude, with a gingham spread she had pulled over her with her good hand, her face a bloody, swollen pulp when the boys entered the room.

The dust raised by the scout's racing horse clogged his nostrils and tickled his windpipe, but the captain ignored it as he waited for a report. The scout appeared more animated than Captain Verlander remembered seeing before.

He spoke in his usual choppy, taciturn way, "Big fight among people. Some have been killed. If we push on, we will be there in another couple of hours."

The captain said, "I'll have the men ready to ride in fifteen minutes. Back in his tent, he used the last of his turpentine to treat his hemorrhoids. He couldn't tell it made any difference.

In a little while, they were on their way. He closed his eyes for a moment and breathed a prayer of desperation that his mission be successful in the next few hours. His hand brushed against his holstered revolver and again doubt and depression assailed his senses and he wondered if he would be using the weapon against the red devils and their perverted leader or would he be using it to end his own miserable life.

The scout flicked his reins and pushed his horse along. From the gunshots he had heard earlier, he hoped some of his people were still alive. He didn't hold out much hope. While scouting, he had again felt a cold chill on his neck and down his back and raced his horse full speed to escape the little crippled white man who could hardly walk but as a rider was as good as any Comanche. The scout felt fear and worry for his people.

Toby and Billy made an interesting contrast. Toby was old; Billy was young. One was experienced; one had encountered so little. One was wise combined with a touch of cynicism that age brings; the other was ignorant of much and still held onto the naiveté of youthful innocence.

Billy had warmed to Toby quickly. He reminded Billy of Sheriff Dan and his grandfather whom he had known as a small boy until the kind, gentle old man had died of the pleurisy. Billy was scared and tormented with guilt and bubbled forth his troubles onto Toby.

At first, Toby listened. He had always been a good listener. He knew Billy only to nod to in town. He had heard of the boys mental slowness but speed and skill with a gun. The first night they spent together under the stars, Toby allowed the man who thought like a boy to place his saddle next to his own and sleep within arms reach.

After hearing Billy tell what he knew about Hiram and his role in the disappearance of Camel, Toby finally relented and revealed his story to his new riding partner.

That day, they teamed up to thwart Rocking H hands from rustling 3C steers. Billy untied the rope corral penning a dozen cattle while Toby bawled his mountain lion cry. They laughed and patted each other on the back as the four ranch hands lashed their horses to escape the deadly big cat.

As they rode back to their camp in a remote area sprinkled with cactus and sharp rock formations, Toby thought hard on what Billy had told him about Hiram and Camel. It made perfect sense to him. Camel was wild, but he would never have stayed gone as long as this if he could have helped it. Recalling the fierce beating Billy described and Camel's continued absence, Toby figured Camel was dead. It saddened him; it did not surprise him.

His bones ached, his arthritis flared up in his joints, he was having trouble placing his boot into his stirrup, though he worked not to allow Billy to see it. Slouching in the saddle, Toby felt the world rested on his tired, bony shoulders. He could not keep up this

serious game he played against the most powerful man and force in
the territory. Sooner or later, he would be caught and subjected to a
horrible death at the hand of Hiram or his sadistic foreman, Bryant.
Well, guess that's the way it is. He would go down with his rifle in
his hand. Never thought he would die peacefully.

Glancing back at Billy, he had to separate himself from him.
Billy was a gentle man with the mind of a young boy. He did not
deserve to die in a hail of bullets or swing from a cottonwood tree
for a fight that was not of his making. He had to figure a way to get
the boy back to his mother.

Deep in thought, Toby did not see the Rocking H rider sitting on
his mount a quarter of a mile away. His hearing was not very good
these days and he did not hear the horses' hooves clatter a hollow
echo on the hard stone. Billy was whistling the tune of Joe Bowers
and feeling more optimistic than he had since taking it on the lam.
He didn't see or hear the rider either.

The judge scowled and growled the meeting to order. In his
usual laconic manner he said, "What do you have to say?"

Around him sat the Arlington's, the McCormick's, Grandmother
Stutz, and A.J. Moniker, Hiram's bank employee who was
extremely nervous, chewing on his lip and fiddling with his glasses.

Mr. Arlington cleared his throat and said, "Your honor, we
appreciate you giving us this time to..."

The judge's raspy voice sounded irritated, "Mr. Arlington, that's
my job. Cut the pretty talk and tell me what's on ya mind."

Mr. Arlington's face flushed red, he was unaccustomed to being
addressed in this roughshod manner. "We are greatly concerned for
the welfare and security of the citizens of Angel Valley."

The judge yanked his glasses off, rubbed them with a wrinkled
handkerchief and said, "Why?"

Grandmother Stutz spoke up, "Because in recent months we
have had our sheriff gunned down, citizens disappearing, citizens
shot, and there are questions regarding the security of our banking
funds."

Mr. McCormick jumped in, "There's something not right here,
Judge. I think ya need to talk with A.J. about the banking."

A.J. Moniker wiped sweat from his forehead with a handkerchief; his coat was wet at the armpits and he wore a silly half-grin on his cherub-like face. He stared at the judge, opened his mouth, but nothing came out.

The judge said, "Out with it Mr. Moniker."

A.J.'s voice trembled, but he said, "I uh...saw my family kicked off our farm. My pa got into debt and he uh...he uh...borrowed money and the sheriff came one day and ordered us off. I was..."

The judge raised his voice, "Mr. Moniker, I'm not interested in your childhood. What do you have to tell me?"

A.J.'s voice was hoarse with fright. He could manage only a whisper, "The books are cooked. My employer, Mr. Hiram Bishop," pausing to catch his breath, he continued, "Mr. Bishop is repossessing farms illegally. The borrowers are not money smart and Mr. Bishop takes advantage of that."

"The judge said, "These are serious charges, Mr. Moniker. Are you ready to testify before a jury of your peers that you are telling the truth in this matter, and can you produce records to prove it?"

The sweating, trembling banker, closed his eyes and nodded as though he could not stand to see the face of the judge when he answered him. He slunk in his seat and appeared to grow smaller.

The judge scanned the group before him for a long minute, "Alright you good citizens have done your duty. I expect what has been said here today to stay right here. Any questions?"

Mr. Arlington cleared his throat and coughed. Grandmother Stutz said, "We are not making any accusations, but everything suspicious we have discussed centers around Hiram Bishop. There are all kinds of rumors floating around town about different..."

The judge interrupted, "Mrs. Stutz, I am not interested in rumors or gossip, just facts. You have made your concerns clear to me. Now leave it up to me to resolve them. Is that understood?"

There were nods, murmurs and chairs scraping the floor as everyone but the judge got up and left the room. The judge sat staring at the closed door for a long time. Shaking his head, he grunted, "Hiram, you arrogant, pious, greedy bastard."

CHAPTER 31

Indians laughed at the way whites got sunburned and how easily they got lost.

Red Deer sat the brown horse that had belonged to Big Boy. He scanned the rocky terrain for the army soldiers who pursued them and for the ugly little white man known as Sans. Red Deer fumed when he thought how Camel had been reluctant to give him the horse. He would not have done it if Father Pollen and Naiche had not intervened on his behalf. Who did Camel think he was, anyhow? He was a drunk skunk whose mama had been a dog and his father a buzzard who loved to guzzle strong drink like Skinyas.

He took a deep breath to slow his anger when he recalled how Camel told him over and over to beware the cowardly white little coyote, Sans. He turned to the west and stiffened when he saw the cloud that told him it was the army on the move. It was coming in his direction. Whipping his horse around, he kicked him in the sides and moved into a gallop to warn his people of the approaching enemy.

He was looking between the ears of his mount, enjoying the speed and not having to walk in the hot, rocky sand, and did not see the glint of steel reflecting the sunlight. The bullet slammed into his chest and knocked him into a somersault off his horse. White alkaline dust rose and then settled on him. Splayed on his back, he looked into the white ball of the sun and saw something that pleased him. He smiled. He did it so seldom, it felt strange.

The Morning People had eaten the weak gruel made up of desert rats and a couple of lizards. They missed Naltzukich's strong, accurate throwing arm so effective in bringing in game.

Little Sun ran up to Camel. "I was standing on the point there trying to follow Red Deer with my eyes. I lost him, but I think I see dust from the west and I think I heard a gunshot."

Camel followed him to the rocky knoll and both stared into the distance with hands cupped over their eyes. At first Camel saw nothing. About to turn away, he saw it. The army had returned to chasing them during the day which meant they would also have to move.

With experience and adeptness the Morning People prepared to move out. Anrelina and Naiche were trying to persuade Father Pollen to ride on a travois hitched to one of their newly acquired horses. They agreed to leave the white woman, Eunice, for the army to find.

Camel stood on the rise once more to confirm the army's location and get an idea how fast they were moving. The dust cloud told him they were coming quickly, be here in another hour. A glint of sunlight caught his eye about a thousand yards out. He lost sight of it for a few minutes and then saw it again. It had to be Sans.

Camel told Naiche and Father Pollen what he saw. Anrelina overheard and said, "We have weapons now we can stand up to him."

Naiche's expression was solemn, "We are not killers, Anrelina; that man is."

Camel looked at Anrelina and said, "He knows like all of us, the only one here he needs is Naiche to find him water. I will take one of the horses and go out to meet him. Whatever happens, don't allow Manuelito and Little Sun to fight him."

Father Pollen shook his large head on his small, shrunken body and said, There must be something we can do to…"

He fell into silence under their stares. Naiche placed a brown, gaunt hand on Camel's arm, "You are a brave man, Camel. The desert has made a new man of you. The desert has the power to kill a man or to make him a man. There is an old legend…" he paused, "But we do not have time for old men's stories now, we must leave this place. May the great spirit go with you, Camel."

Camel checked the cinch on the horse, adjusted the stirrups, checked the .44, placed it back in its holster, checked his rifle to ensure he had a round in the barrel and mounted up. He looked down into the upturned face of Anrelina. She squeezed his ankle and was gone.

Atop the knoll, he could see the small dust cloud made by Sans and the larger one made by the army. He nudged his mount ahead to place him directly in the path of Sans. The terrain was rugged: a mixture of alkaline dunes, craggy rock formations, prickly cactus, greasewood and mesquite. His horse stumbled, gained his footing climbing up a rocky outcrop and almost toppled over scrambling down the far side.

Camel pulled up, listening for hooves. The only sound was a buzzing fly and the blowing of his horse. He knew he had to be close to Sans, but where was he? The country was so rugged. A flash of fear reminded him that if he missed the crazed little killer, he would be turned loose on the Morning People. Since all of his vigilante buddies had been killed, what would he do?

For the next several minutes, Camel searched the sky for dust, smelled for it, listened for hooves, creaking leather, anything to locate Sans. A faint scream sent a shiver of fear down his back. He stopped, listened for it but heard nothing. He yanked the reins of his horse hard. The sound had come from behind him. Riding fast, he reined up as he neared their camp from the previous night. He smelled dust and held his rifle ready. Nothing.

Then he saw it. A body. It was Eunice lying on her back beside a dark rock outcropping. His eyes searched the terrain before him as he rode to her and looked down on her. Her still face was contorted into a grimace of pain. Her large hollow eyes stared into the sky. Sans had disemboweled her.

Camel kicked his horse and raced toward the Morning People who might already have been discovered by Sans. He cursed himself for allowing the killer to slip past him. One, two, three gunshots sounded a short distance away. The trail led into a dry arroyo and a glimpse of colored clothing made him jump from his mount and aim his rifle at it. It didn't move. He walked cautiously toward it, holding his rifle, and holding onto the reins so his horse followed him. It was Little Sun. His crumpled body laid on its side; blood covered his face and head.

More shots. A hundred yards or so ahead, Camel found the body of Manuelito. Rage mixed with helplessness filled his throat.

Sans would wipe out all of the Morning People except for Naiche. He would wait until he was safely out of this barren country and then kill the old Indian.

He kicked his horse and raced ahead. Suddenly dust stung his nostrils and he made a controlled fall from his horse. A shot whizzed by his ear, making it ring. He rolled behind a towering lump of dark rock and peered around trying to spot Sans. A bullet smashed into the rock a few inches from his face, sending stone splinters into his forehead. He felt nothing but a trickle of blood running down between his eyes and onto his nose. Pulling back from the edge of the rock, he scrambled up and cagily peeped through a hole near the top of the rock. At first he saw nothing.

Another shot careened off the rock where he had been a moment before and then several more bullets whined and screamed around him. Some ricocheted off the rock and whistled tunes of potential death. Peering through the hole, he spotted a light puff of smoke. Following it downward, he was convinced Sans was holding up behind a clump of rocks, prickly pear and cholla cactus.

Leaning back, he deftly placed his rifle barrel into the hole, aimed for the middle of the clump and fired. Sans responded with a half-dozen shots from his Evans carbine. Camel hunkered down as lead breezed past him or plunked into the rock formation.

Sans's rifle held at least 30 rounds and Camel knew he was up against a deadly weapon in the hands of someone who knew how to use it. Peeping through the hole, he saw movement but the firing stopped. Sans was reloading.

Camel rested his rifle against the rock, drew the .44, measured the distance between them which he estimated to be roughly fifty yards. Holding the revolver tightly, he ran as fast as he could toward his enemy. His moccasins beat a rhythmic tattoo on the hard, rocky soil. It occurred to him that he could never have run this fast before the desert almost killed him.

He was within ten yards when Sans stood, showed himself and threw the rifle to his shoulder. Camel dove for the hard earth as the bullets ripped around him. He made a smaller target stretched flat on the ground, facing his adversary. His first bullet struck Sans in the shoulder and spun him around. The rifle went flying. Camel leaped over a prickly pear and saw the little humped-back man charging him with his knife drawn. A snarl covered his face and his beady eyes radiated hate.

The next bullet caught him mid-chest and knocked him back into a yucca cactus. As Camel neared him, revolver pointed, he blinked his eyes in disbelief as the little man rose shakily like a broken wind-up toy with blood covering his torso, spurting from his nostrils and dripping from the corner of his mouth.

The next bullet struck him high in the stomach and smashed him into the yucca. Camel stood over him and saw his lips writhing like a rattler whose coils flexed and convulsed after his head had been shot off. The eyes still held to life and hatred. His lips moved but produced no sound. Camel looked to the sky for a long moment and then back down into the eyes of venom.

After a long pause and the lips continued to move and the eyes held their fire, Camel said, "I will not put you out of your misery. You earned it."

Reclaiming his rifle and horse, he became aware that his head and face ached from the rock fragments embedded in his flesh. His ears rang from the gunfire and the powder stung his nostrils. Blood dripped from his nose and covered his torso and front of his pants.

Following the trail, he came upon the Morning People in less than a quarter of an hour. They smiled and ganged around him in relief and rejoicing. Father Pollen asked about Little Sun and Manuelito. Faces dropped as he told them. Father Pollen shook his head, "We tried to stop them from going back, but they would not listen."

Tears streamed from Anrelina's eyes as she tended his wounds. Other than the tears, she remained stoic. Their eyes met and he could see a lifetime of hurt in them. He had an idea. "Father Pollen, do the men chasing us know you?"

He squinted through his specs and said, "I don't know, why?"

"Because there's a dead man back there a ways who could be described as you. Let's go!"

The priest protested as Camel pulled him onto the back of his horse and the two of them rode off. Standing beside Sans's body, Camel said, "I'm going to take his clothes off and you are going to put them on. We'll put your outfit on him. If the army thinks they have your body, maybe they will call off the hunt."

Father Pollen grumbled and Camel had to scold him to hurry, but in a few minutes, the switch had been made. Back with the Morning People, Camel talked to Naiche about his plan. Naiche agreed and told the people to walk in single file and to step in the foot print before them.

Billy laughed and said, "You are Toby the ghost man. You look spooky to me." With that, he laughed harder. Toby smiled at the comment and chewed his rabbit. At first, Billy's constant babble had bothered him. But he now found it enjoyable. Billy was like a child and once he bonded with you, he was your friend for life. *My child is more like it*, thought Toby as he smiled and nodded at something the other said.

It had been a good day. They had rounded up over twenty rustled 3C steers on the Rocking H spread and herded them back to their rightful place. Toby ached from the effort, but it felt good to reclaim what Hiram and his thug of a foreman had stolen.

Looking into the small fire built with dry wood, Toby wondered how long he could keep up the charade. His arthritis hurt him more each day. This was not the way a man his age should be living. His eyes seemed to be deteriorating each day along with his strength. He had always been thin, but he caught a glimpse of himself in a pond the day before and the white bearded, gaunt, hollow-eyed, stranger he saw frightened him for a second. The sudden quietness and the look on Billy's face told him he was daydreaming and had missed something.

"What ya say, Squirt?"

Billy smiled at the nickname, " I said, Toby, you remind me of Sheriff Dan. Did you know him very well?"

Toby spit a piece of sinew and picked at his teeth with a finger, "No, can't say I did, Squirt. What little I did know of him was all good though. I remember somebody saying something about him and it sounded like he was a man who did the right thing." *What I won't tell Billy was that I was sporting with Queenie Beaumont when she told me how the sheriff treated her decently and had never requested any favors.*

Billy's expression grew somber and he said, "Sheriff Dan could always help me to make the right call, Toby. I guess I need your help now. Whatcha think I should do? Ride into town and give myself up to that sorry Sheriff Frank? I did shoot Junior Beaumont and kill him and that makes me a murderer."

Toby saw the tears welling up, "Now Billy, don't go downing yourself. You don't know if you killed him or not. I toldja about the man I saw when I was a boy who got half his head shot off and he was still walking around, alive as much as you and me."

Billy would not be comforted. He placed both hands over his face and his shoulders racked with sobs. "Yeah, you told me that story, but you never said if he had any sense or could talk or think. What must my poor mama be thinking?"

The sobbing youth leaned over onto his side and laid there in the fetal position crying and sniffling. Toby wanted to tell him to stand up and be a man, but he knew Billy's mental state was not that of a man. He scratched his white hair and pulled at his ear. It was a tough situation. He was supposed to be dead and could not show himself and find out if the shot had proved fatal. Billy thought he was a wanted man and could not learn the truth without giving himself away either.

His shoulder hurt as he pushed himself up and moved beside his partner. He patted him on the back like a mother burping her baby. Toby thought of his Indian wife and the way she would pat their baby who died less than a year old. He tried to talk soothingly to Billy the way he remembered his wife talking to their infant child.

Bryant took a draw on a rolled cigarette and said, "Come on, boys, you can dig faster than that. One of the sweating workers who stood about three feet in the hole with another man shook his head, wiped sweat from his forehead with a faded red bandanna and said, "I hired on to punch cattle, not dig up dead people."

Bryant flipped the cigarette away and said with anger, "You were hired to work for the Rocking H and unless you get your ass moving on the end of that shovel, you might end up in that hole permanently."

Two other hands stood nearby. The men were taking turns digging and their faces showed none were happy with the task. In a couple of minutes, Bryant said, "Okay, let's change hands on those shovels. You should be hitting the box any time now."

As the men worked, Bryant turned to gaze at the ranch house and support structures: stable, barn, corral, squat smokehouse, two sheds, one large one and a small one and an outhouse.

He had scoured the house and buildings trying to figure the puzzle of men claiming to sight Toby. At first he wrote it off as fear and hysteria. But lately, he had come to wonder if the sightings were accurate. Only one way to find out…dig up Toby's body.

The man standing on the coffin scraped the dirt off the top of it with his shovel. He looked up at Bryant and said, "Boss, I want to keep my job, but I'm not opening this coffin."

Bryant mumbled several profanities, "Then get your scary ass outta there."

Pulled out by his comrades, all four men stood waiting for Bryant to open the coffin lid. He took one of their hands and dropped to the coffin. It took him several minutes, sweating and cussing to get the lid off. The men's eyes were large and their faces white as they gazed at several good sized rocks resting in the coffin.

Bryant looked up at them and smiled, "Well girls, looks like you had nothing to be scared of, did you?"

The men shook their heads in disbelief and uttered profanities of their own. They helped Bryant from the hole and he said, "We'll leave the grave open because I expect to be burying Toby in it within the next 24 hours."

Bryant left the men washing up at the well and kicked his horse into a gallop. He wanted Hiram to know about this as soon as possible. He would suggest a 100 dollar reward to the man who shot the old coot and this time bury him for real. He smiled. He would do his damnedest to be the man to collect that reward.

Using a gourd, Maggie explained how the earth was almost round and circled the sun. She had one of the black children named Abraham, stand holding a pumpkin while she circled him with the gourd. The other children thought it funny and giggles were heard under the arbor where class was taking place. Maggie wished she could still use the McGuffey Primers and Webster blue-black spellers from the classroom, but knew that was no longer an option. The slate boards for writing and computing would be helpful also but she consoled herself by admiring how these children learned with so little materials or equipment. They used several rag-tailed Bibles for reading and some old Farmer's Almanacs for just about every subject.

Following the science lesson, she sat at the well-built desk that Ben Davis had built for her. He had also built long benches for the students to sit on just like in her classroom. Only the wood of these benches was not polished yet by little wiggling butts. Maggie glanced up at a patch of blue sky revealed through a leafy opening in the arbor. She smiled to herself in contentment. Convinced in her resolve that she was doing the Lord's work, she found herself almost enjoying the personal comfort sacrifices she had to make daily.

Living with Quiermo, Estefania, and their children was not one of them. It was a great relief to be out of Bilbo's house and no longer under the watchful, accusing eyes of his sickly, whiny wife. But everything else had become more difficult since the town council meeting. She walked every where she went and the towns people were giving her the cold treatment.. Billy was not around now to help clean the school building, so she did that. Jeremy, an older student who used to sharpen pencils for her, now had chores to do at home.

It was the Negroes and Hispanics who treated her with kindness, respect and appreciation. Some of her regular students continued to respond to her when their parents were not around. Some of the younger ones, in their innocence, repeated their parent's lurid gossip about her and the pastor.

Two of the children whom she found affectionate and responsive through it all was Ralph and Floyd Manning. She remembered how Ralph had asked her to visit his mother. That was puzzling. Why did he do it? Both boys had seemed nervous and not themselves that day.

Henry Goins offered her a ride home in his mule-drawn wagon and she told him she needed to visit the Mannings. He readily agreed to take her there. Said he would be glad to wait for her. Take as long as she needed. Maggie shook her head and told him she would walk home.

Henry had lost his easy smile and soft eyes since losing his wife, Vera Mae. He somehow seemed smaller to Maggie. His broad shoulders drooped and his eyes held a constant look of pain and sorrow.

As Maggie insisted on dismounting from the wagon without assistance, she was met by Floyd and Ralph. The boys were elated to see her and escorted her into their small, rough-hewed home.

Maggie was shocked when she saw Pearl. The woman's face was swollen, bruised and puffed almost beyond recognition. She sat in bed, her back propped against the wall. She was embarrassed to see Maggie, but in a few minutes, it was obvious her need for help superseded her feelings.

Pearl told her about a drifter attacking her and how Hiram had come along to chase him away and had the doctor out to see her. Listening to her and watching her, Maggie knew that the story was untrue. Angel Valley did not have strangers. It was too remote. She said nothing, but her woman's intuition told her Hiram was responsible.

Maggie prepared supper for Pearl and her boys when Judah rode up. Pearl chose to visit with Judah sitting upright in her bed as Maggie and the boys ate supper. They could hear Judah and Pearl talking softly.

Maggie stood at the door and asked if she could bring something to them. Both declined. Judah looked up at her from the side of the bed where he sat and said, "If I could find who did this, I would kill him." Maggie saw Pearl turn and stare at the long, dark weapon leaning in the corner.

In the excitement, Captain Verlander had momentarily forgotten his painful hemorrhoids. Sitting atop his horse, he looked down on the body everyone thought was the radical priest. He dismounted, squatted beside the body and stared at the face. He was the only man in the unit who had actually seen the priest before. One thing he knew for sure, *this is not the priest, the Reverend Donald Asbury Kelly, that I was assigned to capture and return.*

Standing, he walked slowly around the area. Before this assignment he would not have known how to do it, but now he scanned the ground for telltale signs. His newly educated eyes told him someone had worked hurriedly to brush away prints. That was probably his scout.

His eyes caught sight of a couple of moccasin prints and horse hooves someone had overlooked. Looking around, the only one he saw watching him was the scout. The captain walked casually over and scraped away the prints with his boots. He looked for several more minutes and then motioned for the scout to come to him.

He ordered his men to seek shade under a couple scraggly oaks about thirty yards away as he talked to his scout. "What do you think we have here?"

The scout spoke more fluently than he had throughout the long, hard journey. "I know a group of five riders joined them. They have fought one another. I saw many graves and dead bodies. Men, women and children. This is the priest that led them. Only horses left here, two of them. I do not know who the riders were. Maybe they were riding from Mexico." With that, the scout shrugged his shoulders and fell into silence.

The captain wiped sweat with his sleeve, examined his hat and thought what a convincing liar the man to be. For the first time, he appreciated his scout. Nodding his head in agreement, he dismissed the scout and beckoned his lieutenant.

The lieutenant stood before him, bearded, dirty and scowling in the killing heat. Captain Verlander said, "Lieutenant, it seems someone else has finished the job for us. We've known about the other group and it looks like there was a helluva fight and they have killed one another off. The only ones who have escaped are a couple of the latecomers." He paused, watched the man for his reaction. There was none so he continued, "Did you ever see the priest before?" This question had been put to his men before but he wanted to confirm it.

"No sir. I've never seen any of these people before."

"Well, as I've told you men, I saw the little priest once on the reservation. I was in charge of taking a wagon train of meat to them." He pointed to the body of Sans, "Here is the priest. Helluva way for a man of the cloth to go, huh? But I guess he was crazy and got what was coming to him in the end. These bodies have got to be buried because of this intense heat. Get up a burying party and when it's done, Lieutenant, tell the men we are going home."

The lieutenant smiled for the first time in many days. Matching the smile, the captain realized his hemorrhoids were feeling better all the time.

CHAPTER 32

The Indian's diet included sunflower seeds, Jerusalem artichoke, ground cherry, pokeberry, grasshoppers, bees, beetles, snakes and lizards.

The orange slice on the horizon melded into blue and then black as night fell on the remaining Morning People. The reduction in their number was reflected in the dynamics of the group. Naiche continued to be as stoic as ever, but Father Pollen's dejection was obvious in his expression, silence, and gait. He blamed himself for the deaths. Anrelina, too, was silent but her dark eyes spoke eloquently.

Naltzukich's absence was felt with each decision made and with each meal they ate. They felt more vulnerable without the watchful eye of their scout, Spirit Dog. Little Knife's anger, though it was excessive, always provided a crystal clear picture of why they should break camp each morning and face another day of marching through fields of cactus, stumbling over rattlers and tarantulas, looking over their shoulders for the pursuing army, the brilliant flash of blinding light beaming down headaches, and always...always thirst.

Little Sun's radiant smile and easy manner had counter balanced Little Knife's anger. Manuelito's steady, quiet personality and ability to trade his blankets for needed goods would be greatly missed. Red Deer's smoldering anger and quiet hatred was another missing ingredient from the new recipe. The dead child Mangus and his natural bubbly laugh and inquisitiveness were sorely missed. His mother appeared to be near death. She had not eaten since losing her child and staggered when they marched unless Anrelina held her up.

There was another change. Skinyas was gone. He took with him one of the horses and his tus. It was assumed he had deserted to the army. At first this gave them cause for concern. Was Skinyas going to assist the army in their chase? But after a couple of days, it was obvious the army had turned back.

They rested in a valley of craggy rocks interspersed with sharp, triangular Spanish daggers and ocotillo plants armed with pointed spines projecting outward. A small, muddy pool of water held the group like a magnet. Naiche led them to it but seemed to flounder once there. He was ancient. Was his age and the grueling mental and physical demands taking their toll? Holding his hands out and mumbling as he always did in searching for the life-sustaining liquid, he stumbled on one of the thousands of rocks and fell onto his face. Anrelina helped him up and tried to clean his face as he resisted and fussed about needing to be left alone until he found them water. With much encouragement, he finally allowed Anrelina and Father Pollen to assist him as he sat on an angled rock.

Everyone collapsed from fatigue and thirst. Camel rested atop a flat rock and stared at his moccasins. Without thought he picked up a small dry stick and pushed it into the hard sand. To his amazement dirt stuck to the lower end of it. Digging with his hands, he was scooping up water in a few minutes.

Women filled their tus's as Camel stepped back. He felt a hand on his shoulder. It was Naiche. He stared into Camel's eyes for a long moment before saying, "The spirit is showing you how to find water. That is good."

Camel shook his head in disagreement, "I didn't do anything, Naiche. You are the one who led us here."

The old Indian squeezed his shoulder, ignoring Camel's comment, and returned to his place. That night they ate thin gruel made of armadillo, a couple of lizards, all boiled in sandy water.

The next morning, Camel asked to speak with Naiche, Father Pollen and Anrelina. He had had a dream that he described to them. They listened quietly. They sat for a long time contemplating in silence.

Anrelina spoke first, "It is a generous offer, Camel; it is a good idea. I am for it."

Father Pollen spoke next, "It makes sense to me. I agree with Anrelina."

All eyes were on Naiche. He seemed to be far away. In a land no one in the group could see. Camel felt a twinge of concern for him. He looked as though he could float, he was so thin. His face had something of an ethereal glow to it. He smiled and it surprised the rest of them because he did it so seldom. Indeed, only Anrelina had seen it before.

Naiche stared through Camel as he spoke, "I have been seeking a vision, and you have given it to me." He turned to Father Pollen. You came as the result of a vision. Now Camel has come to us. It has been hard. Very hard. But we know there is a real promise waiting for us. Camel will take us to the promised land we have all seen in our dreams and visions."

The next morning at sunrise, they packed up and headed for Angel Valley. Paradise. It would be a long journey. Camel was a man with a vision for the first time in his life.

Toby knew they were searching for more than steers this morning. They were man-hunting and he knew he was the man. He was glad he and Billy had spotted the pile of sand beside his grave the day before. It was risky but hunger drove them to return to the 3C to get the last of the jerky from the smoke house. Feeding Billy had sapped his supply. Luckily they had approached the ranch house from the stand of trees on the north side and seen that the grave had been opened. Quietly, they had walked their horses back into the trees for a half mile before they rode hard away.

Toby glanced at Billy lying on his stomach a few feet from him. If they had not seen the grave, the boy would have thought they were after him. Toby scolded himself for not having sent him away before this. But, *gosh darn it*, he thought, what could he have done differently? The boy clung to Toby like a calf to a heifer.

There were six riders, all armed and scanning the rocky terrain for old Toby. He whispered to Billy, "Be real quiet, Squirt. Let them just slide on by us." The riders were almost out of sight when Billy's horse whinnied. Their horses were tied off about twenty yards behind them and the riders immediately turned and moved toward the sound.

Toby's pulse raced. *Dammit! This was not supposed to happen.* The riders came closer and he knew he and Billy could not make it to their horses and run for it. He felt sick as he levered a round into the chamber and drew a bead on the closest rider's horse. He said, "Don't shoot unless I tell ya, Squirt. Maybe we can wiggle outta this yet." His words sounded hollow to him. Billy's eyes told him that even he knew there was no way out of this without a gunfight.

The riders spread out and stopped about fifty yards away. The lead rider said something to the others and then spurred his mount forward. Toby recognized Bryant. He rode straight toward Toby and Billy as though he were looking through the rocks and bushes that concealed them.

Holding his rifle to his shoulder, Bryant was now less than twenty yards from them. At this range, Toby stood, raised his rifle and took aim.

"Get down, Toby! Get down!" Billy pleaded.

Toby ignored him. *Come on Bryant, ya dirty bastard. I know it was you who tried to kill me once. Let's get it over with now. Maybe if you're the better man and win, ya will at least let Billy go, he's not part of our problem. It's just between you and me.*

Bryant fired first. Billy saw Toby flinch, and then fire his weapon. Toby aimed for the chest but his trembling arm failed him and his bullet removed the lower lobe of Bryant's left ear.

Even riding hard, Bryant shot better. His shot skidded across Toby's ribs, making him drop flat onto the rock and gasp in pain. Billy raised his Colt, but Bryant skidded to a stop and dropped behind a boulder surrounded by weeds and brush.

The other riders scrambled for cover. They were several yards behind Bryant, lacking their crazed foreman's desire for a fight to the death. A couple of them took shots, but Billy saw no results. He stared at Toby. "Ya hurt bad, Toby?"

Removing his bandanna, Toby stuffed it into his shirt already soaked in blood, "I've been shot worse, Squirt. I'll make it. Now why don'tcha get on that nag of yours and make a run for it. This is not your fight. I'll hold them off while…"

There was emotion in Billy's voice, "Stoppit, Toby! You're my friend, my only friend and I'm not gonna leave ya."

Billy focused on the rock Bryant hovered behind and caught a glimpse of his hat. Aiming and shooting at it, he heard Bryant roar, cuss and scream, "Alright ya old sunuvabitch. I'm gonna finish ya this time and there will be no doubt about you being dead."

In Bryant's hatred, Toby's face now held the spot previously reserved for his father. Killing Toby might be more fun than killing his dad, although he never thought it possible.

Each man sat in his own surrey eyeing the other. The older man was angry; the younger man frustrated. The old one said, "Hiram, you have shot the milk cow this time. Everyone in Angel Valley whose worth a good Goddamn is against ya."

Hiram's face turned red and he said, "Judge, what do ya…"

The judge bellowed so loud, his horse took a step forward, making the handbrake squeak. "I mean Arlington, McCormick, even the old bitch, Granny Stutz, is saying you taking the town to hell on a racehorse. But that ain't the worst of it, your bank assistant is telling me you stealing, screwing the people blind and he has the records to prove it."

The judge held his chest and took several breaths. Dammit, he knew Hiram was a greedy bastard, but he had always given him credit for using good common sense and not going too far. The judge knew all too well the importance of maintaining one's image of respectability while feathering your nest at the same time. Hell, he had turned a poor paying Texas judgeship into a very lucrative business while maintaining a spotless reputation. He had often had to discipline himself when his little small voice whispered that he was going too far. That was when he had to back off and keep himself above reproach. Hell, he had preached this very biblical admonition to Hiram more than once. He had considered Hiram a protégé. His breath rattled and his hands trembled because he was angrier with himself than with Hiram. Why hadn't he picked up on the mans inability to control his appetite? Now he had gotten the whole town against him. And this jeopardized the judge's career as well. Hiram, like so many others through the years had paid him well to look the other way or to make judicial decisions look judicial while they were actually the result of a bribe...one not too large, but appropriate for the situation.

Hiram cleared his throat and said, "Judge, don't worry I..."

The judges eyes bulged and a purple vein in his temple throbbed, "I am worried and you damn sure better be. Restrain yourself man! You can't gobble up the whole damn valley like a hungry horse eats oats." The judge gulped air and continued, "That piss-poor lawman you hired ain't worth a bucket of hot horse shit. And Hiram, you better listen to me and listen good, don't you even sneeze at that bank clerk of yours. Another murder, missing person or land grab in Angel Valley and the damn Texas Rangers, United States Marshall's Office and maybe the whole damn US Army is gonna be seeing you in a federal court. It will be out of my hands. I'm not going down with ya, Hiram!" With that, he pushed his brake off, slapped the reins and bolted ahead.

Hiram sat for a long time watching the dust from the judge's surrey until it was a speck on the horizon. He was not used to being spoken to like that. The judge was the only man in the county who could do it and get away with it. Hiram found himself imagining having Frank back shoot the old bastard. Everyone knew the judge kept a scattergun at his knee in the surrey and in the courtroom. Frank could not be depended on to outshoot the old man in a fair fight.

He pushed the thought from his mind. Leaning back in his surrey seat, he rubbed his massive neck, eyes closed, and said, "A rod is for the back of him that is void of understanding."

That night, Cholla visited with his whip. When he left, Hiram lie on the floor sobbing. The next day he sat at his desk for only a short time. He could not stand to look at A.J. Moniker. He kept wanting to smash his face with his fist and then kick him until he was soft and pliable.

Leaving at mid-morning, he held himself erect so his bruised back did not rub against his starched white shirt. He must remember to talk to Juanita about putting less starch in his shirts when ironing them. Stinky acted surprised to see him so early in the morning and even more surprised when he ordered a beer. Hiram never drank before late afternoon.

Stinky tried to initiate conversation to see if he could deftly pick his brain, but Hiram obviously did not want company or conversation. He shrugged when spoken to but remained silent. He sulked and stared out the window as he drank the day away.

The sheriff dropped by after he closed his store and Stinky pointed to the back room and whispered that Hiram was there. Hiram was no friendlier to him. Just the sight of Frank irritated him. The judge was right. Frank was a wannabe lawman who was no better at it than he was as a store keeper. Frank tried several times to strike up a conversation but was met with stony silence. When the sheriff drained his first glass, Hiram let him know he wished to drink alone. Frank slunk out and shrugged at Stinky who returned an understanding lift of his eyebrows.

Stinky was itching to close at eleven since it was a week night and the place was deserted except for Hiram parked in the back room. But Hiram was so damn moody and mean, he approached him only when he yelled for another beer and then scuried out. At eleven-thirty, he peeped into the room and saw the big man was gone. He shook his head. It was so unlike Hiram to get drunk during the day. He opened the back door and looked around to be sure Hiram had not passed out and was on the ground sleeping it off. Only the star embedded sky and a coyote barking met him. He shook his head again. It was not like the big man. A man who drank all day was a man without discipline. Usually a drunk. A man going down, not up.

He closed the door, placed a board across it, blew out the kerosene lamp and made his way up the squeaking stairs to his bedroom and stock of cheap booze. Across town, Hiram sat at his lavish desk with his head resting on his crossed arms. His nose was flat against his large Bible, slobber soaking the vellum pages as he snored, sleeping in a drunken stupor.

Bilbo stood in the pulpit looking out on the many empty pews. Hiram sat alone in his usual place. The new family, the Stoddard's, sat near the middle. A couple of boys sat whispering on the back pew. Queenie Beaumont sat near the back, her first time ever to attend church service. Bilbo wondered if she was the lone attendant who sympathized with his plight.

He had seen Hiram look back when she entered the sanctuary. A flash of annoyance appeared on the big, square face as he looked at Bilbo. Bilbo leaned against the pulpit, clutched its corners and thought for the first time in his life he might faint. He had worked on this sermon all week. Indeed, lately he avoided people. Remaining all week in his parsonage-prison, he either listened to his wife's whining or studied for his Sunday sermon. Regardless of all the preparation, he still felt completely empty, like a hollow log. Taking deep breaths, he tried to speak, but his voice was barely audible. Clearing his throat and faking a cough, he was finally able to speak. They were not his words, but the words of a stranger.

At the end of the miserable hour, only Queenie Beaumont remained to address him following the sermon. Shaking her hand, he really looked at her for the first time. He saw a woman in her middle thirties, not beautiful, but pleasant looking, and her voice held the sound of a tinkling bell within it. This was not the same sound he had heard her make when she yelled at her kids. Watching her walk away, for the first time he saw her as a living, imperfect human being who had needs. He locked the church door from the inside and leaned back against it. Closing his eyes, he felt tears welling up as his inadequacies and failures washed over him. Queenie Beaumont needed ministry like every other resident of the area, but he was not the man who could give it to her. He could not help anyone because he could not help himself.

Three days later, a weary rider made his way to the train station in Alpine. He wore a black suit gray with dust. His white shirt was yellow and dingy from sweat and road dirt. He carried a satchel and walked stiffly from the station office after leaving without buying a ticket. He walked his horse to the local blacksmith where he sold him. The blacksmith figured him as a gambler down on his luck and was surprised when he failed to adhere to the ritual of the west by not haggling with him over the price.

That night when the train made its stop for water, a lone figure carrying a stuffed satchel ran from a deserted shed. He stumbled and fell, his case emptying its contents onto the moon-washed sand. A cry could be heard over the sounds of the train's engine as the man scrambled to scoop scattered items back into the bag. The last item was a large, black book with its pages gently flipping in the night breeze coming off the mountains. He grabbed it, held it to his chest, sobbed loudly, and spoke to it, "Oh Lord have mercy on my soul." With that he scurried to the train and his shape became part of it as he boarded it.

Maggie had another mission. She cooked and kept house for Pearl and her boys. Judah was an enormous help. He brought a pork hind quarter, hoed the garden, milked the cow, fed the mules and patched fences. Every Sunday he brought his girls to play with the boys. Maggie concluded Judah was the most gentle man with a woman and children she had ever seen. As she cooked or washed dishes, she watched Pearl and Judah out of the corner of her eye as they held hands and talked quietly to one another. Sometimes, they would not talk, just sit quietly watching the children play. It was as though their relationship transcended the limitations of conversation and a simple meeting of the eyes or quiet smile sufficed.

Maggie had to admit that deep within she was jealous of Pearl. She wanted the kind of love Pearl had found in Judah. She wanted what the poor black couple, Henry and Vera Mae had. Was she destined to live the life of a celibate missionary, always tending to the needs of others at the expense of her own? She recalled the men whom she had encountered in Angel Valley. The one who had swept her off her feet was Camel.

Next, she had the misfortune of knowing Hiram. The bullish, pock-faced, pious man who quoted scripture but was Satan incarnate. She gave herself to Camel; Hiram took what he wanted.

And there was Bilbo. Poor, weak Bilbo. Why had she allowed him into her room even though their relationship was platonic? Was it for herself or for him? Were they both simply pathetic figures unable to control their own destiny?

Judah pressed her to allow him to give her a ride home in his wagon but she wanted to walk. It was a long one, but she felt the need to be alone. As a whippoorwill sang its melancholy lament, she thought again of her past and her future. She expected any day to receive a letter from her family back in Connecticut. Hiram had threatened to write several times and she figured he would get around to it sooner or later. What about her conduct in Angel Valley? She had made some grievous mistakes, she readily admitted, but when the children, White, Black and Hispanic looked at her with eyes of adoration, she knew she was doing something right.

A coyote barked in the distance and a nearby dog answered. She could see the adobe she now called home, a single light glowing through the wax paper covering the window that Estefania left burning for her. The sound of horse hooves frightened her. A stand of pine trees stood tall and straight to her immediate right. She lifted her dress and ran to them. She stepped behind the tree as the horseman came into view. Her breath caught in her throat, it was Hiram.

CHAPTER 33

In the old west, the cowboy most often carried a rifle like the Winchester 73 which shot .44-40 ammo. The same ammo he used in his Colt 44.

The morning air was cool and crisp. With the sun breaking over the Davis Mountains to the east and the Tierra Viejo mountains to his back, Camel rode the brown gelding within forty or fifty yards of the mule deer. His first shot dropped the animal to his knees.

Back at the camp, the Morning People were elated to see so much fresh meat. For the first time in a long time, Camel heard excitement in voices and even a giggle or two. Even the child, Chatto, showed some response. He had hardly spoken since losing his best friend, Mangus. Overall though, the cloud of sorrow over the loss of so many of their own continued its impact on the group. The day before, Camel had walked into the bushes to relieve himself and found Father Pollen on his knees sobbing. Naiche seemed to have aged before their eyes in recent days. He appeared to be thinner, his eyes showing confusion, and having difficulty locating water. Anrelina obviously tried to maintain her positive attitude, but the spring was gone from her walk and she was unnaturally quiet for long periods of time, lost in her thoughts.

Their sadness was compounded by the death of Mangus's mother the day before. Anrelina found her dead in the morning. She grieved herself to death. Camel felt that while all of the deaths had impacted the group, the death of the child, Mangus, had a unique and profound effect on everyone. Mangus, a bubbling energetic child had held the hopes and dreams of the future. Camel felt the others had died a little with him. After all, wasn't that what this entire dangerous, risky venture was about...a future for a people who had none unless they carved it out for the next generation.

The group was moving southeast now. The country remained rugged; finding water continued to be a high priority, but things were changing for the better. The terrain held sparse grasses and fewer brown tumbleweeds and dry mesquite bushes. Small madrone trees became more numerous amidst a variety of vertical boulders, Rock lettuce and Cory cactus. Prickly pear and Cholla cactus speckled angled rises to gray, craggy cliffs that towered high above them like long abandoned castles silhouetted against the cobalt blue autumn sky.

Out of thirty-three Morning People beginning their impossible trek, twenty-six remained. Six were known dead, Skinyas' absence continued to be a puzzle. Riding through the wild, beautiful country, Camel thought how all of them managed to stay alive until he joined their group. *Do Anrelina, Naiche and Father Pollen resent my presence? Do they hold me responsible for what happened?* His mood matched the group's and he rode silently, dealing with his own demons.

The cooler weather and gentler terrain allowed them to travel during the day and rest at night. Camel spotted a dozen or so buzzards circling a quarter of a mile ahead of them in the sky dotted with fluffy clouds. Drawing nearer, he saw carrions perched on boulders and tree limbs. In the center, he saw a patch of clothing. He looked down on the swollen body of Skinyas. An empty tus perched a few feet away at an angle, just beyond one extended hand. Camel dug a grave and placed the remains in it. Looking down at his handiwork, he thought, *"That could be me."*

They were camped in a dry riverbed packed with limestone soil. Naiche had given up on locating water. They needed to find some tomorrow because the longer their water remained in a tus, the stronger the taste of pine pitch. Father Pollen invited everyone to circle up around the fire and give thanks. Camel noted about half of the group lolled outside the range of the circle, electing not to participate.

Father Pollen prayed and Camel was surprised to hear his name listed as a reason of thanks. The thought made him uncomfortable. He wondered if the others agreed with their priest's prayer. His

thought was interrupted by Anrelina's high-pitched voice. She
stood tall and slender and chanted. Camel had never heard anything
like it before. There was no harmony and at times she seemed to be
howling like a coyote. Soon she was accompanied by Chee and
others. Several produced gourds that emitted a rattling sound that
complemented their singing. At first, Camel found the sound
grating on his ears, but the more he listened, the better it sounded.
Everyone was now gathered around the circle and appeared to lose
their tenseness and tight-lipped sternness that had been a part of the
group since the final encounter with the vigilantes.

Camel saw Father Pollen retreat to his blanket a few yards away
and as he laid down his silhouette disappeared into the darkness.
The Morning People moved from singing to dancing.

Watching, Camel wondered how long this shindig would last.
He moved toward Father Pollen's blanket and standing several feet
away, tried to determine if he was asleep. The squeaky voice
coming from a dark lump gave him his answer.

"Well, Camel, what do you think of a mixture of Apache and
Navajo music?" Before Camel could answer, he saw the preacher
sit up and lean back on one elbow. "Pull up a rock and sit down. A
body certainly can't sleep with all this ruckus going on."

Camel answered, "It sounds strange to my ears, but the more I
listen, the better it sounds."

There was no response so Camel went on, "I gather you are not
real fond of their music."

The little man gave a weary sigh and said with a tone of
resignation, "Oh, I'm sure it's alright. I guess my Presbyterian
Calvinism gets in my way sometimes."

Camel said, "Do you know what they are singing or chanting
about?"

"Anrelina's first song was a plea for help in our time of need.
The others have been for healing, for strength, certainly they are
qualities we direly need."

The two of them fell into silence as the cacophony of howls,
chanting and rattles filled the cool night air. Father Pollen said,
"The Navajo for centuries have recited a creation history that grants
equality to women. In their myth, the first people emerged from an

underworld. The first man and woman created the sun. They created all things and instructed the people how to live."

Camel did not respond and watched as sparks from their fire rose and danced in the darkness, blending with the stars. Father Pollen laid on his back, his weak arm unable to support his weight, "I commend myself on my flexibility and liberality in accepting their beliefs and I tell myself I have not forced my theology on them, but I'm probably kidding myself. In winning their friendship by fighting for them, I have taken my pay from them in their patience as they listen to me and nod in agreement. Sometimes I tell myself they have almost completely discarded their pagan ways, but then like tonight, I see and hear them and wonder if I've wasted my life and their time and failed to win their souls for our Almighty Lord."

Camel stood, stretched, and said, "You are too harsh on yourself, Father. I too have asked myself if I have brought this calamity on them. You guys were doing pretty well before I staggered along. Now, I've got to make water." The priest spoke, but Camel stepped into the bushes out of earshot which was not far with all of the noise. Music, he reminded himself, music.

The next morning, Naiche accepted a ride on a travois. He did so only after Anrelina cajoled and threatened and Camel encouraged him. Father Pollen refused a ride and still trudged along with a look of determination on his freckled, impish face.

That afternoon, they searched for water. Naiche kept drifting to sleep and was no help. Camel sat his horse and searched the variegated canyons for signs of water. He wrinkled his nose, turned his horse slightly to the south and pushed ahead a couple hundred yards. He stopped and listened. Pushing ahead with the people following him, they came to a flowing creek winding its way among boulders and gray stones of every size and shape. They looked like they had been tossed there by mother nature to act as a protector of the twisting waterway.

An hour later, Naiche, Father Pollen and Anrelina sat on a blanket. She invited Camel to join them. He perched on a polished gray boulder. Father Pollen said, "Camel, it is the thinking of the group that we change your name. It is customary among the Navajos to give a name that is suitable to a person. My birth name is Donald Asbury Kelly. After coming to know me, they asked if I would allow them to change my name to Pollen. Pollen has great significance to them; it represents new life, a renewal, change. After coming to know you, they want to change your name to Moses." He smiled at the look on Camel's face.

Camel shook his head in amazement. "I don't think so, Father. I'm not much of a Bible scholar, but I think it might be downright...uh," He stumbled for the word.

The priest said, "Blasphemous, sacrilege, heresy. No, Camel. Not so. They have heard me tell the story of Moses leading the children of Israel to the Promised Land. They understand that you are not Moses reincarnated. But they see your actions and what you have done and are doing for them and the name seems appropriate to them."

Naiche and Anrelina nodded their heads in agreement. Father Pollen chuckled, "I don't know whether I feel jealous that they selected that name for you rather than me or pleased that my stories have made an impact upon them."

Camel stood and rubbed his neck. "Father, Naiche, and Anrelina, you know the kind of man I was when you found me living with Bones. It seems the desert and you people have made me change my ways, but I'm the one who has benefited from our friendship. We still have a long way to go to reach Angel Valley and I might fall off the wagon and misbehave again. Sometimes I feel that the desert took the desire for a drink of alcohol out of me, but then again I'm not so sure. I don't feel it's right that you do this thing."

The priest struggled to stand, reached his feet and said, "There is more to it Camel. They feel this is one way they are showing their faith in God by putting their trust in you. They feel very strongly about this and mean it as a great compliment, but even more, it is important for their belief system. I suggest that you strongly consider their request. If not for yourself, then for them."

That night, an even larger fire was built and following a prayer and a few words by the priest, Anrelina began her high-pitched song. Soon the gourds were rattling and there was much chanting. Anrelina took his hand and guided him to the middle of their circle while the women danced around him and tossed what appeared to Camel as grains of pollen. He sneezed several times and was embarrassed, figuring that hardly added any dignity to the occasion, but no one seemed to notice. Finally, the activity stopped and Naiche shuffled forward. He placed his hand on Camel's shoulder and said, "From this moon to the last moon, your name is Moses. You are not the Moses of the book, but you are a man who is leading his people to a promised land like that Moses did many, many moons ago."

The next morning Camel felt strange each time someone addressed him as Moses. Riding the top of a grassy spur with the people walking behind him, he smiled to himself as he imagined the folks back in Angel Valley hearing him called by his new name. Gazing at the purple mountains of the Chisos Mountain range ahead of him, he saw the weathered and weary face of Toby. Good old Toby. Always there for him. What's happened to him since I disappeared from town? Did he give up on the ranch, pay the hands off and head out to Santa Fe where some relative lives? I owe Toby so much. Will I ever have the chance to repay him?

Glancing back at Naiche on the travois, satisfied he was alright, he looked at a craggy peak and saw the face of Maggie. He had treated her shabbily as he treated everyone else. Was she still around? She was pretty, intelligent and he found her New England accent only made her more interesting. He had trouble seeing her remain in a small, backwater dump like Angel Valley.

A Red-tailed hawk screamed overhead and a covey of quail flushed from high grasses beneath twin oak trees. Moses' horse jerked on the reins and took a quick step but he held the reins tightly and talked gently to him, calming him down. Lush vegetation loomed ahead of them and a welcome sight. They were getting closer to Angel Valley each day and he worried for the umpteenth time about his promise to take the Morning People to his ranch. What would his neighbors say? Would they insist that the Indians be returned to their rightful place on the reservation? What about the town's sheriff? In his former life as Camel he had hardly instilled confidence in others. Would the town rise up and throw him and the Morning People out? What about Hiram? Hiram. His square face filled Moses thoughts. Although he no longer felt hatred for his old nemesis, he dreaded to think what his response would be toward himself and his friends.

For the next week his new name sounded strange but then he forgot about it. He took to his new name as though it were given to him as an infant. Perhaps, he thought, he liked it. The name Camel had been branded onto him by his justifiably irate father and though he had never consciously considered it, he did not like it. It was demeaning and though he deserved it, he resented it subconsciously. He wished his father were alive to know the circumstances that prompted the Morning People renaming him.

There was more. With his new name came his recognition that the Morning People respected him. They did not see him as a drunk, a womanizer, a gambling cheat, a lazy good-for-nothing, but rather they saw him as one of their leaders. A man who had earned their respect and they would follow him without question or doubt. It was a new and exhilarating experience for Moses. The responsibility was great but outweighed by the self-esteem that he now basked in.

He felt like a new man. But then the gnawing old doubt and fear of falling back into a life of booze, gambling, and women filled him. He shivered as though ice water ran down his back at the thought and made himself focus on his surroundings.

On this morning the air was comfortably cool and the dry desert still made its presence felt with occasional mounds of white alkaline sand and scattered patches of black volcanic soil. A creosote bush was seen snagged to a lone cactus here and there but mostly they were now on terrain holding more green than burnt browns and ash black.

The horse leaned into the hill he was climbing. Moses turned in the saddle and watched the line of men, women and children following him. Their stamina and perseverance astounded him. Reaching the top of the hill, he gazed across the tops of several hills and deep purple mountains in the distance. He eyed the panoramic view before him and marveled at its beauty. He was seeing the big picture and did not see the wagon pulled by two mules down hill about two hundred yards away. He felt a bullet tug at his sleeve and heard its crack echo off the sloping mounds.

The atmosphere rang with tension. Hiram took a deep breath and fought for control. He sat in a straight-back wooden chair too small for his large frame. Across the table from him sat the

Arlington's and Grandmother Stutz. McCormick did not show and he now knew why. The meeting was taking place in the Arlington's parlor and Hiram thought how he would like to smash all of the furniture…cracking each piece across the skull of these cut-throats.

Clearing his throat, Hiram said, "So the two of you were approached by an English cattle company who expressed an interest in buying your ranches. Rather than sell to them, you sold to McCormick."

He knew that was a lie. Each dipped their head in agreement with his statement. He said, "Mac is a friend, but I would like to make an offer before you close the deal."

An awkward silence followed. Arlington's face was beet red, he said in a tight voice, "The transaction has already been completed, Hiram."

Grandmother Stutz said, "You might want to deal with Mac, Hiram. Like you say, we are all friends." Her voice was cold and dripped with sarcasm.

Hiram moved and his chair squeaked in protest. Waving his hands in a helpless gesture, he said, "I don't understand. We have plans, we have…"

Arlington cleared his throat, dabbed at his chin with his white napkin although all he'd had was coffee. "Hiram, Angel Valley has experienced a series of tragedies. No one is to blame. It just happened. It all began with the disappearance of Camel. Our sheriff was murdered in cold blood. Our pastor and school marm were found together in a compromising situation. Now we hear that our pastor has abandoned us in the middle of the night. There is a rumor that 3C cattle have been rustled. There was the recent shooting incident of the Beaumont boy by the Womack retarded boy." He dabbed at his lips again and said, "And Hiram, the railroads not coming here. Alpine is as close as its going to come. Railroad management says there is simply not enough business in our area to make it solvent for them. All things considered, this is too much for our hamlet to absorb and survive."

Hiram stiffened. Arlington knew he hated that word, hamlet, and it was only the second time he had used it in Hiram's presence. The first time Arlington had used it he had been made aware of

Hiram's aversion to it. A fire burned in his gut. The ever dapper, proper Arlington had just insulted him.

There was an awkward silence. Mrs. Arlington mumbled an excuse about having to check on the kitchen and made a hasty retreat. Mr. Arlington coughed and said, "There is even a rumor that the foreman of the 3C ranch died and his grave has been opened. There is supposedly no body and so the question is now being asked whether the man is really dead. Especially since another rumor has it that the man has been seen riding with the Womack boy."

Hiram protested, "We cannot allow rumors to dictate our actions or future. We have to be strong and have enough faith in our Lord, our government and in ourselves that we have established to keep us going through the rough times."

Another tense silence filled the room. Grandmother Stutz spoke, "Hiram, my nephew insists that I move to Houston so he can help me. You know I am getting up in years. And, Hiram, we are all friends here, but we are also realists. Our town has failed. We must move on to something better. I am sure that you will do the same."

Hiram stared into the old ladies cold hazel eyes and thought, *You old bitch! You will live to be a hundred and outlive your nephew by fifty years.*

Hiram rose abruptly. He could not take it any longer. "So you are going to abandon Angel Valley?"

Grandmother Stutz's voice grew icy, "No, Hiram, the vision and possibilities we held for Angel Valley have abandoned us."

Back at his bank, he found that the Arlingtons, McCormicks, and Grandmother Stutz had all emptied their accounts. Hiram spoke curtly to A.J. and walked briskly to Stinky's backroom. He began drinking hard liquor and told Stinky to leave the bottle and he was not to be bothered by anyone. Throwing a drink down, he kept hearing Arlington say the trouble all began with the disappearance of Camel. Camel. Damn, how he hated that man even in death.

Quiermo was explaining to Maggie how his father constructed their adobe. He explained he had mixed goat blood with straw into the pre-cast bricks and sun dried them. The blood gave the floor a glossy sheen that enabled Estefania to mop it and keep it shiny clean.

Maggie's mind drifted as Quiermo talked on. She watched him for cues when to nod, smile, respond, but found herself with Camel again. They were locked in a passionate embrace and she was enjoying it. Why was she still thinking of Camel? Probably, because she had no other decent suitors. But she didn't travel all the way from Connecticut to Texas to find a husband but rather to teach impoverished children. That sounded good, but brought her little satisfaction. Would her mother and grandmother be pleased with her? She had decided that Hiram's threats to write a recriminating letter was just that…empty threats.

Seeing the faces of the white children in school, the black children under the arbor and the brown faces in the adobe shed, she was proud of her achievements regardless of the setbacks and humiliation she had experienced. She stared at Quiermo and then Estefania. She had missed something. They were looking at her and expecting a response.

Wiping her face with a napkin, she said, "I'm sorry, Quiermo, I guess I was daydreaming. What did you ask me?"

He said, "I heard today the preacher, Bilbo Carmichael, has vamoosed. He took his horse and left in the middle of the night. They say his wife is in very bad health and some of the city council members are sending her to Alpine to catch the train back to her home."

Estefania said, "It is good that you came to live with us."

Pearl laid on her side staring at the shotgun. She wiped a tear from her freckled cheek and her lips trembled. Judah sat on the other side of the bed. He rubbed his neck and said apologetically, "I'm sorry, Pearl. That's never happened to me before. Getting old I guess."

She closed her eyes and forced herself to breathe evenly, feigning sleep. He twisted and looked at her for a long while. She fought back a sob as she heard him whisper, "I love you, Pearl."

She remained completely still as he dressed. He closed the porch door so quietly she strained to hear it. That was Judah. Thoughtful, lovable Judah. A couple minutes later, the drum of horse hooves told her he was gone. Pulling herself out of bed, she walked to the old faded dresser and picked up a small mirror.

Holding it close, she examined her face. Around both eyes she still saw color, the results of the beating she had taken at the hands of Hiram. The biggest difference she noted was her nose. It was crooked. The bridge was either swollen or permanently enlarged. The lower part twisted slightly to the right on her face. Pearl had never considered herself a beauty, but had been told by numerous suitors that she was pretty and though it was unspoken, she knew they considered her sexy.

Sure the years in Texas on their hardscrabble farm/ranch had taken its toll on her shape and face, but she had retained a woman's pride in her looks and told herself that with a little care, rest, and dress up, she could still turn a man's head. Not anymore. She slipped a gingham dress over her head, pulled at her lively auburn hair. The boys would be here soon and she had several chores they needed to do. Maybe that would take her mind off of her looks and Judah. She had no doubts about his love and knew her disfigured looks were not the reason for his impotence. No. No, poor Judah felt the anger and frustration of a man who loves a woman who has been violated by another man. His sexual impotence was merely a manifestation of his feelings of inadequacy in protecting the woman he loved.

The one good thing coming from the beating and rape by Hiram was Judah's new resolve to hang on. She still hoped they could make a go of it.

CHAPTER 34

A common saying in the west was , "God created men; Colonel Colt made them equal."

Moses looked down the bushy slope to a man standing on a wagon fiddling with his rifle. He had a long white beard and was struggling with his weapon. Another man jumped from the wagon and tried to hide behind it. Moses could see the man standing had a single-shot rifle. Probably a Sharps .50 caliber from the sound it had made.

Turning back, he shouted to the Morning People, "Down! Everyone get down.!" They obeyed. He drew a bead on the man's chest, but did not want to kill him. He aimed at his gray, shapeless, broad-brimmed hat. The hat went sailing as Moses' rifle bullet kicked it off the man's bald head. Levering another round into the barrel, he shouted, "Don't shoot! I'm a white man and I got a repeater here."

The bearded man either did not hear him or ignored him. He threw the rifle up and took aim. Moses dismounted as the heavy weapon fired. His horse whinnied and he felt a bolt of fear that his animal had been shot. But his horse tossed his head and showed no sign of being hit. Moses took a quick inventory of his people, no one had been harmed. Luckily, the man could not shoot. Stepping away from his horse, Moses aimed and fired again. The man's left leg buckled and he toppled from the wagon.

Mounting up, Moses kicked his horse and raced to the man on the ground rolling on his back, clutching his left knee. Dismounting, he saw the other man hiding behind the wagon was a young Hispanic teen. His eyes were wide with fear as he clutched the wagon rims.

Moses tossed the Sharps single-shot rifle to Chee who came running up. He turned his attention to the old man who was now groaning and cussing.

"Omigod, you heathen, unsaved savages are on the warpath. Well, you can kiss Ol' Charlie's ass becuz I ain't gonna give up without a fight. An ya damn sure ain't gonna eat my mules ya…"

It took a while for Camel to convince Charley he was a white man and that no one wished to do him harm. The leg was a mess and Moses was concerned Charley was going to argue and resist them until he bled to death. He finally agreed to allow Anrelina to look at his wound. The bullet had entered just above his knee and broken the bone. As Anrelina, Father Pollen, and a woman worked on the wound, Moses had an opportunity to assess the other man and the rig.

The young man, named Barboncito, kept speaking in Spanish, "Yo no hago nada. Yo no hago nada. Yo siento!" Moses said, "I think you're saying that you are not doing anything wrong and that you are sorry. Can you speak English?"

The young man swallowed and said, "Si. Yes. I work for the senor. I am doing nothing wrong. Please do not harm me. I only…"

Moses gestured for him to be quiet. "We are not going to hurt you. What are you doing out here?"

The man pointed to a canvas stretched taunt over the wagon bed, "We hunt longhorns for their hides."

Moses lifted the tarp and saw skinned hides stacked high. The wagon was in good condition and pulled by two large brown mules. Most ranchers had turned to importing and breeding cattle from the East and Europe because the longhorns' long, angular, twisted frame held little eatable beef. Their sometimes volatile temperament didn't help either. Most folks now killed them only for their horns and hides.

Watching Anrelina doctoring the old man, he wondered how many more there were like him. Men who had fought the Comanches and Mescalero Apaches. Men who believed with all their hearts that the only good Indian was a dead Indian. His heart skipped a beat as he thought of the people of Angel Valley and their reaction to the Morning People. *Will they shoot before they learn that my friends are harmless?* This was a reoccurring fear that weighed on him more each day as they neared their destination. Was he leading them to a new life or to a grave?

They camped there for the night so they could tend the old man's wounds. Sitting cross legged before the fire beside Father Pollen, Moses noticed the little man with the twisted body and large head seemed lost in his thoughts. As the people drifted off one by one to bed down, Moses started to say goodnight to the priest. He stopped when he felt a hand on his foot.

"What do you think of your new name?" asked the priest.

Moses was silent for a moment and then said, "Felt funny at first, but guess I've taken to it pretty well."

The fire popped and in the distance a owl hooted several times in rapid succession and then was quiet. "I felt the same way when they gave me my name, but it seems natural enough now."

Moses stared at the large bespectacled face that faded in and out with the dying fire. He felt ready for bed but something about Father Pollen's silence and voice beckoned him to stay seated and allow him to have his say.

He shook his head, looked up at the twinkling stars and said, "I pray that our journey will end alright. I have been so angry and frustrated with myself over the horrible deaths of so many of our people. They followed me, trusted me and, in the end, I only led them to their death."

Moses responded, "Father, you cannot blame yourself. You didn't force them to follow you. Little Sun told me how on the reservation they had to line up to receive cow entrails, rotten meat and flour full of beetles. Little Sun was about one of the most affable people I have ever known but he said life on the reservation was a living hell. These people are ready to risk their lives for something better. They are still risking them, like today with old Charley trying to shoot them."

A coyote barked and yelped and another one chimed in and before long there was a chorus of animal voices serenading them. Father Pollen looked at Moses, "Thank you for that. I feel a real kinship with you, Moses, because they are looking to you now for leadership and a better life. I pray not to envy your newfound position."

Shaking his head, Moses said, "Don't envy me, Father. The truth is I worry all the time about what the people back in Angel Valley will do when I show up with my new friends. As you know, I was not exactly the model citizen before I met you, these people and the desert. They might just all die from laughing when they hear my new name. Old Charley today really brought that home to me. Am I doing the Morning People any favors by taking them to my home?"

There was more. He worried a lot these days about turning back into Camel. Camel would get drunk as a skunk, look for a poker game and a willing woman. He could not share these thoughts with Father Pollen.

Both men fell into a long silence. The coyote howling was reduced to a sole poignant wail. The fire was almost out now and Moses could see only a silhouette of his companion. The priest shifted, grunted in pain and said, "They are wonderful people. They are God's children. Everything they encounter, the land, sky, mountains, rivers, everything is holy. That is why they have traditionally resisted Christianity. To them everything belongs to God, not just one day a week or a tenth of what they have, but all of it. Of course many preachers would say I've lost any sense I ever had. The Navajo have their own gods and creation story and an oral history that is similar, in my opinion, to our New and Old Testaments. They have a legend that parallels our story of Adam and Eve being cast from the Garden of Eden, they tell of a great flood and another story reminds me of David slaying Goliath."

He shifted again, trying to find a position without pain, he gave up, sighed and said, "Take their name for themselves, *Dineh.* It's translated, *The People* or *Earth People.* To them, their way of life was the only life. The chosen way."

Fatigue sounded in the priest's voice, "Superstition plays a large role in their beliefs. For example, the Apaches consider a crow evil, but the owl is the most evil bird of all. A good Apache dies and goes to an underworld existence, something like the Old Testaments Sheol, but a bad Apache is incarnated in an owl."

The fire had died to mere ashes and only identified itself with an occasional flicker.   Moses could hear the anguish and struggle within the holy man's voice. Moses heard loneliness too. He could identify. He and father Pollen had chosen to side with people who were feared, hated and mostly misunderstood. In a way though, the two white men knew they would be considered traitors by their own kind and a measure beneath the outsiders they befriended. It was a lonely, frightening position.

Some type of bird flapped his wings overhead in the dark and brought Moses back to the drone of his friend's voice. "…Hogan is round like the sun. The door always points to the east so the first thing they see in the morning is Father Sun, one of their many deities. Directions are very important to them. There are four, so the number represents perfection to them much like the number seven to the early Christians. East is the holiest direction."

Moses said, "It's interesting that you have some Navajo and Apache. How did that happen?"

"Naiche says its part of the Navajo legend that they are related to the Apache. For sure the two were united when Kit Carson modeled himself after Sherman and burned crops and hogans and rounded up thousands of Indians and herded them into a reservation called Bosque Redondo in Eastern New Mexico. Thousands of them died of starvation and disease there. Actually the Navajo, unlike the Mescalero Apaches, did not range this far south. They lived in New Mexico, Colorado and Arizona.   Obviously this group will go anywhere they can simply live like people and not animals." Father Pollen's voice was growing hoarse and Moses wanted to end this but remained quiet as his friend shifted again.

A child cried out. A bad dream. Several coyotes had resumed their barking and yelping. Father Pollen said, "Moses, I'm proud of you. I guess I consider you one of my children too. You and I have much in common and whatever the future holds, you can always know that I admire you and you are in my prayers." With that said, he struggled up and shuffled off to make water and then hobble to his bedroll.

Moses found that he was not as sleepy as he had earlier thought. The priest was right, they did have much in common.   The responsibility of these people, so helpless left to themselves, having been subjected to so much adversity, felt like a heavy burden weighing him down. But it was a weight he must bear. A weight he would bear. It was also an opportunity somehow yet unclear to him to undo some of the bad.

Father Pollen was right, the Morning People were counting on him to lead them to a new life. A life with meaning and satisfaction. He had gradually assumed authority over them. He now acted as scout for them as Spirit Dog had done. He pointed the way for them and provided them meaning as Father Pollen had done early on. He now found water for them as Naiche did before the rigorous demands wore him down. He provided food for them as Naltzukich had done so effectively with her cunning traps and accurate throwing arm. The authority he held brought with it responsibility that both scared him and yet also lit a fire in his heart and soul. Soul. His had been immune to the needs of others for as long as he could remember. He sat staring at the dead fire and smelling the dry smoke for a long time before he made his way to his blanket.

Toby tried once again, " Hey, Squirt, keep low and get on your horse and ride like the wind. I'll keep this group of wild jackasses penned down while ya get outta here."

Billy adjusted his gun, checked his revolver and grinned at Toby, "I said I ain't leavin' ya, Toby!"

The old man frowned, shook his head and said, "Okay, Squirt. Just keep ya head down."

Billy smiled. He could hear the softness wrapped within the roughness of his mentor's voice. When Toby called him Squirt, he knew all was well. Billy watched the old man work his fingers, trying to limber them to combat the aching arthritis that plagued him.

The blast of several pistol shots drowned his voice out. Billy ignored Toby and peeped around a rock hummock. He spotted a man standing behind a boulder aiming a six-gun at them. He heard the shot, heard the bullet skid off a boulder a couple yards from him. Taking careful aim, Billy fired at the man and saw him disappear behind his cover.

Toby squinted, trying to see who was shooting at them, but could not see any shooters. His ribs burned like fire, but he knew as the shock wore off, the would hurt even more. This needed to be brought to a hasty end before he passed out from loss of blood.

Toby watched a rock where he thought he might have seen something and gave up trying to run his friend away. *Dammit, I'm gonna be responsible for this young man's death.*

One thing was clear to both men. Their fate would be determined right here in a rocky canyon a few miles outside of Angel Valley. Billy was proud to take a stand with his friend. Each one had shared his story with the other, just as he and Sheriff Dan Libby had done. The young man believed heart and soul in his aged, wise friend.

Toby narrowed his eyes and rubbed them with his sleeve. His old eyes were giving away on him. He could not see to shoot as he once had in his youth. Another problem was the trembling. His muscle control and coordination was failing him. When he tried to aim, his arms trembled, making his sights bounce up and down.

He glanced over at Billy and cursed himself for the thousandth time for allowing the young man to be caught in a gun fight like this. Toby was an old man. He had lived his life. A full life. He had known the compassion of a loving wife. A warm fire and warm bed on the coldest night. He had broken broncs, ramrodded men, and experienced so much. Billy had not enjoyed any of these things. He felt awful for his inability to direct the young man to a safer position.

Both men fiddled with their weapons, shifted their ammo, but each kept a watchful eye out for movement. It didn't come but the crack of a rifle sent a bullet thudding into a rock a couple inches from Toby. He yanked his hat off and squinted, trying to see where the shooter was hiding. Several shots sounded. Bullets whined, whistled, and screamed all around them.

Billy spotted something to his right. Twisting on his rock, he saw nothing at first. Then he saw a man raise up from rocky brush and level his rifle at them. Billy snapped off a shot and the man ducked behind the craggy rock. He heard Toby fire and work his lever. Looking at the rock the shooter hid behind, Billy scanned it and guessed where the next attack might come from. He aimed his revolver at that point. The distance made it a difficult shot for him and he knew he must aim high. He was right. The man with the gray hat stood to shoot and Billy aimed an inch above his head and fired. The shooter dropped his rifle, clutched his upper chest and went down slowly.

Toby wiped sweat from his eyes with his sleeve and loaded his rifle. He was angry and frustrated. He was not hitting anything because he either could not see well enough or his aim was not steady enough.

He heard some yelling but could not make out what was said. He looked to Billy, "What'd they say?"

"They said, Little Mike has been hit and needs a doctor."

Toby grunted as he levered a shell into the barrel. "You had to do it because I durn sure ain't hit nothing but a couple of rocks and a cactus."

Billy moved back to his original position. He could see the smoke of three different shooters. Two were out of his revolver's range but one was as close as the other man he had hit. He watched the one within range for over a minute and then saw a head and shoulders behind the stick of a rifle. He aimed and fired high and the figure and rifle disappeared from sight. He watched for a long moment and the rifle appeared again and fired a round that screamed an inch above his head. He heard Toby fire, mutter a curse and the rifle appeared again. Billy fired once, cocked and fired again and waited.

There was more yelling and the gunfire stopped. Toby looked at his companion, "Can ya hear 'em?"

Billy nodded, his eyes big, Toby didn't know if it was fear or excitement. Billy said, "They said that R.L. has been hit bad."

After a long silence, one voice was heard above the others. It was Bryant. He was yelling and cussing at his men.

Toby grinned at Billy, "Even I can hear 'ol loudmouth Bryant airin' his lungs at his men. He sounds really mad. I guess most ranch hands don't sign on to get shot."

Billy spotted a couple of men running and snapped off shots at them, but they never returned fire. It surprised both Toby and Billy to see Bryant scramble from his cover and run to a rock formation several yards away. Billy was waiting for his next move and snapped off two shots at the running, ducking figure as he continued to distance himself from them.

"Coward!" Toby muttered. A few minutes later, he and Toby heard horse hooves and saw dust rising.

Both men held their positions for about an hour without seeing or hearing any movement. Billy looked at Toby, "Looks like they had enough and headed back to Angel Valley. We better get you to the doctor."

Toby was silent. His red, wrinkled face, cool blue eyes and white hair marked the experienced cowboy that he really was. After a long moment, he said, "No doctor, Squirt. I'll make it. As for them leavin' it could be a trick."

A few minutes later, Billy's patience ran short. Climbing down from his rock, he stretched and said, "I believe they gone, Toby. Like you say, they don't like getting shot up."

Toby tended to believe his partner and began to ease from his rock perch when a rifle sounded and spun Billy around. He sprawled onto the rocky ground, curled into a fetal position, and began groaning. Toby dropped to one knee to see how badly his friend was hit. He heard Bryant's flat, deep voice behind him, "Drop the rifle, Old Man."

The new family that had arrived less than a month ago was leaving Angel Valley. The husband, wife and two children had their possessions loaded in two wagons, each pulled by four lumbering oxen. He drove one wagon and she drove the other one. A milk cow was hitched to the back of her wagon and two horses and a mule trailed behind his wagon.

Hiram stood in front of his bank, a frown on his face, watching them as they rode past him. One of the boys waved and he waved back. Looking down the street, he saw Stinky leaning on his broom in front of the saloon. Hiram knew he should at least make an appearance in his bank, but he couldn't make himself do it. He strode toward Stinky.

Walking across the dusty area between the buildings, he looked at the few sparse dwellings and for the first time he did not see the potential for a bustling town, a town that he owned and controlled, but rather a tiny hamlet that was in the throes of death spasms. Hamlet. That's right. That's what it was. A hamlet. A dying hamlet.

As he stepped onto the steps of Stinky's place, he heard his name called. Looking across the wide expanse of area they called main street, he saw Frank Mosley standing in front of his mercantile store waving to him. To hell with him. Ignoring the sheriff and bartender, he entered the saloon.

Stinky sat a bottle and a glass on the bar. Hiram was not worrying these days who saw him drink. He sat at a wobbly table and poured himself a stiff one. Gulping it down, he heard footsteps and looked up to see Frank Mosley enter and come to his table. Stinky acted like he was busy, but since there was no one else in the place, Frank let him know he would like to talk to Hiram in private. When the door to the backroom closed, Frank sat down uninvited as Hiram poured himself another drink.

Frank appeared nervous and said, "Hiram, is it true that the city council has disbanded and the Arlingtons and Grandma Stutz have sold out and are leaving the area?"

Hiram stared at his deputy. His whiny voice grated on his nerves. He wondered what he had ever seen in the man. He could chew a better man out of an apple. Gulping another drink, he belched loudly and said, "That's right, Frank. They running away. I guess we are going to have to cull the bad apples until we get the sweet ones." He didn't believe his own words and from Frank's expression, he didn't either.

Frank shook his head and grimaced, "Business is dead over at the store. I ain't had a customer all morning. Yesterday, I had two and they didn't amount to anything." He stared at his boots and said nothing as Hiram belted another one down.

A rooster crowed somewhere and a quail whistled his poignant bob-white song. The two men sat silently; each one despising the other. Finally, Frank got up and walked out without a word. Hiram stared at him. It surprised him that Frank would leave without what he came for...strength in the form of assurance for his weakness and spineless decision-making.

Hiram arrived home early in the afternoon. He told Juanita he needed to see her sister, Carmen. Juanita smelled alcohol on him, noted his red face and wobbly walk. She stepped down from the wooden chair she was standing on to clean the top of the kitchen cabinets and agreed to get her sister. She put away her dusting cloth and set the chair back in the corner. As she prepared to fetch Carmen, she heard a noise that made her stop and listen. Tiptoeing into Hiram's bedroom, she found him laying face down snoring. She quietly walked to her adobe and made no effort to locate her sister.

Hiram woke at dawn with a throbbing headache. He laid very still, hoping the nausea would pass. Sweat beaded his forehead. His heart pounded. Giving up, he lunged to the side of the bed, pulled the lid from the honey pot and puked into it. He puked until there was only a string of thin gruel attached to his lips and the side of the pot. Coughing and gagging, he spit, wiped his mouth with his sleeve and rolled onto his back. His throat was raw from the strained retching. His voice was a whisper, "How long wilt thou be drunken? Put away thy wine from thee."

Judah and Pearl sat on the steps of her cabin. He sat on the lower step while she sat on the one above and rubbed his back. "Thank you for the ham." She said.

The children ran and laughed around them. The laughter and giggles of young ones were medicine to their ears. He reached back took one of her hands, squeezed it, stood and said, "I want you to tell me the truth, Pearl."

She looked at him strangely. He continued, "I figure you have always told me the truth and I want it now. Was it Hiram who hurt you?"

She had prepared for this moment. At least she thought that she had. She feigned a frown and started to deny it when tears gushed from her eyes. Between sobs, she blurted, "No! No, it was not Hiram!"

Finally, wiping away the tears with her apron, she looked up into his sad eyes. They reflected pain and anger. He said, "Your tears tell me what I need to know, Pearl. But you lied to me and..." He turned abruptly and yelled, "Get in the wagon, Girls, we gotta get home before dark."

Pearl moved toward him but he mounted his wagon and never looked at her as he said good by to her boys and spoke to his girls. She saw the look of concern on the boys faces so she stepped back

and bid the girls farewell and thanked him again for the ham. He
slapped the reins hard and the wagon bolted forward.

The girls waved as long as the wagon was in sight. When all
they could see was a speck of dust, her oldest son said, "Is
everything alright, Ma?"

She nodded, smiled and strode back to the house. Didn't Judah
understand she was only trying to protect him? Hiram was a
dangerous man. A deadly man. Men could be so foolish at times.
The thought of something happening to Judah brought more tears to
her eyes.

That night Hiram finished his meal and walked out onto the front
porch to smoke a cigar. He jumped when a quiet, deep voice came
out of the dark, "Hiram, it's Judah. I brought my gun so if you
wanta take it up now, we can. I'm here to tell you that if you ever
hurt Pearl Manning again, I will kill you, so help me God."

Hiram eyes had adjusted to the dark and he saw Judah standing
about twenty feet away. He appeared to be carrying a rifle or
shotgun. He angrily pitched the cigar into the yard. " Why you
ungrateful bastard. All that I've done for you and you go and
threaten me. I ain't never touched that woman. The only thing I've
done is good things for her. I've even…"

Hiram saw the silhouette shift and the weapon appeared to be
pointing toward him. There was a silent vacuum and Judah's flat
voice filled it, "Go getcha little pea-shooter that you hide but we all
know you carry and let's handle this right now if it suits you."

Hiram felt his heart thumping in his throat and he felt he would
burst with anger. He was so mad, he lost his breath. After a couple
of wheezes, he spoke in a high, tense voice, "You and your young
ones get the hell offa my land tomorrow."

Judah said, "We'll get off but it won't be tomorrow. And if you
wanta send that little piss ant you call sheriff to put me off, tell him
he's welcome to come with his pea-shooter too."

Hiram stared at the still, ominous figure. He had never known
Judah to talk like this before. He had a reputation as a quiet, patient
man. Hard worker. Never a trouble-maker. He knew he was seeing
Pearl, but he never thought Judah had the stuff in him to do what he
was doing. He knew he should have killed that bitch, Pearl

Manning. That was his problem, he was too soft. Too generous. Too much of a man of the Word.

Turning, he strode back into his house and blew out all the lamps. He didn't like the idea of Judah watching him like a fish in a bright bowl. Edging to a window, he peeped out to where his accuser had stood. He could see nothing. He cussed, cried, and ended his evening on his knees praying.

CHAPTER 35

In our country's history, many were opposed to free public education. It was seen as a handout to the poor. The goals of public education as written into most state constitutions was to expand liberty, increase prosperity, create better workers and lift the poor and foster equality among all peoples.

The bright, yellow sun glowed its way over the Chisos Mountains before them and brightened the Christmas Mountains behind them. This was rugged country.

The Morning People remained in camp another day to nurse Charley and reassure his young partner, Barboncito. The way Charley cussed and complained, he sounded up to his old self.

Moses was seeing familiar landmarks now and figured they would be in Angel Valley within another three or four days. He decided he would avoid the township and take his friends directly to the 3C Ranch. He wanted to avoid any confrontation with the townspeople. But how to do it? News travels fast and a group like their's would create plenty of news. All of it bad.

In the morning he killed two black-tailed jack rabbits and a javelina. The hog-like creature was not eaten by any white men he knew, because a gland on the animal secreted a strong, offensive odor that affected the taste. But he had seen Nalzukich clean and cook the carcass in a pit and when you are hungry, the meat tastes fine.

Back at camp, Anrelina volunteered to handle the cleaning and cooking of the freshly-killed animals. Moses noticed that Chee watched her closely and no doubt would have liked to help her but that would not have seemed manly.

Moses found himself checking on Naiche. The old Indian laid in the sun on an old scruffy buffalo blanket. Moses guessed that he had had some type of attack or stroke. His right arm and leg seemed lazy and he had difficulty controlling them. He would close his eyes for long moments between words. And sometimes, he would start to say something but fall silent in the middle of a sentence. Moses was glad they now had horses so that both Naiche and Father Pollen could ride on a travois.

Moses accepted a gourd of water from a young Indian woman and then sat on a blanket in the shade of an oak tree. Father Pollen walked toward him in his penguin sway. They exchanged greetings and Moses invited him to sit for a while.

The pastor felt like talking. "Everyone recognizes the names of Billy the Kid, Sitting Bull, Wyatt Earp, but how many do you think ever heard of the Reverend Sheldon Jackson, Father Ravallior, or William Friedman?" Shaking his head sadly, he went on, "These were men who gave their lives to share the word and love of God, but no one cares about them. We want the dramatic, the bloody, the gory. The people back East don't want to read in their newspapers about the accomplishments of Indians. The way they continue to survive under the most horrendous conditions. No, people don't want to be reminded or to even read about that. They want to read about the Ghost Dance and the Seventh Calvary's slaughter of the Lakotas at Wounded Knee."

The Texas sky was cobalt blue. White scruffy clouds slid across it like white sailing ships running before the wind. Was this the beginning of autumn? Moses looked back into the eyes of Father Pollen who smiled, "Getting a little preachy again aren't I?

Chatto ran by being chased by a smaller boy. The men watched the children and the unspoken thought for both was that this is what young ones should be doing. Father Pollen smiled at both children and gave a wave to the younger one who looked back at him. Wanting to change the subject, Moses said, "Looks like ya got a buddy there."

"His name is Stephen. Named after the first New Testament martyr," said Father Pollen. He smiled wider than Moses recalled seeing and said, "Guess I've made some progress, huh?"

Moses watched them and again wondered how they would fare in Angel Valley. He wondered if the school marm, Maggie was still there. Of course she taught the white kids and these Indians would not be welcome there. His thought was interrupted by Anrelina. He looked up at her and squinted. Her silhouette was outlined by the sun, making her appear as an angelic creature.

"Charley says he is going to have Barboncito hitch up the mules to his wagon and they are going to leave us within the hour. He said he will not spend another night camped with red devils."

Both men rose, Moses almost reached out to assist his friend, but stopped himself. The man was badly crippled and would accept assistance when it made a difference to everyone, but otherwise, it was hands off.

They found Charley leaning against his wagon, his wounded leg lifted an inch off the ground. Anrelina had bandaged his injury using leaves and herbs she had gathered from the ground. She had tied it with cut strips from his trousers.

Barboncito had hitched up the mules and stood beside him, eyes wide with uncertainty. Charley glared at Moses, "Squaw man, if ya help me onto my wagon, I'll be on my way. I figure that's the least ya can do since ya the one who shot me."

Moses had avoided Charley for this reason. He bristled at the name but took three deep breaths before answering him. "Charley, not that it's any of your business, but I am not a squaw man. Second, the reason I shot you was because you shot at me first. Shot at me twice as I recall. Now, if you get on that leg it might get infected and you will either lose it or it will kill ya. Why don'tcha stay here…"

Charley's face was beet red, "I ain't gonna tell ya what I think of you. And it tears at my guts to have to ask ya for help, but dammit, I wanna get the hell outta here as fast as Maude and Susie Q can take me."

Father Pollen started to say something but Moses leaned forward, both hands cupped, "Step into my hands Charley and I will put you on your wagon."

As the old man took his seat on his wagon, Moses turned to see Chee standing there with their rifles. Moses nodded to him and took both from him. He handed the Sharps to Barboncito and said, "You hold this until you get out of sight. If he takes it and points it this direction, I'm going to shoot him and it won't be in the leg this time."

A look of relief and appreciation was evident in the young Hispanic's dark brown eyes. He held the rifle, took his seat and slapped the reins. The wagon jumped forward, wheels squeaking. Moses held his rifle at ready as he watched the back of the two men. About fifty yards out he could see the two men scuffling over the rifle. At one point Moses thought Charley had it and raised his rifle to end the job he had started the day before. But Barboncito held it and after a while they were only a speck disappearing over a hill.

Father Pollen said, "Such hate and anger. My, my." He shook his large head as he turned, removed his thick spectacles and wiped them on his sleeve. Moses stood planted there for a long time. He knew what he had witnessed with Charley was only the beginning. How many white men and women would think just like him? Those who had looked at him with contempt before or had ignored him, would now look at him with hatred like Charley had done. By aligning himself with the Morning People, he would place himself in no man's land. While he had come to respect and even love the Morning People, he was still a white man and would never feel completely comfortable with their culture and way of life. No amount of respect for them would ever make him one of them. While the Morning People accepted him, he knew that there were lots of Indians like Little Knife and Skinyas whose feelings toward him would be the same as whites. Some, like Naltzukich, would be people of quality. A feeling of loneliness mixed with fear ran down his spine. Was he ready for this? Was it easy to be the big strong leader out here, but what about back in Angel Valley?

The air was filled with gunpowder, dust and tension. Bryant held the rifle on Toby and grinned, showing white teeth and eyes burning with the brilliant glow ignited by revenge. As blood dripped from one ear, he stood within a few feet of the two men.

Billy groaned in pain. Toby turned to him and said, "Hang on Squirt, you going to be okay." Billy laid in a fetal position on his left side. His revolver, holstered on his right side, had slipped down in front of him. He groaned, whimpered and said in a little boy's voice, "Toby, tell Ma that I love her."

Bryant sneered, "Oh shit, this is making me weep, Toby. The kid wants you to tell his ma he loves her and here you ain't goin' nowhere. Well, I guess that ain't right either. Ya goin' to hell to have supper with the devil."

Toby wiped sweat from his eyes, felt his arm tremble from fatigue. "The boy needs a doctor, Bryant. He don't deserve killin', you know that. He's a good..."

Bryant kicked Toby's knee, "Shut the hell up, you lying, scheming old bastard. Fake your death and then go around killin' Rocking R men."

Toby started to say something but Bryant kicked him in the bloody ribs. The old man grimaced and held his side. "Guess ya notice I was ridin' a different horse before ya killed him Ya got any ideas how this came about, Old Man?"

Toby looked his adversary in the eye but didn't speak. Venom oozed from the hate-filled voice and he knew Bryant was beyond reasoning. He was in his own world of hate and nothing Toby said would make a difference. He glanced again at the moaning youth beside him and chided himself for allowing this to happen.

The smile widened, the voice deepened, "It's time to pay me whatcha owe me, Old Man. With that he pointed his rifle at Toby's foot and pulled the trigger. The impact of the slug sent a shock throughout Toby's tired, aged body. His leg convulsed for a second; he pulled it up to him. His bearded face scrunched in pain as he opened his mouth wide to breath deeply and moaned. Blood dripped from his boot heel, forming a black stain on the rocky ground.

Bryant watched him deep-breathe for a long moment and then said, "Damn sure smarts don't it, Old Man?" He kicked the foot and laughed. Placing the barrel of his rifle against the flat upper part of Toby's other foot, he said, "Let's see how ya like this."

The rifle sounded again and Toby pulled both legs up to his chest and gasped for air. His face was in the sand now and his sun-seared skin tore against the rocky soil. Blood smudged his cheek and nose, soaked his shirt and dripped from both boots. He said nothing. The only sound was Billy's low moaning grunts interspersed with whimpers for his mother.

Bryant's face showed his displeasure. This mean old grizzly bastard was no fun at all. A horse whinnied and he looked up at their mounts standing thirty or so feet away. He recognized Toby's old horse. "Hey, Old Man, ain't that your ugly-faced horse over there? Yeah! Yeah, I would recognize that mule anywhere." His eyes lit up as he saw that he had Toby's attention.

Toby opened his eyes, straightened his legs, wiped the blood from his eye and said, "Bryant, you ain't all bad. Please don't shoot my horse, I beg…"

The rifle blast silenced him as he turned to see Babs fall to her knees and then roll onto her side. Blood ran down one shank.

Bryant laughed hysterically. Now he was getting somewhere with the old bastard. That was his weak spot, his horse. "Hey, ya horse don't like getting shot in the leg either, Old Man. Let's see what she thinks about one in the hind leg."

Bryant aimed his rifle but got a kick on his shin from Toby. He cussed, laughed, stepped back, aimed and fired again. Toby heard Babs snort, whinny and then snort several more times. Pulling bullets from his pocket and loading his rifle, Bryant laughed wildly, "Damn, Old Man if ya horse don't sound just like you do. Let's see what happens with another leg."

Watching Toby for his reaction, he walked slowly towards the fallen animal and grinned as Toby begged him to leave Babs alone. Bryant looked down, placed the rifle within a few inches of the horses hock and fired. He looked back to see Toby bringing Billy's long-barreled revolver up. He spun as he raised his rifle at the same time a slug whizzed by his head. The gun barrel wavered in Toby's shaking hand. The grin returned to Bryant as he leveled his rifle at Toby. A surprise kick from Babs knocked his leg out from under him and he toppled to the ground. Still clutching his rifle, balancing on his knees, he cussed and brought his rifle up again as Toby's next bullet found his shoulder. The impact of the lead spun him half-around and he fell over, still holding to his weapon. He cussed and made another attempt to raise the rifle when a bullet tore into his brain and a white light was the last thing he saw.

Toby's hand filled with the big handgun, dropped to the ground and he looked like he was going to pass out. But he found the strength to hold to the gun and crawl to Babs. He laid down and placed his face close to her so she could see his eyes. He rubbed her head and talked gently to her. They laid there for a long minute with him running his hand through her mane and telling her how much he loved her. He placed the muzzle of the revolver to her head and pulled the trigger.

The tumbleweed that shuddered, rolled and paused for the next light breeze in the middle of the town's one street was the center of attention for Angel Valley residents. A. J. Moniker stood at the banks window with hands clasped behind him and studied the weed as though he thought it might be on its way to the bank to make a much needed deposit.

Stinky stood with both rail-thin arms draped over the swinging doors of his saloon and puckered his lips while watching the erratic drift of the peculiar weed.

Barney Womack stood with one foot propped onto his cold stone firebox. He chewed a splinter of wood and thought how he had no blacksmithing job, so what the hell else was there to do except watch the damn tumbleweed. He certainly didn't want to go upstairs and listen to more of the wife's crying about Billy.

Frank Moseley blew dust from a clothing display and stared at the weed lolling along and it made him think of his business…going no place in a hurry.

Queenie Beaumont stood looking out of a dirty window above the saloon. Stinky had suggested a business deal and she had agreed to it. But there was almost no business. The night before she had had one customer, a drunk ranch hand who had quit the Rocking H and was heading north. The night before that, she had no business at all. The tumbleweed reminded her of her life…drifting aimlessly.

Ben Davis sat in his wagon about a hundred yards on the dirt street outside of town clucking to his mule. He had come to town to see if there was any carpentry jobs but found nothing to do. The tumbleweed made him think of moving along himself. Perhaps there was work for a skilled carpenter in Alpine.

At the end of the wide dusty street opposite from where Ben Davis sat, Hiram stood smoking a cigar, watching the weed roll and stop, roll and stop. Somewhere a shutter or door banged against a wall and between the sight of the tumbleweed and the sound of the lonely echo of the banging wood, Hiram saw a ghost town. His eyes moved from the weed to his cigar. This was his town. He owned it lock, stock and barrel. So what? What did it amount to? Nothing. Everyone in town owed him but they didn't have the money to pay him. A scripture from...he could not recall the book but it went something like... "And if thou sell ought unto thy neighbor, or buyest ought of thy neighbor's hand, ye shall not oppress one another."

Tossing the cigar away, he moved toward his bank. His feet felt heavy. It was a tremendous task, requiring all of his strength to make himself keep walking. He had an almost overpowering desire to rest on the wooden walkway that he stepped up on. He needed to catch his breath, gather his thoughts and try to recall scripture that would inspire him and enable him to turn things around. But he kept moving, putting one foot in front of the other until he stood at the entrance to his bank.

A breeze blew at his bowler hat and he slowly reached up to hold it on his head. Did he hear the distant echo of laughter in the wind? Was it the shrill, hysterical snickering of demon banshees, evil creatures that had united to bring him down? His senses told him the sound he heard was the wind howling around the edge of the building, but his spirit told him it was the doing of something or someone that was intent on destroying him and rejoicing in the prospect. Suddenly, he did not want to be exposed to the malignant stench within the very air that he breathed and stung his nostrils like boiling, bubbling sulfur.

He opened the door quickly and stepped in to face A.J. Moniker. The little weasel had always made sure Hiram found him at his post behind the counter in the past, but lately he had been taking liberties that incensed Hiram.

Ignoring the little ass and his greeting, Hiram said, "The banks closed as of now, A. J. Your position no longer exists. Get your things, give me your keys and...and..." He walked around his employee, brushing against his shoulder roughly and sat at his desk.

Looking out the window, he saw that the tumbleweed appeared to be stalled directly in front of his bank.

Slumping in his chair, he was oblivious to the sounds of his employee getting his things together. He asked himself for the thousandth time how it all came apart. Each time he did, he always began and ended with the same name, *Camel*. Lunging up and out of the door, he headed for Stinky's place. He had to get that useless drunk out of his head. The wind blew hard and he looked back to see the tumbleweed had rolled up the wooden boardwalk and lodged against the door of his now defunct bank.

Ephraim extended his calloused hand to Judah who took it and mumbled words of empathy, "Sure will miss ya. We'll be following ya any day now. I been holding on until my mare foals."

"Come on kids," yelled Ephraim. All of the children moved toward the wagon. Their faces looked more like the adults now. Ephraim helped the youngest one up to sit between he and his wife while the others found invisible niches on the side of the wagon where they perched. Two large mules pulled the wagon and tied to the back was their milk cow, Patty, whose tail swatted at flies. As the wagon rolled slowly away, Judah, Pearl and their children watched silently as the Stoddard family moved from the area and out of their lives.

Judah felt Pearl move close to him and he placed his arm around her slim waist. He looked down into her permanently battered face and smiled. It hurt him each time he saw her broken nose and the purple bruise around her eye that seemed to have become a fixed part of her features. They still had not made love since her beating. She continued to deny that Hiram did it but he knew better. Each time she came to him, he saw the big man abusing her and it killed his desire.

Pearl looked into his face and gave the hint of a smile. She smiled very little these days. She knew her smile was different now. Looking at Judah watching the children play, she saw again the double-barreled shotgun resting in the corner of her bedroom.

Maggie swept the school floor for the third time. She had stacked the heavy wooden benches, her desk and chair against one wall. Looking down at the paper she pulled from her pocket she examined the inventory of slates, pencils, and horn readers for the third or fourth time. She was procrastinating and knew it. But it was hard to say goodbye to the stark wooden floors and walls where she had worked for the last year. Mr. Arlington had visited her at Quiermo's pueblo and told her that the township had dissolved and there was no longer a budget to pay her. Mr. Arlington's face held its usual redness with embarrassment as he observed the humble surroundings Maggie now called home. But he was polite if a bit aloof and even offered to pay Quiermo to drive her to Alpine so she could catch the train to return home. He hinted that he would finance the train fare if she needed it. But she graciously refused his offer and told him she was now working with the Mexican and Negro children. He seemed almost offended in hearing it and made a hasty getaway, taking just enough time to ensure that he avoided any chicken droppings.

Hearing steps on the porch, she looked up. It was Hiram. She stood, her heart in her throat. He looked different. His black coat and pants were dusty and rumpled. His bowler hat rested at a weird angle on his head. His beady eyes took her in and then surveyed the room. He looked back at her. She could see him lean and then right himself. He was drunk.

The broom handle was made of white oak and a bit heavy. Billy had made it for her and she felt she had to use it. Picking it up, she measured the big man, the distance between them, how long it would take her to clear the door, and stared back at him. They stood there for a long moment, she could hear him breathing and smelled the sour whisky on his breath.

"I thought you would have been long gone by now," he said. "Did you hear that we are no longer officially a township? We have no money to…"

She spoke over him, "I heard. I have cleaned the building and I will leave an inventory of supplies on the desk."

Moving to the desk she laid the papers on it, still holding the broom, she picked up her bag and started for the door. Hiram stepped forward blocking her path. She said, "Get back, Hiram! I'm leaving."

He reached for her and she swung the broom handle at his head. He tried to block the blow, but it whacked him on the head, knocking his hat off. He cussed as he rushed for her. She brought it down again with all her might. He grunted in pain and stumbled past her as she sidestepped and ran for the door. Dropping the broom, she ran through the door. She heard a crash and furniture falling. Glancing back she saw him crumpled on the floor, holding his head as blood ran down his face.

She ran until she saw Quiermo coming for her in his buggy. She slowed to a walk, fidgeted with her hair and took several deep breaths to calm herself. Quiermo looked at her with a question in his eyes, but did not ask.

CHAPTER 36

The wild mustang of the plains was a hardy, though small horse used by the Indians. He could run fast in short distance sprints but was no match for the larger grain fed horses of the U.S. Calvary.

"It's Billy Womack! It's Billy!" The shouts made Stinky appear at the door of his saloon and Frank Moseley stepped outside his mercantile store and into the street to see this strange sight.

Frank muttered, "I'll be damned!"

Junior Beaumont ran toward the small house that the doctor occupied. He yelled for the doctor and after a long moment the physician appeared at his doorway. Junior was overcome with excitement. "It's Billy Womack, Doctor, the man who shot me and the old man is Toby Smith, the foreman of the 3C ranch. He was supposed to be dead, but he faked it. Looks like he really might be dead this time."

The doctor shook his head. He had already dealt with four gunshot wounds in the short time he had been here. *What kind of place is Angel Valley?* The first was Junior Beaumont. The next was Toby at the 3C ranch. The last two were Rocking H hands, involved in a shootout that morning. One of the last two men had been seriously wounded and was recovering on a cot in the doctor's living room. The other had been picked up in a surrey by Hiram.

The doctor had told Hiram, who had been instrumental in convincing him to come to the Valley, that he was packing his clothes and medical bag and heading to El Paso. Surely not all places out here were as wild as Angel Valley.

He looked at Junior, his first gunshot wound patient and admired the red thin scar that was barely visible on his forehead before disappearing into his hair. The bullet had removed hair and a layer of skin from the skull, but had done no serious damage.

The doctor walked down his steps and frowned at the grisly sight. A young man who was pale and appeared to be either dead or unconscious was held in the saddle by a ghost of an old man who had both thin arms wrapped around the youth's waist. Dried blood discolored the shirt of the young man and the old man's boots were covered with it.

Junior took the reins of the horse and led him to the doctor. As the horse stopped, both men began a slow slide to the ground. Junior and the doctor reached to soften their falls. At first the doctor thought he had just seen two dead men ride up to his office. Billy's pulse was barely detectable. He searched even longer for Toby's and almost pronounced him dead when he detected the slightest flutter of his heart.

Barney, Billy's father appeared and helped the doctor carry Billy into the doctor's house. Next, they carried in the limp body of Toby and placed him on a mat. Frank Moseley observed it from across the street. Locking his store, he made for Stinky's, since that's where Hiram was spending most of his time these days.

In the saloon, he found Stinky sitting behind the bar. Hearing the sound of bedsprings squeaking overhead, he looked questioningly at the droopy-eyed bartender who shook his head, "Hiram's spending time with Queenie. We damn sure ain't gonna make any money like that."

"I thought he saved himself for that little Mexican jumping bean over in Adobeville," said Frank.

Stinky rolled his eyes and spit into a spittoon, "Carmen. I wanted to see if we could get her in here, but he, pointing upstairs, wouldn't hear of it. Now, he says she's gone back to Mexico. He wouldn't tell me, but one of his men who was high-tailing it outta here said she took off with one of his ranch hands, a dapper Dan type. Damn if everything ain't turned to shit for him lately."

Frank glanced upstairs where the noise continued and said, "Not just for him. I'm not doing any business at all. How about you?"

"Ya know I ain't doin' nothin'. This place has gone to hell and I can't keep the doors open like this. Ya probably heard that Granny Stutz and Arlington laid off all of their hands except for skeleton crews. Ya know he's (pointing upstairs) lost all but a couple of his ranch hands. They say it's too dangerous to work around here anymore. How about old Toby and Billy ridin' in here all shot up? Where's Bryant? I know he's been gunning for the old man ever since he dug up his grave."

Frank stared into the warped mirror and said, "I don't know. His men said they left him out there shooting it out with Toby and Billy. That's what I need to see Hiram about. How we gonna handle this…arrest 'em or what."

The noise upstairs ceased. A second later, Hiram's voice roared, "Stinky!"

"Aw shit. He's gonna drink up all my good whisky." Stinky grunted reaching for a bottle and headed up the stairs.

Frank considered following Stinky up the stairs, but decided against it. He walked slowly out of the saloon and, for the first time, thought how he could escape town with the merchandise loaded into a wagon without Hiram catching him.

Back in the store, he went through the motion of straightening clothes, dusting items on shelves and was thinking how he could load up in the middle of the night and…he did a double take. A stranger rode past his store window. Walking to the window to stare at the lone rider, he thought how bad things were. There were so few strangers in town now that a new one attracted attention.

The rider hitched his dappled gray to the hitching post, brushed some of the road dust from his canvas Levi's and walked stiffly, like a man too long in the saddle, into the saloon. Stinky was surprised to see him and after pouring him a drink asked where he was coming from. This was not saloon etiquette, but Stinky was so elated to have a paying customer, he forgot himself.

Tossing the drink down, the stranger said, "Ojinaga. I saw a strange sight yesterday. A bunch of Injuns walking this way. Seem to be led by a white man." He shook his head as Stinky poured him one on the house to keep him talking. "I didn't think you folks had any Injuns down here anymore."

Stinky studied the man. He seemed to be sensible and sober. "Are you sure? Cuz we ain't had any Indians around here for a long time. Got plenty of niggers, greasers, and half-breeds, but no Indians."

"Well, you gonna have some in a couple days because they were heading this way."

Maggie listened with interest as Quiermo repeated the story he had been told by Ben Davis. A group of Indians was heading for Angel Valley. They were led by a white man dressed like an Indian. A little later, as she helped Estefania clean up the dishes, they received a visit from Juanita, Hiram's maid and cook. She told the same story, but added something that made Maggie take a deep breath.

"They say the group of Indians is mostly women and children and they are led by a white man named Moses. But someone else said it was Camel Campbell leading them. He has gone Indian." She laughed at that.

Quiermo, diverted his eyes from Maggie and said quietly, "I have heard that too, but we must remember that it is only a rumor."

Juanita smiled, "I like it because it makes Mr. Burro Hiram very mad. He must hate Camel very much. He turned red and had trouble breathing when Stinky told him what he hears about Camel leading the Indians here."

Maggie had finished her work and stepped out into the starlit night. The weather had a tang of autumn in it and the smell of smoke in the cool night air reminded her of Camel. She tried to tell herself she should not get excited. Like Quiermo said, it was only rumor so far, but that did not rein in her emotions or hopes. It was foolish she knew, but she still clung to the hope they could enjoy a future together. A shooting star glowed as it made its way across the sky and she took it as a good omen.

Hiram rested on his knees, bent over a wooden chair, his head laying on his hands. He gasped from the pain Cholla had inflicted upon him with his whip. His voice broke into a sob as he said, "More, Cholla. The old devil still has me by the throat and I'm gonna beat him if you have to wear out your whip."

Cholla took a deep breath, raised the whip, but then slowly the arm came down. "No, Senor Hiram. I will not hurt you anymore. This is madness and I cannot do it."

Hiram's voice held a weariness and a touch of madness thought Cholla. "Beloved, follow not that which is evil, but that which is good. He that doeth good is of God: but he that doeth evil hath not seen God." Third John, uh, I cannot remember which verse. Cholla, it does not matter. I will double your pay tonight, whip the evil out of me and help save my soul. Do you hate me so much that you would send my soul to hell?"

"I cannot save your soul, Senor. Only you can do that."

Daylight was dawning. Hiram had not slept a wink. With bloodshot eyes that blazed with hatred, he stood watching the eastern horizon lighten. If Camel was coming to Angel Valley with Indians, Hiram must stop him.

CHAPTER 37

Some of the nicknames used for prostitutes in the 1880's were...soiled doves, prairie flowers, scarlet ladies, calico queens, frail sisters, and come-on girls.

The word spread like wildfire. Camel was leading a group of killer Indians into Angel Valley. They were fierce and bitter children of the Comanche, Mescalero Apaches, Cherokee and Cheyenne who were returning to reek vengeance upon the whites who killed their grand parents and parents.

Another rumor held that Camel had gone crazy from alcoholism, escaped into the desert where he joined up with a group of Half-breeds and Indians who were as crazy as he. Together, they would ferment a revolution made up of disenchanted, ignorant Mexicans and dirt-poor Texans. People who were too lazy to work and earn their own land, but who would fight to steal the land from those who had earned it honestly.

Still another story was told about Camel getting drunk, lost in the desert, and being taken prisoner by a group of rampaging Indians who had escaped from their reservation in Oklahoma. He was being forced to lead them to Angel Valley so they could scalp the men and rape the women.

Stinky reported to Hiram that he figured Camel was bringing redskins back to take over the town so Camel could set up his headquarters in the saloon. He vigorously rubbed a glass and watched Hiram from the corner of his eye as he said, "Way I figure it, I better move my stock and get on up to Alpine and then I can come back later after this thing is cleared up."

Someone suggested Camel planned to unite the niggers and Mexxies with the Indians and they would take over Texas and then march into Mexico. There was even talk that Camel simply aimed to turn Angel Valley into the gambling and carousing center of the southwest.

The talk accelerated the migration from the area. The half-dozen Quaker families living almost twenty miles east abandoned their settlement and headed in a northwesterly direction. Two old maids who lived on a small goat farm north of town led their goats north and no one ever heard from them again. Some of the Mexican-Americans fled to Mexico. Quiermo and Cholla were on the road every day hauling families to Alpine who had no other transportation.

The second topic of gossip was the blazing gunfight involving Toby Smith and Billy Womack fighting Bryant Williams and Rocking H hands. One story had over a dozen men killed and twice that many wounded. Another held that Toby had been buried alive by Bryant Williams but had been dug up and saved by Billy. Later the two made a stand against Bryant and his men and killed them to the last man. Someone said that Bryant had been badly wounded and was wandering around blind and shooting at anyone that approached him.

One topic included in all of the stories was the involvement of Hiram Bishop. He was not the religious, church and civic leader that he appeared. He was also bankrupt. His bank was closed and all of his ranch hands had abandoned him. He had set Queenie Beaumont up as a prostitute in the upstairs room of Stinky's, but no one could do business with her because Hiram had homesteaded the place. He was a scripture-quoting hypocrite and the disciple of the devil. He should be run out of town like he ran all of the disappearing people, like Camel, out of town. There had been rumors kept under wraps for some time about strange things occurring at his house late at night involving the Mexxies, but now the rumors were talked up for all to hear and expound on. It was unsaid, but running Hiram out of town would eliminate many people's debts and make life far more bearable. But who would remain in Angel Valley? Many of those people had already left or were preparing to do so.

Hiram, the sheriff and the two remaining Rocking H hands stood looking down on the body of Bryant Williams. There was a long period of silence broken only by the screech of a hawk overhead. Hiram looked at his employees and said, "Bundle him up and bury him under that big oak behind the bunk house."

He looked at Frank and started to say something, but instead turned and walked toward his buggy. The part-time merchant and sheriff did not follow him. In the past he would have followed like a puppy dog and waited for his master to give him his orders, but not now. It was obvious Hiram had lost his power. Frank had seen the look in the hired hands' eyes.

I would bet a silver dollar once they bury Bryant, they'll ride fast and far from this territory. And why the hell not? This is no longer Angel Valley; its Death Valley.

Hiram mounted his buggy and without looking back, slapped the reins and headed back to town. He was keenly aware of the lack of respect demonstrated by Frank. *The little turd! He's nothing but a sorry store-keeper and a sorrier sheriff.*

Reaching down under his seat, he retrieved a bottle, chugalugged it and stuck it between his legs. He knew what kind of welcome party he would throw for Camel.

Billy stood stiffly beside his mother. The bullet had grazed his rib and tore muscle and tissue. The doctor wrapped his torso in a tight bandage that limited his movements. He and his mother looked down at Toby who lay white and still. The doctor spoke softly, "I had to remove one foot and I might have to remove the other one. I should know by tonight. He's so weak that it doesn't look good for him."

Billy felt hot tears stream down his cheeks and wiped them roughly with his sleeve. "He's my friend and I don't want anything to happen to him. Please do everything you can for him, Doc."

The doctor looked like he had not slept in a long while. Bleary-eyed, disheveled hair, stubble chinned, he nodded, "I am, Billy. Now, why don't you and your mother go home and check back with me about dark and I will tell you how he's doing."

Back at home, Billy's father, Barney, called him to come downstairs with him. "Billy, I guess ya know now that ya didn't kill Junior Beaumont. Ya creased his skull and he bled a lot, but he's up and runnin' all over town like always. He's pimping for his old lady right now."

Billy studied his boots. He was a mama's boy and his father's gruffness always unsettled him. But now, for some reason, he sensed a difference in his father. Barney said, "We got some talkin' to catch up on, Son. Tell me what ya know about Hiram, Frank, Sheriff Dan and the whole works."

Billy looked into his dad's eyes and saw acceptance and understanding that he had not seen before. He began with Camel's disappearance and told how Sheriff Dan's shotgun was pointed in the wrong direction as it lay on his body. The sheriff was left-handed, not right-handed. His voice trembled as he told how he and Toby had survived and about the final shootout.

When he finished, tears streaked down his cheeks again. He wiped them quickly not wanting to be cuffed by his father. But instead, he felt Barney's rough hands massaging his neck. "That's fine, Son. I understand. Now why don't ya go upstairs with ya mama and get some rest.

Billy tossed and turned. He kept seeing Toby's features so white, thin and still. Since Sheriff Dan got killed, Toby was the only one he could confide in totally. He didn't want the old man to die. He finally dozed off as he recalled the conversation he had with his father. Dreaming of Dan and Toby, he smiled in his sleep.

CHAPTER 38

On a ranch the bronc-buster was usually a teenager who was sometimes also called a hardfall or a fart-knocker. The bronc-buster who broke the horse usually named him.

Moses felt like a strange-looking bug being studied by lots of people. He looked into the tired, weak eyes of Naiche who was sitting on a folded blanket, leaning against an oak tree. He shifted his gaze to Father Pollen. The little preacher stared back through his thick spectacles. Finally, he looked into the large brown eyes of Anrelina. They all said the same thing. This group was unanimous.

Anrelina broke the silence, "Moses, we appreciate all that you are doing for us, but our question is a fair one, don't you think?"

Her question resonated again within his tormented brain and soul, "Moses, why are we traveling so few miles each day? We know that you have had to fight for us already and we have to take measures to be careful, but it is like we are going to live out here for the rest of our lives."

Father Pollen's statement seared his brain, "Moses, are we like the children of Israel and doomed to roam these wastelands for forty years? Are you not going to take us to the promised land of your ranch as we discussed? Must we wait for a generation to pass and have another one, a Joshua, take us further?"

He first felt anger. Second, he felt indignation. Third, he felt guilt because he knew they were right. He was dawdling. He was fearful of showing up in Angel Valley with this group. *It's not that I'm ashamed of these people. I respect and care deeply for them. So what is it? Am I ashamed of my new name? Do I fear facing all*

*of my old demons in Angel Valley? Do I not want to face Hiram? Is
there an element of truth in all of these?*

Father Pollen said, "Moses, we want you to take a day, a week,
however long you need to decide what you are going to do."

Moses opened his mouth to protest, but Anrelina said, "We will
not leave this campground with you as our guide until you go away
and take some time to decide what the moons ahead hold for us. If
you do not return, by the new moon, we will know you have gone
on. We will understand and accept it."

Father Pollen added, "We will do that, but we will also be very
disappointed. But whatever you do, you will remain in our prayers."
He limped away and Anrelina followed. Only Naiche remained
because he lacked the strength to leave. Looking up at Moses, he
nodded, smiled slightly and grunted. Moses tried to smile, gave it
up and headed for his horse.

Mounting up, he heard his name and saw Anrelina coming
toward him with something in her hand. It was a piece of the mule
deer he had shot wrapped in a leather skin. Their eyes met; he felt
small. Looking away, he rode toward a bluff in the distance, all the
while struggling over why he was having such difficulty doing what
he knew was right.

He spent the night on a bluff. He could barely see the flicker of
the Morning People's fire. He thought of the differences between
the red and white culture. Indians built a small fire and sat close
whereas whites built a larger fire and sat further back. Munching on
the grilled deer, he watched the stars as they began to appear. The
night sky was blue-black bejeweled by the twinkling stars. The
Milky Way brightened to its full luster and between it and the full
moon, the night held a silver glow.

His hobbled horse cropped the short Texas grass as Camel
stretched on the ground and admired the heavens. *I know why I'm
stalling. I'm scared. I'm scared of what the people of Angel Valley
might do to the Morning People. But there's more to it. I'm scared
to face the people for myself. Will they laugh at me?*

Was he strong enough to face the towns people? Would he find
that Camel was not dead, only sleeping until he tasted whisky and
held a deck of cards? And what about holding a woman? The
thought of being with a woman, a real woman like Maggie made

him restless, like a penned up stallion corralled next to a brood mare.

What about Anrelina? He never thought he would go for an Indian, but she appealed to him. She was a striking woman, and had a presence, a purity, a way of looking at him that made him want her, but at the same time made him want to be a better man.

Unable to sleep, he jumped up, startled his horse and her snort scared him. He laughed aloud, and talked quietly to her as he rubbed her forehead and jaw. The laugh was hollow and did nothing to ease the restlessness within. Taking his rifle, he walked a hundred yard circle around his camp, decided he was only wasting time and finding no relief, laid back down. It was a beautiful night but he could not appreciate it. Struggling with his thoughts and doubts, sleep was elusive and came to him late as a lone coyote barked and yipped in the distance.

Back at the Morning People's camp, Naiche snatched sleep in spurts. He could not find comfort regardless how he moved or shifted. Forty feet away, Father Pollen mumbled a torturous prayer. He felt his disciple and protégé was slipping away. Perhaps he was already gone. A half-dozen yards away, Anrelina lay on a blanket staring up at the night sky listening to others breathe deeply in sound sleep. A tear glistened in the moonlight and she wiped it away.

The sun was above the horizon when Moses opened his eyes. Saddling up, he headed east without looking back at the Morning People's camp.

Maggie stood beneath the arbor with her hand on a child's shoulder. Giving soft, low encouragement as he struggled with an addition problem, her mind drifted to her memories of Camel. One of his surprising traits was intelligence. He hid behind the wide grin, handsome features and magnetic personality. His knowledge of many subjects surpassed Bilbo's.

She had spurned his first advances, but did finally allow him to engage her in conversation. As they talked of politics and places of interest, he impressed her. She liked a man with intelligence. She liked Camel because he combined smartness with humor better than any man she had ever known.

Then one night it had happened. He used his charms on her and she succumbed. She learned from him even an intelligent man can be a scoundrel. How many other women had had to learn the same lesson?

Standing before the group of Negro children, she paused to recollect her thoughts. She must concentrate on this arithmetic lesson and less on Camel. Or was it Moses? Could he have lost his mind as one of the rumors suggested? Time and again she had heard that the desert was capable of doing strange things to people. It could cure some of terminal illnesses. It could kill others in a very short time, and others it merely drove to madness.

Explaining an addition problem to a beautiful big eyed child, she considered again her options if she encountered him. If he showed no sign of recollection, would she have the strength to move on? What if he had grown mad and transformed into a monster? Should she try to help him? Would he hurt her? That idea made her see the face of Hiram and that broke the chain of thought for now.

Frank Moseley sat his horse in front of Judah's cabin. He had ridden out of town with his .32 holstered to his hip as Hiram watched. Before turning into Judah's, he had unbuckled the belt and placed gun, holster and belt into his saddlebag. Judah had responded to his yell after a long minute by rounding his cabin carrying a shotgun.

Frank wiped sweat from his forehead with his sleeve although it was not an especially hot day. "How are things with ya, Judah?"

The ensuing silence made Frank shift uneasily in the saddle. He watched the big-barreled shotgun closely. *Damn! Why would Hiram insist I do this now?* Hiram has lost *his ass and everyone knows it.* Why in the hell did he allow himself to be bullied by fat-ass Hiram?

Judah ignored the question. His voice was steely, "I know why ya here. I already told Hiram I would leave as soon as I can. That should be within the week. I'm not leaving a minute sooner. You turn around and go back and tell him that."

Frank looked at the shotgun and felt sick. He well knew what one of those things could do to a man. His breath came jagged and quick but he looked into Judah's face and knew he was dealing with

an honest man. *Dammit, calm down! He's not gonna shoot ya.*
Smiling awkwardly, he said, "I hear ya, Judah. I'm goin' right now
and I'm not comin' back. Hiram can do that if he wants to."

Judah spit and said, "That's fine with me."

Riding back to town, buckling on his gun, Frank thought how it
would take Hiram to make a peaceful man like Judah ready to shoot
it out. He had to get his merchandise on a wagon and get the hell
out of town. What about tonight? He would wait until dark, pull his
wagon behind the store, load it up and be halfway to Alpine or
Marathon by daylight. While the merchandise actually belonged to
Hiram, Frank figured he had earned it in recent weeks by risking his
life for Hiram and so far getting only shit in return. That would
change tonight.

The doctor shook his head in amazement. "Toby, you are either
the luckiest man or the toughest one I ever met. I have an idea it's a
little of each."

The old man laid on his back and responded with a weak smile.
His voice was a hoarse whisper, "I've had more than my share of
luck, Doc, that's for sure. I guess I'm too danged ornery to die, so
ya just gotta make a fence post outta me."

Looking over at Billy, the doctor said, "You can have a few
words with him, Billy. We mustn't tire him out, he's still weak
from loss of blood. The good news is that I did not have to take that
other foot."

Billy smiled from ear to ear and went to his partner's side.
"Hey, Old Man! Ya ready to go ridin'?" Remembering what had
happened with Babs, he lost his smile, worried that he had said the
wrong thing.

But Toby looked at him with his clear, blue eyes and said, "Hi
Squirt! How ya doin'?"

Billy reported to him in an excited manner how he had not killed
Junior Beaumont, just creased his skull. He had decided though he
would not give Junior any more shooting lessons because he did not
trust him holding his pistol.

The doctor shooed Billy away so Toby could get his rest. When
the youth had left, he looked at Toby, ordered him to rest and then
returned to his back room to complete his packing. As soon as Toby

was able, he would be leaving and the doctor would say good-by to this cursed hellhole where people shot one another for sport.

Toby closed his eyes, but did not sleep. He thought of the conversation he had heard yesterday. The doctor had assumed he was asleep and had talked to someone at his door about some white man leading a group of Indians to Angel Valley. That was interesting news unto itself but what really perked up his ears was when he heard someone say that the leader was Camel, but he had changed his name to Moses. *Camel? Leading Indians? Changed his name to Moses?* Toby's first thought was that Camel had been on a long binge and lost his mind in the bottle. To lead people required perseverance and discipline, two traits that Toby had never associated with Camel before.

Toby's body told him he needed to sleep and regain his strength but his heart pumped hard with the excitement of even more news he'd overheard. Hiram was busted. Toby never considered himself a vindictive man. But by durn knowing Hiram had bellied up was like the cool water the doctor had given him when he was burning up with the fever. It was good!

His contemplation led him to combine the two events and men. Camel returning with Indians and Hiram leaving the country. That could mean the 3C reclaiming its stolen herd from the defunct Rocking H and resume ranching. But what about the Indians? How would they fit into the picture? He was still puzzling over this question when his tired, torn body assumed control and transported him into a deep, healing sleep.

CHAPTER 39

Some whites who observed the treatment of the Indians during the latter part of the nineteenth century wrote scathing accounts of the situation. In 1858, Bishop Henry Whipple wrote, "A Plea for the Indian." In 1868, Lydia Child wrote, "Appeal for the Indian." In 1881, Helen Hunt Jackson wrote, "A century of Dishonor." Three years later she wrote, "Ramona." Each one of these books told a sad, sordid story of how whites brutalized Indians in their attempt to contain, christianize, and train them to compete in a capitalistic economy.

Riding in the open country, Moses admired the variegated canyons, rock towers, and the purple Chisos Mountains. This was wild, untamed country and he had always loved it, but now he found that even the beauty of the land could not rid him of faces he saw as clearly as if they were standing before him. He saw Father Pollen looking up at him in that inquisitive way he had and he saw the deep-set eyes of Naiche with the wrinkled face and presence that so impressed him. He saw all of them, but one more than the rest...Anrelina.

Slowing his mount to a walk, he saw Anrelina nursing the sick ones, encouraging, preparing food, always moving and always helping someone. Pulling on the reins, he stopped his horse and sat still. Most of all he saw her feeding him when he was almost dead from thirst. He saw the way she looked at him, sometimes when she did not know he was aware of her eyes on him. *She probably sees me watching her too when I'm not aware she knows it.*

A couple of hours later, he sat on a bluff and scanned the area for the Morning People. At first he did not see them and felt a flush of fear. Then he spotted the group. Breathing a sigh of relief, he rode at a trot toward them.

Several of the women and children immediately surrounded him. The women smiled at him and giggled. The children excitedly poked his legs with their fingers. He looked for Anrelina and saw her carrying a large, fat bull snake. He thought how she had replaced Naltzukich in hunting for whatever was available to feed the group. Chee followed behind her smiling his pleasure over her accomplishment. Moving toward Naiche who sat on his blanket where Moses had left him, he encountered Father Pollen. The little gnome of a man grinned, showing crooked teeth and his eyes beamed behind the thick spectacles. He reached out for Moses who bent and hugged him.

"Welcome back, Moses, I have been praying for your safe return."

"Thank you, Father. It's good to be back. This is where I belong. And we need to hit the trail early tomorrow morning for Angel Valley."

The priest adjusted his spectacles, "So you have found peace with your decision?"

"Yes I have. Are you people ready to follow me?"

"Yes we are, Moses."

Anrelina stood before him without the snake. She placed her palm to his face and smiled like he had never seen her do before. Turning, she was gone.

Moses looked at Naiche and was surprised to see the old Indian sitting with his head drooped on his chest. Moving closer, he heard him snoring. He looked at Father Pollen.

Making a face reflecting resignation, he whispered, "He's been like that all day."

Moses squatted near Naiche and spoke softly in his ear, "Naiche, I'm back."

At first there was no response but then the snoring ceased, the eyes opened and the head lifted. Moses looked sadly into the tired eyes that held little of the fire that had always been there. The eyes focused on Moses and a withered hand found his arm. Moses held the hand and said, "We're heading for Angel Valley at first light. I'm going to take you home with me."

Naiche did not speak for a while. Finally, he said, "Moses, lead us to the promised land."

"I will, Naiche. I promise you."

Maggie tried to act disinterested as the talk around the table centered around Camel or now Moses, leading the Indians to Angel Valley. She fooled no one. Chewing on a banana pepper, Quiermo said, "The talk is that Camel will be here with the Indians in two days. There are so few people here now that it is thought that it would take only a handful to overtake us."

"Senor Hiram will not like that," said Estefania.

Quiermo swallowed, cleared his throat and said, "Senor Hiram is not the important man that he was. His bank is closed, there are no workers left on his ranch, and others are still leaving."

Estefania corrected the boys for playing and said, "Who else is leaving?"

The new sheriff, Senor Moseley, is packing up his goods. Our blacksmith, Senor Womack is filling up his wagon and Senor Stinky is…" His voice trailed off.

"What about Senor Stinky?" Estefania gave the boys another look and turned her large brown eyes back onto her husband.

He chewed his refried beans too long, finally answered, "They say he would have been gone before now but Senor Hiram will not leave his business. I think that after I make a run tonight, he might not be spending so much time at Senor Stinkys."

Estefania scowled, "What are you saying, Quiermo?"

His face flushed, he took a deep breath, "Tonight I will be taking Senorita Beaumont and her boys to Fort Stockton. Cholla would be doing it, but she…he has left.

The two women looked at each other and broke into laughter. Quiermo had had enough. He took the boys outside with him as Estefania and Maggie cleaned up.

A few minutes later, the Negro farmer, Henry Goins, pulled up in his buggy to take Maggie to the Saltflats to teach the children. He was usually quiet, but this afternoon he appeared troubled and seemed to want to talk.

"I don't know about this talk about bringing Indians here. I was a buffalo soldier years ago and we whipped the Apaches and

Comanches and I never thought I would hear about Indians around here again." He shrugged his massive shoulders, "We might have to be moving on if there's trouble. I'm getting a little old to be fightin' 'em these days. Since I lost my Vera Mae, the chillun got no one to take care of 'em but me."

"I don't think Camel would be bringing anyone to the Valley that would hurt us, Henry. Did you hear that he has changed his name to Moses?"

"Yes'm, I heard about his new name." He shrugged and shook his head, "I don't know about that either. Mr. Camel or Moses never did anything to harm me or my people, but he never did anything to help us either."

It occurred to Maggie that this illiterate Negro farmer had summed up Camel's life and contribution quite succinctly. She decided to keep quiet and defend him no more. She continued to wonder what would happen when Camel, or Moses, appeared with his Indian friends. Would he be different? If so, how? Would he be crazy as some had strongly suggested? But the one dominating thought was the question of whether Camel would even remember her. She tried unsuccessfully to focus on the reading and numbers lesson she would be teaching the children today beneath the arbor, but she failed miserably.

Hiram stood naked before the window above the saloon looking down onto the tumbleweeds blowing through town. *I hate those damn things.* Was it the way they drifted along without any responsibility or worry? They never accumulated anything but dust and maybe a sandspur or two. Squeaking bedsprings made him turn around. Queenie slipped into her white slip. She said, "I can hear the boys calling for me. I better get home and see what they got into this time."

Listening, Hiram heard Junior's voice calling her name. Pulling her dress over her head she buttoned it and said, "I need some money, Honey. The boys gotta eat."

Plodding over to a rickety chair holding his pants, Hiram reached into his pocket only to find it empty. His face grew red; he roared, "What the hell's goin on here! You stole my money, you whore."

Queenie's eyes grew large and her expression one of exasperation. "Hiram, you've been drinking for days now. The only one you've given any money to is Stinky and he's said the last couple times he brought you a bottle that you owe him."

Hiram threw his pants down and yelled, "That's a damn lie! You little whoring bitch! Thou shalt not bring the hire of a whore, or the price of a dog…"

Queenie grabbed her shoes and tried to leave but Hiram clutched her upper arm. She screamed and tried to hit him with her shoe heel but he slapped her and then threw her into the wall. She bounced off it. He kicked her in the stomach, and while she gasped and writhed in pain, he slung her from the room and slammed the door shut.

She moaned and laid on the landing for a long while until Stinky came up the stairs and looked at her. "Damn, Queenie, he busted ya up pretty good. Ya need help getting' up?"

She nodded and reached out with one shaking hand. He assisted her down the stairs and out into the bright autumn sunlight. Blood ran down her face from a ripped forehead and she held her stomach with both hands. Junior appeared and said, "Did Hiram do this to ya, Mama?"

Leaning on him for support, she mumbled through busted lips, "Go get Quiermo. We're leaving now."

Hiram sat on the edge of the bed and thought for the hundreth time that his troubles began with Camel, or was it Moses? And that bastard was bringing savages to Hiram's town. Scratching his buttock, he giggled. The bastard would find that the town was all gone. There would be no one here to give a damn what he did. He and his bunch of riff-raff savages could…he stopped and realized he was breathing deeply. His face was hot with rage. Regardless of the condition of the town now, it was still his town and by damn that no good drunk was not going to take it from him. At the window, he saw several more tumbleweeds invading his street…his town. *Come on Camel or Moses! You're just like these no-good weeds! Not good for a damn thing! And if I can…I'm gonna stop ya!*

Floyd's eyes were big with excitement, "Mama, are we gonna go into town tomorrow to see Camel and the Indians?" Before she could answer, he continued on excitedly, "I heard that the Indians are gonna go back on the warpath. Do you believe that, Mama? Are you gonna take the shotgun?"

Wiping her brow with her sleeve, she said, "No, Floyd, I don't. There's lots of gossip among the few people still around here but I don't think there's going to be any trouble with Indians." From his expression, she wasn't sure he was happy or dissatisfied with her answer.

Ralph spoke up, "We gonna go into town tomorrow to see 'em, Mama?"

"Let's see what Judah thinks about that." She thought how much she depended on his decision-making now and what a relief it was to have a good, strong man to depend on.

The two ranch hands sat their horses talking quietly. One was saying, "You tellin' me that Hiram promises each one of us a hundred dollars and the pick of his corral if we shoot Camel before he gets to town?"

The other nodded and looked away, "Yeah, that's it but…"

"From what I hear, Hiram ain't got no more money than you or me," said the other. "The last time I saw him he looked worse than a jackrabbit stomped on by a thousand steers."

Their eyes locked and simultaneously they said, "To hell with Hiram!"

CHAPTER 40

"From the time of the Gadsden purchase, when we came into possession of their country, until about 10 years ago, the Apaches were the friends of the Americans. Much of the time since then, the attempt to exterminate them has been carried on at a cost of from three to four millions of dollars per annum, with no appreciable progress made in accomplishing their extermination."

Annual Report of the Commissioner of Indian Affairs to the Secretary for the year 1871.

The Morning People stood on a hill a little over a mile away looking down onto the town known as Angel Valley. In the clear, cool atmosphere, it seemed much closer. Camel had dismounted and stood with Father Pollen at his right, Anrelina on his left, and Naiche before him sitting up on his travois. He looked up at Moses and smiled for the first time anyone in the group could remember. "Do not be hurt by my words, Moses and Father, but I can smell the white eyes from here."

Moses and Father Pollen exchanged smiles and Moses thought how he had not heard that term in a while. His heart pounded and his breath came fast. This was it. Would he lead his friends into a death trap or a new way of life? He could see a small knot of people at the town's edge awaiting them. He also saw the glint of sun on metal several times and knew that meant the towns people were armed. He could not blame them. He just hoped and prayed they held their fire, saw what a harmless group it was and gave him a chance to explain their intentions.

Telling Chee to secure his weapon, he did the same. He wanted to invite no misunderstanding. He and Chee also led their mounts rather than rode them. Moses took a breath and said, "I hope the people are hospitable, but we'll only know by going down there and looking them in the eye."

Feeling someone grip his hand roughly, he looked down into Naiche's burning eyes. "You have become a man, Moses. A good man. You have beat the demon whisky and found God. Whatever happens now, you have done well, my son." Moses squeezed the calloused hand. He felt his eyes moisten. He had never heard Naiche call him son before. He had never acted like a son to any man before.

It was time to go. Stepping out, he said, "Come on, Morning People, I want to show everyone my new friends."

In Angel Valley, people sat in wagons, stood in small groups, or sat on the town's train platform. Maggie was pleased to see people from throughout the area, including Adobeville and the Salt Flats. It was apparent to her that these people were not a community. They were separate groups who had never been under the same roof before. White, colored, and brown people knotted together and gave cursory nods to each other. It occurred to her that perhaps this was the real reason the town was disintegrating. The number of weapons on display frightened her but she prayed they would not be used.

At the outermost area stood Hiram and Frank Moseley. Hiram had discarded his black suit as he had discarded his hypocrisy. He held a full bottle of whisky in one hand, a cheroot in the other with a pistol stuck down the front of his pants. His trousers were rumpled and his white shirt stained brown with sweat and grime.

Frank stood close to his mentor though he looked uncomfortable. His pistol remained in its holster with his hand on the grip. *Why didn't I get outta here before now?*

As the group led by Moses approached, the silence grew heavy and tense. Maggie stood on tiptoes trying to see through the yucca and cacti that blocked her view. As they came into sight, she was aware of the smallness of their group. Her eyes sought Camel or Moses. Her heart sank. He was not present. Had it all been just one more rumor surrounding Camel's mysterious disappearance? Hand shielding eyes from the sun, she refused to give up yet. Her eyes searched the group and returned to a man in the front leading a horse. Could that be Camel? Moses? His hair was shoulder-length and almost completely white. His tanned skin contrasted sharply with his white hair and stubble of growth on his face. He dressed like an Indian with leather breeches and a brightly colored Navajo blanket worn like a poncho over his shoulders. She was unsure it was him until he turned to a young Indian woman at his side and smiled at her. Yep! Those white teeth told her it was Camel, or Moses.

Moses held up his hand, halting the group about thirty yards away. Maggie was amazed at how quietly the group had moved toward them. Now the silence weighed heavily on everyone and stood like a cold, white mountain of stone between the two groups.

The silence was broken by Toby's deep, crackling voice, "Is that you Camel or are these old eyes playing tricks on me?"

The smile flashed, "It's me, Toby. It's good to see you my friend."

Toby's voice was heavy with emotion, "It's good to see you. I hear you go by the name of Moses these days. Is that true?"

Father Pollen piped in, "It is true. Camel came to this group as a drunk and cheat. Between the desert and the Lord, he's a new man. Like Moses, he saw a burning bush in the desert. Like Elijah, he fled to the desert to save his life. Jesus went into the desert to face Satan. This man saved our lives more than once so we decided to give him a more appropriate name."

Moses allowed his eyes to move over each group and then said, "This is Father Pollen. He is a Presbyterian minister and a help to anyone in need. This is Anrelina, another friend and leader of our group. These people I think of as the Morning People because another fine man, who is now dead, gave them that name. They are all my friends and going with me to the 3C Ranch. I can tell you they will be good neighbors and a help to this community and I hope that you will allow them to live their lives in peace here in Angel Valley." He paused and looked around to see what kind of response he would receive.

Hiram's voice roared in rage and sarcasm as he moved toward Moses, "Humph! How wonderful! I want to be the first to offer you a welcoming gift, Moses." His voice rose even louder at the mention of the name. He extended a full bottle of golden liquid to his hated adversary who now stood about three feet from him.

Moses stared at the bottle. This was the moment he had feared. Hiram waved it under his nose, "Come on Moses! Let's have a drink for old times sake."

Father Pollen's squeaky voice sounded, "Please do not do that, Sir. It's…"

Hiram glared at the funny looking little intruder, "Shut up! This is between me and your good sober leader, Moses, or is it Camel?"

A horse whinnied somewhere and a shutter slapped against a wall and then silence settled over everyone. Hiram still waved the bottle within an inch of Moses's nose. After what seemed an eternity to Maggie, Moses grinned the way Camel used to do and said, "I can't do that, Hiram!"

Hiram sneered, "Sure ya can! Come on, I know ya want a drink. Have one, have the whole bottle."

Moses held his grin showing his white, even teeth and looked into Hiram's eyes, "You know why I can't do it, Hiram?"

"Why? Why can'tcha do it?"

Moses paused, allowed Hiram's words to hang in the air. "Because you look like you need it more than I do."

Hiram swung. Moses easily ducked the haymaker. Hiram had been on a week's drunk and had eaten little. He had lost weight but it was not a healthy loss. Moses was almost fifty pounds lighter, lean and strong. Hiram cursed and swung again. This time Moses leaned away from the fist, stepped inside as it slipped by and pushed the big man hard. He went stumbling backwards and fell on his back.

He cussed, cried and pulled his pistol. As his arm extended with his weapon a gunshot rang out. Billy's aim was accurate, the bullet smashing Hiram's elbow. His arm dropped and hung helpless at his side. Moses stepped forward, picked up the pistol and handed it to Father Pollen who took it and held it as though he were holding a stick of dynamite with a lit fuse. The gun appeared large in the small man's hands.

Toby's voice rang out again, "Keep that gun out, Billy and put it on Frank Moseley. If he reaches for his, you make sure you stop him. This is the time to tell everybody whatcha know about Sheriff Dan Libby."

Billy seemed to grow in stature and self-confidence. He pointed his pistol at Frank and said, "Pull it out gently, Frank, and drop it on the ground."

Frank's expression was one of fear and frustration as he did as Billy ordered. The young man said, "I tried to tell our judge what happened with Sheriff Dan but I couldn't make him understand me. Maybe I can do better with you folks. Ya see, I saw the killer leave our town, I watched Frank head out in the same direction and then Sheriff Dan followed them. We all know the killer and the sheriff got shot. You thought the sheriff and killer shot one another. But it didn't happen that way. Ya see the sheriff was left handed. Frank forgot that or didn't notice it. He had to be the one who killed the sheriff and laid his shotgun across him pointing the wrong way."

There was silence except for Hiram mumbling and cussing as he clutched his injured arm. Toby said, "Anything else the folks need to know, Billy?"

The youngster smiled, "Yeah! Me and Frank held Camel, I mean Moses, as Hiram beat him. We then put him on a wagon where he was carried to Marathon and put on the Southern Pacific Railroad."

Hiram scrambled to his feet, oblivious to his bleeding , dangling arm. "You little dumbass, retarded shit! There ain't a word of truth in anything ya say. The judge didn't believe ya and nobody here does either."

Several voices joined Toby, "Yeah we do!" Judah, holding Pearl's shotgun, had stepped away from his wagon bearing Pearl and their children. A. J. Moniker, who had his things all packed and planned to leave with his wife that very night had joined the chorus. He adjusted his glasses and said in a trembling voice, "Hiram also stole your money by cooking the books and forged papers to steal your land."

Junior Beaumont shook his fist and screamed, "You beat up my mama, you sunuvabitch! I hope you burn in hell!"

Several angry voices sounded together. All aimed at Hiram and Frank. This went on for a long while until Judah gained everyone's attention. He jabbed his shotgun toward Hiram as he spoke, "This man has done terrible things. Things that we cannot talk about. He has treated women in an indecent manner and he has lied, cheated, stole and done it all to us while he's quoted scripture to us and been a big shot at the church. Again voices sounded in support and Maggie noticed that the residents from Adobeville and the Salt Flats were joining in also. It occurred to her that this was the first time she had seen the town act in unison...all rising up against Hiram and his henchmen.

This time Toby was heard. He told about witnessing Fuzzy's death and how he was convinced it was the handwork of Hiram's ranch hands. He told how he had witnessed Bryant Williams and his men rustling 3C steers and how they had tried to hunt him down. He ended by telling about Billy joining him and their gunfight with Bryant and Hiram's hired hands.

A thumping sound made everyone look to see Hiram lying face down on the dry sand. Again quiet settled on the group. No one moved to help him. Slowly, one, then two, and then several people began to drift away. Wagon axles and leather squeaked, springs creaked and singletrees and doubletrees rattled to the sound of "Yaaaaa" yelled by drivers at their horses and mules. Dust rose as single riders, wagons and buggies made their way back to their homes, most determined to pack and leave the area.

Within the dust and movement, Frank bent quickly and retrieved his pistol. He lifted his weapon toward Billy who had kept his eye trained on the crooked lawman. Billy's gun bucked in his hand as his slug tore through Frank's knee cap. Dropping to both knees, Frank grimaced with pain but raised his revolver again. This time Billy's bullet caught him in the throat, clipping his spine. His head tilted at a bizarre angle as he toppled backward kicking up grayish-white dust.

Toby's voice was quiet and encouraging, "You did good, Billy. Ya tried to stop him without killing him, but he wouldn't have it."

Billy holstered his gun and smiled faintly at Toby as each of his parents took one of his hands and led him toward the stable. They left town the following day. It was rumored that Billy found work as a deputy in Pecos. Another story had it that he married a girl in El Paso and worked for his in-laws. The story that many liked the most had him working as a trick shot in a traveling circus.

Maggie and Moses each moved to Hiram's side. Father Pollen joined them. Ben Davis and Henry Goins helped them lift the semi-conscious Hiram to his feet and take him to his house. Maggie bandaged his wound and bemoaned the fact she knew little about what she was doing. Hiram was pale, having lost lots of blood. He laid on a grand sofa in his living room and the Morning People stood outside waiting for Moses and Father Pollen.

Everyone, including Maggie, left Hiram on the sofa with water on a side table. Outside, standing on Hiram's steps, Maggie and Moses looked at one another. She wanted to ask if he remembered her, she had not heard him call her name.

He said, "Maggie, it's good seeing you. You're still helping folks, I see."

He did remember. But his words lacked the warmth or passion she had hoped to hear. Did she really want the old Camel back with his romantic sweet talk and dashing ways? Perhaps what she really wanted was a more responsible Camel. Looking at this lean tanned man with long white hair and an air of resoluteness somehow disarmed her. She felt flustered and at odds with herself.

Her answer sounded weak and barely audible, "Yes. I am still teaching children and..." *What else is there to say to you?*

He smiled, but it was not a Camel smile. It was a Moses smile. What it lacked in charm and personality, it made up for in a presence emanating strength and resolve.

He bounded down the stairs and strode off with his group following him. She saw him lift Toby onto his horse and lead it as his new friends headed with him toward his ranch. Blinking, she stood on tiptoes, shielded her eyes from the sun with a hand and tried to determine if her vision was accurate. *Is he holding hands with that pretty Indian girl? Yes, he is.*

Hiram hurt all over. His arm burned in pain, his head throbbed and nausea swept over him. He laid and listened to people's voices. Horses whinnied and a mule brayed. He knew they were packing and leaving Angel Valley. Good. They were not people of character anyway. It took a special man, a man of strength and conviction to establish a town. And by damn he had almost done it single-handedly.

As dark settled, the sounds diminished, but some continued to be heard. He thought he heard Stinky's voice. Stinky owed him money. Where was the little weasel today when he needed him?

His pain grew worse. But the greatest pain was inside where no bullet had entered. No blow had harmed him. The pain was in his heart and soul. He had failed. All that he had worked for had disappeared. As the night darkened and the moon rose, he laid on the sofa staring upward. He needed help. He needed relief from his pain. With his injured arm across his stomach, the other forearm resting across his forehead, he whimpered like a small child.

Hearing footsteps, he moved his good arm and looked with wide hurt eyes at his visitor. In the semi-darkness he made out a figure wearing an overcoat and hat pointing a shotgun at him. His whimpering became sobs. After a long minute, the figure turned and with quiet voice said, "You ain't worth it."

Outside, the visitor raised a boot to the stirrup and a shock of long auburn hair streaked with gray fell from beneath the hat.

With all of his strength, Hiram sat up. Fighting nausea, he struggled to his feet and made his way to his bedroom. With his one good arm he opened a mahogany wardrobe, leaned against it breathing hard, reached in, felt for a moment and pulled out a small dark object. Making his way to bed, he sat hard on the side and looked out of the window. There was his town. In the dark he could still see his town as it had been. A small but growing place with lots of potential. But the moonlight revealed a figure moving back and forth from a wagon to the saloon. He knew it was Stinky sneaking out in the middle of the night. Stinky's actions spread the light of reality onto the scene. This was now a dying town, soon to become, at most, an outpost for supplies or most probably a ghost town.

He watched for a while and then bowed his head and mumbled a prayer. He raised the object to the side of his head and a blast filled the room. The sound spilled outside where it was heard by the saloon keeper and a few others who could not sleep. They were waiting until daylight to leave town. No one was surprised and no one checked on him.

EPILOGUE

Five years later Angel Valley was almost a ghost town. The single viable business preventing the town's total demise was Odom's Saloon and Sundries housed in Stinky's former saloon.

All of the townspeople had evacuated to other areas. Maggie returned to Connecticut and a year later married a Congregational pastor. Judah and Pearl had abandoned their places and headed for Marfa where rumor had it that ghost fires from long dead Apache Indians could be seen burning nightly. Billy accompanied his family to Abilene where he landed a job as a trick shot in a circus and married the bearded lady. Henry Goins, the former buffalo soldier took one of the Navajo women from the Morning People as his wife. After Father Pollen married them in the church where he conducted services the first and last Sunday each month, they left for Tucson.

The Salt Flats became deserted shacks that began their inevitable descent back to dust. Quiermo and Estefania moved along with the other residents of Adobeville to other locations: Fort Stockton, Marathon, Van Horn, and Ojinaga.

A few remained. Ben Davis, the Negro carpenter, became a member of Moses' extended family. He took a Navajo woman as his wife as did one of Ben's sons, Wiley. McCormick purchased most of the land in the area from the former owners, the Arlingtons, Grandmother Stutz and, of course, Hiram's ranch. He had several nephews who helped him run cattle on the vast territory and two of them married women from Moses' family.

Naiche surprised everyone by living for almost a year after arriving at the ranch. He died in peace, satisfied that his people had found a new and meaningful life.

Toby hobbled around on crutches and directed work until one morning he did not show for breakfast. Moses found a horse and saddle missing along with a rifle and gunny sack. He tracked him for several miles. With the Chisos Mountains resting before him, he turned back. His old friend had decided to end it his way and Moses would not interfere. He was thankful for the times he had seen the look of pride in Toby's eyes as he had watched the prodigal son return and be all that his father had wanted him to be.

On a beautiful spring day when the cacti were in full bloom and blue bonnets blossomed, the little church filled with smiling people to celebrate the wedding. Father Pollen beamed through his thick spectacles as Anrelina and Moses made their way down the church aisle to the altar.

Some years later, when one of the Morning People left the ranch, Moses would joke to Anrelina that he would soon have no more Morning People. But Anrelina would place one hand on her swollen abdomen, take the hand of the little girl beside her and say, "There's Naltzukich and me and one more on the way."

THE END